DEBORAH BROMLEY

THE CHANNELLING GROUP

THE CHANNELLING GROUP

This book is dedicated to Helen, Alison, Mandy, Chrissie, Lucy, Ros and Colin

You inspired me

Contents

Deborah Bromley is a hypnotherapist specialising in *Life Between Lives* (LBL) hypnotherapy which was first documented by Dr Michael Newton in his bestselling books *Journey of Souls* and *Destiny of Souls*. Deborah contributed to the subsequent book *Memories of the Afterlife*. This book is fiction and is her first novel.

Deborah wanted to write contemporary fiction that was faithful to the spirit of her experiences of the afterlife, using the essence to give life to the fantasy and finding out what would happen if you added your imagination. Spirit guides, soul groups, channelling, life between lives and the afterlife all feature in this book but the story is, fundamentally, about a group of women and their (extra)ordinary lives.

Prologue

When I think about what happened now, it all seems so completely obvious. I wonder how I didn't spot it, yes, me, who considers herself so in tune with these things. At the time, of course, we were all caught up in the events. And what momentous events they were. When I look back, though, it's clear the mistake I made was to take things at face value. If you've never doubted what you see with your own eyes, it's an easy mistake to make. I've now learned to question the obvious explanation, at least that's what I tell myself. Besides, at the time, we were actually all looking the other way, absorbed in our own lives.

She had (and still has for that matter) an ethereal quality I thought was something to do with her soft hair and her lilting voice, with just a tiny trace of the accent that became more pronounced when she was excited about something or passionate about what we were doing. The way she came to join us was mysterious, too, but I was just grateful for another person to join the group, so we had enough to make it worthwhile. She was there when we needed help; when we realised we were out of our depth. She just arrived.

Now and then I see her. She has unusual clothes, they don't fit in with the style she had before and she seems to be living in a different part of the town. So when I am least expecting it, perhaps sitting in a queue of traffic or picking the kids up from school, I find myself looking at a long raincoat (looking like it came from a charity shop), but with that astonishing hair again, floating above her collar like a cloud. Her face looks changed too, she has a different look, perhaps it's even a different face, I wouldn't be surprised, but the tell tale dimples are still there and I know it's her. None of the others know that I look for her all the time.

I remember when we were practising together, the things she said to me, the way she looked into my eyes. Even when I told her I wouldn't say my question out loud but only think of it in my mind, she answered straight away with no hesitation. That time she was holding my hand, I felt myself moving through time and space, outside any experience I had ever had before. We were sitting in Beatrice's living room at the time, the others were chattering away, but I was focussed on what I wanted to know, the questions I needed answers to. The sounds of the others talking, and sometimes laughing, faded for me. I only had eyes and ears for her. Time stood still. Space had no meaning. Only the brightest light I have ever seen. Too quickly I lost concentration and we were back in the present. So I smiled, stretched my arms and then we both got up and moved away. I looked back at her and for a brief moment her face disappeared again in a burst of light. That was when I understood what was happening, I hadn't imagined it. That's how I know we have to keep going, because she came to help us for a reason. I don't know yet what that reason is, but I intend to find out.

Chapter 1 - At the vets

The tabby cat spat and sank her claws into Beatrice's hand without warning, right into the soft ball of her thumb so she couldn't move without making it worse. Suppressing the urgent need to swear loudly and, firmly gripping the paw in question to prevent more damage, she eased the claw out. A bead of blood formed at the site of the wound. Affronted, the cat yowled at her but meekly submitted to the indignity of the cat basket.

'Mummy, you're so cruel, she doesn't feel very well, you know.'

'She bloody well felt fine to me! Just get in the car while I wash this under the tap. I don't want to bleed all over the car seats.'

'Can I carry her?' The younger child danced around with excitement.

'Only if you keep her level while you walk. Put her in the back of the car and be gentle.'

'Alright Mummy, come along little lumkins, my baby. I'll make you comfy.'

Emily heaved the basket up making an exaggerated performance of the task and huffed and puffed her way out of the kitchen. The poor cat was rolling around in the basket like a sailor in a storm.

She moved over to the sink and ran cold water on her wound; it stung. She thought of her evening ahead. She wondered how much chance there was of getting out later without being covered in bandages. Well, never mind, at least the poor little sod was now in the car. 'I'm glad I'm not that vet,' she muttered to herself.

Alexa, her elder daughter, was observing her from the doorway, leaning nonchalantly against the frame. Her dark, straight hair was smoothly framing her cool, intelligent face. She rolled her eyes in distaste and shuffled out in slow motion, her preferred speed of perambulation.

They piled into the car and Beatrice reversed out of the drive. It was starting to spit with rain and the windscreen was greasy and hard to get clear. She experienced a sense of restless foreboding. It wouldn't have been her choice to have the children along with her on this trip but, as usual, she didn't have any alternative. Alexa had refused to stay at home and sit with Emily so that meant they all had to go together. The drive up the lane and out of the village was as beautiful as ever, trees now vibrant with reds and golds, but her mind was focussed on the point of their journey. In the back, the cat was keeping up a persistent and pitiful dialogue with Emily.

'There, there Fluffy, it's all right.'

'Meaoiw ... eaiow ...'

'You'll soon feel better, don't worry.'

They drew up at the surgery and parked the car, it was nice and quiet, just as she had planned, because the afternoons at the vet were not usually very busy. Fluffy smelled a bit rancid after the journey but Beatrice bent down and put her nose up against the wire door and whispered to her cat. 'You old fraud, you'll outlive all of us, won't you?' In her mind she added, 'just make sure that this time, it isn't anything too serious.' The cat opened her toothless mouth and treated her to a warm, poisonous, but loving, blast of cat breath.

The children were rapidly settled in the large, bright waiting room and had soon forgotten the purpose of their visit. Emily was riding a rather odd looking, fur covered, rocking sheep and Alexa was thumbing through the 'pets needing homes' book, no doubt with a view to a fresh onslaught on her mother's conscience, before begging for another cat or, even better, a dog. Beatrice knew poor old Fluffy hadn't got much life left but she was dreading the moment when she had to decide whether to take that final step or struggle on with more tablets and injections.

The girls had only known Fluffy as an adult cat, a bit old and not at all playful. She had been rescued by Beatrice many years previously from a house full of rather irresponsible male students. The cat had been left behind by a previous occupant according to a grubby youth who was lolling on one of the lumpy sofas. It seemed to Beatrice that none of the young men had any idea how to look after it nor any interest in its welfare. Nobody had cared for the cat - it looked thin and unloved. She was there for a party, one of those impromptu things you heard about from a friend. Before Facebook made house parties into hostile raves that attracted the police. She was bored and listless by eleven o'clock, unimpressed by the company and anxious to get away without seeming rude but, simultaneously, entranced by the pretty tabby. It looked like it needed a good feed. Sneaking back early the next morning, when everyone was sleeping off their hangovers, Beatrice rescued it. She just marched in and tucked the cat under her arm as it sat among the unwashed glasses and beer cans and crisps trodden into the carpet.

Fluffy she had called her, in the absence of anything more inspiring. The cat looked as if it had very mixed parentage, but the spark of affection she felt as she sped away from the horrible student house with Fluffy staring shocked out of the front windscreen, that spark made up for all the dull days and nights of her life at the time. She was lonely waiting for someone interesting to come along, preferably someone with whom she could build a life. As it was, she just kept increasing her gang of furry companions. Fluffy joined the rest of her collection and had soon clawed her way up the pecking (or purring) order until she was the one who slept on the bed every night, regardless of which of the others had staked a prior claim. Fluffy was a deep and contented sleeper and didn't jump on Beatrice's head in the mornings which was a bonus, whichever way you looked at it.

She sat quietly meditating on these memories in the vet's waiting room, a place she had been many times before, as she said goodbye to her feline friends of yesteryear. All those feelings were with her now in a rush. She was weak, helpless and grieving for her losses. All those years on her own with her furry family of pets, before she had met Bill. Those years of struggle and loneliness. And Fluffy, waiting at home at the front of a queue of wriggling pussycats, with a cuddle and a purr.

'Mrs Abington,' called the vet. He stepped out of the consulting room with too much eagerness and looked directly at her.

'Wait here children, don't make too much noise,' she whispered. Alexa snorted and looked down again at her book. Emily was involved in a rambling, imaginary conversation with the stuffed sheep and both children looked utterly unconcerned about Fluffy's fate.

Inside the consulting room the vet was putting on his latex gloves and wiping down the black rubber treatment table. There was a lot of dog hair on it. She lifted the basket and placed it on the wet surface, undoing the straps. Fluffy stubbornly stayed hunched right at the back. Emotion was tightening her throat and making speech impossible.

'What seems to be the matter with you, old girl?' The vet was unrelentingly cheerful.

She couldn't talk. A sob was threatening to break loose in her mouth. She inwardly commanded herself to breathe deeply and get a grip, if only to stop the humiliating tears that would inevitably follow.

'I think she might have to be put to sleep. She hasn't been eating and I know, after the last time, you thought she might have something more serious, you said you might have to see if she has a growth.' The words tumbled out.

The vet didn't look at her but just coaxed the old cat out of the basket where it stood on the black rubber table, skinny, shedding multicoloured fur and smelling.

'Let's have a little look, shall we?' He was gentle and kind as he carefully palpated the abdomen and listened to her chest, looked into her mouth. The tears thankfully receded. The vet gave no clue in the tone of his voice to help her predict his verdict on poor Fluffy. He turned away and picked up a shining metal bowl and pulled on a length of paper tissue.

'I'm afraid she's extremely ... (sick? unlikely to survive? Beatrice's mind raced) ... constipated, Mrs Abington. Her bowels feel completely impacted with faeces and given her age, she probably hasn't got the strength to squeeze it all out. I'm afraid this is going to be rather unpleasant for both of us.'

The vet reached behind him for a tube of, what looked like, yellow axle grease and spread a good dollop on his index finger. With one hand he restrained the cat while the other slipped effortlessly up poor Fluffy's impacted back passage, without hesitation. So much for good manners. A wave of relief flooded over her and a small giggle followed. Crisis over and at least this time she hadn't blubbed like a baby. The past, however, with all its power to take away her calm and controlled exterior, had been awakened from slumber. If she had ever thought her memories were truly in the past.

Later on, one greasy bottomed cat, still alive and kicking, emerged from the consulting room and the children cooed and fussed over her. Behind her, she heard the familiar snapping sound of the vet's latex gloves as he peeled them off and discarded them. Beatrice was feeling like she had avoided a death sentence. It was silly how you allowed yourself to get so worked up about these things. She was a grown woman, over forty, reasonably successful in her career, with a reputation for toughness, feeling as if the world was now wonderful because she didn't have to have her manky old cat put to sleep.

'We've got to give her lots of Weetabix to get the poos coming out,' she explained to her youngest, 'then she'll feel like eating more. I've just got to pay and get some medicine for her that will help. The vet said she was quite well, really, and her chest is clear so she's had a little reprieve.'

'Tell me again about the poos coming out,' Emily begged.

'They were like little black raisins, all hard and dry, no wonder she felt horrible,' Beatrice said. She could relax now and see the funny side.

'Can I see them?' Emily was determined.

'No, darling, they went into the special bin to be thrown away.'

'I don't like raisins.'

'I know you don't sweetheart.'

'Do I have to have them in my lunchbox? Chloe has them and she likes them, she says I'm silly for not liking them.'

Alexa made an exasperated huffing sound. She plugged herself into her iPod and closed her eyes.

By teatime, when all the fur had been vacuumed out of the cat basket and the cereal cupboard had been scoured for a box of Weetabix, Beatrice remembered it was getting late and picked up the phone to call Rose. They had a book group meeting that night and she needed to know the catering arrangements.

'Do you want me to bring anything?' Beatrice asked.

'Nothing at all, it's all laid out already.'

'Are we drinking?'

'You bet, I've got three bottles and we've got to finish them all, but also some soppy non-alcoholic muck for the lightweights.'

'OK, well, sounds good. I hope everyone is coming. Maybe I'll walk over and then I can get drunk. Have you read the book?'

'Sadly, yes.'

'You didn't like it then?'

'I'm not telling you, you'll have to wait until I tell you in the proper context of the group.'

'Spoilsport. Anyway I also have a few things of my own to say about the last choice.'

'Using words beginning with F and C, perhaps?' Rose chuckled.

'I'm going to keep you in suspense.'

'Oh well. I'm sure we'll be in the minority. Everyone else seems to drool over those clearly 'made up for the money' accounts of spirits and the afterlife. All of them simpering and bleating about spirituality and being true to your feelings. If I have to say nice things about Dierdre Gleam and her bloody dead relatives I shall be sick.' Rose made a realistic vomiting sound.

'You are quite right of course but you really are a horrible person as well.'

'Thank God for that, I thought I was losing my touch. I won't be too horrid though, not tonight. I would never have thought Hils would enjoy that stuff. But it shows we are all so different, and without that, well, life would be unspeakably dull.'

'OK, well I hope your choice is something good. Or Dierdre Gleam will get her dead relatives to haunt you!'

'I'll see you later, then.' Rose signed off, abruptly.

Beatrice whizzed around the house, in housework mode, picking up bits of discarded clothing, pencils, little pointless drawings and many pairs of shoes. She found four pairs of socks stuffed down by the side of the sofa and an old cup, half filled with cold cocoa, on the floor by the standard lamp, waiting to be kicked over. The children were arguing about what unsuitable television to watch and all was well. Bill would be home any moment and she could slip away unnoticed. It was dusk, her favourite time of day, when the light from the setting sun made everything glow with an amber tint. The grey surface of the road outside disappeared in the fading twilight and seemed to turn into liquid, shifting and insubstantial. Birds were preparing for bedtime and their songs were urgent and purposeful as they called to one another. The air was warm. The man across the road had lit a bonfire and the smoke was drifting across towards her house in the light breeze. The rain that had threatened earlier had now cleared and the evening promised to be fine. Closing the door, she separated herself from her indoor life and concentrated on the scene outside. There, in the distance, were the oak trees at the other end of the village from her house. Nearer were smaller ornamental trees and shrubs in the many well kept gardens nearby. She loved this feeling of being enclosed by nature. Gerald from the bungalow was putting his car away, she waved. It was very, very peaceful, apart from the racket and occasional squeals and swear words from her own house. She wondered why no-one ever complained about it. Perhaps they were too polite to say anything but had, mentally, marked her down as an ineffectual parent and disciplinarian, not quite one of us, you know. Perhaps social services had a file on her. Who cared, anyway? It was about time she lived a little and took a few risks with her life.

At that very moment Bill's car came around the corner. He parked, collected his briefcase and bounded across to her.

'Nice day, darling? What's for dinner? How's Fluffy? How're the kids?' She filled him in on the details while he foraged in the cupboard for crisps and poured himself a large glass of red wine. Formalities over, she eased herself out of the comfortable domestic scene, popped on her jacket and slipped out.

Chapter 2 - In Rose's rather grand living room

'I see you've tidied up.' The lounge looked immaculate and smelled of fresh flowers.

'You know something, Beatrice, you can easily go off people.'

'You love it really. Did you get a new cleaner then?'

'Look, I did it myself, OK, just because I'm not obsessive about having a clean house does not make me a bad person.'

'In your opinion.'

'Weirdo.'

'Freak.'

'Loser.'

'They don't say that anymore.'

'No, you're right. Talking of teenagers.' Rose changed the subject. 'How is the lovely and charming Alexa?'

'Ah, you know she had work experience? Five days hard slog with no pay.'

'Sounds very much like being a wife and mother to me, except it goes on forever, not just five days.'

'Well, after she finished her week she calmly explained to me she doesn't want to work at all. She made it sound like she would be soiling her hands if she lowered herself to get a job. Anyway, she says she wants to marry a rich guy and would I keep an eye out for one, that way she won't ever have to work.' As she was talking, Beatrice had the uncomfortable sensation of putting her foot in it. Rose didn't work, after all, and Charles was rich. It was too late to take it back. She had only told Rose because it seemed like a funny story.

'Tell her from me it's not all it's cracked up to be.'

'Sorry, tactless me.'

'Doesn't matter. Is she serious, though, do you think?'

'No idea, you can never tell with Alex.'

'I could speak to her? I think she still views me as a kind of auntie. Oh, that reminds me, could she babysit for me next Wednesday? We've got to take the boys to a sports evening at school. So Grace needs a sitter.' Rose's boys went to a posh single sex school where sport was considered more important than exam results.

'I'm sure she'll be free. She loves coming here. You have more interesting snacks. And Sky.'

'Ask her to ring me? It won't be a late one. Drink?'

'Yes please, white, I think tonight.'

Beatrice stretched out on Rose's nice squashy sofa and looked around. She was first, so that meant they could talk freely before anyone else came. Lots of yummy food was laid out on the side table, she spotted a box of truffles too, would Rose notice if she ate a few now? The house didn't really do justice to Rose's personality. It looked as if a mysterious style consultant had worked hard in the background, changing the sofa choices, reorganising the pictures, selecting the curtains, matching up the rugs. This wasn't Rose, she knew it for a fact. Anyone who had been on the receiving end of a lift in her car (first remove three sacks of rubbish and food debris from seat before you get in) could spot the disparity.

They had known each other for at least ten years, since that fateful first day at the primary school, when their respective children had huddled behind both their skirts and refused to go in. The reception teacher had been patient, but firm. 'Could the mummies please move gently away and say goodbye to the children? And then we can get on with the day.' Rose and Beatrice had looked at each other. They had each spotted a kindred spirit, slightly subversive, mildly anti-authority and determined not to be told what to do by a menopausal primary school teacher with an attitude. It was Alex who pre-empted a fight by looking up at Beatrice with tears in her eyes, chin wobbling, ominously. 'It's all right Mummy, I'll be brave and go in on my own.' She took Rose's boy and walked towards the teacher who, by this time, was wearing a smile of nauseating smugness. Rose, who had been brewing up for a withering put down turned towards her and winked. 'Fancy a drink ... it's not too early for alcohol, is it? To either celebrate this new phase of our lives or drown our sorrows, whichever appeals most.' Rose stared, looking around for anyone who wanted to disagree with her. It was loud enough for everyone to hear. The reception teacher shook her head and, gripping her new charges firmly by the hand, retreated into the school building. Beatrice knew from that moment they would be marked down in the staffroom as troublemakers. The women quickly became very close friends. It was Rose that had begun calling her just 'B'.

Now, in Rose's beautiful lounge, they settled down for a cosy chat before anyone else arrived. Beatrice wanted to know more about the book choice.

'Well, what is this secret book you have chosen for us?' Rose reached across and pulled out a shiny paperback from a pile on the table.

'I've selected a few possibilities, but this is the one I really want us to read.'

Beatrice looked at the familiar title. She had recommended it to Rose last year. She was puzzled, though.

'You realise if we read it, then we will have to do it. Do the exercises and so on, as a group.'

'Yes, I know,' Rose beamed at her, 'that's exactly what I intend to happen.'

'Really? I'm all for it, it would be great. Not sure about the others, though.'

'We'll just gang up on them. You told me I should read it ages ago but, I thought that if I was going to read it, it would be better to do it in a group and then we could all practise together. Get some good energy going.'

They sat in silence for a few moments. Upstairs, Rose's husband could be heard yelling at the children. He clearly had not yet mastered the knack of the effortless bedtime routine. Rose would have to train him.

B was not so sure about the book choice. 'Perhaps we should just all read it first? I don't know how the others would feel about committing to lots of group practice. What is your second choice if no-one wants to read that one?'

'It's about shamanism in South America and it's over 600 pages long.'

'Hmm, you know how to get your own way, don't you?' They both slumped back onto the sofa, laughing and smiling.

The book Rose had chosen was called *A Course in Channelling.* Beatrice had read and devoured it over a year ago. It had been recommended to her by the girl who ran the mind, body and spirit section of the bookshop in Buckingham. If you were serious about spirituality, this was the defining work you should read. The girl was very believable, not at all spotty and peculiar, so B took her advice and bought it. Her usual diet of past life regression books and spiritual self help guides had long since been exhausted and she was ripe for something new. When she read the introduction she couldn't believe her eyes. The book was a set of instructions and techniques that would enable you to connect with (how exactly would that feel?) and channel your own personal spirit guide. She was excited and anxious all at once. It could be beyond her capabilities, though. Perhaps only gifted people could do this? She knew a few of them already. Not being remotely sensitive (about as sensitive as a house brick), she had never had any supernatural or tangible spiritual experiences. But there was a desire inside her that needed to find an outlet, coupled with a persistent feeling that she was on the brink of discovering something vital, life changing. Organising a reading group based on spiritual books and discussing their meaning was, she supposed, a natural progression from her solitary endeavours. She found she was learning much more from having different perspectives, too. So, the group of her friends had come together. They had drunk a lot of spirits (naturally) and read a diverse selection of books, starting with her personal favourite - *Siddhartha* by Herman Hesse. When she had read the channelling book on her own, she was dismayed by her attempts to find the right frame of mind, the concentration required to practise the various meditations. She was keen but a bit lost. And not sure if she was doing it right. The book was sitting on her bedside table waiting to be picked up again.

The book group, however, had really taken off and been better and more fun than she had anticipated. It was good discipline to read things other people had chosen and the simple rule that whoever hosted should choose the next book meant they had all been to each of the friends' houses and read some fascinating books that would not, ordinarily, have been to her taste. There had been a lot of deep discussion too. It was amazing what you found out about people when you were all on a similar wavelength and trusted each other. Rose had told the group, one dark evening last winter, about her childhood terrors when her family had moved into a different house. It wasn't a particularly old house either. She had been plagued by disembodied voices and dark shapes in her bedroom at night. She had been too frightened to tell anyone. Then Hilary had talked about her experiences when her grandmother had died and how she had known it was going to happen beforehand; she was confident she had some skill with precognition. Jill had admitted to being able to communicate telepathically with her sister, more so when they were younger. But it had recently become stronger again despite her sister living in Canada and she wanted to know why. In comparison with all of them B felt a bit second rate. She was the one who had organised this group and all she could contribute was theoretical knowledge. Nothing to confide or offer as proof. Just a desire, a wish and, if she were honest, plain envy of the other friends.

Beatrice had also come to understand, though, there was a downside to spiritual sensitivity. Her friends seemed to be floored by the emotional side of ordinary life. It sounded like their lives were like a human rollercoaster, full of ups and downs. They just didn't appear to have a tough outer shell like she had. When they talked about their feelings, she couldn't empathise, she'd had never felt these intense feelings herself. She must have a control mechanism or protection, whatever it was, that stopped her from going too far or getting hurt. Lately, however, she had begun to wonder what she might be missing.

It was still early evening and the other group members had not arrived yet. Rose walked over to draw the curtains, then sat opposite her, she looked on edge. As if something was bothering her.

'Aren't you a little bit apprehensive about what may happen, if we do this channelling thing?' B asked her friend.

'Like what exactly?' Rose looked at her, distractedly.

'Well, the ghostly presences you told me about, you know, when you were a teenager.'

Rose now looked directly at her and screwed her eyes up before speaking. 'Listen, I need to own up to something, I think. If I don't do this channelling and find out what it's all about I am going to go stark staring mad,' she said. 'Since Easter, I think it started then, something weird is going on. In my head. It happens when I'm on my own in the house.'

'In this house?'

'Yes, don't worry, it's not the house, I'm sure of that – it's me, I think.'

'What happens, then?'

'Whenever I am on my own, usually in the bedroom, it starts. It always catches me unaware, so I sometimes forget and I get sucked into it. I start to get little lights flashing in the corners of my eyes, just on one side. Then if I look hard enough, the light gets brighter and I get a horrible tight feeling in my chest as if I want to gasp. But I can't breathe. It is huge and overwhelming, but not frightening as such, as long as you don't mind holding your breath.'

'Sounds like the start of a migraine to me, have you seen the doctor?'

Rose reached across and patted B's hand.

'Don't look so scared, I'm in fine health. It's not migraine, I assure you. And before you ask, I haven't got a brain tumour either. I have actually looked up every imaginable symptom on the internet.' She continued. 'It starts with the lights. Almost like they are dancing round to catch my attention. Then, if I look hard enough, it changes, opening like a golden tunnel and I don't know where it ends. It fills the room, or just my mind, I can't tell which. Up until now I have been able to snap out of it and rush downstairs and do something trivial like put the TV on or sort out the dishwasher. It seems so long ago , those ghosts, or dark energies when I was growing up. I feel sometimes as if it was just my overactive imagination. Or hormones. This is totally different though.' Rose was looking distant now.

'The truth is B, I am intending to follow it very soon. I don't think I have much choice. It's a very powerful feeling and *compelling* – it's pulling me in. I have looked at accounts of people who have died and come back, you know, near death experiences, flat lining, whatever you want to call it, and it sounds like that. I think about it all the time and I'm starting to avoid being at home alone. I don't feel any different in myself. It's as if something outside is calling me, wanting my attention. But it's all happening in my head.'

'This is way outside my understanding. Shouldn't we try to find an expert? They must exist. College of Psychic Studies? Something like that?' Beatrice was quietly panicking.

'I'm glad you said we. I feel quite alone and bit worried.'

'Don't be. Let me see what I can find out about getting help.'

'But it's so intangible, though, isn't it? It's in my head. I'm not sure I could explain it or trust someone I don't know. You are my stability. I know that you will help me; you're so knowledgeable and down-to-earth. If one day I don't come back or I'm found in a heap with my eyes glazed over and a stupid grin on my face I'm trusting that you will know what to do.'

'Oh no! Rose, I don't know what to do! I'm the last person you should ask.'

'Look, I've read a bit of the book, OK? It's so logical and believable, it talks about control and how you train yourself to be in control of these phenomena. I'm too scared *not* to do it. Maybe I'm too sensitive, I don't know.' At that moment they were interrupted. The doorbell rang and Rose got up, looking both relieved and, to Beatrice anyway, exhausted.

Hilary, Jill, Lesley and Gwen were on the doorstep, full of energy and gabbling all at once. Hilary had a box with a warm and slightly disintegrating quiche in it and Lesley had booze; they tumbled in like schoolchildren. Gwen looked like she had been in the Edinburgh Wool Shop sale section again and, by way of contrast, Lesley was urbane, cool and colour co-ordinated, her elfin face alive and her peachy curls jiggling as she spoke. Jill beamed. Gwen scowled behind her dark fringe and her rather masculine spectacles. Lesley marched in, gripping a bottle in each hand and holding a large bag of pretzels between her teeth.

Later, Beatrice and Rose explained they were going to read and study this book that was, basically, a course to teach you how to become attuned to the spirit world, make contact with spirit guides and then, if you wanted to, do readings for people.

'By spirit guides, do you mean dead people?' Hilary didn't look impressed.

'I'm not sure if spirit guides have ever actually been people at all, I think they are perhaps wise beings assigned to people to stop them from screwing up.'

'Do we have to do much practice if we are going to do it? I'm not sure I can spare the time. I've got a lot of work on at the moment.' Hilary was reluctant. The others were unsure.

'Well, I don't mind meeting more often. I really enjoy getting together.' Jill seemed enthusiastic.

'Isn't it dangerous, like the Ouija Board? Could we contact bad spirits by mistake?'

Beatrice had wondered this herself. But she knew she had to be positive.

'Polly and Pippa aren't here tonight but I'll phone them and see what they think.'

'I haven't seen Pippa for ages. What's happening with her, then? And is David any better?'

It was beginning to disintegrate. Gwen was staring at her. Not in a nice way. Something is not right, she thought. Next to Gwen, Lesley was chatting animatedly with Jill about something. Jill. Beatrice knew she had applied for a full time job at the hospital. Hospital. Oh shit. What an idiot. In a horrible flash of understanding the full implications of what they were planning, contacting spirits, dead people or whatever, struck her. Gwen wouldn't mention it out loud but her anguish showed on her face. Her dearest friend Lesley would be doubly affected by this. And what if they stumbled upon something, messages, a spirit guide, who wanted to speak to Lesley directly about her loss? How could they protect her?

Rose stood up and swept her hands up in a gesture of finality.

'I think it is time. We talk about spirituality, isn't it right that we actually do something, rather than intellectualising the subject? I'm going to do it and B is going to help me, so we are going to work at it together. I'm not scared of a bit of work; with my family I'm used to it. I know this is the right thing to do, so let's just get on with it.' Rose looked as though she would not brook any arguments. And as she observed the assembled friends, Beatrice wondered what they were really thinking. Lesley looked just the same as always. You would never know. Beatrice would have to think about this very carefully. Rose turned her back and reached for the chocolates. She passed them to Jill and smiled. Beatrice hoped Rose wouldn't notice that she had already eaten a few of them.

Chapter 3 - Staring out of the window

Pippa stared out of the window until her eyes hurt. The air was damp and the dustmen were due soon; she could hear the clump and the alarming grinding noise of the dustcart, it was a little way up the road. The children had just gone out of view, on their way to school, and there was a deal of mess to clear up before she could leave. Her camera and lighting gear were dumped by the bed.

Her eyes felt dry, desiccated, after last night's bout of weeping. The skin around her eyes was tight and sore. David was in the spare room but not awake, not that she had looked. He hadn't made any sounds yet, at least. Would she dare go off and leave him alone all day or should she call someone and ask for some help? But what could she say? What possible explanation could she give to anyone for wanting someone to come and sit with her husband and watch him to make sure he didn't do anything stupid? Anyway, if someone called round or phoned they might make it worse; precipitate something. Pippa couldn't face another of those terrifying drives back to the house wondering what the hell she might find. Then trying to cover it all up. If she made a good start now she could be back before the children came home from school and she could smile and make dinner and make it appear to them that it was just another day. An ordinary day in their family life. It wasn't just another day, though.

Last night she had found a half written note, in his handwriting, that gave her an inkling of just how low he was and what he might be capable of doing. She assumed he had been disturbed as the note wasn't finished. But it was addressed to her and it was lying on the little bedside table. She had anguished with herself. Should she destroy the note and hope he had forgotten or should she leave it and risk the reminder of what he was thinking about? The kids never went into his room anyway so she wasn't really worried about them finding anything. She had chewed the inside of her cheek and tried to unravel the racing thoughts in her head. Finally, before bedtime, she had decided what to do and retrieved the note from his room. It was still screwed up in her pocket. She had then clattered down the stairs and into the living room to resume family life, such as it was. When she came through he looked up and smiled wanly at her; she bent over his slumped frame. He was still snuggled up in his track suit bottoms and pyjama top but he had his soft cream jersey over the top, so he looked all warm and cosy and lovable. Her throat tightened and her eyes pricked. Not again, no crying now. He should be comforting her but he couldn't, he had nothing left at all. She had stroked his hand, it was slightly cool as if it wasn't being used for anything, redundant, pointless. She had rubbed harder to warm it up and spoke as cheerfully as she could.

'Cup of something, then David? Ovaltine? Horlicks?' David shook his head as if nothing could make him feel better. 'Well, I'll make one anyway, maybe you'll feel like it then?'

That had all happened last night. Now, after a restless night's sleep, she was in a worse state of indecision and turmoil than before. She quickly ran through her choices and reviewed the things she could do. It was two months before his next hospital appointment. She could phone up and ask for it to be brought forward. She could speak to his CPN but he was on holiday and wouldn't be back for another two weeks. She realised she had not recently checked how many tablets were in the pack. Maybe he had been missing them, or hoarding them? The dilemma was without hope of a solution. Because, in the back of her mind, she knew what the consequences of asking for help would be. The possibility of another stint of inpatient treatment and the inevitable worsening of David's trust and no guarantee of any improvement. They had changed his medication last time and while the old wore off and before the new kicked in there had been a week where her poor husband had endured (what she imagined was) mental torture. Pain beyond endurance. His eyes had told her everything she needed to know. The situation was unfixable.

'Dare I leave him today?' She stared even harder out of the window.

'Dare I leave him and risk the consequences?' She took a deep breath and realised that, actually, she had no choice.

'Pippa, Pip, shall I help you get the stuff out of the car?' Julie, her assistant, bounded across the path and panted like a puppy. Pippa heaved her camera and the tripod out of the back and then bent over to where the lighting gear and her laptop were stowed. There were bits and pieces all over the back seat and she directed Julie to take them carefully inside without dropping any of them. The studio was set up and ready from the previous day when they had shot a group of dance students who wanted some action photos for their portfolios. So young and hopeful they were, it had made her feel twenty again and with everything to look forward to.

Julie, as a workmate, was just perfect. A thorough antidote to her current problems. She had never met such a relentlessly enthusiastic and positive girl. She would be on her way next July, off to University and all those handsome buff guys or whatever you called them these days, 'hunky blokes' she thought, showing her age. What on Earth was she going to do without her? She felt the start of a feeling of mild panic in her chest.

The studio was small but big enough for a good shoot with enough space for action shots. She had cleared a whole area on the ground floor with nothing in it, no twee cushions or silly backdrops, no rocking chairs or ridiculous props, just clean white space, just what she needed to capture her subjects, her models, her customers. Today they had a selection of children coming in. This was a very special occasion as the children in this case were disabled with learning difficulties of various kinds. They were coming in as a whole class from a special school to do some individual portraits, group shots, and then to do a whole class action shot which would hopefully be used for the school brochure and website. I'm really looking forward to it, Pip thought, it will do me good.

She popped to the loo and stared at herself in the mirror. She looked horrible, pale and lined but, if she smiled hard enough, her face looked almost normal. 'How can I get through today and tomorrow and the day after that when I feel so totally rubbish inside?' The thought banged at the inside of her head.

There was a lot of noise coming from the front of the studio and she emerged from the loo to see a group of small children standing in the foyer, methodically peeling off their coats and outer garments while twittering away in happy excited voices. The teachers and carers had serene, kind, almost spiritual faces. The children were shooed and shepherded into the waiting area and Julie found enough chairs for the adults to sit down. The children were mostly sitting cross-legged on the floor looking expectant; their little shiny faces all scrubbed and pink and pretty. They had their best clothes on and some shirt-tails were already escaping; some socks meandering down small plump legs. There were two boys in wheelchairs and one sitting on a chair with a teacher gently holding his hand.

Pip felt overwhelmed with humility. She spread a broad smile over her exhausted features and hoped it looked genuine. Her mind clicked into action and she started to sort out the best pairings and groups of children, thinking about poses and props that she might use. There were two little girls that had matching rosy cheeks and were wearing quite clashing clothes. That would make a good shot. One of the boys had a hand knitted multicoloured scarf on; I should like to get him to keep that on, she thought. Those childish smiles were just so infectious; she could feel herself warming up inside. This was going to be a good day after all.

Chapter 4 - Trying to get in touch

From: Beatrice
Recipient: Pip

Hi Pip
We all met up for our book group the other night and I was hoping you would come, does that mean that you don't want to be involved anymore? We have decided to do something different, called 'channelling', it is where you get in touch with your spirit guide and get messages about stuff in your life that you want answers to. It was Rose's idea but I've already had a try and I liked it and want to do it together. I don't want to push you but it is a bit of a commitment.
How's David? Has he had his hospital appointment yet? What about his work, are they being sympathetic? I'll leave it up to you anyway
Love as always
Bxxx

From: Pippa
Recipient: Beatrice

Hi B
Work going well. Glad you all got together but I don't feel able to commit to anything in the evenings at the moment. David is the same. His consultant said we must expect it to take time. These new generation antidepressants are not a quick fix. I just am going from day to day. The kids don't know yet how serious it is but in a weird way they are accepting of what is happening. Life goes on, you know? I think I might have to get some more help. A carer maybe, just for some of the week when I have bookings that are going to go on all day. You probably know where I can get some advice about this. Would I have to pay or can I get some help with the cost? Don't know how to go about it. Come to the studio and we can have lunch, Julie

can hold the fort. I have so much I want to tell you and I'm sure you will give me your best and wisest advice, Pipxxx

Beatrice ground her teeth and wrung her hands. Bugger. What can I do to help? It was much worse for Pippa than she thought. In contrast, Beatrice counted her blessings. Her house was warm, the people in it comfortingly easy to get along with and all of them well and moderately happy. Bill was the best husband anyone could want, nice to look at and with hair too which, at his age, was very welcome. Her lovely children were secure and safe. What more could anyone wish for? She thought about Pippa, her dear friend, and wished she could think of a way to help her.

Pippa was at home again dry eyed at her computer plodding through mountains of emails. Emails from firms wanting her business. Emails from newspapers with special advertising deals. Emails from colleagues wanting to sell old equipment or go halves on some new stuff. She quickly deleted all the spam and trawled through the e-zines, before scanning the individual mails and leaving, in her inbox, the ones that she really wanted to look at. She re-read the mail from Beatrice. She was just the right kind of friend; she knew when to push and cajole and when to let go and give Pippa space. She so wanted to get on the phone right now and meet up with her, share a drink at the pub; away from the house. She so wanted to tell her what was on her mind but, in truth, just thinking about it exhausted her. In a way she thought that if she talked about it to B, (who would then want to take some sort of action), it would make the whole sorry situation real and worse. There was a fine line, she thought, between hope that things were going to go back to how they were before and acceptance they never would and could get much worse.

Now, as she sat there, with everyone safely tucked up in bed, she could pretend to herself things were normal. They were a normal family, her and David and their two lovely children. David had just been going through a bad patch, that's all. Overwork and a new demanding boss, that is what she was telling people who enquired. 'How long has David been off work?' Friends asked her, sympathetically. 'Oh, it's about five months now. They are being very understanding. There have been a lot of staff off with stress related illness at the company since the takeover; HR are really very good. They can't wait for him to get back but I want him to have a really good rest first.' What a complete load of bollocks. David was never going back. David was just waiting for the chop to come. David wouldn't even notice when it did come, he was so locked into his safe, sad little world. He had almost shut down completely this time. Nothing stirred him, nothing made his eyes light up. The old tricks that Pip had used in the past to distract him, to motivate him, had failed miserably. He used to respond when Pip said she wanted something doing in the house, a new project, something he could build, like a complicated shelving unit or that water feature and gazebo in the garden; it had helped, she was sure. If only I could imagine what it really feels like, what thoughts go round in his head? Why are his thoughts and feelings different to mine and why do his thoughts make him feel so down, so depressed, unable to function and without hope? *Low mood* they called it. It was hard to believe, after all the advances in modern medicine, they knew nothing more than that. No doctor or book or research on the internet had been able to tell her.

But Pippa *had* known what she was getting into right from the start. She couldn't pretend to herself that she had been fooled into thinking David was an ordinary boyfriend with a normal family . His mother had suffered with clinical depression for as long as David could remember. It was an open family secret. She was scarily expert about her disorder and all the treatment she had received over the years. Pippa knew there could be family similarities and she and David had talked about it endlessly. He was honest about the problems he'd had as a teenager. *Two years* it had taken him to get better then. But, of course, depression like that didn't just happen, like an unfortunate accident. She knew the difference now between what David had and other depressions that were termed 'reactive'. In his case it was a part of the sufferer, like their eye colour or the shape of their face. David's inner world was imprinted on him long before Pip came along. His brain chemistry was part of his genetic inheritance. If she was honest with herself about her own attitude at the time, it was sheer arrogance on her part that drove her on to agree to marry him. 'I can cure him of this,' she told herself. 'Just let me show them how clever I am.' What an idiot.

Chapter 5 - Jill gets a cold

Somewhere up her sleeve was a screwed up bit of tissue, probably toilet paper, it would have to do, to mop up the snot from that last sneeze. Her nose was sore now and red around her nostrils which made her look slightly unappealing as a health professional at the cutting edge of the modern NHS and the new Assistant Ward Manager for Charlton Ward. It was a small twelve bed semi-acute ward for elderly patients, with four side rooms for more vulnerable patients. Oh, how excited she was! 'I love this work,' she thought out loud, 'even when everyone says it is too stressful and too messy and I know I will be totally unappreciated and get shouted at by all the consultants and most of the patients too.' And she knew, in the back of her mind, that there would be sadness. That came with the territory. But her refresher training was still clear, her bank nursing of the last few years had stood her in good stead, and the fond memories of previous work with the elderly made her feel empowered and determined. All my patients will receive the best care that the team can offer, she affirmed to herself.

She picked up the letter that had come yesterday, confirming her successful appointment to the new position and her lovely new salary. Much better than the unpredictable earnings from bank work. It made her heart beat faster. It made her glow inside. Just another little step along her personal road to security and stability. All her own work. Who cared what Max thought? Who gave a damn about him, anyway? Not me, that's for certain. He can rot in hell with his mincing, bloody skinny, whiney-voiced girlfriend. She kissed her beautiful letter, sniffed, coughed, blew her nose again and went to get her mobile to text Max and tell him where he could shove his latest offer to settle the last few years of maintenance. He had not paid one penny for Theo when he left, it had all been down to her and her own earning efforts. But her solicitor had teeth and the threat of court and a claim on his pension had brought him back to negotiating. He was still a complete miser though, she thought.

Jill was upstairs looking at the heap of clothes on her bedroom floor. Her room was just how she liked it, full of sun, comfortably messy with a big pile of books stacked up on her bedside table. She toyed with the idea of getting back into bed and just having another chapter of her current book, just a last little chapter, before making a real start on sorting herself out for her new job. There would be a different uniform to order and all the bits and pieces that went with it. She wondered if it would be too optimistic to order a size 14, or should she stick with a more generous 16 and be damned, leaving lots of extra space for food pleasures to come.

Her dressing gown was grubby, that needed washing too. She flung it off and added it to the heap of screwed up clothes and then bundled them all up in her arms and proceeded to feel her way downstairs to the kitchen to sort them out for washing. How she relished the freedom of her aloneness. Naked and handsome and abundant, she bent and squatted down among the washing pile, revelling in the wicked sensation of abandon. She sorted the whites and colours and shoved the first load in. She stretched up, high on her tiptoes, looking down at her brown legs and white belly, golden soft hair tickling her shoulders. Jill marched over to the sideboard and grabbed the neck of an old bottle of cherry brandy, taking a large gulp. 'That's more like it,' she hummed and ran off back upstairs to get dressed.

There was a special shop Jill liked to go to. It was called Crystal Cave and it had all manner of fascinating things to buy. There was a massive amethyst in the window, facing into the shop area, and when you stood near it you could feel a blast of energy almost akin to heat. It made your face feel irradiated. She had always been drawn to crystals and anything at all to do with energy healing. Today she felt a desire to stand and bask in that crystal heat, just to remind herself of the sensation. She also needed something to speed up the process of healing her cold or she would not be starting work on Monday.

The thin girl with the brown plaits was behind the counter; she looked as if a breath of wind would blow her away. To the side was a large trunk with all kinds of small, different coloured stones, all mixed up together. Jill knelt down and eased her hand into the smooth sea of minerals. She was looking for a stone that she didn't have already, but her gaze was drawn to another hand, small and pale, plunging into the mass of stones and letting them trickle through delicate fingers. Another customer was crouching down, doing just the same as her. She looked up, surprised, and stared into the heart-shaped face and cool violet eyes of a young woman, probably half her age, who was staring straight back at her. Jill smiled, she loved new faces, new souls.

'I can't resist them,' she explained.

'Neither can I,' the girl replied.

Her beautiful pale rosy lips were so perfectly formed and slightly moist, Jill almost wanted to reach over and touch them. This girl had a cloud of silvery blonde hair, so fine and beautiful compared with Jill's own, rather ordinary, blonde. It curled around her pretty young face.

'Are you looking for a particular stone?' The girl was asking her. 'Or can I make recommendation for you?' There was just a slight trace of accent. Spanish maybe, certainly European. How thrilling, thought Jill.

Jill replied, 'I just wanted to see if there was anything special today for my cold, I'm just fishing around really, tempting myself to buy something.' Jill avoided asking her where she was from, despite bursting to know the answer.

'I know not how fishing can get you crystal; I know that a good meal of fish can make you stronger when you have this cold,' the girl said, grinning broadly as she did so.

Jill had no idea what to say next. The girl was so charming. She turned back to the crystals.

'My name is Krystina,' she said 'and today I choose for you this stone,' and handed Jill a smooth pebble of rose quartz, just like many she had already but, when she held it in her hand, the stony coolness was unlike any of the other stones in the trunk. It was icy cold and, even when she put it into her other hand and held it for a minute, it remained like an ice chip, unmelting. She slipped it into her jacket pocket and it was a relief to get it out of her hand which throbbed where the crystal had been. The girl, Krystina, just smiled at her and slowly opened her own hand and there was a black rock with lines and speckles in it. 'Today, this one is what I need, I will buy for you the cool stone for that is what *you* need,' she said and with that she moved swiftly to the counter and paid the thin girl with plaits and was gone. Jill gaped after her like a goldfish in a tank.

'She's the one that does the psychic readings, up there on the board.' The plaited girl spoke. 'She's from Slovakia, I think they're in the EU now, but I couldn't put money on it. She's a bit dramatic, even for me.'

'Thanks, I'm not sure we English are used to being spoken to, unless it's about the weather, of course.' Jill moved over to the notice board and looked at the list of meetings and classes.

Krystina
Introductions to your Spirit Guide
Also Private Readings

That's a coincidence, thought Jill, that's just what I'm going to learn how to do! As she walked away, out into the autumn sunshine in the street outside, she was aware that her nose hadn't run since she put the stone in her pocket. She fingered it suspiciously. It still felt cool but not icy like before. 'What a load of nonsense,' she muttered. 'I must pull myself together and stop letting my imagination run away with me.'

Chapter 6 - Rose listens at the door

It was a lovely evening and the weather had been beautifully fine for the last week. Charles was looking at the news and Rose decided to pop upstairs to check the children before going out for a walk around the garden, just to drink in the last warm breaths of late summer air. She paused on the landing. One of the children still had their TV on. It must be Grace, she's probably asleep with it on, she thought. Rose moved to put her hand on the handle to creep in and quiet the noise when she stiffened. Grace was talking animatedly to someone. Her voice was alternately high and excited, then low and murmuring. Rose walked straight in.

'Come on young lady, what's going on! You should be asleep by now.'

Grace was sitting up in bed, staring at the opposite wall talking nineteen to the dozen about her last birthday party.

'And then Mummy had got a magician, but he didn't have a real rabbit like I asked for, just a pretend one. Mummy told me that it isn't allowed 'cos of cruelty nowadays. So then we had the magic and it was really cool. Jessica got frightened by a big bang but I liked it. Then we had a proper tea Granny, just like you maked at your house with jelly and peaches with custard. I said they were goldfish and Mummy laughed.'

'Grace, wake up now darling, you're having a little dream.' Rose went over and squeezed her arm.

Grace turned sharply to face her, 'I'm not asleep Mummy I'm telling Granny about my party. She couldn't come because she was buried, remember?' The child beamed up at Rose and then turned back to face the wall again and began to talk, then stopped and nodded from time to time.

'Take care Mummy, Granny wants you to look out, just in case. She's off now, back to her friends. I asked her to come back again another night, is that alright? Mummy, say something. Granny is saying goodbye.'

Rose sat heavily down on her daughter's bed, at a total loss as to what to do next. Grace snuggled down into her pillow, looking calm and serene.

'I love Granny, you know.' And in a moment, her child was fast asleep.

Rose's heart was thumping uncomfortably in her chest. What was going on? Grace was only four, too young to be pulled into this. Was it something to do with her? Had she unleashed something? She didn't dare tell Charles, he would go absolutely ballistic, even though he was usually so calm and dependable. She gingerly rose up off the bed so as not to disturb Grace. She needed thinking time.

She grabbed her cigarettes and let herself out into the garden. The heady smell of late roses and the sharp aroma of nearby bonfires were lost on her. She felt sick with nerves. Over to the little bench at the bottom of the garden, she sat down heavily and sighed. 'Think clearly!' she commanded herself out loud. 'Right, let's get this straight. I can't stop myself from being sucked into what seems to be a sort of parallel Universe of energy and my four year old daughter talks to dead people.' She took a long, thoughtful drag and blew the smoke out. 'I'm planning on doing a group, sort of hippy style, a crystal waving meditation course to help me to find out what is going on with me and, what is more, I'm going to do it with a bunch of total amateurs who haven't a clue what is going on either.' She started to smile. 'What a stupid fool I am. I obviously haven't got enough to do, wanting to mess about with the spirit world, like this. Perhaps I'd better talk to B about this again and see what she thinks.' She stubbed her cigarette out and lit another one.

She stared at the little copse just outside the boundary of their property. There was a strip of land that belonged to the village, it just provided a bit of privacy between the houses and the golf course. As she looked at the pretty scene there seemed to be a light, it looked at first as if there was someone with a large torch or lamp. You could see some movement and the light was white but with purplish tones in it. Without warning the light grew and became brighter and brighter. The radiance was almost unbearable. Rose couldn't breathe, she was lost, gasping and gaping like she had been hit on the chest. She experienced the sensation of being sucked upwards.

The brilliance was closer and the heat and power drew her up and out of herself. She wasn't breathing at all now. It was all happening so quickly. Is this what dying is like? She was helpless. Then a purple blob seemed to appear through the haze of brightness. She felt a strong feeling of connection. She was drowning in love and for a moment she wanted to go, to leave and go all the way with this wonderful feeling. At that moment a voice came into her head 'Be clear and confident, it is all as we planned. You will remember more as you connect more, do not allow your fear to stop you.' The anonymous but familiar voice resounded in her head.

And then it stopped and she was aware of the birds again and the smell of wood smoke. Her cigarette was still burning between her fingers. She squinted at the copse. Nothing, there was nothing there at all. It had probably lasted all of five seconds. She stubbed her cigarette out and stood up, shaking. As she looked towards the house, she saw Grace waving happily at her from the upstairs bedroom window.

Chapter 7 - The handsome Dr Farkas

It was Wednesday morning and Jill had been on her shift for about an hour and a half. She still felt mildly out of her depth, partly exacerbated by the brimming confidence of nurse Holly who was clearly very competent indeed and was making her feel old. Holly was very slim, a strong athletic slimness that was accentuated by the fitted uniform. Her bottom was probably the pertest behind Jill had ever seen. She wanted to squeeze it to see if it was real. She needed to stop distracting herself with these stupid thoughts and concentrate on what she should be doing. Forms, why were there so many forms? And where are the ones I actually need? She looked up, checking to see the state of the ward. There were two University of West Buckinghamshire students in that day, looking a bit lost with their files and clipboards and wanting some direction. Rounds would be starting soon and an admission was coming in, anytime now, with the bed not ready. This is the challenge of my chosen career she told herself. No patients in her care could be left to do things independently. Bathing, toileting, feeding, drinking, medications, getting comfortable, in bed or in the stupid, slippery, upright chairs they provided. All this had to be done and she was determined to get on top of it, be there *before* a patient needed help. It was a small thing but it was important. Her eyes scanned the room and in an instant she could see the tasks and the order they needed doing.

'Holly, can you find me some more of these forms, please? And then' ... she quickly rattled off the next round of tasks and Holly, she noticed, looked bright and willing and ready to follow her direction. It was all going to be alright. I am good at this, she told herself, I just need to get used to the way things are done on this ward and find out where they are hiding all the bloody forms!

The admission was coming in and the rattle of the bed coming down the corridor alerted her. At the doorway, walking in front of the new patient, stood a man of about 30 years old with clear blue eyes and a mop of romantic dark hair. He was likely to be one of the consultants she hadn't met yet or one of the A and E team. It was hard to tell who was who without a uniform. She had realised, since returning to work, that her preconceptions about consultants were completely outdated. They should all be old and dressed in a three piece suit with a bowtie! Surely the newer ones she had met were highly intelligent beings that had done their training when they were about 8 years old! And why were they all so handsome? Maybe their innate intelligence made them more handsome. Then she remembered Mr Walsh the ENT man. Ew.

'Hello there,' he glanced at her badge, 'Jill. Good to meet you. Can I call you Jill? I'm just bringing the patient up myself so I can update you on her status and order more tests. Her notes.' He offered her the file in his hand. It was a lovely hand with fine black hairs softly covering the back and tantalisingly disappearing under his shirtsleeve. Jill's arms were suddenly made of rubber and her tongue was glued to the roof of her mouth.

'Doctor Farkas, sorry, I should have introduced myself. From downstairs. A and E. You were expecting us.' He looked at the patient in the bed. She was black and blue from the top of her head all the way down the side of her face and her arms outside the covers were in plaster.

'Can we sit for a moment? Miss Ethel Toddy. Came in around 8.30am. The carers found her. She thought she would get up in the night for the toilet but she had an argument with the hoist which has made a mess of her, I'm afraid. Think she was on the floor, or wrapped round the hoist, anyway, for about five hours. She has Parkinson's so hasn't been walking for about two years but, of course, in the night one forgets such things. I have the most recent care plan in the back of the file here.'

'Ouch!' It was the only thing Jill could say.

'Yes, ouch! Exactly. Anyway, it's all here so as long as you are happy, I'll leave her with you. Daughter has been with her but I think she is getting her some clothes from home, that sort of thing anyway.'

'Yes,' her brain was only capable of monosyllabic responses.

'Yes, you are happy then? I have to rush back now. Lots of poorly people waiting in A and E that I can then send to you Jill.'

'Yes,' she could just about hold it together. Dr Farkas leapt up and was gone before Jill could breathe again. Oh God! She bit her lip and hesitated, suddenly feeling huge and leaden and plodding. She felt her colour rising. She had never seen such a gorgeous man, and he was so much younger than her. It was humiliating to be so affected by his gorgeousness. By the time she could take the few steps to Miss Toddy's bedside, Jill couldn't help but notice most of her staff were standing open mouthed and staring at the corridor where the handsome doctor had just exited. Sitting beside him, Jill thought, was like being close to a warm fire in winter, or a beam of sunshine when you were used to languishing in dull shadow. He was just shamelessly gorgeous and might be unaware of the stir he was causing.

Dr Farkas, it turned out, was something of a hospital sensation. He was on a temporary contract from Hungary and was hoping for a suitable permanent vacancy to come up. A and E had many such staff and she had learned there was a review going on which had deterred UK based doctors from applying for the several unfilled senior positions. It seemed the hospital was relying on these enthusiastic doctors from abroad to keep things going. The usual sticking plaster on a broken arm approach.

'Dr Farkas charms all the patients and most of the staff too,' Holly was beside her now and between them they were going through all the necessary jobs so Miss Toddy could be admitted and made comfortable. Her hospital nightie was already soiled with blood and other nameless fluids, so they settled comfortably into the routine to clean her up, drawing the bed curtains as they did so.

'Dr Farkas then. He seems nice.'

'Nice, are you mad? He's a red hot sex god and I'm shotgunning the first ride on his ... '

'Holly, don't you have a boyfriend already? And isn't that an engagement ring I see on your finger?' Jill smiled and poked Holly in the ribs. They were well muscled. Like her bum.

'Yeah, yeah, yeah, I get it. But it doesn't seem fair. It shouldn't be allowed. How can I go home to Sam, who is really lovely, don't get me wrong, when I've got wet pants from Dr Farkas coming round all the time.'

'Ssshhh, voice down, not everyone is asleep or unconscious you know,' Jill warned, although she could hardly stop herself smiling.

'OK, sorry.' They continued whispering.

'So does he come round a lot then?'

'Yes, he's always popping his patients up here, and coming back to see them. I tell you, I'm having dreams about his hairy hands on my arse.' Holly hesitated, before continuing.

'Thrusting.'

'Thrusting?'

'Mmm, don't you ever get dreams like that?'

'Well, not for a few years anyway,' Jill admitted.

'Just you wait, you'll get the dreams, just the same as all of us. Perhaps you'd better get some extra panties in and keep them in your locker.'

'Ew ... fortunately I think I'm too old to be affected like that.'

Holly burst out laughing. 'Not past your sell-by date yet, I'll bet.' And she held up a handful of the hospital incontinence pads they used for all the patients.

'Maybe these nice pads would be better for you? Make you feel more *secure*. He may be back at anytime ...'

A voice piped up from outside the curtain. 'We can hear you, you know. We may be old but we're not all deaf!'

Jill and Holly sniggered simultaneously. Oh dear. Found out by the patients.

'Pantie-wetter, that's what he is.' Holly whispered.

'And we are all going to be alright,' the voice from outside the curtain called out 'because we are *already* wearing the incontinence pants!' There was a ripple of laughter and Jill realised that most of the ward had been listening in.

By midday Jill was flagging. There had been a steady and tiring stream of minor issues arising from things that were outside of her control. She had realised with a sinking heart that she had not been keeping up with the hospital time recording system, weirdly called 'One Space'. It was all done on the computer, hence the inexplicable lack of forms. All time, including student hours and bank hours had to be logged accurately by her as the nurse manager on duty.

Temporary staff and students as well as all the ward team (there were so many of them revolving weekly - it was mystifying) had to log their hours, sickness, holidays, courses, CPD, meetings - you name it, it had a code. The nurse manager then had to verify and sign off individual staff member's action logs. It was simple when you were just working on the ward but once meetings, training, professional development hours and all the rest of it were factored in, multiplied by the staff and students under her authority, the mess began to swim in front of her eyes.

'I'll bet there is even a code for going for a pee,' she muttered.

'It's called *general admin, non clinical,*' Megan, who was bashing away at the other work station, helpfully supplied.

Jasminder came up behind her. 'You'll soon get on top of it. Don't worry, at least you are doing it. The last girl we had, and she was only a girl really, she never did it at all! It took them four months to find out! None of our holidays had been authorised. It's amazing we even got paid! And that's only because payroll are so inefficient they didn't notice either.'

'I just can't get my head around why there are so many codes. Surely most of these aren't needed at all. Who thought them up? It's bonkers!'

'The problem is, my love,' Jasminder patted her arm, 'we have all the time and action codes on there for the whole hospital, everything that is done by everyone, including the elusive Chief Exec right down to the cleaners. But I have a secret print off of the ones we need, so as long as you don't tell anyone, I'll let you into the club of secret 'action code list holders'. Just don't tell anyone outside Charlton. In case it's against hospital policy!' She winked.

Lunch had finished and all the patients had been freshened up ready for visiting. This was a quiet time for the staff when they could grab a bite and catch up with each other. Jill took herself off to the small office to eat a sandwich, thoughtfully provided by Holly. She hadn't had a chance to explore all the drawers, cupboards and cabinets, so she took her break standing up with her notebook open on the desk and scribbling down all the key information she came across; the box files with the most important subjects typed on the front were her priority. She had only spent a week of induction training with the Ward Manager, Sue, and now hardly ever saw her. So she decided to play detective and find things out for herself. Sue was obviously a keen proponent of the flow diagram. All the policy and procedure files were prefaced with multiple flow charts showing who did what in what order. Everything had to be learned, Jill realised. And in her own time, there simply was no time for any of this during her shift. A soft knock on the door and Jas poked her head around.

'Vomit alert. I've sent two off to get cleaned up but everything's covered in it. Mrs Peake in bay 7. Can you help so we can sort it out before visiting? Sorry!'

'No, that's fine. I'm just coming.' Jill could easily tear herself away from the procedures without a backward glance.

Much later, and with a stream of sick down her own skirt and tights, Jill sought out something to put on for the rest of the afternoon. She walked swiftly towards the laundry which was located right over the other side of the site and collected a set of scrubs. Ducking into a staff room nearby- it was empty- she started to peel everything off in her haste to get out of the stinking uniform. No one was about so she sat on a bench and went to take off her tights. They were sticking to her legs; she would have to shower, C. Diff was still a problem and also Norovirus despite it being months until the peak winter vomiting period. She got up and looked outside in the corridor for the nearest female shower and toilets. She couldn't see any. She'd probably have to go out again and find where the dedicated female shower area was but she wasn't confident about the layout at this end of the hospital. She had to get back quickly though; indecision, she hated it. She couldn't put her sick covered legs into these nice clean scrubs.

There was a hand sanitising unit by the exit door out into the hospital. That would do for now and she could then find a shower and make a good job of it. She pumped the gel out and rubbed it onto her slimy leg. A brisk wipe with some paper towels and she could get on with it. She wouldn't touch a patient until she'd showered properly but for now at least she could pop the scrubs on and find that changing room! Just as long as no one came in. It was spookily quiet. She pulled the poppers of her uniform apart and started to peel the damp fabric off her body. She felt exposed and vulnerable in her bra and pants. More gel and more paper towel. She wiped and sanitised her shoes. She was just shaking the scrubs out so she could get into them when there were voices close by. Quick, her heart was thumping. She was rushing now. The trousers were starched and firmly stuck together. She couldn't push her foot into the leg fast enough and make it go down to the end.

The door opened just a few inches and she could see a hand, a male hand. It was a hand she had seen before, only a few hours before. She remembered the soft dark hairs and the long pale fingers. For a frighteningly long moment she mused to herself, she had never realised how distinct and personal hands were, almost as individual as faces. Dr Farkas pushed the door wide open and walked right in on her. He stopped. He stared. 'Don't come in Alan, there is damsel in distress in here and I need to help her.' With that he pushed the door closed and walked purposefully over to her. Jill was mortified. Her plump, dimply thighs were bare and exposed. Her pants, off white and cutting into her fleshy belly, were barely covering her arse. She couldn't look at him. He firmly took the trousers from her and pushed his arms down each of the legs in turn, easing out the starchy fabric so they transformed back into normal clothes again. He handed them to her and turned his back while she struggled to dress herself with a bit of dignity. By the time she had the trousers on the top was ready for her. Then he looked straight into her eyes without smiling at all. 'I always love to help a woman in need.' He was kind but gently mocking her. 'Put it on, then I can walk back with you, there is something I would like to talk to you about.' She pulled the, now warm, tunic over her head and slipped her clean shoes back on. He made a neat parcel of her dirty things and wrapped them up with the wet bits on the inside. He produced a bin liner from his pocket to put the things in, gave her a suggestive wriggle of his eyebrows and tucked the wrapped parcel under his arm. They walked out together. Dr Farkas' colleague had gone away and they were alone, for the moment. He turned towards her and put his hand on her shoulder. She could feel the heat on her skin, it was spine tingling.

'Call me Zolli, short for Zoltan,' he grinned. 'You are lovely, nurse, do you know that?'

Jill felt her entire digestive system, from her stomach right down to her bowels, turn to jelly. They continued walking along the corridor, greeting colleagues as they went. Other doctors and the more senior staff gave her looks which ranged from puzzlement to something she thought might be disbelief. He passed the parcel of her uniform to his left side so he could gently guide her through doorways by placing his beautiful hand in the small of her back.

'I was going to the shower first,' she said.

'Oh yes, of course,' he checked the directions in the corridor and propelled her down a side hallway.

'In here I think.' He handed the parcel back to her and held his nose, pulling a silly face.

'You wanted to talk to me about something?' Jill was confused.

'But I have already, nurse.' He nodded good bye to her and a lock of dark curly hair flopped across his forehead.

She showered in a haze of happiness and walked back to the ward with her sicky uniform in one hand and a smile so wide it hurt her face.

Chapter 7 - The computer class

'Oh damn and blast and sod it!' The young girl at the next work station sniggered as Lesley cursed thoroughly under her breath. The screen had, unaccountably, gone blue and then blank which meant she must have accidentally clicked on something that had closed the application down. She prayed that she had saved the work. The lecturer was relentlessly pressing on with the class and everyone else was glued to their screens. Lesley reached over sideways under the desk so she could restart the machine. She felt like a complete fool for the millionth time that evening.

'Now, cascading style sheets are what we are going to look at next, so click on the right hand panel where it says design and look at the drop down menu.' Lesley scrabbled to put her login and password in.

'Click on edit and cut and paste the document name into the K drive and press return.' It was all going too fast.

'Let's check the code so go up to the left hand top where it says view code and look at it. Can you see where it says 'body' about half way down? That is where I've just inserted some code to set up three nested tables for the text that you've already got on your web pages.' Lesley sighed and just stared at her screen.

She couldn't catch up now. She'd have to stay behind at break and ask for more help. She didn't mind, though; she didn't really want to stand around the awful drinks machine with the intriguing class mix of nerdy teens and already competent web designers.

The lecturer continued. 'Go to page properties at the bottom of the page and you can add some colour and change the default font. Put a heading in and then save it. Now we're going to save that and link the pages you've made to this master style sheet.'

Oh damn and blast and sod it! Lesley thought the rude words rather than spoke them. It was a better strategy by far or she would get a reputation. Not that she looked like a woman who would swear all the time, quite the contrary. Her apricot blonde curls and pale, pale complexion made her look like a startled cherub that had accidentally dropped down to Earth for a little amusement but forgotten how to get home again. She had the knack of smiling sweetly all the time, even when blindingly furious, which often made strangers want to pat her or offer to hold doors open for her. When she thought about this afterwards it made her feel aggrieved. If they only knew what was really going in inside her, the thoughts she harboured, they would be shocked and hurt.

She couldn't possibly catch up with the rest of the class now so instead she allowed herself to indulge in a little light daydreaming; or perhaps night dreaming seeing as this was night school. She had progressed well with this course and she was happy with the work she had done at home. She thought about the images she had loaded onto her practice site today. It was going well and soon she would be in a position to ask for contributions from the small group of friends she had made at the hospital, friends in a similar position to her. They all knew she was doing it but not really how it was going to work so she was waiting to make a print out to pass tactfully round, perhaps when they got together for a coffee. It was such a sensitive issue, she needed to proceed very, very carefully indeed. There was a fine line between her noble intentions and a website that was just plain morbid and depressing. So she hugged her project to herself and allowed a feeling of pleasure and satisfaction to grow in her chest. She would be strong. She would get over it. She would make something good come out of it. She never wanted anyone to go through the ordeal she and Colin had endured without any help or support at all.

Because that was the utterly horrible reality. No help at all. You imagined, if things got worse, there would be some kind of extra pastoral support, a sort of parallel service that would step in with counselling or useful advice or putting you in touch with others who had been there before. But that didn't happen. There was just the consultant, looking tired as usual, and the nursing staff who looked just the same. The care was just the same, the same stunningly high tech standard of medical care but, she had felt there was a point in the preceding months, the months that they had struggled through, where there was a sort of *distancing*, an emotional chasm had started to yawn openly between them and the medical staff. She knew what it meant but hadn't dared say anything to anyone. Hope was fading. Staff were gently withdrawing, ready for the end. It had been like a weight around her heart. Damn, damn and blast. A tear had trickled down her cheek and plopped onto the keyboard. She mustn't cause a short circuit. She must stop thinking about it all now and concentrate on her web design course. Enough time for tears later when she would be on her own. Colin would be out late at a meeting in the city and she could go home to the empty house and sit in Jack's old bedroom and just allow these feelings to overtake her.

Much later she drove her little car up the driveway and pulled in to the space at the side of the garage. A minute or two later another, much larger, vehicle was cruising very slowly up the close, headlights on full beam, and she was annoyed and blinded by the bright lights. A dull green car with mud slashes up the sides eased onto her drive and parked sideways across the tarmac. Lesley shook her head with exasperation. Gwen would be looking for a good long chat and a few glasses of wine before she could reasonably get rid of her. She pasted on her trademark bright smile and walked over to the driver's side of the dirty estate car.

'Hello Lesley.' Gwen boomed as she scrabbled around the passenger seat for her bag and what seemed to Lesley like a huge mound of papers and books and rubbish.

'Thought I'd pop in and keep you company.' Gwen looked at Lesley very shrewdly over the top of her spectacles. Lesley continued to smile but she knew Gwen would not be fooled, nor would she be put off. Oh well, Lesley loved her old friend really, she was just like a comfy old pair of Wellington boots. You took them for granted and left them by the door, muddy and disregarded. You never cleaned them or cared for them but, by golly, when you needed them to go outside in the most filthy weather, or when the dogs had got loose in the field, that was when you really bloody needed them. Like now, she thought. I'm like a loose dog, like the ones you see on country roads sometimes, lost and terrified, running along, just running without any idea where I'm going, I've just got to keep going. Gwen knows this and she has even perfected the knack of turning up and making me mildly annoyed to give me a sort of antidote to my relentless activity or morbid misery. And if she knew that I sat in

Jack's bedroom and wept whenever I could find time by myself she would probably move in with me and monitor my every move. It occurred to Lesley that she had better stop thinking these alarmingly honest thoughts as Gwen had already confessed to being psychic. She may even be reading my mind now, thought Lesley.

They sat in the conservatory while the dogs had a run in the garden. It was dark but the glow of the lights from the back of the house cast a beautiful gentle amber radiance over the grass that gave it an ethereal appearance. Bonny and Jess were jumping in the air trying to catch late summer insects. Gwen got up, without a word, and went out of the side door and picked up a large stick and started to throw it. The dogs were ecstatic with joy. They tumbled over each other to get to the stick first, snapping and snarling in a frenzy of competitive barking and pushing. Bonny was first and Jess went straight down on her haunches to wait for the stick to be returned and thrown again. Lesley became absorbed in the game and relaxed into her chair.

'When was the last time I did something so simple and pleasurable?' Lesley wondered out loud. 'It must be many, many months since I've thrown a stick for my lovely dogs without it being a chore, a drag that has to be got over as quickly as possible.' She turned the realisation over and over in her mind, like a heavy stone but she couldn't make it feel less cumbersome and weighty.

Eventually Gwen and the dogs came in, all damp and dewy and panting and Gwen sat down heavily and looked down at the floor. Lesley hoped that there would be no awkward conversations tonight. She didn't feel up to it.

The wine glasses and opened bottle were on the table now and something caught her eye on the floor in the pile of stuff that Gwen had brought in. It was the channelling book she was supposed to be reading. She had forgotten to buy it. The next meeting was planned for about a fortnight away. She wasn't sure she could be bothered.

'Is that the book we've got to buy?' Lesley asked.

'Oh yes, I've read the first part already and I thought we could talk about it together, unless, of course, you want to talk about something else ...' Her friend looked embarrassed behind her glasses. So, Lesley mused, she had come tonight with the intention of talking about *it*.

'I haven't even bought it, honestly, it just slipped my mind. I'm not really sure if I want to do it anyway. It all sounds a bit too flaky. Do you think B will be offended if I drop out?'

Gwen had spent the last week anguishing about whether it would be a good or a bad thing for Lesley to learn how to do this channelling. In the end there seemed no clear answer. Gwen had concluded she had to trust whatever spiritual powers were at work. They would not, surely, expose her friend to further heartbreak. The more she read of the book, the more she was impressed by the honesty and purity of the likely results. Intention. If you intended things to work out well there was a good chance they would. Gwen was now more worried about Lesley's apathy towards life in general. She struggled to interest her in outings or meals out. The book group was the one definite commitment she would consent to but her mood tonight was not encouraging.

'Oh, don't drop out, just give it a go. I do think you'll find it isn't quite what you think.'

'I don't know. I have a feeling I won't like it.'

Gwen leaned forward.

'What if I read a bit to you; you can see if you change your mind.' It was a bit like being a child again and a tug of desire to be mothered swelled up inside Lesley.

'I'll just read the first chapter while you lean back and relax, I don't mind, really, I'd like to do it for you.' It seemed churlish to refuse. What else had she got to do with her evening?

'Alright, that would be nice, thanks.'

Gwen reached over for the book and opened it, pressing the pages open and stretching the spine. As Lesley looked at her she noticed the amazing illustration on the front cover. It was an image of a figure in a flowing gown, like a dancer, looking up, holding an arm outstretched to the side. In the distance was a multi coloured radiance of light, a star, intense and shining. A beam of sparkling light was bridging the space between the light and the figure. A connection of light between an earthly body and something more divine. Inside the figure there was a glow of lilac light in the shape of a flower with petals opening, placed right where the heart would be. It was a hypnotic scene. Gwen cleared her throat and began to speak.

'Channelling is the term we like to use now to describe the method by which individuals can connect with their spiritual guide or guides and by doing so communicate their wisdom to the world. It is possible to learn how to become a competent channel. In the past people held those who were able to channel in high esteem, as though the channels themselves had special powers or were separate in some way. They were called mediums. Now we prefer the name channelling as this demonstrates that the person is a conduit and means by which energy and wisdom can come from one dimension to another. This time now on Earth is a very special time. It is the time of the conscious channels who can bring forth spiritual messages while remaining in a conscious, open, knowing state. Earth needs this higher wisdom to move into a more spiritual era, for Earth is changing and we must assist with these changes by changing people's hearts.

This book is a manual for those who wish to learn this skill. It requires dedication, hard work, practice and above all, an open heart. Channelling is a very humbling process. It is not possible to make a connection with the world of spirit without becoming intensely aware of the deep love and care that our guides and other wise beings have for us souls on Earth. When we connect with these beings we are shown a glimpse of the great oneness, of the 'all that is'. It is a deeply moving experience for us here on Earth to know and understand the unconditional love that radiates down to us during our earthly struggles.

So, if you are wondering whether you are able to succeed and learn how to channel your guide or another high entity, know that you have been drawn to this process through the loving gentle direction of your guide, who knows you are ready and that this is the next stage in your personal spiritual journey.'

Gwen looked across at Lesley. She looked very peaceful. Gwen wondered if she should stop now. All at once Lesley opened her eyes and sat up. The two friends stared at each other.

'Thank you, Gwen. Thank you from the bottom of my heart. I understand what it is I have to do. I need this, right now, at this point in my life. Rose is a very perceptive person and I'm glad she suggested it rather than say, Hilary or Jill. I might have been very dismissive if Jill had got on her new age soapbox and pushed me into it.' Lesley sighed and looked up at the night sky through the glass roof panels. It was clear and inky black.

'When you were talking just now I had a strong impression of myself in the future, really helping all those other bereaved parents, but in a positive way. I can't do it on my own though. I've been having ideas and doing my web design course but I'm still directionless and I have trouble raising any enthusiasm. I need guidance. I want someone to hold my hand and help me. Give me a boost. I just wonder if I have a spirit guide who might be willing to help me do this, what do you think?'

Lesley's pale little face was earnest and questioning. Gwen felt a lump come into her throat.

'I think that is exactly what you will find, my dear,' she said.

Chapter 8 - Beatrice makes a new friend

It was pouring. Sheets of persistent cold rain beat down on the pavements and parks of the elegant town. The late summer weather was finally finished and autumn had set in properly. A few days ago it had been very windy and a fence panel had come down in her back garden. Bill hadn't got time this week to sort it out so she was just nipping down to the fencing contractors to get someone out to do it for her.

Beatrice was glad to be out of the office this afternoon. Her Director had come whistling down the corridor, jangling the change in his pocket (why do men always do that, she wondered?), wanting to discuss why there was an underspend in the salary budget when the Department had made such a big fuss about understaffing in April and had got permission to recruit two new posts that B hadn't filled yet. She really wasn't in the mood to go into detail about how obstructive HR were and how the job specifications HR had written were so unattractive that they had not had any applications worth pursuing. It was perhaps just as well she had put him off. The way she was feeling at the moment she might have told him what an incompetent idiot she thought he was. Not a good strategy for a successful career, she mused.

'I am outspoken it's true. I should just keep my opinions to myself,' she thought out loud.

Beatrice pulled the car into the wood yard. The car park, such as it was, was a mixture of mud and sawdust. She picked her way gingerly towards the office, balancing her large golfing umbrella in one hand with the, rather damp, measurements on a sheet of scrap paper in the other. Her good leather handbag was getting wetter by the second – it would be ruined. The office was a small shed with the door wedged wide open. A gnarled old gentleman was sitting fiddling with a calculator and jotting figures down on a sheet.

'Hello there,' she called out, 'it's Mrs Abington, I called earlier about my fence panel.'

He looked blankly at her. His face was brown and deeply lined, like a sultana. It gave a pleasant impression.

'Hello there, I'm Mrs Abington, I phoned about an hour ago?' The old man reached into his top pocket and twiddled something.

'Hello, my duck, can I be of assistance? I jus' had to turn me 'earing aid on, ye know. I'm still not quite used to it. My boy, he's the one that wants me te 'ave it. I quite likes bein' deaf, it stops me old lady from disturbing me when I's reading th' paper!' And with this he grinned widely and started to chuckle and giggle until he had to wipe his eyes. Beatrice couldn't help herself and she giggled too. What a nice old man he was and such a contrast to all that poisonous office crap she had left behind.

In the end she accepted a strong sweet cup of tea, plonked her damp bottom down into a dirty old armchair by the electric heater, and engaged in a long and convoluted conversation about the merits of oak over treated softwood for fencing, whether trellis should be curved or straight and the new fangled fashion for painting them there fence panels blasted silly colours like what those television gardeners do.

'It's not natural,' Harry, for that was his name, said. It was a very satisfying afternoon in that little shed cum office, smelling of creosote and wood shavings, passing the time of day with Harry.

When she had ordered her fence repairs she set off back to work feeling much brighter. The weather, however, was much worse and the rain was pelting down in the way that only English rain seems capable of. The roads were awash with surface water and the sky was grey and leaden. She had a bit of a walk ahead of her from the car park to the office and she was already a bit soggy from the woodyard. Had she remembered to pick up her umbrella and was it in the back of the car? She glanced around to check the back seat when she hit a large deep puddle and the car jolted, aquaplaned a bit, and she had to grip the steering wheel hard as it wrenched out of her grasp. A huge spray of water arched out from the nearside wheels. The wipers struggled to cope and as the scene cleared she saw a small, pale, wet figure, in her rear view mirror, standing on the pavement looking shocked and angry. Oh bugger. I've drenched a pedestrian! Beatrice pulled over a few metres ahead and popped on her hazard warning lights, then raced out of the car back to where the soaked girl was standing, still gasping for air through a dripping curtain of rain soaked hair. The spray had gone right up over her head and she was totally sopping.

'I'm sorry, I'm really so sorry, I didn't see the puddle.' The girl coughed and looked quizzically at her. She seemed unable to speak.

'Are you alright? Apart from being soaked through, of course?' They were getting wetter by the minute.

'Look, will you let me drive you home so you can get dry?' B moved closer towards her and held out her hand. 'Please?'

The girl smiled a sort of crooked smile.

'That will be better I think than being drowned rat, am I correct?'

The girl was obviously foreign, Eastern European probably, perhaps a foreign worker from the expanded EU. B felt even more guilty and even more remorseful. It was likely the girl was wearing her only raincoat, maybe her best set of clothes. I've just ruined her entire wardrobe.

In the end she settled for dropping the girl off at, what she said, was a friend's house close by. The drive was awkward and as they progressed in the renewed downpour the girl kept glancing at B from under her dripping hair. There was a wet puddle on the floor of the car just down by the handbrake. At last they arrived outside a very attractive and well kept Victorian terrace in a rather fashionable part of the town. There were a selection of stained glass suncatchers in the front bay window; they looked hand-made and pretty.

'Thank you, you are very kind.' The girl went to open the passenger door.

'Should I just wait and see if your friend is home?' B was still concerned.

'He is at work but I have key, you no worry.' The girl was firm.

'Can I know your name? Let me pay for your dry cleaning bill. Please?' The girl smiled her small quizzical smile again and B was suddenly aware that outside the damp car, the sun had come out.

'No matter, I will wash clothes. My name is Krystina. I work at the crystal shop in the arcade. If you come in to see me I will recommend crystal for you.' She pressed a business card into her hand.

Beatrice smiled back. 'Thanks, I would like that very much.' Would she really? No, B had never bothered with all that crystal stuff. It was for fools. But to make amends she would go along, probably with a huge bunch of flowers.

Back at the office, it was late, so most of the staff had gone home. Beatrice checked her emails. There was a brief message from Jill to phone her and could she come round for a drink on Friday? That would be very nice. Another message, this time from Gwen about the proposed second channelling meeting and could everyone go to her house as she thought her old car would be in for a major repair so she would be housebound that week? She'd have to fix it with the others. Gwen's house was comfortable but cramped and a bit bohemian. That might be a problem if they wanted to do a bit of practising. They'd all have to squash into the small space. The first meeting was planned at Beatrice's house next week. She was quite looking forward to it. She hoped the others had actually had a look at the book or Rose might feel a bit put out.

Her thoughts strayed to the wet girl Krystina. She wondered if there was a nice crystal that would help everyone to focus on something, better than staring at a bloody candle, like it said you had to in chapter three of the channelling book!

She would definitely be visiting her sooner rather than later. B shut down her computer and put on her coat. It was still very damp and rather smelly from earlier on. In her pocket was the card, slightly soggy now. Krystina. Very interesting.

Chapter 9 - The Education Welfare Officer

The meeting, hopefully, was not going to be too difficult. Hilary had put on what she considered to be a cross between a sensible suit and something more up to date. Unfortunately she had ended up looking a bit like an accountant with bad dress sense, which was not her intention. She wanted to look like she was a concerned mum, but not a pushover. The EWO was about 15 years younger than her, about a size 8, and she looked as if she ate parents for breakfast; probably lunch and dinner too.

She had put on a light makeup and had cleaned the soil out from under her finger nails but, when she looked in the mirror of the ladies toilets, just by the Head's office, she looked like she had put her make up on in the dark. The foundation was just a bit too pale for her tanned outdoor skin; she had bought it last January and used it only once since then. She was hot as well. Despite the fact that it was only very early November and still relatively warm for the time of year, the heating was turned up to baking point. No wonder the children all had asthma, their little lungs were being dried out like crisps. She stood in front of the mirror examining her reflection. No point in trying to splash her face, that way led to disaster.

'Deep breath now,' she muttered to herself. The effect was disappointing. Her small breasts hardly filled out the suit jacket. She looked as though she could do with a good meal. Under the badly fitting jacket her little body was lithe and sinewy, testament to her outdoor life and her work. She was strong, too, but not verbally, and she knew she would have to keep her wits about her. Now she had to go and do battle with the EWO.

She had already met the woman last academic year when Gemma had been caught smoking at the back of the science block. There had been some suggestion that the kids were smoking something a bit more lively than Benson and Hedges. She wouldn't have been surprised, Gemma was quite capable of testing the water to see whether she like it or not. Her beautiful girl, independent, clever, her reason for living. Now, she assumed, she was attending some sort of follow up appointment. As far as she knew, all was well in Gemma's world. Her daughter seemed to be on a nice even keel. No boyfriend at the moment but she looked as though anyone would want to go out with her. She was secretly proud of her, especially as she had such a duffer of a mum to model herself on. She had only just started having her hair done properly after Gemma dragged her to the hairdressers and made her have a proper cut. She took another deep breath and calmed herself, ready to go in for her appointment.

The Head's office was very comfortable and there was a tray of tea things laid out. Hilary felt a slight twinge of panic. Maybe it was going to be a longer meeting than she had thought, perhaps there were matters to discuss that would require a cup of strong, sweet tea to counter the shock! Outside, the late autumn sun was beginning to lose its brightness. It was nearly 3.30pm. She surveyed the empty paths and playground of the school site. Soon the bell would go and children of all sizes would come to life and start to leave, banging along the corridors, shouting in the changing rooms, kicking a stone along on the tarmac outside. Gemma was staying behind at school tonight, in the library, she'd said. All was well. Now what had they got to say to her?

They were smiling. It must either be very good or very bad indeed.

'Welcome Mrs Bartholomew. Thank you for coming today to help us to help Gemma,' he pressed the fingertips of his large hands together in a sort of steeple shape.

'She has a lot of potential, you know, and when we see her,' at this point he turned to the side and smirked in a knowing way at the EWO who smirked back, 'she is a very able student. But.' He looked down and paused, frowning, at the sheets of paper in front of him. They were computer print outs, records of registrations, according to the upside down heading. He shuffled them around, as if by doing so he could make them into something else.

'There is no way of dressing this up Mrs Bartholomew. Gemma's absences have reached a level where we now have to consider whether to refer her case up to the truancy enforcement unit at County Hall. I appreciate you have been very sincere in your assurances that you will guarantee her attendance, I have seen copies of your letters. But Gemma is now slipping away from school at morning break, it appears. The records from the individual subject teachers show that she is here at morning registration, all smiles. Even her homework diary has been marked up to date. Then she stays for the first two lessons and thereafter, we simply do not see her.'

Hilary suddenly felt like she had been hit in the chest. She didn't know what to do next, her mind was scrambled.

'What?'

'Gemma's earnest promises to us, it seems, have been completely meaningless.'

'What? What letters are you talking about?'

'Over to you, Brenda.'

'I'm sorry I don't understand!'

'It's quite clear Mrs Bartholomew. I was alerted to the absences again towards the end of last term but my workload with other children meant that I had little time to look at Gemma's case again until now. The Head and her Year Head have been trying hard to get her to admit she is truanting. But she just clams up. Every morning, it seems, she promises to stay for the whole day but by lunchtime she has gone again.'

She continued. 'I sent you letters on 16th September and then again on 25th. You replied to me within days; I was happy with your commitment to tackle the problem. When it didn't improve I left at least three telephone messages during October and then this was my last letter.' She rotated an official looking document with the county crest at the top and allowed Hilary to read the dreadful contents. It was an official final warning letter.

'I haven't received any of these,' Hilary was almost shouting, 'and I never wrote any letters back either.'

The EWO looked again at the warning letter. 'This is the correct address, isn't it? This one was recorded delivery, as the regulations stipulate.'

'I'm sorry, there must be a mistake. I really, I mean I am being absolutely straight with you now, I haven't received any of these. I didn't know. I thought this was about something else, related to the smoking thing last year.'

'No, sadly Mrs Bartholomew, this is much more serious. For many years now it has been a *criminal* offence to fail to ensure that children of a statutory school age attend school, unless there is a special exemption order in force or the child is excluded or taking part in approved home tuition, but this last option requires pre-registration with the LEA and approval has to be granted following an education sub- committee meeting convened for the purpose. This meeting that we are having now is the last part of the necessary process before referral for prosecution.'

She wasn't smirking now. It had gone very quiet. She realised the children that had been milling around outside had evaporated. The school was suddenly a very different place, empty, deserted. She wanted to run out and find Gemma, to confront her, to hold her and see if she was real, to see if she was this person they were talking about.

'I still don't understand. Why haven't I had any of these letters you sent?'

'I really couldn't say.' The Head took off his glasses and cocked his head on one side, like a parrot.

'You see, we have no choice really. We, as a school, are measured on our truancy record. There are boxes that must be ticked. Aside from the criminal aspect of the law now, our league table position is affected by truancy figures.'

Hilary felt all the air rush out of her lungs as if she had been punctured. She had no idea what to do. Indignation had been replaced with a growing feeling of being hopelessly out of her depth. She couldn't say anything, she didn't know what to say. She had to see Gemma. She was worried, there must be something very, very wrong indeed. Let it be simple, youthful bloody mindedness. Let it not be something she couldn't deal with. Let her be safe.

'I need to go now. I have to collect Gemma, then I can find out what has been going on.'

'Gemma is not here Mrs Bartholomew, I thought you realised this. She has absconded from school. Just the same as almost every day since the beginning of term. We are trying to be fair with you but this just isn't making sense. You surely know where your own daughter has been hiding out?'

Oh God! Let it be alright. Let her be at home now. Hilary stood up and walked out of the stuffy room, into the corridor and out of the front entrance door.

Behind her the Headmaster was calling. 'We will have to take action now, Mrs Bartholomew. It won't wait any longer.'

But she was gone. The November wind hit her in the face. Her heart was pounding and time was slowing down. She couldn't get her car keys out. She dropped them. As she bent down to grab them she felt herself go light headed; there were watery noises in her ears and she felt sick. She stumbled down to her knees, the tarmac was gritty, her hands were grazed. She couldn't grip the keys. Her heart was thumping in her chest. She was going to have a heart attack. She looked at the hard tarmac and knew that she would soon be slumping down onto it. It looked strangely comfortable. This was it then. She'd never see her precious darling again.

Chapter 10 - Be still my beating heart

Jill's legs were hot and itchy. The varicose vein behind her knee was throbbing nastily. Fortunately, she had on some very fetching maximum support hose and, if she surreptitiously managed to sneak her feet up on the vacant chair opposite her, she could rest them for half an hour and the throbbing might go away. In front of her was a rather tasty looking jacket potato with cheese and coleslaw and a large mug of tea. Heaven. It was a late lunch break and the staff restaurant (so called) was quiet.

The catering staff were bashing the large metal trays about as they cleared the ravaged remains of the cottage pie and cauliflower cheese away and made way for the tea things. Scones, apple crumble slice, treacle tart. How comfortingly familiar these simple items were. She had settled back into the old routine now. She felt so relaxed about the job that she hardly gave it a second thought. Her early worries about fitting in were gone. Even Holly and her were mates. What a revolting phrase. Sounds like condoms. She smiled to herself. She mustn't seem to be having an internal conversation with herself, people may think she'd escaped from the psychiatric wing! And dressed up in a nurse's uniform to boot! Get a grip of yourself woman, she reprimanded herself.

Her feet were stretched out on the opposite chair and her toes were wiggling contentedly under the plastic table cloth. She was reading an old Woman's Realm summer holiday edition, special holiday fiction. It was quite engrossing. Then she became aware of something just out of the corner of her eye. It was a small movement, a flash of white. She looked up but couldn't immediately see anything at all. Within the magazine, the heroine was having a very serious conversation with her doctor. There it was again. Like a flash. It was just like a light bulb blowing. Probably time to go anyway, she checked her watch. Another five minutes. Then, as she looked up again, Doctor Zolli, as she now knew him, was standing opposite her, with his hand on the back of the chair, the one with her feet on!

'I don't seem to be able to sit down and look at my favourite nurse.' He tugged pointlessly at the chair.

'Oh sit down, please, sorry, oh please do, I'm just putting my feet up, it doesn't matter, I'm sorry, please do, no really.'

'I love it when you are flustered.'

Oh, that's why he kept popping up in these awkward moments. He wanted to embarrass her.

'I was just getting ready to get back.'

'So I see.' He surveyed the remains of her lunch. The dishes were almost scraped clean.

'Where I come from, we admire a woman who knows how to appreciate her food.'

He was laughing at her now, she thought. I can't sit here and listen to myself being patronised. But she stayed glued to her chair. She sucked in the roll of fat that bulged over the top of her belt.

'I have a little problem,' he continued. 'I need to ask the advice of a nice lady and I choose you. I hope I do not give offence?'

He looked so engaging, as he tried in vain to pull the chair out, that she forgave him. He was only a child really, she should not be so prickly. He was just being friendly. She moved her legs and slipped her feet back into her nurses shoes.

'Go on then, I need some excitement in my dull old life.'

'Your life, it is not dull, surely. You have family? Nice husband and children perhaps? You have nice holidays and two cars?'

'Oh Dr Farkas, you *overestimate* me.'

He looked quizzical.

'It was a tiny witticism, a bit of irony - joke I mean.'

'What is the joke? I have been told I have to work at the English humour.'

'Well, it's not a joke really. I was just trying to make light of it. I don't have a happy family life at all. You couldn't be further away from the truth.'

She looked firmly at him. No point in beating about the bush. If she and he were to be friends in any shape or form, then he might as well stop thinking she was a middle aged matron with a plump behind and a comfy well upholstered existence with a doting husband and lots of money.

'Oh.' He waited.

'I am a divorced mother of one, a son who is away at University. I have just gone back to work full time after four years doing a bit of bank nursing and I live in a small house about a half mile away, so I can walk to work if I like. Saves money.' She looked for his reaction. His face was expressionless. Jill felt like an idiot, she looked away for something to distract her. She hurriedly turned over a new page in her magazine. Without looking up, she said, 'How are you finding our weather here in the UK? Is it different from Hungary?' She kept her eyes down, looking at the words swimming in front of her.

'It is similar, not too much different. But colder in winter and hotter in summer in my country. You have more rain. I like it though. In Hungary it is very cold in the winter. We have snow, sometimes until March we have it. Then all the grass it is brown and dead, rubbish is in the street and you pass by the frozen bits of food and cigarette packets every day. They don't move. Nobody clears it up. That is when I get fed up, everything brown and dirty. But then Spring comes and I wake up one morning and the snow has gone. The brown dirt and all the rubbish is wet and soggy. Then in a week it is green. Men come and clear it all up; then suddenly it is hot. Quite hot and I leave my coat at home. Winter, spring for a week, then summer. That is my country. It rains in the summer, just when you think it will never rain again. Not like here when it rains every day. I saw you last week, in the rain, you have umbrella and you are singing as you walk along.'

He took her by surprise. He put his hand around her jaw, leaned over the table and twisted her face to look at him.

'I saw you last week singing under your umbrella.'

'Was I?'

'Yes, I could hear you, it was so loud. I have my car window open as it steam up. You look happy.'

His hand was still cupping her chin.

'What do you want with me?' She pulled away. This was becoming awkward.

'I would like it if you can show me your country? Would that be OK? I am needing a good companion in this place. Someone who is nice and can be my friend.'

'But you have loads of friends! Everyone talks about you, you're a hospital legend. Dr Farkas is so pleasant, he is so popular, he must want to stay in England. He works so hard at his job!' Jill was surprised at the bitterness in her voice.

'So that is what they say about me ...'

'Well, not in so many words, but you definitely give everyone the impression that you are, well, if I'm honest, not stuck for friends. Am I right?'

'Are you right? I do not think so, I am in need, dear nurse Jill, if I may call you that, of a little bit of home comfort, as you say. A happy face to look back at me. When I have time off I feel not so good, a little homesick but, if I have you as my lovely friend ... then we can have good times together.'

'Yes, if you feel like that, I think we can.' Jill thought again. 'Are you sure?'

'Why not?' He grinned. 'Are you saying you are not nice lady?' He then proceeded to pull a funny face, imitating horns coming out of his head and stuck his tongue out to the side like a demented lunatic.

'I'm not hard up you know, I said I am divorced but I'm not desperate.' She joined in the game and rolled her eyes up and blew a raspberry, very loud.

'Then we can be clowns together; be my friend?' He took her hand and stroked it.

'Go on then, you are obviously crazy, so we had better stick together.'

He stretched up and sighed. He looked tired now. His curly brown hair was sticking up in places. She wanted to smooth it down.

'What shall we do tonight then?' He asked straight out.

'Tonight, tonight? What, already? I thought you meant sometime in the future.'

'Nurse I have to be severe with you,' he looked at his watch. 'You are late back from lunch and I cannot cover for you, keeping me talking like this. I cannot excuse your naughty behaviour. You had better go. I will come around to your nice little house at 8 o'clock sharp.'

'But, but ...'

'No buts, we will sit and talk and eat maybe.'

'You don't know where I live ... yet.'

'Oh yes I do ...'

And with that he got up and turned to walk away, but not before giving her an enormous wink.

Later on that day, Jill found herself wondering whether she had been dreaming. She hadn't seen Dr Farkas for weeks and within the space of half an hour he had invited himself to her house for dinner, she assumed for dinner anyway, and then what afterwards? Should she be getting worried, nervous? Or just treat the whole thing as a joke. After all, what did she know about his home circumstances, his life, his wishes?

If she was in Hungary, for example, and feeling a bit lonely, she would probably choose someone older and bit ordinary to make friends with. Yes, that was it; she wasn't threatening to all to him. With that thought, she heaved a huge sigh of internal relief. He probably wanted to moan about the stream of blonde and sexy girls he's forced to go to bed with. Or that several jealous husbands have been coming to the hospital threatening to punch him. So the best strategy for her would be to lay in a bottle of wine, just one though, and make something nice and homely to eat.

With that she marched out into the ward and checked all of her staff were gainfully employed and all her patients spick and span. Well, almost all of them. The curtains were closed around two of the beds (toileting, no doubt) while Mrs Greenish in bay 2 was tipping water from her sippy cup all over her hair.

Chapter 11 - The first proper meeting of the channelling group

'I've got so much to tell you all.' Everyone started to gabble at the same time.

'Me too, things have just been manic.'

'I have some very thrilling news, too.'

'I've only got bad news, I'm afraid.'

'Oh no, sweetheart, what's the bad news?'

'It's Gemma ...' and with that, Hilary's face fell.

'Oh Hils, don't cry darling. Do you want to tell us, or shall we change the subject?' Beatrice was round to her chair like a flash and was patting her as her friend tried to get control of her feelings.

The others leaned forward attentively to her story as she sobbed and snuffled.

'I was called in to see the Education Welfare Officer last week, to school, you know. The Head was there too. I didn't really understand how serious it was. They want to prosecute me. They say Gemma has been bunking off, truanting, since the beginning of term. I couldn't believe it. They say she's been coming in every morning. They've got the records, as well, to prove it. But she's been leaving at break. I don't understand, the school is pretty secure and they have teachers on the main gates too. Anyway, they sent me some letters and written final warnings, which I didn't get, I'll tell you about that later. Then I thought I couldn't sit and listen to them being so bloody patronising and not believing me, so I left. Then when I went to get into the car; I was going to go home have it out with her anyway, or hear her side of the story, I came over all funny and started to feel faint. I had to sit down but my heart was absolutely pounding. I don't really remember much more, I was feeling really terrified. The next thing I knew I was lying down on a sofa in the sixth form common room. Some sixth formers had found me passed out on the ground in a heap and carried me inside. They were so sweet; there was a tall lad who had actually carried me, he was just lovely and so kind. Anyway, to cut a long story short, I'm all right, but Gemma and I are not really speaking. She knows I know but she won't talk about it.'

'Didn't you go berserk?'

'Actually I was quite shaky when I eventually got home, I had to go down to Casualty for a charming two hours, hoped maybe to see you Jill, although I know it's such a big hospital. God, how I wanted to see a friendly face, but hey, there you go. I had an ECG and my cuts cleaned and it seems it was just a bloody panic attack, hyperventilation, so I'm a nervous wreck.' She laughed, and then they all laughed.

'What a horrible thing to happen but why won't Gemma talk to you? What are you going to do on Monday, presumably if she keeps doing it you're going to be in more trouble?'

'There are only so many times you can shout at a teenager when she locks you out of her room and turns the music on full blast, you know. She only comes out when I've had to go out on a job. I'm just having all these one sided conversations and she is blanking me. Look, I don't know, I just don't know.' Hilary looked desperate and B could see she was beginning to panic again.

'Yes, Hilary, do you want me to speak to her?' Beatrice could instantly see how this was very serious indeed and needed some fast action.

'Come on, let's talk about something else and see what Hils thinks a bit later.'

They all pulled back a bit, everyone rearranged themselves on their chairs and sofas so that Hilary could relax a bit more and have a bit of space.

'Who's got something nice to tell us?' Beatrice again, taking charge.

'I have.'

'Oh good, come on then.'

'Is it about Max, has he developed sudden erectile dysfunction, for example, or a huge wart on the end of his nose?' Rose had disliked Max, Jill's ex, on sight.

'No,' Jill was beaming, 'I've got a romance.'

'What!'

'You dark horse.'

'Come on, then, have you bagged a goaty old consultant, loaded and as randy as hell.'

'No, you won't believe it when I tell you. I'm not sure I believe it myself. I'm having a romance with a younger man, one of the temp A and E doctors from abroad. He's Hungarian.'

'Bloody hell!'

'How did that happen?'

'God! I'm envious.'

'How old is he then?'

'Well, he's about 30, I think, certainly not much older. He is really very handsome and he's a bit lonely in England so he made friends with me.'

'How handsome?'

'Brad Pitt level, Colin Firth? Even, dare I say it, Hugh Grant?'

'Do you know, Lesley, your taste in men is absolute crap!'

'He doesn't look particularly English, I must say. He reminds me a bit of Ralph Fiennes, yes I think that's about it. But he is more, sort of, clean shaven, not quite so broody. And he has these Slavic cheekbones and floppy dark curls.' Jill blushed slightly.

'For God's sake, I am going to explode in a minute. Are you going to tell us what has actually happened?'

'You mean, have I ... have we ...?'

'Yes, we want to know.'

'Yes, you have to tell us.'

'If I'm honest, I want to know too.'

'Definitely.'

'Just get on with it.'

'Well ...' Jill was astonished by the intensity of their entreaties and their bright expectant faces.

Jill didn't want to give details. It was too fresh and, in a sense, too precious to share with anyone yet. And she knew that if she tried to describe what had happened it would come out all tawdry and cheap and spoiled. He had been the perfect gentleman. But it was clear right from the moment he stepped into her hallway and touched her cheek, that there was to be no hiding place. She had been totally wrong about his intentions.

He came into her house from another wet evening. His raincoat was splattered with dark spots. He shed it and hung it up on the hall rack. Then he turned towards her, smiled and began to advance. She was trapped between him and the stairs. She couldn't back away without taking a step up, that would look odd. He touched her cheek and cupped her chin, just like he had that afternoon. She felt weak.

'Shall we begin?' He spoke softly and his face moved towards hers and he just looked into her eyes, looking deeper and deeper and deeper, until she felt as if he was examining her very soul. She couldn't speak. Then he opened his lips slightly and breathed a soft breath into her face, it smelled of flowers. Her legs were jelly. He moved so slowly towards her, gazing into her eyes as he did, that she couldn't even breathe.

Then he kissed her. It was like being caressed by the sun, he just joined his lips with hers and the pressure was so gentle and sweet. He moved her mouth to open it a little more and the taste of his mouth was so cool, so cool and fresh that she wanted to be drawn inside. His face was so soft and so gentle. He had her cupped in his hand but then he moved it, and his hand touched her back and began to stroke her across the shoulders, over and over. He moved his other arm around her and enveloped her. She was being drawn into a place of pure emotion. She was powerless and powerful all at the same time, she couldn't stop if her life had depended on it.

They were moving together very gently, swaying easily with each other, just lightly and in complete synchronisation. Then she saw light, like a star but far away at first. She had her eyes closed but she could see it as if she was staring at the sun. It was like being exploded, there was no other way to explain it. But his hands around her, enveloping her and holding her so safe, so strong, made it alright. She could look into the light and it did not hurt or make her blink. She had lost a sense of her feet. She could have been floating. Then it seemed as if his kissing changed pace slightly. She felt as if he was all around her, which he was, his arms anyway, but it was like she couldn't tell which part of her was the front or the back or even if she had a front or back. Or which part was being kissed. She was being opened up like a flower and light was pouring into her. And she never wanted it to stop, ever.

'So you all want to know the details, do you?' Jill formulated a stock reply that would satisfy her audience. They nodded their heads enthusiastically.

'Not yet,' she said, 'but very, very soon. You'll have to wait until I'm ready to tell you.'

'Spoilsport.'

Conversation then moved on but Jill was aware of them looking at her from time to time. She had actually spent quite a long time looking at herself this morning in the mirror. There was no doubt about it, she did look different. She felt completely different. He was coming around to see her again, later on that evening, after the meeting. About half past ten, he had said. Oh how was she going to concentrate on what they were going to talk about? There was no uncertainty in her mind now. Tonight there would be no reservations. She couldn't resist him even if she tried. Inside her, something had woken up. She wasn't sure that it was lust, exactly, but it was a sort of energy that she hadn't felt before. It tingled inside her middle. Tonight it is, then, she thought to herself.

Rose was talking about some strange experience that had happened to her a few weeks back but Jill was only half listening. She had been in the garden, when it had been a bit warmer, and some kind of time warp, or out of body thing had taken her over. It doesn't surprise me, Jill thought. Rose had always seemed to be a bit ethereal and anyway, she was B's friend really. I don't know her all that well.

Lesley was looking much better than she had last year. She looked as though she had been to the hairdressers too. Perhaps I need to go and get my hair restyled, Jill thought. Something younger, perhaps a colour on it, as well.

They were waiting for Polly before they could begin properly. Polly was Hilary and B's friend from another reading group that was a bit too serious for Jill. Polly was the kind of person who was always late, that annoyed Jill, however, the others didn't seem to notice. She couldn't say why she wanted to get away at 10ish, because then they would all be twittering around her again asking for details. She was starting to feel a bit nervous. Beatrice was looking at her, she looked back. Beatrice then just got up and clapped her hands and everyone stopped talking.

'Let's start, shall we? We could be waiting ages for Polly, no doubt some domestic crisis has come up, if she comes later, it doesn't matter, does it?'

She continued. 'I want to talk about the book for a bit, I know it was Rose's idea but I'm the one who read it properly about a year ago and did the meditation tapes, so I sort of know what we are in for. However,' she cast a knowing look around the room, 'if I know you lot at all, you will all be astrally projecting around the road by the end of the evening and I'll still be sitting on my bum in the lotus position!'

'Oh, bloody hell, we don't have to contort ourselves into that do we?'

'No, just be comfortable and well supported and have a straight back.'

'I did a Buddhist mediation course when I was at Uni,' volunteered Hilary, 'and I found sitting on the floor quite comfortable in the end.'

'You keep your ends to yourself!'

They all settled down and B decided to get everyone talking about what they had read so far. They were reading the book three chapters at a time and then planning to practise doing the recommended exercises from the book, which were a series of guided meditations. Beatrice actually felt quite anxious about how it was going to be received. Gwen was looking apprehensive.

'I know someone who goes to a Spiritualist Church. She's an old friend of mine from college and when she found out that I was going to do this she had a real go at me about it. So I have read the first bit of the book but I'm not sure about going any further. I was enthusiastic at first, I know, but now I want some reassurance.'

'What did she say, anyway?'

'Apparently, when you dabble in these sorts of things you have to be protected and because we are amateurs then we might be opening ourselves up to malevolent spirits that she says are just waiting out there for a chance to tune in and that's how they get their kicks.'

'What?'

'I'm amazed that some people believe that rubbish.'

'Has she been brainwashed, this friend of yours?'

'Actually,' Polly said in a very loud voice as she stood in the open doorway, 'I have heard much the same thing from someone I know who is practising medium.'

They all stared at her as if she had just beamed down from another planet.

'This woman said we are stupid to be trying to contact guides or spirits because we should leave it to the professionals who know what they are doing and have had proper training. Quite honestly the woman is the most flaky character I know, love her dearly as I do, so I told her to stop being so protectionist and that I'd report her to the clairvoyant's union for restrictive practices.' Polly flopped down on the sofa in a cloud of Givenchy, something musky, and proceeded to pull off her long leather boots.

'Have I missed anything yet? I can't wait! Have we conjured up a spirit at all?' She stared at the assembled group, who looked suitably stunned, from under her very long sooty eyelashes.

Beatrice stood up and stretched her arms out, 'Let's get started, shall we, and then we can chat afterwards and see if anyone has connected with a dark spirit?'

'Mmm ... I hope I get Torquemada,' Polly purred, 'I need help with my sado-masochistic bedtime routine.'

'Poll, you are the pits.'

Beatrice checked that everyone was sitting in a comfortable spot, Hilary opted for the floor with a large cushion. The curtains were closed and B was happy that any nosey neighbours wouldn't be checking them out. She moved to turn on the tape.

They were all quiet and had closed their eyes. The sound of rhythmic breathing was audible from Hilary's corner. Eventually some very peaceful music started to drift out into the room and the sound of a female voice, very calm and very reassuring, spoke out clearly and with a persuasive authority. The meditation was beginning.

'Now ... get comfortable, with your back straight and supported and your hands laying gently in your lap. I want you to breath in and as you do so I want you to imagine that your whole body is becoming more comfortable and more relaxed with every breath you take. As you breathe your upper body is gently rising so that your spine is stretching out and you feel lighter and more alert with every breath. Feeling your shoulders relaxing and your neck relaxing and your head relaxing as you breathe in and out.

Now I want you to visualise the area around your heart, your heart centre. You can feel it inside you and imagine you can see it as a centre of energy, glowing and radiating heart feelings in your body. Imagine the energy as a green colour and as you do so I want you to feel that green powerful heart energy radiating out into your body with wonderful feelings of love and joy ...

Now move the focus of your attention up to your head, to that place we call your third eye, right between your eyebrows, and imagine a centre of radiant blue energy glowing there. You feel the energy and, as you do, your connection with your natural ability to sense other worlds is growing stronger ...'

Rose was starting to feel very disconnected from her body. She could hear Hilary breathing, still quite loudly, to her right and Jill was sitting next to her on the left. She could feel Jill's energy, it felt sort of warm and yellow. As she looked into the black space inside her head she could actually see a yellow glow on the left side of the inner screen. It was quite comforting really. Things were going well. She was aware of herself sitting on the sofa but she couldn't really feel her body, it just felt as though it were anaesthetised, like she had taken something. She knew her feet were on the floor but she couldn't feel them being there, but it wasn't an unpleasant feeling. She wondered whether anyone else was feeling like that or was it just her? Jill coughed quietly. B was sitting directly in front of her but she couldn't feel anything there. She knew she should be concentrating but, actually, the sensations she was feeling were rather compelling. The gentle voice of the speaker was flowing in the background.

Hilary was wedged up against the wall of the lounge and the slight discomfort was keeping her focused and concentrated on following the instructions. They were imagining a beam of light energy coming down into the top of their heads now. She could almost see it and noticed how her head suddenly felt lighter and as if it had moved up by a few inches. She was feeling very motivated to do this properly. Gemma will be all right, she thought, and as she did so, she lost her focus and noticed how much her back ached, rammed as it was against the wall. There was a moan from her left. Then a sort of thumping sound. She was curious. She opened her eyes by a few millimetres. Everyone was still and in their meditation positions. She looked at Rose. She looked a bit odd. Her face had a sort of contorted quality and it was a strange colour as if she was holding her breath. She opened her eyes fully and looked more carefully. Beatrice was also looking and motioned her to keep still. Rose actually looked very ill.

'I can't do it.' A strangled sound escaped Rose's lips.

'What can't you do?' B whispered

'I can't hold him.'

'Do you want to stop?'

'I can't stop it.'

Rose's face was looking very odd. B stopped the tape. Polly opened her eyes and moved across the room to sit in front of Rose.

'Open your eyes.'

'It won't stop it happening.'

Gwen was looking very frightened indeed.

'Tell it or him to go more slowly.'

Beatrice reached out to hold Polly's hand and then touched Jill's shoulder and signalled that she should hold hands too.

They started to breathe deeper and keep pace with Rose who was now looking distressed. She whispered, 'Breathe with her, then slow it down.'

'He's here and he wants to come in.'

'Can you not control what's happening? Tell him you can't take it.'

'He's impatient.' Rose's voice was very distant. The only sound in the room was the breathing. It was as if all time had been suspended. All eyes were on Rose.

'He means me to connect with him, he is very powerful and has been waiting a long time.' Rose still looked ill but her voice was calmer.

'It's OK, he is moving away.'

And with that she opened her eyes and started to shake her hands and feet out. They all waited.

'God! That was stunning.' Rose's eyes were shining. 'It was definitely him, my guide, I caught a glimpse of him, very old and wearing a long robe. He is so powerful, I can't believe it.'

'What did it feel like? You looked horrible. I thought you were dying.'

'Yeah, I envisaged a trip to casualty with a grey limp body that I couldn't explain!' Polly was shaken. 'They'd definitely have detoxed you for drugs!'

'I feel fine now. Honestly. Don't worry about me.' Rose looked at their faces, it was a shocking sight. B was staring blankly, Hilary was plainly terrified, Polly was fidgeting uncomfortably. Jill face was a mask of deep concern.

Jill was indignant. 'It's really not a matter for jokes,' she said, 'although I can't imagine what my colleagues in A and E would say if we had needed to take you down there.'

'Oh come on, I'm fine really.' She stood up and did a little shuffle from foot to foot. 'You're making a meal out of it. I enjoyed it, I didn't feel at any time that there was any problem. Really.'

Beatrice felt deflated and anxious. She got up to make a pot of coffee and picked up the tape player and ostentatiously took out the tape. She hesitated. Half of her wanted to tuck it into her pocket. They were looking at her.

'Let's get rid of this now, then, before we do any more damage.' There was a murmur of consensus. It had gone too far and they had only just begun. She took the meditation tape out with her into the kitchen and gently slid it into an inner pocket in her briefcase. Then Rose was behind her.

'I know now what I have to do,' she said, 'and I think we should keep going.'

'You're crazy. The others are petrified, you saw their faces. They'll never agree.'

'Are you worried?' Rose wouldn't drop it. Beatrice felt as if it was all her fault but she was perplexed; her natural common sense fighting with the feeling that she ought to be more concerned.

'No, honestly, I'm not. My experience is that you cannot harm yourself. The spirit world is just not like that. But you even scared *me* tonight.'

'I know, but it felt perfectly fine, it was an experience I even felt I recognised, you know.'

'I do know. Oh blast! I do want to do it properly but, if you are going to do your dying swan act every time we turn the tape on, nobody will agree to be in the same room as you.'

'So let's keep going, I need you to help me.' Beatrice was the most level headed person she knew.

'OK, I kept the tape, it's over in my briefcase. Let's just keep quiet about it for the moment, shall we?'

When they got back into the lounge, Jill was putting her coat on. She looked like she was in a hurry.

'I've got an early start, so I think I'll get going,' she said, 'let me know what we are doing, won't you? Rose?'

'No worries, I'll give you a ring.'

The evening broke up rapidly. Lesley and Gwen went off together. Polly stayed behind with B to talk into the night about her latest crisis. By the time Polly was ready to leave they had polished off two bottles of wine and B had to call a taxi. It took ages but she didn't mind. Bill had gone to bed long ago and she wasn't worried about disturbing the girls, they slept like logs.

Polly and B waited outside the house for the taxi to come. The recent wet weather had cleared and the night was ice cold. Polly drew her beautiful cashmere coat tighter around her while B hopped from foot to foot in her slippers and an old cardigan. Soon it would be December and the round of shopping and children's parties and present buying would begin in earnest. Polly was telling her about some friend who had met a much younger man and was actually going to leave her husband and move in with him.

'What, and leave the children?'

'Yes, she's completely dotty about him. I just can't get through to her, it's as if she has lost her wits.' Polly wasn't renowned for her tact, so Beatrice assumed she had given this woman a total haranguing.

'So much wrong done in the name of so called love.' The taxi drew up, lights blazing and Polly piled, somewhat unsteadily, into the back seat and set off.

The dark crisp night closed in and suddenly it was very quiet and still. There were no lights on in this part of the village and the sky was able to shine clear and bright without the insidious orange glow of suburbia. Her house looked comfortingly warm and sleepy, long and low under its slate roof, cottage windows hiding its slumbering occupants. She knew she would have a blinding hangover the next day.

'Oh well, better get off to bed then.'

Chapter 12 - Gemma

Another school day. Another tiny step towards freedom. Then Gemma could stop worrying about it. Today she would go to the area behind the DT block and stand with the smokers for a bit. She had been one of them before, they were an OK crowd, they were cool. Then she could break off to go to the loo, if she went to the girls loos in the PE changing rooms then she could walk back past the overgrown path and she'd be just in the right place by the time the bell went. Then she would be safe. She would meet Ally at lunchtime who would bring the work with her for Gemma to copy. Only a few months now until her exams. It would be alright, she knew it would be, as long as she could avoid questions being asked.

Mum was downstairs. That was going to be the main problem. She couldn't see how she could arrange for it to stay the same for a few months more. She'd collected all the letters, so Mum hadn't had to know. But last week Mum had been to see the Head. Smug bastard. If only he knew, that would wipe the smile off his face. Mum must have had a phone call. I need to find out what she knows but I can't ask her. She has been looking at me in a stupid pleading way and saying 'We have to talk,' or 'You're in a lot of trouble.' If only she knew just how much trouble. Avoidance. That was her only strategy. Avoidance. Say nothing. Do nothing. Keep a low profile, as Ally would say.

Beatrice had decided, after last night's drinking session, to take the day off work. She had also promised Hilary she would go over for coffee to see if they could come up with anything useful to get Gemma to talk or even stay in the same room as her mum for longer than a minute. However, the severity of her hangover made her concerned she was still over the limit from the previous late night with Polly. God, Polly could knock it back. It reminded her a bit of her time at University. They used to go to all nighters and just drink and dance and party and goodness knows what else. Then at four o'clock in the morning, they all used to wander over to the other side of town to the fruit and vegetable market and go in, wearing their party clothes, to the café, for a fried breakfast. Now that was the way to avoid a hangover, lots of fried bread and egg and bacon. Yummy.

Her head was splitting. Alex was looking at her from over the top of an open packet of salt and vinegar crisps. That was her breakfast. B couldn't even open her mouth to nag, she might be sick. All that thinking fondly about egg and bacon, she wasn't up to it at all, and anyway, it was too late for egg and bacon now. Alex looked particularly beautiful today, her hair was freshly washed and her beautiful willowy figure made her look like a model.

'Can you pick me up from town tonight Mum?' She asked.

'Sure, what time?'

'I'll call you.'

'Alex, if you were in any trouble would you tell me?' B sneaked the forbidden enquiry in before Alex could clam up.

'Yeah ... but I'm not in trouble, OK?' Alex turned her head away and B could see her lips curling in distain. Parents. Yuk! How gross!

Later, Beatrice phoned Hilary to rearrange their coffee and chat. Then she waited until the children had set off to school, Alex walking determinedly down the lane and Emily having to run a little to keep up with her, as if Alex wanted to get shot of her as quickly as possible. Beatrice summoned up all her energy and opening the kitchen window, yelled after them. 'Make sure you take her right into school, won't you?' Alex turned around and gave her a scowl.

Once the house was quiet, she heaved herself up the stairs and looked at the unmade bed. Bill's pants and socks were sitting in a little pile on the floor where he'd left them last night. She felt aggrieved. She would have to tidy them up later. For now she needed a little sleep, just an hour so she could rid herself of this ghastly pain in her head. She looked down at her morning attire, floppy gym pants and grey jersey top; she thought about putting her nighty back on but, in the end, just fell into bed and pulled the covers over her eyes. Ugghh. Never again. Why do I always forget how horrible alcohol makes me feel the next day? Why would anyone want to do binge drinking?

Hilary was also waiting for the house to be empty. When B had phoned earlier, to rearrange their get together, she felt really let down. Selfish Polly had kept her friend up late and now she had to wait. She'd put off her morning gardening client until tomorrow and now she had time on her hands. Time to think. Time to walk around the house. Time to walk towards Gemma's bedroom. Time to think about whether to search for anything to give her a clue. This was not in her nature, really. Her heart was thumping. She felt both excited and ashamed of herself. The door was stuck on something, a pair of socks, pink and black, slightly grubby. She pushed further. She mustn't disturb anything, she looked at the ball of socks stuck under the door and pulled them out, tucking them into her pocket to replace on her way out. The bed was unmade. Books were stacked in neat piles on the chest of drawers and the desk. Novels, some of them were from her bookcase downstairs, she hadn't missed them. There was a scent of perfume and a kind of singed smell, like a saucepan had been left on. The house phone was on the floor by the bed and as she picked it up, tutting, she caught herself and put it back again. She spotted the hair straighteners on the window sill, they were still hot but, thankfully, not still switched on. Hilary began to relax. Where to start? She checked her watch, 8.50, she would give herself half an hour and no more. If she couldn't find a clue in that time she should stop. It was deceitful, after all, and, anyway, Gemma would find out what she had been up to if she gave any clues away. Worry about that later.

She turned her attention to the wardrobe. She looked inside. The clothes were tightly packed on the rails and quite a lot of things were neatly arranged on the floor in boxes of varying sizes. Shoes were wedged in pairs, with elastic bands round them, down on the left hand side. Hilary opened the boxes one by one and looked inside. She was looking for a diary or a box of letters maybe, she had no idea really. She didn't want anything to fall out as she didn't want to have to rearrange things back in and get it wrong. All the visible boxes had innocent stuff in, old school work mostly, by subject and well organised. That's my girl, Hilary thought.

She pushed through the boxes towards the back of the wardrobe. There was something, it wasn't too big and it seemed to have a lid.

Without pulling it out and working blind she eased the lid off and pushed her hand inside. There was a lot of space. She pushed further and worried about breaking the lid, it felt like a shoebox, not very solid. There were papers, some thick, some flimsy and what felt like photos. Using her fingers like pincers she manoeuvred a photo out of the box. She pulled it out into the daylight. It was a photograph of a horse, a pony really, against a background of a field with some trees in the distance. A photo from when Gemma was small and rode a horse every Saturday morning. So, just a box of old photos and stuff from her childhood, in all probability. She eased a space in between the clothes and sneaked the photo back. Where next?

She bent down and looked under the bed. It looked reasonably clean, just with a cereal bowl on the floor by the bedside table. This morning's Golden Nuggets. Must resist the urge to clean it up. On to the desk. The computer. What could she find out by looking at the computer? It was switched off so she pushed the power button. While she was waiting she looked at the desk contents. It looked spookily like the desk of someone who was a well organised scholar and was up to date with her work. There was a neat pile of exercise books. Chemistry was on the top. She opened it and looked at the tidy notes. They were very neat and had a beautifully labelled diagram of an experiment. Electrolysis of copper sulphate solution. There was a date. Tuesdays date. But she hadn't been at school on Tuesday except first thing in the morning. The book looked full and well kept. With sheets stuck in. But no marking. No teacher's ticks or notes or encouragement. It was faintly heartening that Gemma was, somehow, making an effort to keep her studies up. She flicked to the back. There was a sheet of something that hadn't been stuck in yet. It was just handwriting. A note from a friend maybe?

Will you be able to come to the library at break time today? I don't want to press you but it is quite important. I know you are busy with your course work darling but spare a thought for poor little me. I miss you so much xx

That was all. Who was it from? No name. The handwriting was neat and small, with a left slant. It looked like it was from someone older, not like Gemma's childish round script. Perhaps a sixth former? She had met the sixth formers, they were like another race, tall, clear skinned, dressed in their own clothes, well spoken. But this note had a feeling of pleading, or that the sender felt neglected. It made her feel uneasy.

She refolded the note and put it back, the computer screen was up and ready for her to put in Gemma's login and password. Blast. Don't know either. Her watch showed that her predetermined time was up. Nothing to show for her search yet but, in a funny kind of way, she felt lighter. Gemma was not stuck in a deep abyss of something. Her room showed that she was keeping some kind of order. She hadn't found any drugs either. Her shoulders relaxed a little. Her chemistry book, then a biology book, a book of modern poetry and a DT file, all looked, to Hilary anyway, as though Gemma was working. Working hard too but no sign, in any of the books, of any teacher's marks. It was puzzling but she didn't feel as disheartened as she had expected.

Beatrice felt much improved by lunchtime and resolved to decline all alcohol for the rest of the day. Perhaps Hilary could make her a sandwich. She was the kind of person who often had unexpectedly delicious ingredients in her fridge. Being a professional gardener she was also very particular about the provenance of her food, so no supermarket lettuce today. Things were looking up. While she was driving along - the traffic was light - she thought about what could be going on with Gemma. Part of her was amazed. Gemma had been a lovely little girl, especially in comparison with Alex who could best be described as 'challenging', even as a toddler. She was thoughtful and polite and had grown to be a very attractive in a pale, slender kind of way. She knew Hilary was very aware of her daughter's inner beauty and how lucky she felt to have such a wonderful child. But now it all seemed to be unravelling.

Hilary had been a single parent even before the term had been invented. She thought about the current fashion of pitying and pandering to the young for their mistakes in getting pregnant. Hilary had received no help or support, only scorn and derision. B's thoughts meandered around the terrifying array of birth control methods and products available to the young at the parents 'personal and sexual health' workshop she had been obliged to attend when Alex was in year 9. She had actually been made to hold a large pink and rather unnaturally shiny vibrator. It was about as far from reality (particularly in size) as it was possible to get. It was a totally disgusting evening made worse by the obvious enthusiasm of some of the fathers in the gathering. Bill had unaccountably been working away that night, how coincidental!

Her mind drifted back to Hilary and the subject in hand. By this time she was at the traffic lights at the junction of the main road and aware that she had not actually noticed getting there. Hilary's own story was that she had been conned into having sex by one of the older boys at their Grammar school. He was quite advanced for his age and very charming. He actually had a neat little moustache at the age of sixteen when all his contemporaries were longing for a hair or two to shave away.

Beatrice racked her brains to recall the details and piece them together. At the time she and Hilary had gone over and over it, trying to see a way to make it right or to push the blame onto the boy. As far as she could remember he had taken her to town after school one evening. They had, according to Hilary, bought some cider from a shop. She had waited around the corner, he looked old enough so it was not questioned. It wasn't as hard to get hold of booze in those days. They all did it if they could. Hilary and the boy had gone to the cemetery. It was a popular destination for their age group and held them spellbound with the atmospheric Victorian monuments and the tingle of anxiety as it got to dusk. You had to endure a frisson of danger not knowing what was lurking just outside of your eye line. Hils and the boy had drunk the cider. Hilary was unusual in that both her parents worked; she was not going to be missed at home by a mother in an apron.

They had kissed. They fumbled around a bit. It was quiet. It was very quiet. He knew what he was doing and basically he did it to her. And she let it happen. She was strangely pleased about it (this had shocked Beatrice, it seemed as if Hils had known all along what would happen). They were completely alone. There would have been no-one to call out to, even if she had wanted to. He was strong but very, very persuasive, according to Hils. And that was that. Virginity flushed down the toilet by an oversexed schoolboy like a used tampon.

The group of Hilary's girlfriends found out later on during that week. Beatrice and Hilary had a close knit set of good friends. They were in a double physics practical lesson. They knew Hilary had been out with him but were unprepared for the shock admission. None of the girls had even got past breast squeezing, it was a kind of unspoken rule, nothing below the knicker waistband until the summer holidays before you were 16. There had been a few sweaty attempts to break through this boundary by some of the wispy beard brigade but the group had been adamant. Anyway, everyone knew that if you did it you would get 'into trouble' as all the mums called it. (They were unanimous on this point.) They knew what 'trouble' meant from their biology O level course.

Amongst the detritus of the physics experiment with clockwork cars on a lab bench, a stopwatch and a chart on a clipboard and not too much teacher supervision, they listened horrified to Hilary's tale. The beast, the animal, he had transgressed the rules and obviously planned his assault, below the knicker line, with precision and callous disregard for Hilary's maidenhood. B was especially angry. She had meant to be first. Now the thrill of telling the others and their looks of glowing admiration had been stolen from her by mousy Hilary, who never wore any make up and certainly had not been practising the appropriate moves with the seriousness that B had, several times a week, with her 17 year old boyfriend, Carl.

Now, at the roundabout, Beatrice winced at the memory. She had been a horrible and precocious teenager with much too high an opinion of herself. Hilary had really been duped, of course, not believing that anyone would want to do it with her in the first place but Beatrice had been furious that this boy, who they all knew and liked (or so they thought), could break the *rules*.

Hilary would not be drawn on the gory details, except the after effects. So none of them were any the wiser about what it felt like to *do it*. Hils would only say it was 'unspeakably disgusting' and afterwards she couldn't believe how messy it all was. Bodily fluids. Fortunately for Hils her parents had not returned from work when she got home so she had the house to herself and could wash it all away. It was funny how these little details stayed with you after all these years, B thought, as she drove up Hilary's road. She remembered the feeling of righteous indignation on her friend's behalf, or perhaps jealousy that Hilary had been the chosen one. And how she planned to get revenge on the boy in question.

B's arrival outside Hilary's house cut off her daydreaming and she sighed. She had actually got no nearer in her thoughts to any idea of how they could make progress on the Gemma thing without confronting her or making a scene; two strategies that she knew from bitter experience with Alex were the opposite of what was required and, anyway, Hils was just not that kind of mum. What they needed was a big clue or a lucky break. She locked the car, walked up the path in the beautifully landscaped front garden of her old friend's house, and knocked on the large and well polished brass knocker.

Hilary looked a little dishevelled and sheepish.

'You were expecting me now, weren't you Hils?' B was worried she had not made her revised plans clear.

'Yes, yes, of course, come in quickly, I want to tell you something.'

Hilary shuffled along the hallway and into the kitchen at the back. B was hoping soon that the suggestion of lunch might come up before they really got down to talking about Gemma.

'I've been rummaging through her room this morning, feeling as guilty as hell. What do you think I found for my compromised principals and furtive activities? Bloody fuck all, that's what.' This was strong language indeed for Hilary.

'You must have found something, after all, what has she been doing with her time all these weeks when she's been bunking off? She must have accumulated something, receipts for coffee shops maybe, or bus tickets, something that gives us a clue as to where she is going. Did you see anything like that?'

'No, but I did see something odd. Her school books are up there, well most of them that I could see, and they are all up to date with essays and drawings and science experiments, just as if she had actually been to the lessons. But no teacher's marks of course. I was quite glad. She seems to be keeping up her work but where and when is she doing it? I'm relieved that my Gemma hasn't lost her wits even though she is making me so angry at the moment with her non-communication. She's even started sending me texts so I can't ask her any questions. Like ... she texted me last night to say she would be back about eight but not where she was or who she was with. I texted back to ask these vital questions and how she would get back and I just got a reply that said something like 'Yeah, right, see you later Mum.' What's that about then? God I'm beginning to feel as though I'm being unreasonable for wanting to know what is going on.'

'Don't be stupid, you've been threatened with prosecution! I'd be livid, fuming, I'd have wrecked her room by now and probably wrung her irresponsible little neck as well!'

'That's not my style you know, B, I'm stuck in my neo hippy, trendy, muesli eating 1970s mentality!' The two women giggled.

'That reminds me, I was having a lovely reminisce as I drove here. All about our 5th year and the start of it when you were un-ceremoniously deflowered on a flower bed in the grave yard!'

'You make it sound so romantic ... gosh what a grotty experience that was. I often think about the way you punched the boy in the face right outside the sixth form common room just when old Smithson was coming out of the door. Your face! It was priceless, you were squealing with the pain and trying to look indignant and brave while pretending that nothing was going on. I felt really blessed, having you as a friend then. Remember? He had to get his mother to come and pick him up at lunchtime, what a loser!'

'Yeah, I never knew punching someone could break your fingers. Look, my ring finger is still knobbly around the knuckles where it broke. The things I did for you, my girl.' B reflected for a moment. 'What hell you went through with your mum and dad, though, and the termination. My mum was so kind to me around that time and I can't help thinking that she felt really sorry that you'd drawn the short straw with your family so she compensated for it by being sweet to me. It's funny how things turn out, isn't it? If we only knew then what we know now.'

'Mmm, if I'm honest though, I did allow that episode to make me finally decide I was damned if I was going to suck up to my parents anymore and do what they wanted. I think I saw they were more interested in what their friends thought than my welfare. My mum actually accused me of leading him on, she said something like, 'You'll never make me believe that a good looking boy like that would look twice at you if you hadn't offered it to him on a plate!'

'Bitch!'

'I know,' Hilary sighed, 'I'm glad they moved away to Yorkshire in the end. At least they gave me a good excuse not to go with them.'

'Remember the way your mum used to try and pretend you weren't in when I called for you. And how she used to hang around in the hallway and try and get me to go away, then when you called out that you were just coming, 'Just coming, Beatrice,' and she'd give me that peculiar look and walk off in a huff?'

'Peculiar is exactly the right word for her. Do you know she has started writing poetry, like that stuff you get in birthday cards? My sister sent me some copies. I couldn't believe what twaddle she was coming out with. None of it was anything other than rank hypocrisy.'

'Ah, hypocrisy ... sneaking around our daughters' bedrooms and ruining our liberal credentials ... sounds like we and your parents are like peas out of a pod.'

'Don't say that,' wailed Hilary.

'OK, just joking. Sorry, I'm being cruel. Polly made me have an awful hangover. It's not my fault. Now, what's for lunch then?'

'Lunch, oh ... lunch. I'll have to dig something up. Not literally you know, just from the fridge. Let's do that and talk about little Miss Trouble later.'

'And while we are at it, a nice glass of something would go down well, too.' B's resolve disappeared without a second glance. Hair of the dog. That was a much better philosophy than abstinence.

Alexa was sitting on her desk at school in the lunch break, calmly applying another coat of mascara and then squeezing the eyelash curlers in what looked like a torture ritual of some kind. She was all alone. Thinking. The other girls were outside somewhere, doing something of no account, she thought disdainfully. She was mulling over some fragments of conversation she had heard at home, on the evening when all her mother's friends had gathered downstairs to do their silly book club thing. Then she had overheard her mother and father having a sort of random discussion about Gemma, a friend she had known when she was little, they were at nursery together.

Gemma, it appeared, was in trouble of some kind. Something to do with school but Dad had mentioned the possibility of prison. Someone was going to go to prison! Her ears had pricked up but she couldn't find out any more. If she had asked then they would have told her it was none of her concern which, indeed, it was not. However, she was not her mother's daughter for nothing and the prospect of a bit of digging out of facts and seeing what she could pick up on the 'grapevine' as her mother would have said, made her feel secretly excited. Actually, she would just go online and see who could talk. Someone must know something. In her mind she fast forwarded herself into a future time when she could bask in the reflected glory of being able to inform her mother (haughtily of course) that she, Alexa, knew more about it than her mother did! What a pleasant prospect. Anyway, her curiosity was piqued, she had to know more. It made yesterday's revelations about Daniel's girlfriend and the courgette seem pretty pathetic.

Later on she met up with her group of friends, the only ones to be considered cool in her year, outside the school gates. Alexa didn't want to betray how interested she was in the topic so she hedged around the subject a bit.

'Yeah, right, have you heard about that girl from Hollingbrooke Upper?' In her voice there was the slight inflection necessary to show her distain and pity for anyone who was not fortunate enough to avoid going to such a place.

'Nah, what girl?'

'What's she done, then?'

'Is she friends with Jade?' Jade had been another unfortunate who had left the school when her parents fell on difficult times.

Alexa's antennae were on red alert. She hadn't known Jade well, she was short and spotty for a start but she could soon get to know her. Yeah, like, later on when all her mates were online and someone could add her.

'Dunno really, she might be.'

'What's the big deal then, Alex?' Her friends were always on the look-out for useful information.

'Just heard a rumour, probably nothin', nothin' to get in a sweat about anyway. I'll check it out and speak later, OK?'

'OK, laters, then.'

'Laters ...'

And with that the group drifted apart.

Hilary was out in the garden, looking for a few last sprigs of mint that she might put into the impromptu couscous salad she had made for their lunch. B was sitting in the rear window and looking benignly at her. Hilary was thinking gently about the topics they had resurrected. That first sexual encounter in the cemetery, the cemetery for God's sake! She had never been able to suppress her utter disgust, no, worse than that, her contempt for that boy, the way he had so little control over his body, his sexual impulses. How stupid she had been for thinking it would be interesting to find out what sex was like. It was like being an animal, jutting and pushing and not normal. But now she knew that it was very normal and that people actually liked it. People, men (and women too) looked at photos of sex for pleasure! She felt apart from those people.

She unbent her shoulders and looked up around her garden, now *that* was what beauty was all about, not fumbling around naked, it was so undignified! That first feeling had never abated. She had gone along with the other girls' own first times and laughed and joked and alluded to secret pleasures but, really, she was just repelled by it all. Even more so now, in her forties. She had endured the termination and, with it, her thoughts about her future altered. They would not include a husband and children, she was sure. But that idea reversed when Gemma was conceived. Beatrice was pregnant with Alex, blissfully in love with Bill, and happily married. Rather naively, Hilary thought she should join her. She thought she could have some kind of mutual kinship with Beatrice. Something deep had stirred inside her and, as she was seeing someone casually at the time, she jumped into bed with him, fantasising madly about a baby. Pregnant within two months, she had dumped the man concerned like a shot (he had been very upset) and blithely moved forward into single parenthood with all the confidence of a woman who knows deep in every fibre of her being that she will never have to have sex with anyone again. Mission accomplished. Job well done. Funnily enough she hadn't realised she had wanted a child until B was actually pregnant. She had never spoken about her ambivalence regarding the physical side of love. People seemed to assume she was unfortunate because she couldn't get a man. Her peculiar job, for one thing, meant she didn't meet many men, thank God! Then, after Gemma was born, she could hide behind her baby. A good bit of subterfuge; no man wanted to take on a single mother and another man's child. Ah! She rubbed her back where she had been bent over and, taking the mint back into the house, she noticed B had closed her eyes and looked as if she was napping.

'You took a long time …' She wasn't asleep, just closing her eyes.

'Just mulling over what we had been talking about.'

'Me too.'

'What should I do then?'

'What should you do?'

'Bedroom rummage draws a blank. Can't think of any other places to look right now.'

'Her bag, the one she will be carrying when she comes home, then.'

'She'll put it in her room and I'll have to sneak it out.'

'But do you think it can be done?'

'I'll give it a shot but I'm not taking any risks. We are on very dodgy ground, us two, and what if she decides just to go, completely? Leave home. I'd be devastated.' Hilary blanched.

'How? She's only just 16.'

Hilary was now spooked. 'I must go slowly. I wonder why she won't tell me what's going on.'

'Let's think, get a bit of paper.'

'OK.'

They sat huddled over the kitchen table. On the paper they wrote:

Pregnant
Drugs
Boyfriend
Bullying
Hates school

Bored with school
Crime, shoplifting for example
Prostitution

'Come on you're getting silly now.'

'Does she have any money of her own, do you give her an allowance, does she have a bank account?'

'Why?'

'Well it would tell us if she was getting any cash from whatever she is doing and wherever she is going. Receipts, card purchases, that sort of thing.'

'Good thinking but no bank account yet. Right, she has £10 pocket money per week that I give her in cash. Apart from that, if she wants clothes or toiletries, for example, she just asks me and sometimes I get them for her. Usually with clothes she tells me how much she wants and I give her cash. I get quite a lot of cash from clients. But, hey, you know I am not at all well off, she kind of knows not to ask for much and I think she is quite thrifty. She's certainly careful about her things, very particular about looking after her clothes, ones she likes and wears a lot.'

'Hmm ... then we need to see if she has suddenly got money, that will give us a clue.'

'Alright, I'll ask her if she wants any more money, say an increase in her pocket money, I can say I want to put her on an allowance, that would be safe ground to talk to her about, don't you think? Yes, it appeals to me and then maybe she'll open up a bit more; she won't just walk off if I'm offering her more money, surely?'

Hilary was looking more animated, better really.

'Yes, I think that is a very, very good starting point. I can't believe you just said pocket money. That's so last century, darling.' B patted her friend on the arm and winked. Gently does it, she thought.

Alexa had logged on and started her usual chat to her mates. She was waiting for a particular group of mates to come online; mates who would know Jade and other people from Hollingbrooke. Downstairs the phone rang. Her mother answered. Alexa listened quietly from just behind her door.

'I just remembered something. There was a note, from someone from school, it talked about meeting in break or something. It was clear from the tone that she has a close boyfriend, maybe someone has a crush on her. It has 'darling' in the note. I thought that the handwriting looked quite mature, as well, not like the round loopy writing of teenage girls.'

'You probably stumbled on a note from a secret admirer. That's more promising, isn't it? Can I see the note? Have you still got it?'

'No, I couldn't keep it, silly. And I can't remember the exact words. But the note made me think it was from someone close to her, like a lover? 'I miss you' it said. Perhaps I'm reading too much into it, unfortunately I had to put it back, so I can't check. Do girls call each other darling these days? I can't remember.'

'No. It's usually 'you bitch', or something worse. Girls are absolutely vile to each other, even when they're friends.'

Mmm ... I suppose you're right.'

'Well, add it to the bloody list then, my girl, the plot thickens.'

As Hilary twisted towards the kitchen table and picked up her diary, where the list was being secreted, the ball of socks fell out of her pocket and dropped unnoticed onto the floor and rolled away. Gemma would pick them up later and wonder how her bed socks came to be lying on the kitchen floor. But her worries were so great the socks would soon be forgotten.

Chapter 13 - An unexpected meeting

Zolli had got it into his head he was a neglectful boyfriend and lover. He loved going to Jill's little house. He loved her comfortable living room and her very comfortable bedroom. She cooked like a dream and loved to eat as well. Sometimes he caught her watching him over a steaming plate of pasta or a home cooked casserole. Her face was flushed with pleasure; his pleasure made her happy. Her pleasure then made his heart expand with love for her.

When he was single, he had worked his way methodically through the hospital restaurant menu. He had purchased such delicacies as fish and chips. He knew the differences between Pizza Hut, Pizza Express and Dominos (the latter was on speed dial) and had tested, for research purposes only, McDonalds, KFC, Burger King, Nandos, two tandoori takeaways and several Chinese establishments as well. Krystina made him eat in the kitchen with the back door open. She was not good with food. She never wanted to share or sample the meals. The strong smells of takeaway food made her feel nauseous, she said.

Now he was dining with Jill most evenings, his gastronomic experiences were embracing new and exciting possibilities. He recalled the goulash Jill had prepared just for him. She had been shy and secretive but the aromas coming from her kitchen had already alerted him to the treats in store. Had it been authentic? He didn't care! The beef was certainly less gristly than any he recalled eating in his homeland. But the correct tang of smoky paprika, that was hard to get right. Hungarians were paprika mad, it was like a religion. Home grown and home smoked and dried - each village, each house almost, had its own special and uniquely flavoured spice.

He walked into a deep puddle that splashed up his trouser leg. One shoe was soggy. That should teach him to concentrate on the task in hand. He was on his way to purchase a gift for Jill. And he knew exactly what he was going to buy her. A slow cooker. A three litre slow cooker with an automatic keep warm function. She had been reading a catalogue of kitchen wares and had marked this one out. She left the brochure open on the coffee table, perhaps it was on purpose. This was her desire! He would bring this gift to her, he would surprise her tonight. It was expensive but he could just anticipate her delight when he presented it to her. And what stews, soups, sauces and, yes, more tender goulashes, she could conjure up. He would even help with the meat and vegetable preparation; they could do it the night before and just turn the cooker on the following morning before work.

A loud horn sounded by his ear and he jumped. He had been so engrossed with his dreaming he hadn't noticed the green man was flashing and had turned to red. But he was close now to the indoor mall and ducked into a clothes shop which acted as a walk through to the main shopping area. Rows and rows of women's clothes were set at angles to frustrate his progress through to the shop he wanted on the other side of the mall. He ducked back and forth, sweeping jumpers and blouses out of his path. Young women with babies in buggies blocked his way. Girls with their eyes firmly locked on their phone screens walked into him! He was out of his depth.

Finally, he exited into the main mall thoroughfare. Lakefield Homewares, his destination beckoned. He breathed a deep and relieved breath. Contact with crowds of people, energies so diverse and often, to him, unbalanced, made him feel uncomfortable. He had to protect himself for his own good. Distractions were everywhere. He could see too much, feel too much. He could see the damage in the people around him. But it was not his job to interfere. At the hospital he had free rein, but here, it was almost worse. Hard to bear.

In the shop he was transfixed. There was so much *baking* equipment. He was obviously such an amateur in the baking department. Cupcakes, cakepops, traybakes, muffin tins, decorating icing, colours, sprinkles. A bread maker! He was swept away on a tide of happiness, realising he could buy any of these divine (perhaps that was, for him, an ill advised adjective) baking accessories for Jill. And she would be just as excited as he was! Reluctantly he moved away from the aisles of pink gorgeousness (because almost all of the cake based packaging was pink) and went further into the shop looking for his slow cooker. He had written down the name and model number.

'Can I help you, sir?' A homely lady was looking at him, her head cocked on one side.

'I have the name of my product here. That is right?' He showed her his piece of paper.

'Ah, yes. The Lakefield *own brand* slow cooker. I have one myself. Sooo useful.'

'Can I buy now?' Zolli was intoxicated with keenness.

'Of course, I'll just get one down from upstairs. Would you come to the till, sir, over here?' She rang up the purchase.

'And can I interest you in our extended warranty?'

'Oh, I am so happy, now. I will have it all.'

'So would that be the superlux five year, guaranteed next day engineer call-out cover, Sir?' She was determined.

Zolli found his Visa card and duly handed it over. How he loved everything about this shopping experience. He resolved to do it much more often.

Two women waiting behind him were talking quietly to each other. 'They never pass up a chance to flog you something extra, do they?' 'No, they are shameless but I heard they make most of their wages from the warranty extensions. They must be so poorly paid anyway, you've got to feel for them.' 'Mmmm. But him so obviously foreign too. Turkish most likely, look at his eyes and curly hair. Do you think he knows anything about consumer rights? He can probably cancel it if he goes online within 7 days. Shall I tell him? It's 23 pounds extra after all.' 'No, let him be. He looks over the moon with his cooker. Seeing a man buying cooking equipment, that's made my day. Or maybe he's ... you know ... batting for the other side, as my Ron would say.' 'Gay men aren't the only ones interested in cooking, Bren!'

Zolli was almost in stitches by this time and could hardly contain himself. He turned round and beamed. 'It's a present for my lovely girlfriend. She will love it, no?' Both women looked stunned but quickly recovered. Zolli had effortlessly captured their hearts. 'Oooh, she will love, she will, don't worry about that.' Both women were now completely bowled over by him.

Ten minutes later Zolli clutched his oversized carrier bag and a cake pop starter set he hadn't been able to resist buying. He envisioned wintry afternoons holed up in Jill's kitchen, maybe she would have flour smudged on her nose. Or buttery fingers. He would lick it all off, of course. He set off for a different way back, through Boots. Safety in pharmacies, he thought. It was busy and he glanced around, just making sure he wasn't walking into an energy minefield like before. His elation had made him feel less threatened, so he moved quickly through baby and child, hair products, slimming, men's shaving things and was making for the door when a sound stopped him. He knew that sound and knew it was directed at him. It was a whine; a sneering kind of whine. As if to say, 'Oh, look who's here. One of *them*. Think you can take me on, tough guy!' Zolli breathed. The small ones always had the loudest voices and the stupidest insults. He turned and cast his eyes in the direction of the sound, looking to see which unfortunate human it was attached to.

Phillipa and David had just come from an outpatient appointment with a new consultant. Mr Hameed had left (as was the way ... change the doctors ... don't tell the bloody patients anything) and a Norwegian doctor had replaced him. This was a surprise and it turned out to be a welcome one. More blood tests, a review of medication and a promising chat about possible drugs David had not tried yet. David was down, though. He was the one who had to put up with the turmoil of any changes. The withdrawal of one drug and the desperate week or so while his body adjusted to the new regime. They had been given a booklet about Lithium. It wasn't new but was worth trying. They had to read the booklet carefully, cross check any possible contraindications they were aware of (the list was long) and if they were happy and could factor in the increased blood testing they could order a one month supply. David's GP would monitor his progress, or one of the nurses. His CPN would visit weekly. If he was going to have side effects they would be potentially serious immediately.

Phillipa was hopeful. She needed something new to hang on to. So, as they drove away from the outrageously overpriced hospital car park, she decided to cash the prescription first and do the paperwork and make the GP appointments later. What was another two quid for parking in town when you'd already parted with £4.80 at the hospital because you were ill. It made her fume.

It was hot and stuffy while they queued at the pharmacy counter but Phillipa wasn't put off. This medicine could not be dispensed by one of the ordinary assistants. The pharmacist was coming out to talk to them. They had to wait. David wanted to sit down somewhere and was shuffling towards some plastic chairs. He was tired and looked like he was carrying the weight of the world on his shoulders.

Zolli made eye contact, if you could say the source of the whine had eyes. It's serpent like coils were wrapped around a man's neck and body. The man looked weighed down with the dark energy he was carrying. But, as Zolli focussed intently on the creature, the coils began to melt. It was going back inside to hide. Too late, though. A command was all it took and he saw it uncoil at speed, twisting and stretching out until it had separated from the man and was fading, whining as it went, towards whatever dimension was the right destination for the creature. 'Nasty, dirty little hitchhiker,' he muttered. 'Take that!' He would have to apologise to the man's guide, of course, but, hopefully, he would not have affected too many plans. Maybe his being there at the right time *was* part of the plan for the person concerned. He couldn't help himself anyway. It was like kicking the school bully, sometimes you just had to do it. And I'm just using my *free will*, he said to himself. That is the wonder of Earth life. He observed and released many such beings in the hospital. People in the know called them *spirit attachments*. He considered it part of his calling. Frequently all it required was just a kind word, some reassurance about the next step towards a better dimension, and this was enough to send the energy towards its destination; releasing the host of that extra burden of existing in the world coupled with unwanted, but attached, earth-bound energy. Each energy had its own agenda, thoughts and feelings. The effect could be catastrophic but he had also witnessed people in happy co-existence with one or more attachments inside them. Occasionally, however, like now, he saw malevolent energies, posing as physical manifestations of their distorted thoughts. A serpent. How glad he was that it was very uncommon. If people could only see the energy of the world around them, would it help them to understand living better? Most likely they would freak!

He stepped out of the shop into the fresh air, feeling alive, feeling optimistic. Something very good was about to happen, he knew it! And it was probably connected to chicken casserole and maybe even dumplings!

The kitchen was warm and comforting. Pippa had just taken out an apple crumble made from next door's late apples. It had been a good year. The freezer was half full with blackberries, rhubarb and misshapen strawberries, the stragglers of the crop. She had photographed them in a line, from the tiny ones not worth eating right up to some awfully gruesome shaped whoppers. The picture had been printed and framed for her office. Her strawberry patch had yielded double the bounty this year, edible and artistic bounty. You wouldn't want to eat them as they were, however, made into a sauce, perhaps with a pavlova at Christmas? She thought about Christmas. If she could be bothered. If they invited anyone, that is. Cooking did keep Pip's spirits up and the kids loved home cooked puddings. When she was in her kitchen she could pretend everything was normal. David would not bother her there. He was dozing in the dining room, right now. Joshi had a friend round for X box; she was making them play with head phones on. There were still whoops and the odd curse though filtering through the hall.

David stretched. He had his arms way above his head, feeling really rested and ... quite peckish. He noticed the smell in the house, his wife was cooking something. His mouth watered. It was an alien sensation. A good sensation. But he wondered why he was having it now, after such a long time feeling so subdued and miserable? A thought came unbidden. A nice hot cup of tea and some of that cake or pudding or whatever was on offer. Then maybe he would put some shoes on and see what state the shed was in. The idea made energy pulse through his body. He had a sense of looking forward to something. A feeling he recognised from a long time ago. He cracked his knuckles. Pippa really hated him doing that.

Chapter 14 - Rose can't wait any longer

Charles had taken the children to the go kart track, although how suitable that activity was for entertainment, she really couldn't specify. They all seemed to be keen, however, and after issuing Charles with stern instructions NOT to allow any of them to do anything silly or dangerous (at which point they all rolled their eyes in a collective display of scorn), she let them go.

The truth was, it gave her the free unfettered day she had longed for. Today she was going to go for a reading with the woman that Beatrice had recommended from the crystal shop. Nobody need know anything about it. Not even anyone like Gwen or Jill, who might think that she was being either foolish or, indeed, playing with fire after what happened before at the meeting. Bugger them all, thought Rose. I can't run my life according to what anyone else thinks. I just hope I'm still located on this planet when Charles and the children come home or I've got a bit of explaining to do.

She had sensibly enquired whether this woman, Krystina, her name was, had a free space on Saturday. She had. What time? A choice of times in the afternoon. Good. It was all fixed then.

Rose spent the late morning in a sort of frenzy, partly inspired by a faint sense of guilt, (quite pleasurable, though), sorting through the children's wardrobes and filling up some charity bags with clothes for a collection next week. Altogether it was a very cleansing process. Perhaps she would learn to be tidier. Unfortunately, she was not prone to guilt as a rule and, as this emotion seemed to be her driver in this case, she doubted how long-lived this tidiness idea would be. So, perhaps not, she mused. It was past midday. She was still in her dressing gown. The dishwasher was waiting to be emptied. Half filled bags of clothes were piled in heaps on the landing in a haphazard way. Too late, she must get dressed, and would have to sort it out later. The unpleasant prospect of having to explain why she had turned the house into a jumble sale while her family was out took the edge off her anticipation.

The day was one of those exquisite late autumn days when you could only marvel at the clear deep blue beauty of the sky, the winking sunlight that dazzled you as you drove along between the deep shadows cast by the buildings and the trees on the main road. The grass seemed to be very green, a kind of olive green, she supposed this was from the particular quality of the light. The branches on the trees were bare and clean now and the earth was dark brown and moist from the recent rain. In the village, fires were being lit in cold grates ready for a comfortable afternoon watching the rugby or maybe a nice black and white film. Put the kettle on then, my dear. Come along and sit by the fire. She could imagine the comfy scenes behind the dear little front doors.

In just two hours it would be as black as night and the sky would be filled with the sounds of birds, starlings chattering, singing, calling, flapping. She liked to think of them tweeting to each other excitedly making their travel arrangements before migrating to sunnier climes. Passports? Something warm for the journey? Compass? Torch? No need, I can fly by moonlight. Eaten plenty of juicy flies to keep you going? She pulled out of the junction and turned the car towards the town, smiling at her own imaginary images.

She walked across a large paved square and the crystal shop was tucked away in a corner of a gloomy arcade. As she drew nearer the scent of perfumed candles and incense sticks made her nose twitch. The slim, watery looking girl was serving behind the counter, flicking through a magazine in a desultory way. Rose was beginning to feel nervous.

'Mmmm? Can I help you?'

'I have an appointment with Krystina at two o'clock.'

'Ah, a 45 minute session is it?' She looked pointedly at her watch as if she were communicating with a small, rather stupid, child. 'Up the stairs and take a seat in the corridor.'

The corridor upstairs had three blue plastic chairs lined up against the wall. It was dark and cold but rather stuffy. A bulb in the ceiling rose had been (unaccountably) painted dark red. The floor was laminated and she could see the scruffy gaps around the skirtings where it did not fit properly. Never mind.

From behind one of the doors there were muffled sounds, two voices, both female, engaged in some sort of conversation. It reminded her of her childhood experiences of going to the doctors. There had been a heavy velvet curtain that covered the door at the surgery. The doctor in her childhood would sweep the door open and the huge curtain would billow out into the waiting room. When he had enticed his next victim in, the curtain closed ranks again and all the voices became muffled, subterranean, concealing stories of nasty leg ulcers that weren't healing, or trouble down below. Despite the atmosphere in the corridor, the backs of her knees were sweating.

The voices became more animated and suddenly, as the door opened, it was as if she had come up from underwater and the sounds were clear, confident, the client was happy, satisfied, saying her goodbyes.

The most radiant looking woman she'd ever seen looked straight into her eyes. She was fine boned, with high slightly Slavic cheeks. She had a cloud of fine blonde hair that swirled and ruffled around her face and collar. Light shone through the cloud even though there did not seem to be any real light in the corridor. Her almond shaped eyes were the most dazzling lilac colour. She smiled a crooked smile at Rose and called her name. It was as if she had been waiting an awfully long time to hear that sound, hundreds of years perhaps, but now it was time, she was on the brink of something.

Alexa was getting tired and fed up. What had seemed like a good idea (and a way to annoy Mum) was turning out to be more troublesome. Not only that, she was trying to do some physics homework that she couldn't really give a toss about. There were questions about resistance. What was the formula for R? V over I or was it VI? She flicked angrily through her notes trying to find the answer. Ah! V over I. Now where was the calculator? Nowhere. Use mobile. Battery low. Shit. The screen made that intriguing little twitter that heralded another message. She clicked to minimise it without looking up, then had to go back and retrieve it. Bullseye. Jade had come online. A mutual acquaintance had done his stuff, great. Her attention was full on. Bugger the physics. She would now try to use all her skills to prise the necessary gossip from poor Jade.

Hi Jade, can you tell me if you know Gemma from your year?

Yeah, she's in my class but she's never here. Dunno why.

Wots going on with her, exams are coming soon, dusn't she care?

She's not my mate really.

Who is her best mate then, I need to know

Why, you haven't got it in for her have you? She's OK just not in my group.

Nah, no sweat, don't get in a stress about it. Just got a message for her.

Who from

Just someone I know who fancies her, wants to get with her.

You can call Ally, she's her mate.

Can I message her?

She's not online much best txt her. You sure you're not getting at her?

Nah, I'm cool.

OK, numbers **********

Ta much.

Alexa then had to spend a dull ten minutes conversing with Jade about the school and sympathising with her about the troubles at Hollingbrooke. Art rooms out of bounds because someone had broken in after school and nicked some stuff. All the girl's loos were disgusting and often blocked deliberately. You had to report it to the caretaker who was a creepy, pervy kind of guy.

Alexa was finally able to plead her faithful physics homework and sign off. Deep breath. Dial number. Put on phone voice (keep unremitting note of contempt out of it).

'Ally. Jade gave me your number. I'm a friend.'

'What, who's Jade?'

'Jade from your year at school?' She sounded very wary indeed.

'What's up, who are you anyway?'

'I've got a message for Gemma.'

There was a long pause, then a hesitant cough.

'Gemma who?'

'Gemma from your class who is in trouble.'

'How do you know about that?'

Then a click and silence.

Fuck. Fuck, fuck, fuck, shit.

She threw her physics book on the floor and stalked off down to the kitchen to forage for something stodgy to eat. Blow the diet.

'I have a message for Gemma.' Rose blinked and held her breath.

'I see her alone and she is very worried, much worried. Wait, I hear the answer.' A pause, eyes closed.

'There is another older person, a woman who make her scared, she is scared. She worry many hours.'

'Can I ask a question?'

'OK.'

'What can we do, or her mother, what can she do, to help her? She is in trouble, her mum is so worried.'

A pause, eyes closed.

'I see a school. Library place. Gemma and woman. They are talking . Gemma she is upset. I think woman she have power over her.'

'What can be done?' Rose was holding her breath so as not to interfere with the flow of information. The girl had been working hard for at least twenty minutes. 'OK, I get jumbled message. Gemma she is standing in front of school I see before. She is walking in through the iron gate. She have big book with her, under arm.' A pause. 'It is good thing, she smiles. That's all.'

'Is that something from the future, or something that has happened already?'

'We ask for the future, do we not? I only get pictures so rarely. Usually it is words, like for you.' She smiled and started to laugh. 'That was shocking from guide was it not? Very stern with you he was.' Obviously this was a clairvoyant inside joke, Krystina wiped her eyes.

'OK, I tell you now, I feel it was a vision from the future, her coming to the school with big book. The past was her with woman. This is the problem, I think.'

'So this woman, how did she look to you, what kind of woman are we talking about?'

'She is small, with short red hair, like so.' She made spiky movements with her hands. 'She wears jeans and a tee shirt, Yes, that is right. Can she be teacher, you think? I think she is teacher.'

Her phone suddenly burst into life. She silenced it.

'Time is up now, other client is waiting.'

Rose was so disappointed.

'Can I come back later, I need to talk about the things you said, messages from my guide?'

Krystina put her hand on Rose's arm.

'No worry for you, I come to your meeting. It is already planned.'

'What meeting, when, what do you mean?'

'Next week, at your channelling meeting,' (she sounded the word like Chanel No.5), 'I am your expert. I guide you all now.'

She got up and briskly opened the door for Rose to leave, pressing the tape of the session into her hand.

'Listen to this later. You will be surprised.'

With that Rose found herself out in the square with birds chattering, swooping, flocking together, it was already dark, inky black and frosty. How could that be? She had only been inside for such a short while.

Chapter 15 - A shock in the night

She was lying awake at 3 am. It was the darkest part of the night. The gritting lorries had been out at tea time yesterday so it was going to be a very cold start in the morning. It already *was* morning. She sighed and looked at the lights on the clock radio. Still 3am. It clicked wearily to 3.01 She couldn't get up and have a cup of tea without waking the dog up, which would then lead to a futile dog/human discussion about whether or not it was doggy breakfast time. This in turn would probably waken one of the kids and then it would all become too complicated. Another sigh. Sighing wasn't going to get her back off to sleep. She hated this time of the night. She was thirsty and fed up and wanted, just for a moment, to be able to stop thinking about her problems.

Someone was rustling about outside the house. It might be her imagination or maybe a fox, the dog would normally go ballistic if a fox dared to come near the house. It didn't sound like a burglar. Her heart started to speed up. Reluctantly she got out of bed, God it was cold. No sign of her slippers. Nip over to the window and peep out, not making it obvious in case it was a random axe murderer.

'Don't feel like being murdered in my bed tonight,' she murmured to herself.

She held her breath so it wouldn't steam up the windows and peered out from a crack in the curtains. A sharp intake of breath. Panic. David was outside doing something with the car. What the hell? He's got a suitcase! What's going on? How did he get out there without waking me up? She was standing so still her muscles ached with the effort.

'David, David, what are you doing?' It came out like a tiny whisper. 'Look at me, I'm here, up here, look at me, tell me what is going on?' Pippa was paralysed with indecision. He was carefully spraying the car windscreen with de-icer. You could tell he was trying not to make a sound. He wasn't supposed to do this, do anything, he is depressed, he can hardly get out of bed each day. Deep breath. Courage. Face it.

She grabbed her big dressing gown and located her slippers and tiptoed out of her room. The stairs were in pitch dark. A quick glance in his room. Oh my God, he'd cleared the room and made the bed. What did that mean? She gathered herself and walked down the stairs. The front door was slightly ajar. She pushed it open and was hit by the blast of icy cold air. He was still fiddling with the car, he was doing something inside it, but the engine wasn't on yet.

'David, David?'

He looked up, startled, annoyed.

'David, what are you doing out here, it's the middle of the night?'

'I'm going away.'

'What, what! You can't! What do you mean, where are you going?'

'You can't stop me now, I'm going, I've made up my mind.' It was so final.

'But you're not well. You've only been on the treatment for two weeks, it's not safe, you need your blood tests, I've got to look after you. What are you thinking of? What about the children?'

He slumped down in the driver's seat and appeared to be having some sort of discussion with himself.

'Phillipa, we cannot go on like this. I may be ill, I think I am ill, oh I don't know but ... but I can't stay here like this, just waiting to ... I don't know what will happen if I stay.'

'But,' she was pleading now, 'you can't manage on your own. Who will look after you, who will keep you safe?'

He grasped the ignition key.

'I've explained it all in my letter. You'll find it on the hall table.'

He pulled at his seat belt strap and clicked it into place.

'I don't believe you. You're not thinking straight. I can't let you go, I have to stop you.'

'You can't stop me. There is no law that says just because I am a depressive, yes I can say it out loud - it's not something I have to be ashamed of - that I cannot make decisions about what kind of life I want to have.'

'Have you taken your tablets?' Her eyes narrowed and she noticed him gritting his teeth.

'Not that it is any of your business but, no, I took them a couple of times and decided against it all. Something *has* changed Phillipa because I can think for myself now, that's what I want to say to you.'

'But, but, you've seemed just the same, I haven't seen any change.'

'I haven't shown you anything about what I'm really feeling for months now. Anyway, like I said, I can think for myself, it's as if a veil has been lifted, and now I'm doing this for myself. I have chosen to leave you and to be depressed when and where I like and not to cover it up like a disgusting disability. That's what I feel like, felt like,' he corrected himself, 'before, popping those stupid pills, it's inhuman. I want to be able to be myself now. That's what I want, and if that means being unhappy or black or totally miserable, then so be it. It has got to be better than being medicated ... and being controlled by you.'

'But you seem better now, you're responding, showing the signs of recovery, you're angry, expressing your inner feelings, that's a fantastic sign. David please stay, please?'

'You disgust me with your pseudo psychobabble. I'm a person Pip, not a bloody syndrome.'

He started the engine and slammed the car door shut. She couldn't let go of it, her fingers gripped the handle. He looked straight ahead and revved up. Soon everyone would be looking out to see what was happening. Tears were streaming down her freezing cold face. He moved the car forward, she couldn't get her hand off the door handle quickly enough and suddenly he accelerated and her fingers were wrenched away. He drove down the road and the brake lights flashed and then were gone.

Disbelief.

Numbness

Cold, right into her bones.

Her hand felt funny, sort of hot but without any real warmth.

She looked at it. It looked strange. She shook it a bit, two of the fingers wouldn't go straight. Her middle nail was bleeding. She sucked on it absently. It felt odd in her mouth. The nail was gone, just flesh, it felt strangely bumpy.

The road now was deadly quiet. No lights had come on. Nobody to tell her what to do next. Just her funny hand that she couldn't use to pull her dressing gown cord tighter. She turned now to face the house. All dark. Her house. Her life. Not his. The letter. She blanked the thought from her mind. She looked over towards the front door.

'Mum. It's alright. I'm here, come inside.' Joshi. In his shorts, shivering, holding the collar of the dog to stop him bolting after David.

'Come on Mum, I'm not coming out to get you.' The dog whined, sadly.

She put one foot in front of the other. Josh put his hands on her shoulders and pulled her towards his chest. He was just slightly taller than her.

'It's OK Mum, I saw it all.' He pulled himself away and looked at her. He knew.

'I don't know what to do,' she said.

'It's OK, Mum, I think you need to get your hand seen to first, then we'll decide what to do.'

Chapter 16 - Krystina

Time was going very slowly for her. It was frustrating. She had been working on this problem for a long, long time. That's how it seemed to her. She was used to quick results. Another thing that made her very tired was the travelling. Going from her house to the shop and then walking about doing all the things she had to do, it took so long and she was constantly surprised at how tired it made her. She had to remember to eat. That was just stupid, not to eat. Then she had understood in the last few weeks that the tiredness and the not eating were related. She had to get used to it. He had told her she was not looking after herself properly.

Zolli had been looking at himself in the mirror, adjusting his tie. Silly things ties, what were they for, exactly? He had called her over and told her to look at herself.

'Look at your stomach.'

'Yes?'

'It's concave, you look starved, and your trousers are actually falling down!' Zolli laughed and turned towards her and bent down, tugging her jeans at the knees until they slid down her legs.

'That is not good. You are not following the rules, Krystina.'

'It's OK for you,' she smacked him on his chest, 'there is all that food already made for you. All you have to do is to sit down and eat it. For me I have to remember to stop working and not make for another booking, always I am busy so this is hard. Then I have to go about 10 minutes walking to get to sandwich shop that makes good sandwiches for me to eat. I cannot eat these ones in packet. I have to watch them being made, then I know it's OK.'

'You are just lazy, just like an ex-hybrid, I've known loads of them like you. You just won't make the effort to do it properly. Get your head out of the clouds, girl. We are not on other planets now.' He grinned and went over to the dressing table to slap some smelling stuff on his face. 'Stop trying to pretend that you are somewhere else. You aren't! This is Earth! Get over it!'

His breezy acceptance annoyed her a little. Also she suspected that his work was a lot easier than hers. This time anyway. She knew he had just come from a very tricky contract, she had been filled in on the main points but not the details. He stubbornly wouldn't talk to her about it. That was annoying too. She had brought down with her the love of chewing over and dissecting every tiny detail, every nuance of what had happened, sitting with her friends and going over it all again and again until you had perfected your response. He wasn't interested in this. He just liked to focus on the job in hand, forget about the past. That could all be discussed later. Much later for her. She already had signed up for three more jobs on Earth after this one.

'How much longer have you got on your mission this time, then?' Krystina asked, hoping for him to spill the beans as they said in this part of the world. He squeezed her pretty dimpled cheek and caressed her chin.

'You are far too impatient to know the end of things. Get to like, no, to love, the *doing* of it. Stop thinking ahead. Be in the Now! Ha! I'm getting the hang of this thing called 'chillin'. One of the nurses was explaining it to me yesterday.'

'I'm out tonight.' She enjoyed telling him this as she was trying to dampen his obvious pleasure in his assignment.

'Progress?'

'Yeah, I'm in already. It took so much time though.'

'There you go again,' he was lecturing her now, 'getting impatient, just go with the flow.'

'You really know how to be annoying, don't you? If I was that lovely girlfriend of yours I would punch you so hard that you would not have that stupid grin on your face any longer. There is a word for you, it's smug! Ha! Smug! That's what you are.'

'OK, I sympathise with you, that is what I do well at work. A little smile here, a little tender look there.' He turned his face to the side and looked at her from under his impressive lashes.

'I just want you to know how I feel. We are supposed to support each other. You won't even tell me what your mission is about. We should be sharing ideas and making it better for both of us.'

'You will just have to wait for me to tell you, the time is not right yet. Look,' he sat down, 'I know you work very hard for this. Tell me about your progress.'

'I'm connected with my people, the ones I am going to help. I can influence them now.'

'You are so clever. I knew you would do well.' It was the right response this time to stop her asking him questions.

'Yes, I made several good connections but the third time it really paid off, so I was able to put the idea into her mind that she was wanting to get to know me. And trust me. She was very transparent. It wasn't hard really. I used all my skills though and I showed off a little.'

'How?'

'Just a little light mind reading, then telling her future.'

'You're loving it really, aren't you?'

'Now I feel I am getting somewhere. You know, I just wish sometimes the instructions were more clear.' She broke away from him and started to dance a little around the room. She was very beautiful, he thought.

'I know what I must achieve,' she continued, 'but it is getting there that is more difficult for me. I think I remember what they said and then when we are here I cannot recall all the detail. Sometimes even the desired outcome is too vague for me.'

'That,' he grinned at her, 'is because we are supposed to use our skills, our initiative, to decide how to proceed as we go along. Then we can make adjustments when things go faster or slower. Like when you just happen to be in the right place at the right time, then you can change the plan, it is easy and so very enjoyable.' He was thinking about the very lovely and enjoyable evenings he had spent over the last few weeks with Jill.

'Anyway,' Krystina poked him in the ribs, 'now I also have somewhere to go in the evenings, the group they all belong to, so I do not have to wait here on my own with no-one to talk to. I can find enjoyment too.'

'I'm glad for you, my sweet thing.' And with that he kissed her in a absent-minded way and sped out of the room to go to work, striding up the road in the cool winter sunshine.

Chapter 17 - Bliss

Jill was examining herself in the mirror. She was at home in her bedroom at the front of the house and sunshine was streaming in through the windows. The light was angled across her bed, throwing the soft pillows and squashy duvet into pale relief. She looked at it again. What pleasure. No! That wasn't the word, what *bliss*, yes, that was right, she had experienced in that bed. She toyed with the thought that she might just slip back into it and relive some of the blissful moments. She could hardly believe it was happening to her. It was as if time, something that had always seemed to her so solid, so dependable, had suddenly taken flight and was becoming elastic and slowing down or speeding up. She sighed. That was probably the huge quantity of daydreaming she was doing. Not at work of course. At work she was in a sort of state of amber alert. Mildly excited, ready for a chance encounter, if it should arise. But of course they had to be discreet now, now that they were lovers. She nearly fainted with happiness as she allowed this thought to inhabit her mind.

He only had eyes for her. It was as simple as that. He was punctual, reliable, every time she texted him (and that had at least slowed down from the obsessive numbers of messages in the early days, when she was so unsure) he was courteous, texting back almost immediately (she avoided ward round times, for obvious reasons) with a simple message of love. She could find no fault with his attentiveness. She had started to actually *believe* that her company could be wonderful, her home the most special place to be, her body, warm and willing and fascinating. She stripped off her pyjamas. She looked at herself full length in the mirror. She was incredibly voluptuous, there was no doubt about that. But she had lost at least twenty pounds since she had begun her job at the hospital. What was it now? Just over three months ago.

She had collected her size 12 uniform from the stores last Friday. What a double triumph for her. A normal, beautiful, comely size at last and not one pound lost through misery or anxiety or depression, like when Max had left. Ha! She hadn't even thought about him for weeks now. Who cared what he was doing? He couldn't hurt her now. It was as if she was being nourished deep inside, layer upon layer of love, building up and covering over all the raw wounds of her miserably smashed-up self esteem. She felt lighter, more alive, but not in that sort of brittle, on the surface, 'put a false smile on your face', kind of way. She was smiling inside now - from the inside out. The outside still looked the same (apart from some little dimples on her cheeks that had suddenly appeared) but there was a composure, a surety about the way she walked, the way she talked and held herself. There was no denying it, love was the answer. What was the question again?

Her legs looked firm and muscled, her awful varicose veins had seemed to recede with the weight loss. Her belly was just nicely rounded. She had thrown all her terrible pants away many weeks ago. Actually, some of them were under the sink, doing polishing duties as makeshift dusters. She had then gone to La Senza and experimented with different designs and styles. Even thongs. What a horrible sensation that had been, like a cheese wire, not to put too fine a point on it. Finally she had found that the girly boxers were her style, so you could just see her navel, but the very tops of her thighs were covered in pant, some stripy and stretchy and others a bit frilly. Once she had seen how nice they looked she had spent nearly £40 on them! And bras. What could she do about those awful bras in her drawer? There was nothing in La Senza, well, nothing that would have fitted her. So she went to Marks and Spencer's just to see whether there was anything that would fit her and was delighted to find an amazing and pretty choice. The woman in the changing rooms was rather keen to get in there with her and do all manner of things to her breasts but she had resisted and found a style that encased her ample bosom very nicely. She bought a dark pink one and a cream one that had lace on the upper part of the cup. It was a bit scratchy but she would put up with it just to get the look, the one she was seeing now in the mirror, the look of a beautiful woman. For the first time in her life she was actually feeling that she was a beautiful woman. She shook her head to clear her mind. Could she accept this, even get used to it?

Theo was coming home for the holidays. He knew his mother had a new man in her life. He was faintly surprised; he hadn't troubled to hide his disbelief on the phone, but he would soon find out for himself that his mother, the one he and his father had grown used to pushing around and treating like a sort of servant, had thrown off the shackles and was living a life of happiness. A slight feeling of unease fluttered in her chest. What would it be like when they met? Zolli was almost in Theo's generation. She hoped her son's manners had improved. Perhaps she should do something about preparing Theo properly, a letter? No, a text would do the trick. She rummaged in her bag for her phone. It was switched off for a change and when she had switched it on the new message icon was flashing.

C U 2nite. Luv Z.

Mmm, she was warm and ready and could hardly wait. Not in the mood to send a difficult message to her son, she went back to the task of choosing the right clothes for her last proper evening in before the Christmas vac and the arrival of Theo.

Zolli was looking particularly handsome and his hair was curling deliciously around his ears.

'Where have I seen a guitar in the house? I know I have but I can't see it now.'

'No, I put it away, I thought I would have a good tidy up a few weeks ago and so I put it back in Theo's room, it's his.'

'Will he be annoyed if I play it, do you think?'

'No, of course not. I didn't know you played the guitar.'

'I am full of surprises.'

'I'll get it for you.'

She scrambled out from under the covers and grabbed her dressing gown. Scampering down the cold corridor, towards the room at the back of the house where Theo had made his home, she threw back the door and surveyed the tangled and unkempt array of possessions. He had made no effort to move in properly, it looked like a jumble sale had happened and never been cleared up. The guitar was just behind the door. It was very cold indeed in the house - the heating had been off for hours. They had been in bed since eight o'clock and had not worried about the temperature outside.

'Here it is,' she propped it up against the wall on his side of the bed. 'What are you going to play for me?'

He ignored her while he bent his ear to some extensive tuning of the strings. Then he burst into a sort of gypsy melody, fast and furious and full of the dance. Then a slow and tantalising piece in the same style, while he looked at her with liquid eyes. She recognised some of the melody.

'Some Hungarian dances for you. Designed to make your blood fire up and remind you of your homeland. That is, if you are Hungarian of course.' Then he changed style completely and started to strum some simple chords, in a minor key, then picking the notes out individually until she knew what it was. Softly he began first to hum and then to sing. A song from her youth. 'It was 'You've got a friend'. James Taylor.'

He looked deeply into her eyes as he was singing. She had a lump in her throat. How did he know how special this song was to her?

'That's one of my favourite songs of all time. How do you know it?' He put the guitar down and turned towards her.

'When I was a young boy, my mother used to have two records that she cherished. They were American and she kept them hidden so that the family didn't know she was being influenced by that terrible culture. All free love and long hair and drugs. She had obtained them from a boyfriend of hers who had travelled to the USA as part of a University swimming team. How he got them back through the border guards we never knew. But anyway, when we were on our own at night, she would get them out and we would play them and listen and just imagine what it would be like to live in that country, be able to get in a car and go to the beach with the top down, or just to be able to sing a simple love song to someone without worrying whether it was safe to do so. I didn't really understand at the time. She told me I must never sing the songs or tell anyone we played them. She would get into a lot of trouble if anyone found out that we had them.'

'What kind of trouble?'

'Ah, we lived in the country about a hundred kilometres from Budapest and it was very controlled. They took the party very seriously in our village. We had a big statue of Lenin in the square that the local community had saved up for years to buy and the police and officials made sure everyone said the right thing and did the right thing. Later I knew friends who had lived in Budapest and they were much more open about hating the Russians, they talked and took risks. Their parents were fashionable and hosted evenings where they would plan what they would do when the Russians were thrown out. So, you can see, we were afraid that someone would call and ask us about her records. Even someone that you knew. No one could be trusted, not even your own grandmother.' He treated her to one of his wicked grins.

'Your own grandmother would snitch on you to the police?'

'Yes, if she thought her own daughter was departing from the party line. Remember my mother had no husband, that was bad enough, my grandmother thought that I was being corrupted and maybe that my mother needed persuading to be a better party member, get more involved, do the right thing, not sit at home thinking subversive thoughts and teaching her little boy how to think for himself.'

'What happened?'

'I only know what my mother told me afterwards. She was asked to go and account for herself in front of the local committee. I only remember going to stay with my grandparents for a week, maybe longer, I don't know. She kept feeding me with soup and dumplings and her house was very dark and cold (patriotically cold, I think) and I had to sleep in the same room as her and my grandfather. It was terrible. They were so old and dark and humourless. Anyway, thankfully my mother was a very clever woman and had a way of talking that charmed the old men of the local party. I don't know if she had to offer any favours, I have thought about it since I have found out what happened, maybe she did, I don't care, it would have been worth it to her to sleep with a few old stuffy and frustrated party officials if it meant she could go home and keep her relative freedom. She came for me on the afternoon of a particularly bitter cold day, it was snowing outside, sleety and grey and thoroughly depressing. She burst through the little door of the house and grabbed my arm, really tight, and yanked me out into the wet slush. I had no coat on. We half walked, half ran back to our flat and she bolted the doors. She put the fire on and clasped me in her arms, she smelled funny, old and dusty, and she hugged me and hugged me until I couldn't breathe.'

'How would you like to go to the city, my little Zolli?'

We packed that night and left as soon as it was dark. We went to stay with a young group of friends that she had known before I was born. It was difficult but, eventually, she found a job working in the office of the main Budapest daily newspaper, she was just a clerk, sorting through files and keeping records but it allowed us access to a flat in a panel building. You could only get one if you had a job in a state run industry. It was better than nothing and we could start afresh. Let's stop talking about it now. I want to sing you another song and see if you know this one too. It will be our little guessing game. So tell me what you know about the last song I sing for you.'

'James Taylor. You've got a friend. Written for Carole King, I think. I used to listen to it a lot, too. When I was an awful 13 year old I used to lie for hours on my bed listening to this. I thought it was the most romantic song ever.'

'You amaze me with your accuracy and insight. Now, for your next test.'

He re-tuned the guitar and began to sing, quietly and with feeling.

It was a song about being young again. Thinking yourself to be like you were when you were a child and thought about things in an uncomplicated way. The words were so simple, so effective. She thought about Zolli's youth. His formative years. How different her own young life had been. How impossible it was for her to know what it really felt like for him to be like that young boy in the song.

He paused. She didn't know the song but it did sound typically American, of the same era. California, long sunny days. The Eagles, one of her favourites? But this sounded more reflective. She guessed.

'Crosby, Stills and Nash?'

'So close, but so far.' He resumed and this time he closed his eyes and seemed to be transported. The gentle melodic guitar and his soft plaintive voice entered her heart. For that moment she felt something amazing, unlike any feeling that she had before.

He was now singing about taking that youthful way of thinking and doing it now. Thinking like a child. Making every day have that special magic that only children can conjure up. She was moved but discomforted. The words spoke of being unhappy with life as an adult. A longing for a former time. Was this how he really felt inside?

The last chords remained suspended in the air for, what seemed like, minutes. He didn't move. She couldn't take her eyes off him. She was holding her breath. It was as if this moment was full of his emotion; she sensed he was about to tell her something of great importance.

He opened his eyes and licked his lips, it was coming. Then his eyes cleared and he seemed to change his mind.

'Don't worry, my darling. If I am intense for moment, it is just my highly strung Hungarian nature getting the better of me. So do you know it now?' he asked.

'No, I've heard it before but I don't know who wrote it.'

'Ah, interestingly it is co-written by our dear Carole King, what a talent. But it's a Byrd's number. 'Goin' back'. I love the line about magic carpets. And it's a song that's very dear to my heart.'

She felt suddenly tender; she felt she had seen into a hidden part of his mind or his heart. So she leaped out of bed and went and sat close next to him. Putting her head on his shoulder she asked, before she could stop herself, the fateful question that had been spinning in her mind for many weeks.

'What will happen to us?'

'When?'

'In the future.'

He sighed.

'Yes. I know I shouldn't ask but, when you sang, it pierced my heart. Do you want to go back to some other time or place. You haven't told me what you *feel* about your life and how it has ... ended up, here.' She hesitated, in a moment her fear would take over and prevent her from finishing, 'I want to know.' She sat up and drew away.

'Ah.'

'Does that mean something bad?'

'No, just that I can tell you about the past but the future is something I am not very good at. Can we talk about it another time, perhaps when we are fresh and can take time over it?' He gently placed his hands on her shoulders and turned her towards himself. His eyes were liquid and shining.

'It's just that when you sang ... I ... it made me think ...' She could not finish. Zolli sighed. Always the inner emotions give themselves away. He inwardly cursed himself for allowing her feelings to get so out of control.

He spoke gently. 'Well, I can tell you something that I do know, and that is that I do *not* know what the future will be, I do not have the gift of fortune telling. But I wish you to trust me. I also wish that you will understand that I do everything I do just for you. It is all for you.' He smiled, he looked at her, he waited, he smiled again, waiting for her response.

She was confused, uncertain. What did he mean? It sounded as if something was going to change. Unable to speak, she fixed a watery smile on her aching face, in response to his, then, flustered, got up, and started fussing about straightening the bed.

Later on, after he had entertained her by putting on her frilly dressing gown and making Ovaltine and toast for two and they had eaten it hungrily, she lay awake until she heard the milkman outside, thinking, wondering. What had he meant? She had wanted a simple statement of love or commitment, something like planning a holiday in the summer, even if it didn't happen. Now she was consumed with doubts. That old enemy fear and worthlessness resurfaced. She began to recite her personal mantras, I'm too old, I'm not good enough for him, I knew it all along, I'm not interesting, I'm too fat, he'll find someone else. She finally fell into a fitful slumber circulating these thoughts around her mind.

Chapter 18 - The surprise

She was excited and nervous. They were all coming back tonight. In the end it had been decided to stick to her house for the meeting. Bill was pretty reliable about keeping out of the way and Alexa was on an overnight stay with one of her more respectable friends whose mother could be trusted not to allow children to drink neat vodka and end up with alcohol poisoning or to go out stalking boys while wearing skimpy strap tops and leggings (how did they make a fashion comeback?) and thereby catch pneumonia. Emily, her baby, could be bribed to stay in her bedroom as long as there was sufficient chocolate and a reality television programme on the TV. Tonight it was 'Make me beautiful – tummy tuck special' followed by 'Brat Camp'. This was clearly a perfect viewing combination for a ten year old. Beatrice congratulated herself again for ensuring that she had no friends who had chosen social work for their career.

Her nervousness stemmed from her knowledge that Krystina was coming to lead them. Rose had gone for a reading the week before last and inviting her had suddenly seemed perfectly natural, actually Krystina had invited herself. Beatrice was glad. She had felt nervous about being caught in the middle of Rose's manic determination to connect with her guide at all costs and Gwen's (and Hilary's for that matter) grim predictions of doom and devil worship. So tonight Krystina had agreed to talk to them from the perspective of someone who has the psychic gift and has learned how to use it. Then she would advise them and indeed lead them in the right direction. She was also glad that Krystina had phoned her in advance and she had been able to sound her out about her worries. Since that evening, nearly two months ago, she had been on a sort of mission to research the possibility of any harm coming to them. It had not proved difficult to find books and articles on the internet about the 'dark side' as many referred to it. Indeed she had come across a terrible book that gave real life cases of people who had dabbled in the spirit world and come to grief, gone mad or even committed suicide. It seemed a popular subject. But part of her rebelled against all this doom. Something that she had learned from the channelling book was that the negative side of spirit contact was all generated by human energy. She had discovered authors who were convinced that the power of negative and fearful thought could almost give life to dark energy. It was a worrying idea, the possibility that thoughts, something we think only exist in our heads, taking on a life of their own as a sort of entity made of negative energy.

Her conclusion was that there was nothing sinister or frightening about the messages from the spirit world, it was the human mind that distorted them and turned them into something to fear or a weapon of control or power over others. Deep waters, she thought, do I really know what I'm talking about? Probably not. She was in the kitchen and suddenly felt a huge need to eat a piece of bread and butter. Fluffy was sitting in a pool of light, like a sphinx, beside the bread tin. She smiled with her feline eyes and observed Beatrice from her vantage point. She buttered the bread by gouging out a large lump of butter with a blunt knife and pressed it impatiently into the spongy white square. She quickly folded it over and stuffed it into her mouth. Anxiety. 'Meiow,' went the cat in agreement. And indigestion in about an hour. B wondered if there were any Rennies left in her bedside drawer.

Krystina had been most forthcoming on the subject of the dark side. In fact, when Beatrice had mentioned it, she had agreed wholeheartedly that it was important to take precautions. She talked a bit about 'managing the energies' and 'protecting the heart chakra'. Then she asked B to allow her to explain to the group in person and that seemed to be the best way forward.

The dog next door was going berserk. Several cars had drawn up together and Beatrice licked her lips, wiped her buttery hands on the tea towel and went outside to greet them. Jill was on her own looking totally remarkable, radiant and slim. Gwen and Lesley were parking a very dirty green estate, easily recognisable as Gwen's old wreck and behind them, getting out of a taxi, was Krystina. She looked amazing. She was wearing the most beautiful pink and lilac coat that looked as though it had something like silver thread in it. She lit up the road.

Her hair appeared to have moonlight trapped in it.

When Rose had joined them and they had waited a little while for Hilary, Beatrice had a chance to notice how Krystina had already introduced herself and had drawn the women towards her, they were clustered around her, feeding hungrily on her words. She was wearing, around her neck, the most enormous piece of jewellery, silver, in the shape of a hollow triangle but shaped and curved. Set inside the centre was a large cloudy stone, polished to a perfect sphere. They were all asking about it and Krystina took it off. The sphere appeared to be suspended, without any means of visible support, inside the shaped silver. Krystina held it up to the light and lightly touched it. It spun. She could just see the tiny spindles holding it in place.

'I bring this with me to assist us tonight. It is Selenite, simple and pure. It helps with deep soul memories, meditation and even accessing past life material. I have a bigger one,' with that she reached into her huge handbag and retrieved a very large and stunning looking stone about 20cm in diameter. She then fetched out a wooden stand made intriguingly of three gnarled pieces of wood that fitted together to make a kind of tripod. The crystal orb was placed on the stand and moved to the centre of the low table. Everyone was staring at it.

'Can we touch it?' Jill asked

'Of course, you can hold it if you like, but later, touch it later, when I can tell you more about what we are going to do tonight.'

Krystina was in control. She gathered them all towards her.

'I have come here to work with you all. I know what it is you wish to do and I can help you. I am teacher for this channelling and I know already how to do it, so I light your way.' She looked up again to ask for assent. All the faces were nodding slightly in agreement.

'Where to start? I have traditional upbringing in Slovakia, was Czechoslovakia but now split in two. My mother she have the gift and look for it in me. It was terrible secret because of the way people think in my country. My mother she have to train me never to tell or show my gift to anyone. But I know she is pleased, her child who can do these things just like she can. We spend many hours practising together, often when my brothers and sisters go to bed. We never talk about it in front of others. The first thing she tell me is never to have fear. I can see that, as a child, she must stop me from feeling scared or from worrying about the things I can see or hear. But I tell you this, fear is the problem. It is our human problem, it stops us from enjoying so many things. For us, we need to know that fear will stop us connecting with the spirit world. Fear will make doubts come in our minds. Fear will make us dismiss what we hear and tell us we are inventing it all.'

'But isn't a little bit of fear a good thing, surely it stops you from making mistakes or going too far?' Gwen was not convinced.

Krystina turned to her and Beatrice could see that her eyes were almost black with intent.

'No my friend, fear is your enemy, it makes the human heart darken. Fear is in the heart of the tyrant, fear is eating away at the child who will not speak out about being bullied, fear stops us from loving each other, fear spawns anger and then humans lose all self control.' She was speaking very clearly and directly. 'I mean you to understand this, maybe you do not feel it in your heart yet, but soon you will know what I mean.'

She collected herself and went on. 'I have many experiences as a child, maybe you have them too, I don't know. Children are more open to these things. I learn the hard way that my fear, perhaps when I see dead person standing in my room at night, is just about me and my limits. It shows me how much I have yet to do, to learn. After my mother - she train me about this – show me what to do, I never tell her about my own feelings, she knows and I know, it is something to be overcome. Why I tell you this now? You have fear. So ... get rid of it, it is pointless and useless thing. Fear have no place in spirit world.' She paused. There was no dissent.

'I show you now how it is done and, as I can do it easily, I can talk at same time. I need volunteer, not Rose, she already have reading.' Hilary shifted uncomfortably in her seat and, by doing so, drew attention to herself. They all waited for her to offer. Krystina reached across and touched her hand. 'My friend, you will help me?' Hils blanched, then nodded.

'Sit opposite me and others can arrange themselves to the side so I can explain. First I am going to get myself centred, I do this by arranging my posture so.' She moved forward slightly in the chair so her feet were both squarely on the ground and her back was upright. 'Next I arrange my spine in a straight line, with all my bones sitting neatly one on other. Why do I do this? It is for two reasons. To make energy flow up and down spine, so all of my body is connected properly to each other part. Also, then it is easier to keep in good posture over long period when you have to concentrate, if you slouch it is more tiring.' B doubted she could ever sit upright for more than a minute, she was the Queen of slouch. 'Now I am closing eyes for a moment to just check my chakras. I see them in my mind first and check they are spinning in the right way. From the bottom upwards. You must pay attention to all in turn, no point in attending to heart opening if the base chakra is weak and have no energy, must put energy where it is needed.' She was getting fired up again. 'Make your foundation solid, then all will be OK. When I finish this exercise I am ready to tune in. I am going to show you the basic procedure tonight and you can practise. I do this automatically, you understand, but I show you also beginner's way.'

She closed her eyes again and started to breathe more deeply. Very rhythmically and smoothly she breathed in and out. 'I connect with my higher self now. I am concentrating on one thing, the energy of my breath, this centres the mind and brings necessary focus. I now keep my mind concentrated on my breathing but I open eyes, like this,' she snapped her eyes open and they beamed onto Hilary. Her eyes were shining and unblinking. 'Now I connect with my subject,' she took Hilary's hand, 'I am completely in one mind now, I am so still inside that I have no thoughts, no interference. I ask subject to form a question. You have question?' Hilary gaped like a fish. 'Question please?'

Hilary was appalled. She felt like a worm on a hook. There was no hiding place. All the others were smiling at her in a sort of benign but patronising way. Spinning around in her head was the question. The one she was too terrified to ask. It was rattling around in her mind. There wasn't another thought in her head. Just this one question. In the hall, the phone rang. She could hear footsteps overhead and Bill's gentle low voice answering. Then the sound of someone coming downstairs. Still she couldn't speak. The door handle creaked gently and Bill's slightly bemused face appeared around the door. He didn't say anything, he just closed the door quietly again. She held her breath.

'You have fear?' Krystina's voice, disembodied now, floated towards her.

'Yes,' her dry, papery voice was insubstantial.

'I help you.' She took Hilary's hand more firmly and breathed in deeply while keeping her eyes focussed closely on Hilary's eyes, held in her crystal gaze. Hilary's lips opened and her voice sounded, shaky at first, then clearer.

'Tell me what is happening to my daughter, her name is Gemma.' There, she'd said it. Krystina closed her eyes quietly and then opened them again.

'I have seen her already in my mind. I wait now.' She seemed to stare into the middle distance, then closed her eyes very slowly again.

'She is standing in the playground of school. She is alone. (That is metaphor, I understand.) There is dark space to her side, near her head on right side. I ask now.'

She seemed to be carrying on a silent conversation with herself. 'Now I channel. You see what happen for yourself.' She seemed to stiffen and she breathed very deeply. Her whole demeanour became more upright and her facial muscles relaxed. When she spoke her voice was smoother and her accent was barely discernible.

'She is wiser than her years, your child with the human name of Gemma, and she is progressing through a time of great change. Her darkness is to the side of her and she is moving away from it. Her darkness has a human dimension. Her heart is pure and she is preparing for a great shift of her energy in a short time span as you know it. It is no accident that she has chosen a path of emotional challenge. She aligned herself with an emotional being who is stuck in a place of dependency and darkness, seeking to bind her to earthly love that considers ownership and control as part of the loving process. She has already passed through her lesson of letting go of these qualities, for they have no place in her future. To do this she has learned about aloneness and she is now stronger.' Krystina paused. The group were still hanging on every word, every sigh, waiting for some phrase that they could understand or relate to Hilary or Gemma. Krystina spoke with her own voice again, lighter and higher and this time with a little impatience.

'Are you willing to give me name?' Krystina asked herself under her breath. Then she answered. 'The name you seek is ... Ruth. I reveal her now.' Silence. Breathing. Sweating. Aching from holding their positions so still and quiet.

'OK, I have it now,' Krystina opened her eyes. 'It is clear. I tell you what I see so you can have all the data that we are given. I see woman with girl who is Gemma. They are looking at pictures, like things stuck on paper, there is some fabric and shiny stuff. Woman has very short red hair, she get it from dying it. Ha! She almost like Polish woman with hair colour like that! I see her eyes, she have power over girl, there is the darkness there. Next I see letter, writing not clear but I feel letter is full of fear and other feeling, dark feeling like bad smell. This woman she want to hurt girl but emotions not body. She takes letter and puts it in envelope, I see her have sick pleasure on face. This woman she is problem with daughter. Find the woman and see the problem.' She looked around at the assembled group. There was a gentle discharge of baited breath and they moved and shifted in their seats.

'I'm sorry but that doesn't tell us anything at all. You just made a few lucky guesses.' Gwen was indignant.

'No wait,' Hilary reached over and grasped Krystina's hand, 'tell me what my daughter looks like, just describe her to me, humour me.'

'She is tall, taller than you. Her hair is fair. She always look down, her head it is like this,' she cocked her head to the side and let it droop a little so she looked a little furtive, something that on her face looked absolutely comical. 'She have blue eyes, very wide and open and she have a brown mark on her leg, right at the top.'

'How did you know that?'

'She show me just then, in my mind, she laugh, she is happy.'

'What does it mean then?'

'That is what we do now, my friend, we discuss. I ask you all, what do we learn from this? She is in trouble but it is nearly behind her. She plan it! She is clever cookie. That is her soul talking, not her human bit. She learn to get away from human trouble, that is good, so we do not worry too much. The trouble is the woman. I think she teacher. I feel trouble is because girl will not do what woman want. She nasty bitch, I think! She want her life, she collect lives, she collect souls like trophies, she want power but, girl, she get away. I like her already. When can I meet her and buy her drink?' Krystina's eyes were alight with pleasure.

'OK, let me get this straight. She has been in trouble with a teacher called Ruth? Is that right? You said Ruth earlier. She has short bright red hair. She means trouble and my Gemma stood up to her.' She paused. She hadn't really explained to anyone properly, except B, what was happening with Gemma. 'And my beautiful girl has been skipping school, missing this most important GCSE year, nearly getting me prosecuted, refusing to discuss it with me, pretending that it wasn't happening because of a red haired teacher called Ruth? I can't believe it.'

'OK, you have choices now, I tell you it is nearly over, so maybe time is good to ask her?'

'She wasn't being very communicative this evening before I went out!' Hilary was indignant.

'Ask her, ask her tonight, say name and what she look like, she is Art teacher I tell you, she will let you understand her now.'

'I can't believe it, somehow, it doesn't seem important enough, she'll just clam up like she usually does.' Krystina shrugged and looked mildly bored. Beatrice sprang up and suggested a coffee break or maybe a nice glass of wine. The tension was broken and they all started twittering and chatting among themselves. Bill could be heard clattering down the stairs again and he stuck his head around the door for the second time.

'Polly is going to be late but she is definitely coming. Pip left a message this afternoon on the machine, I think you should listen to it.' He looked crumpled and dear over the top of his specs. He pushed the phone again in her direction. She really didn't want to be bothered with Polly now and Pip, well, she needed time to think before answering the message. She was acutely aware of Hilary looking very bewildered. She was retreating away from the crowd and looked as if she wanted to get away quickly. B stood resolutely between her and the door, she brushed the phone away and Bill sighed. He turned and went back up the stairs.

'OK, but I don't see why I should be your bloody answering service.'

Much, much later, Beatrice was lying on her back in bed. Her mind, understandably, was racing, sorting through all the events and the snippets of conversation, the disembodied voices, the looks on the faces. Bill had been asleep when she had eventually come upstairs. She did her best not to wake him, undressing in the en-suite, and sliding sideways under the covers. He grunted but didn't acknowledge her. Bugger, she thought. More damage limitation tomorrow. Mental note to phone Pippa first thing, she could get her at the studio if she missed her at home. Now her thoughts turned back to the evening's events. After they had broken for a coffee it had become a bit chaotic. She had cornered Hilary and asked straight out about what she thought, and then enquired gently about her feelings.

'I wanted to know, you know, but, actually now, I feel humiliated. Everyone will be asking me things - look at them,' they looked and could see the animated, gossipy expressions on the assembled faces.

'My problems are being dissected like on Jeremy Kyle,' she looked down sadly. 'Anyway I'm going now, I'd rather think this out on my own. Part of me wants to drive like a maniac to find this so-called woman Ruth, or whatever her name is, and have a good shout at her, but another part wants to crawl under a stone and hope it all goes away. What would you do?'

Beatrice placed her arms lovingly on her friend's shoulders. 'I would go home and have a big lump of cake or a doughnut, take a swig out of the sherry bottle and take the dog for a very stressful walk. But I suspect that you will do something much more considered. And you haven't got a dog.'

'Yes, I think perhaps I will. And you haven't got one either.'

With that she was gone and now, in the middle of the night, Beatrice was in agonies of anticipation, waiting to find out what, if anything, had happened. Was it too late to text? Actually she was so strung up, she probably needed to do something to take her mind off this mad thought merry-go-round. She slid out of bed and crept out of the bedroom. Her handbag was in the hallway, she grabbed it and went into the darkened living room. The phone said 1.30 when she switched it on. Oh the joys of texting, she didn't feel at all guilty, as she knew Hilary would only pick it up if she too were lying in bed, sleepless and restless, just like her.

R U awake?

Beatrice sat for a bit looking at her legs. It was an unpleasant sight. She had scaly dry patches on the front of her shin bones. She started to pick away, absently, at a corn on her little toe. It was all very unsatisfactory. Then the blue light came on her screen and the text tone sounded.

gr8 2 stupd old women cant get to sleep.
Wts up thn? Did you spk to hr?
Yeh, wanna no wht happned?
Yup

She pressed the green call button in a flash.

'Hi, what are you doing up at this time?' Hilary asked.

'Worrying about you, of course.'

'Ah, well, worry no more, my friend, it has all become clear. The only reason I can't sleep is I'm just waiting to make sure Gemma is asleep, she was very, very upset. We've had Horlicks and a hot water bottle. I'm just sitting here in the dark waiting to poke my head around her door and make sure she's off before I turn in. So I'll keep my voice down, actually, I think I'll go in the kitchen.'

'Well don't keep me in suspense. What happened?'

'It was easy in the end. I just came in and she was curled up on the sofa watching some American rerun, Scrubs, I think, anyway she looked up and I sort of spurted out 'Ruth', I couldn't stop myself. And then she crumpled. Oh, B, It's so sad. I feel so proud of her but so sorry too. Her first outing into love and it ends up like this.'

'What do you mean, love?'

'Well that's part of it, she had so much to tell me, it all tumbled out in a back-to-front rush. I think I've got everything the right way round now.' She sighed, then resumed. 'She fell in love, or thought she did, with the Art teacher, a woman, this Ruth. I know, you're shocked and I am too. I never thought she had feelings like that, for women. Or maybe it was just a pash. Or is that old fashioned? I don't know, then it all went so horribly wrong that I think she hasn't really thought about what that means in the future. I mean does it mean that for her it is *women*? I don't know, actually I'm lying, I didn't dare ask. Let me explain.'

Eventually, with some awfully explicit detail that made B feel very uncomfortable and distressed, Hilary told her the unhappy tale of what had happened. Gemma had fallen in love with her Art teacher. It happened right at the beginning of the previous summer term. The teacher noticed and after a few ambiguous conversations it seems they agreed to meet away from school. No pretence at it being anything to do with art, no come up and see my etchings or anything. Gemma was quite open about what they had done together. It was bed and lots of it right from the start. They were passionately in love and stole many late afternoons at Ruth's flat. Ruth was 24 and had only recently finished her NQT year. According to Gemma she was very beautiful and so very fascinating. They had become completely absorbed in each other but maintained a distance at school. However, as the autumn term began, Gemma realised that she should start spending more time preparing for her mocks, which are just after Christmas, and she was also behind with coursework, so she wanted to see Ruth less often.

Apparently Ruth didn't take this too well. She started to keep her for longer when they were together, it seems lunchtimes were also involved, and she was late back for school a few times and it was noticed. Ruth started leaving notes in her bag that could be discovered by anyone, teachers even, as they sometimes had to turn out their bags for random checks. Ruth became more demanding and unreasonable and Gemma backed off a bit. Then, one night in October, Gemma had a phone call from Ruth to say she had taken an overdose. Gemma had to go round there and find her. It had been just a cry for help, so she had said, and there was a lot of making up and sobbing and so forth. But that had not been the end of it. Ruth had got it into her mind that Gemma was tired of her and so there started a terrible game of testing her. Accusations of other affairs were flung at her. Gemma soon realised that she couldn't keep this up and the only way she could think of was to get out and avoid her.

She was frightened. This woman who she loved had turned into another person. She wasn't sure how she felt anymore, except this awful and constant feeling of dread.

'I'm giving you the story as best I can remember it. Gemma had reasoned that if Ruth couldn't find her at school then she was safe from the notes. Gemma stopped answering her calls. I don't think she had thought it through properly. There had been one awful incident where Ruth got a friend to phone her at home and say Ruth was in hospital, intensive care, except Gemma was cleverer than Ruth had given her credit for and, by then, she had ceased to feel any love for her and she phoned the hospital first. There was no emergency. No patient called Ruth. It was obvious to Gemma by then that she had to keep out of her way and that Ruth was not the love of her life. I just can't believe she kept it all to herself. I can't understand how I didn't notice.'

'Oh, Hils, I'm so sorry.'

'What for?'

Silence

'For all of this worry and for Gemma? To find out so young about the horrible side of love?' B responded.

'That's all right then, as long as you weren't going to say about her being a lesbian, because if you did, well, you know, I would have to shout at you.'

B was quiet. She could hear Hilary panting slightly and she felt her anger.

'I'm really glad, dear Hilary, that it seems that your lovely girl has a great deal of both good sense and courage. Does that sound a good enough conclusion? Because that is how I feel. God, it's late, I'm so strung out and I bet you are too.'

'Strangely calm now, actually, but I think I'll be a wreck in the morning. Which is probably in about four hours!'

'Let me ring off and you can go to bed. If you want to talk tomorrow, or for me to do anything, I could come down to the school with you?'

'Not yet, Gemma has to decide what to do first, it's not my decision.'

'Yes, of course,' secretly B wanted to march up to the school with her friend, like an avenging angel.

'Hils, just one thing, do you remember what Krystina said about the Ruth woman? Something about collecting souls? Does that ring a bell with you? It is an odd thing to say.'

'She sounds like a completely horrible woman and I want to kill her, but don't quote me on it. I feel so angry but so helpless too.'

'It's understandable. You mustn't blame yourself though.'

'I know ... but it's hard.'

'So much to think about.'

They both sighed.

'Speak tomorrow then.'

'Bye.'

B sat hugging her knees in her freezing cold living room, thinking how uneasy she felt.

Chapter 19 - Misery be mine

When do you actually realise you have been a complete numbskull, an idiot of the highest order, someone who would get barred from the stupid people's club for being too dumb? She winced when she remembered the things she had thought and said. How ashamed she felt. How arrogant, how unfeeling, how cold she had been. How bloody superior she had been. Pippa thought back to all the times she was going about her daily life believing she was so hard done by; that *she* was the one who was suffering and *she* was the one who was making the sacrifices to stay in the marriage. She had cast herself as the victim - so noble, so self sacrificing, so pitiable. How nauseating. All along she had been deluding herself. She had been constructing an emotional prison from which David couldn't wait to escape.

Had it been like this all along? Her mental strength, her natural assertiveness insidiously eroding his self-esteem, his manliness, until there was nothing left? Had she undermined him, day in, day out, with her bright, unnaturally cheerful demeanour? In the last year she had designed a mental theme for herself, a sort of record playing inside her head. It kept telling her what a good person she was to put up with so much, telling her how much she was sacrificing to keep things ticking along just like normal. What a special sort of person she was to be able to take on that responsibility.

She felt sick. She was sick. What kind of person does that to another? Why couldn't I see that it was all my doing, right from the start?

She had, lined up in front of her, two pieces of paper, one folded and grubby, one flat and white. She picked up the folded one. It was David's letter to her. She knew it off by heart. It was the most hurtful thing she had ever read. The words seemed to be written by someone she didn't know. But that is the whole point, you dumbhead! He is a different person, you don't really know him, you just chose to ignore it, that's all! It's no wonder he couldn't wait to get away from you! This precipitated a fresh bout of pathetic weeping. When she was done she drew towards herself the other piece of paper. There were a few lines already written down with ticks placed against them.

Explain to children
Phone Mum
Phone B
Appointment with bank
Solicitor?

The question mark nagged at her. She really didn't know whether to see a solicitor or not. What would she say? David hadn't indicated in his letter where he was going or what he was going to do, just the express instructions that she must not contact him and the reasons why he felt the way he did. Should she mark the leaving date so that, if she never heard anything again, she could say she had been deserted? She could get a divorce?

At the back of her mind another little thought had been hanging around. She had pushed it away many times so far on the grounds that, based on what David had said to her, this would be a very unlikely event to happen. But now that she had been alone for four days without contact of any kind, the thought wouldn't go away.

Police

She wrote it. It looked ridiculous. Her heart began to thump. She crossed it out. She folded the sheet of paper and put it in her handbag. Out of sight, out of mind.

She made desultory preparations to go to work. There were no bookings that day. She had some studio sessions to edit and put into a slide show for the customers. She mulled over what she was going to do as she loaded her gear into the car and set off. Just the thought of doing those simple tasks overwhelmed her. She was struck by the notion that, despite all appearances to the opposite, nobody ever really knew what went on inside other people's lives.

There was a collection she had prepared a few months ago, the memory came to her unbidden. A happy family, they had brought along their dog. It had obviously been groomed and coiffed for the purpose. She had liked the children very much, they didn't have that kind of sugary sweet demeanour that would look so false in the photographs. The boy had an engaging way of looking at you from under his eyelashes, a kind of ironic glance that had been a perfect foil to the formal settings the mother and father had wanted. At the end of the session she had persuaded the parents to let her take some action shots, rather than posed shots. The kids were set to the task of tumbling about in the studio, running towards each other at speed so she could capture the moment when they were about to collide, the girl wanted to do cartwheels, the boy pretending he was behind the wheel of a car. She had put together a separate show of these action shots so that the family could enjoy then without feeling pressure to compare them with the posed selection. Her favourite had been a shot from above of all five of them, including the dog, lying down supine in a circle with their heads all in the centre. The dog was draped across the boy while being bribed with a dog snack she was holding in her hand and waving about to catch its attention. It was a marvellous testament to their family happiness.

In the end they had bought all of the action shots, they had wanted them on CD, she had a special deal for this, so they could make prints and use them as e-cards and screen savers and so on. She felt she had given them something special, of course she had got what she wanted too, a nice fee, except the money was not what the whole transaction had really been about. It was about opening up to the possibility that things are not quite how you see them. Like being able to see things, my life, your life, from a different angle, or even better, from above. 'See the bigger picture,' was one of Beatrice's annoying little homilies but, really, she was right. Her thoughts meandered back to her own life. I didn't see the bigger picture; she now knew this to be true. I was so wrapped up in being the wife of a depressive and keeping it from everyone I knew, (for whose good exactly?) I couldn't see the truth.

Dry eyed now after the preceding days and nights of anguish, she turned her mind to the future.

'What should I do now?' She waited for inspiration. Silence. As she drove to work she noticed the trees were giving way to houses and the start of the built up area in which the studio was located . A voice, maybe her own, maybe not, resounded in her head.

'Do what you do best and do it well.' My photography, my life, my world. She breathed deeply and as she did so realised she had been holding her breath up to that point. She had released something, a little fear or inhibition. Good.

Chapter 20 - The subsequent meeting of the channelling group

'Where are we then?' Beatrice sighed to herself.

She was chewing her pencil and leaning over the kitchen worktop, while jotting notes on some paper. After the last dramatic get together it had been decided they would come together every fortnight. In between, everyone was to read the book and practise with their tapes. Several of the group were working in pairs. She was practising alone in her lunch breaks.

She had met Polly one evening for a chat and a bottle of wine. Polly was very lovable, despite her irreverence. You couldn't tell what she was thinking at any given moment, and when she chose to tell you it was always surprising. B knew that Polly shocked Gwen, who disapproved of her wholeheartedly.

Polly always made her conversation entertaining. Even if she had to relate something really awful or (worse in Polly's eyes) tedious, she would intersperse her narrative with liberal irony, sarcasm, misplaced pathos, self ridicule and so on. It was like being in a bright intellectual light - very nourishing for the mind. Pol had indicated she wanted to do the channelling as well and so had some catching up to do.

The medium, Krystina, was coming tonight, but not to every meeting, as it tended to make everyone think of pressing questions that required immediate answers. It was stopping then from practising or having useful discussions. As Krystina had repeatedly pointed out, they were there to learn how to answer their own questions, not to rely on 'flaky, kaftan wearing, Madam Zelda character'. She had a wonderful intensity and seriousness when doing her channelling or 'readings' as she called them. Then, when she interpreted the information, her language was splattered with all kinds of endearing colloquialisms that she had picked up. B supposed she got these from chatting with the thin, drippy, hippy girls in the shop below. 'Get over it' was her current favourite, something she shared with B's daughter Alex. It was the classic way of telling parents where to get off. Particularly useful, Alexa had told her, when wishing to humiliate parents in public, in front of their stuffy friends. She giggled to herself – half appalled by Alexa's arrogance but half pleased she had spawned such an utterly terrifying child.

OK, back to the list. She wrote down all their names. Then she wrote down a sort of running order:

Progress so far – where we are up to
Obstacles, problems etc.
Krystina to explain trance states
A practice reading, who to volunteer?
Meditation to finish

She chewed her pencil again and looked thoughtful. Bill had said a few choice words again last night. He thought they were all utterly barking mad. Not only had they already stirred up stuff that should not have been disturbed but she, Beatrice, along with this Krystina woman, were deluding themselves and the others. It could only end in tears, or worse. He was worried about Hilary, he admitted it. B hadn't been able to tell him everything (he would have hit the roof) but she had reassured him that it was actually Krystina who had helped to uncover sufficient details to allow the drama to be resolved.

Hilary and Gemma were due to go to County Hall next week to speak confidentially to the Head of Student Welfare, the EWO's boss. Hils had listened again to Gemma's tale and they had together decided the best course of action for Gemma would be to own up to a serious difference of opinion with a teacher, details of which she would not discuss, that made it impossible for her to continue at the school. A phone call to the Principal of the local college had elicited the information that Gemma could sit her subjects under their jurisdiction, as they offered all her core curriculum GCSE's plus IT and languages. The deadline for entry was in April, so there was plenty of time to spare. She would have to forgo her geography, though. She didn't seem too put out. In fact, when B had seen her the day before yesterday, she had looked lovely. Gone was that pale, haunted look and in its place was her former shining, clear eyed, beauty. B could see why any man or woman would want to capture that inner radiance and keep it for themselves.

Beatrice stood up and stretched her arms over her head. It was really turning out rather well. Should Bill be concerned? No, he's just blustering about something he doesn't want to understand.

Tonight they were going off to Gwen's house. Guaranteed quiet, though likely to be on the cold side and with a liberal splattering of mud and dog hair in equal quantities. As a precaution, she had two bottles of decent wine in the fridge for afterwards (no likelihood of decent wine at Gwen's) and she had bought some ready prepared nibbles from Waitrose on the way home. She would go straight there as Krystina was being taken by Rose.

Gwen lived in a small village just close to a large and beautiful country park where she loved to exercise her dogs. She was a bit of an enigma really. B knew her through Lesley, who knew her through some local club or committee they had both belonged to. There was a connection somewhere. The village lights could be seen in the distance, after negotiating a labyrinth of winding roads and following confusing road signs. She wondered why anyone would want to live in such an out of the way place. It didn't even have footpaths for God's sake! She parked as close to the main road as she could, which thankfully had sufficient streetlights and, clutching her wine and nibbles like a desperate alcoholic, made her way to Gwen's front door.

She was first. Gwen was bright and cheerful (and looked very well, too) and showed her into a sweet little lounge with a log fire and two squashy sofas. She had even lit candles. B was impressed. Gwen's dogs could be just be heard barking in, what sounded like, a far off room. Settling herself down with her list and a welcome cup of tea she waited for the evening to begin.

By nine o'clock they had all arrived, established where they were up to, and what they felt was holding them back or otherwise stopping them in their channelling progress. Then Pippa arrived unexpectedly. She just walked straight in and picked up a chair from the dining room and sat down. Just like that. She looked around the room.

'Sorry I'm late. I want to join in, have I missed too much?' As she looked from face to face, you could see the tracks of the tears she had plainly been weeping as she had walked in. B had never seen her looking so helpless and vulnerable.

'Don't ask me anything, please, I'm just here to be part of the group and to see what I can get out of it, God knows I need something! But I'm not here to put anyone out, so just ignore me and carry on.'

Krystina immediately took over.

'We are just going to start doing some practice. I am going to talk for a little while about trancework. Does that suit everyone?' They all looked at Pippa, she nodded.

'Trancework is the foundation of all channelling and all mediumship. It is like learning to walk, you have to do it before you can do anything else. Do not get silly ideas about trance, it is just a method, a technique. So that is what I explain to you today. It is in book also, see, I have read it too, that is what I do for you.'

'When I do a reading for someone or I channel, then I have to go into trance. This is not trance like you may think, that is why I explain now what I mean.' She gestured for them to look at her. She lifted her elegant hands and tapped the sides of her head.

'I have two minds. I have conscious mind and unconscious mind. It is your conscious mind that is listening to me now. Just notice it, it is listening and making sense of the things I am telling you. It is like a little computer, like a laptop, just like that. It do clever things but not have much memory. I tell you, it is always awake when you are awake, and it go to sleep when you go to sleep. That is fascinating is it not?' She grinned to herself.

'It has a job to do for you. It must take in all the data about your world and process it, it make decisions about things, it decide what to do, when to speak, how to act, all of those things. But it is not the full story. You have unconscious mind too. You are not aware of it because it doesn't talk to you like conscious mind do. But I tell you, it is powerhouse, it have all the data in it. It has programmes that do all of the things you need to do in your life, like drive your car. It has the operating programmes on it for your computer mind. It runs you! It is awake when you are asleep. It never sleep. I prove it to you. You all have babies?' She looked around, animated. They nodded. 'When you have a baby, you ever notice how you wake up just before baby cry? You are already awake when baby want milk. That is your unconscious mind, it keep watch for you, the unblinking eye. When baby make little snuffle, it hears and it wakes you up.' She tapped her head again.

'I am losing point. Trance is the skill of making your conscious mind go to sleep but you stay awake! That is what I mean. Then we have access to that wonderful unconscious which is so powerful, it can do anything. We put little mind to sleep and get big mind out to play.'

'I don't understand.' Polly grumbled.

'Neither do I. How can you be awake when you are asleep, you just told us that the conscious mind is awake when we are awake, so how can we stay awake if it goes to sleep, it just sounds ridiculous.' Gwen was indignant and the baby analogy was lost on her.

'It is skill that we have to learn. That is all. Let me think of other example. I know. You drive car. You drive same way every day, to school maybe, or work. When you get there you don't remember driving there but you not asleep. You are in trance and your beautiful unconscious mind is running your driving programme. It drive car for you without you doing anything. Everyone do automatic driving, it is well known.'

'That's right, I do that all the time. In fact, I go the same way whether I'm going to school, work or the shops, the car goes all by itself. So am I in trance then?' Hilary asked.

'Yes, a little, you are in light trance. So you see, if you can do that, then you can practise and get better at it so you can have deeper trance. I want everyone here to be able to have deep trance with eyes open. Ha! I must be mad woman, I think. I know, I stop talking and we practise. All happy?' Nods again, however, not very enthusiastic ones.

'You follow instructions. Sit like this,' she moved forward in her chair and centred her weight so her feet were planted on the ground at an even distance and her back straightened as she did so. She wriggled her shoulders and placed her hands palms upwards in her lap.

'Take deep breath and close eyes. Now focus all of attention on breathing. Just breathe in for four beats and out for four beats. Keep doing this while following the feeling of the breath.'

'Now feel the energy in spine. Imagine that spine is a white shaft of light that is conducting energy from your base right up to top of head. Imagine it, then feel it.'

'Now, when you breathe, you imagine the light moving upwards when you breathe in and taking energy with the breath, so energy is moving upwards into your head. Breathe in and push up. Breathe in and look up with inner eyes. Start looking inside your head. See light. Feel light, move light up, like a wave of energy.'

B was concentrating on the feeling inside her head. She was familiar with this technique and had practised similar meditations many times in the past, then tonight, for the first time, she was aware of seeing light inside her head. She had never achieved this before. Not only could she see it, it was like looking at the sun, it was actually warm and glowing brighter and brighter.

'Now stay focussed on breathing. In a moment I am going to ask you to open eyes but you *must* stay focussed on breath. Your eyes open but you stay inside. See if you can do it. Open eyes now.'

B opened her eyes. Immediately she felt the tug of the scene before her, making her feel as though her attention was being sucked outwards. But she kept feeling her rhythmic breath, in and out. It was a strange but compulsive sensation. Her eyes felt as though she was squinting against a bright light. But the room was dim. There were assorted candles dotted around and she allowed her gaze to wander from light to light. The others were variously staring ahead or had eyes closed. Rose caught her eye. In a moment her concentration was broken and a small giggle formed in her throat. It burst out.

'Oh damn, and I was doing so well.'

'That's OK, all doing well. How does that feel?' Krystina enquired.

'I really liked it, I felt sort of detached and in control.'

'Me too, but I couldn't keep my eyes open for long, I kept wanting to close them again.'

'When I opened my eyes, I could see everyone's auras. It was amazing.'

'What do they look like?'

'What colour is mine?'

'How can you do that?'

'Have I got an aura?' They gabbled. Some time was then spent while they talked about what everyone's auras looked like. Beatrice re-experienced that annoying stab of envy she had often felt in the past. She was miles behind everyone else.

'Tell us how to see auras,' she asked Krystina.

'Ah! It is no big deal. It is just like adjusting the focus on camera, you understand. Aura, it is here already.' She waved her hands around her head in a sweeping motion. 'It is your radiation that you are giving off as you go about the daily life. You just do not have this thing in focus. Some do, you don't. I tell you how.'

She made Jill and Polly get up and go out of the room. Then she moved the small sofa to the left, thus making a space with a blank wall behind. Then she got Jill back in.

'Stand just there. Now come over here,' she positioned B directly opposite, about ten feet away, which was about all that could be obtained in the small sitting room. She picked up a walking stick that was leaning against the hearth. 'I place stick here, in front of eyes and now I ask you to focus on it very strongly.' She positioned the stick about six feet away from B at eye level, directly in front of Jill.

'Now keep looking at stick with eyes but *see* Jill standing against wall, so. Can you do that?'

'Ah, I get what you are saying, if I keep my eyes focussed, then Jill is a bit blurry, wait, let me just see, no almost feel what is there.' She stayed still for a minute or two. Krystina moved the stick a foot closer to the subject. There was something, she was not sure she could see it though. It was as if she knew it was there but her eyes didn't seem to have anything to do with this knowledge. She closed them.

'She has a lot of yellow around on the left side and I get the impression that she has a sort of patch of green lower down on the right. Is that what you can see?' She opened her eyes again and, this time, the impressions were clearer.

There, around Jill's head and part of her body, was the most amazing light and, as well as the colours she sensed previously, there was a lilac flush just at the top of her head.

'I thought it would just be one colour and more round, I like that green patch it is really ... humming.'

Hilary was excited now. 'So what you're saying is that I should, like, make my eyes focus in the middle distance and so the person is out of focus and then you can see it? She was bubbling. 'Can I try next?'

Polly was made to come in. They shuffled around so they were all on the side of the room opposite her. The walking stick was duly waved about.

'Try doing this,' Krystina instructed, 'close eyes, then open, look up, down to side, anywhere and then look at Polly, do it about three times quickly and see what you can see.' She paused. 'You see, you are using a different part of mind to do this. You are not really using eyes. It is like using inner eyes, they have not had much exercise so are a little rusty. It is best to confuse physical eyes then inner eyes work better. Look, we stop now. You practise at home. We must talk more about trance.'

'Go back to seat and get into position again. Close eyes and take breath. Focus on your breathing, all as before. Now I want you imagine a ball of energy locating just around stomach area. Solar Plexus area. It may be small or big. Just see it in mind, now. Then as you breathe in, make it like breathing on a fire, you make it brighter, like breath is bellows. Make it bigger as well. Count for ten breaths ... now open eyes but keep in mind that ball of energy.'

Polly was feeling very good indeed, almost like a sort of natural euphoria, it was fantastic. If channelling could make you feel this high, why would anyone want to take drugs? She was just thinking this idly when she realised she had stopped thinking about her energy ball, and was in fact looking at Krystina and wondering if her hair colour was natural. Oh Bugger. She closed her eyes again and tried to reconnect. Yes, it was still there, open eyes, keep mind blank. Krystina snapped her fingers. She was clearly in charge and this gave

Beatrice a little sense of relief. It was wearing, sometimes, to feel everyone looking to you for a lead.

'Look at me now? Everyone back here in present, good. Now we go in pairs. First you need some easy questions to ask. I have paper here, we write down questions.' She was brisk and efficient.

'What is your name?
How old are you?
Are you married? Name of husband?
Children? Name and ages of children.
Work. What is your job? Boss's name?'

'That will do, just write it down and now I show you what I want you to do.' She bustled them along like they were small children.

Krystina sat opposite Lesley and instructed her to go into trance. Then she got her to open her eyes, all the while coaching her to stay focussed inside. She was looking intently at Lesley, her eyes narrowed. The group were silent and hardly breathing.

'Tell me your name'

'Lesley'

'What age are you?

'Thirty seven'

'You have husband?'

Lesley sounded as though she was talking in her sleep. 'Colin.'

'You have any pets?'

Breathing deeply, 'Two setters, Bonny and Jess.'

'What colour am I thinking of?' Without a pause, Lesley answered. 'Red, bright red.' Krystina snapped her fingers. Lesley looked up. 'Did I get that last bit right?' Krystina smiled, 'You did, my friend, you did.'

Gwen had been holding her breath. Please, please, don't ask her about any children, her knuckles were clenched and white. Krystina suddenly flashed a look at her and smiled. She knew already about Jack. Gwen could relax.

'OK, this is simple, you try it and then I tell you why this is most important skill of all. When you can do this, you can do readings, it is easy. Ha! I am *so* good teacher.'

'Why are we asking questions that we already know the answers to?' Polly was a bit disappointed, she wanted to be challenged.

'This is a practice, yes? I not want you to engage conscious mind to find answers to difficult questions, I need you to practice talking in trance and listening in trance. No more questions. Try now.'

Somewhat chastened, the ladies glanced at each other, nodding heads, subtly signalling to their preferred partners. Beatrice looked at Rose who was fiddling around in her handbag. She poked her hard in the ribs. Rose knew who it was that would do such a thing and elbowed her back. They got up and found a quiet corner by the large table lamp.

Jill was paired with Hilary and Polly with Gwen, a combination of opposites. Pippa, now dry eyed, was being patted gently by Lesley who had pulled up a hard chair from the small dining room next door. Everyone was whispering.

'How are you doing, then, my old chum?' B asked her friend as they got themselves comfortable.

'Not bad, actually, I've been practising quite a lot, in between mountains of ironing and ferrying children to a thousand activities and back. No, really, I've found that you can practise with the tapes while you're doing the ironing. Don't laugh. It's fun and the time goes quickly and you look up and your ironing is done!'

'Don't you have to keep your eyes open? I mean to do the ironing.'

'Of course, what do you think I am, a total idiot? Anyway, it doesn't seem to matter if you have your eyes open or closed, you can still meditate.'

'Mmm ... you're ahead of me there. I've been doing it in the car at lunchtimes.'

'What, in the car park under the Council offices? I'm surprised you haven't been pounced on by a pervert. I wouldn't stay in that horrible underground dungeon for longer than I had to.'

'No, it's not too bad now, they've got a new company running it and there are wardens and new lights. Anyway, it's the only place I can get some peace. Hey, did you really see Polly's aura?' Her voice dropped down to a barely audible hiss.

'Mmm .. what about you?'

'Yeah, what colour did you see?'

'Orange, mostly, is that what you got?'

'Absolutely, it's a first for me, I'm really excited.'

'You're so easily pleased, my dear.'

They became aware that their chatting was noticeable in the silent room. All the others were working quietly.

'Come on then,' Rose whispered, 'you go first.'

Beatrice duly closed her eyes, then unbent her back and got into position. It all seemed very natural and easy. She went through the different stages, taking her time. Rose was talking quietly to her as she breathed.

'Now, open your eyes.' She acquiesced. Rose was just to the left of her but not directly in her field of vision. She felt very centred, very in control.

'Tell me your name.'

'Beatrice,' she breathed it out without thinking, it just formed on her lips.

'What age are you?'

'Forty-two,' without missing a breath.

'What is your husband's name?'

'It's Bill,' a deep breath now, she felt as though she wanted to close her eyes.

'Do you have any children?'

'Yes,' breathing deeply again, 'Alexa and Emily. They are beautiful.'

'Keep focussing,' Rose continued, 'I have a problem that I don't know the answer to, can you advise me?'

B was momentarily flummoxed and started thinking but recovered sufficiently and closed her eyes again. She just waited. A minute went by. She licked her lips. A package of thoughts came into her mind, like a total solution, readymade. She felt unsure, she knew what it meant but didn't know how to express it. She saw a picture, that would do, it was like a symbol of what she felt the answer would be.

'I can see a large tree, it has many leaves at the top, but the bottom leaves are brown and falling. I've also got some words coming. The only way I can explain it is that this represents two different parts of your life and I think there are two choices,' she was talking freely now, 'you can feed the roots at the bottom or you can cut the dead branches back. Yes, that's it. But the tree must survive. Oh yes, I know, you are concerned with the top leaves but you must work at the ones that are going brown.' She opened her eyes. 'I've told you that in a metaphor. Actually, I think I know what the real literal answer is.' Rose looked alarmed.

'It's obvious really, isn't it?' She continued, 'look, if I'm wrong, you will just tell me, OK?'

'I'm just unnerved that you think you know what the question was.'

'Ah, yes, I can see that would be a worry,' Beatrice was very confident now, 'it's like I don't know the exact question but just the general flavour, and then I've put two and two together. Can I tell you now?'

'Go on then.'

'The answer is to do with your life, probably to do with Charles, something like you are only interested in the green leaves, the exciting stuff, like what we are doing now, but you need to go back and rejuvenate the bits that are going brown, like everyday stuff, and being with him, being a wife. There, I've said it. Am I close?'

'My question was - should I agree to go on the weekend away that Charles has booked? My guess is that the answer would be a definite yes.'

'Yes, exactly, I think. Simple really, not rocket science. If you had asked me that just in everyday conversation I would have said you needed to get up close with that man of yours, he's far too hunky to be neglected. What's that saying? 'Men are like fires, they go out if they're left unattended', very apt.'

'Well, I think we did quite well. What did it feel like for you? Did the earth move?'

'Actually,' B resumed, 'it nearly did, it was strange, I felt a rush and I just felt the thoughts all come at once. Now when I remember it, it felt like it was coming in from my left ear, you know, sideways. Odd, but true.'

By this time all the other pairs had finished and they spent a happy half hour talking about their different experiences. Pippa looked very much cheered up. Lesley talked animatedly about her questions and answers.

'So now we have chance to see what simple trance is like. All is good?' Krystina looked around the room. 'We stop now, it make you tired. I am used to it, I have to keep clear head for many hours every day. But you are still beginner. So we stop.'

They all looked crestfallen.

'But I've got so much energy,' Pippa blurted.

'Look, I know you want to carry on. This can get quite addictive, you know. I am an addict already! This I do all day long, and now in evenings too. We stop. You have wine and crisps. I need to get home now. But first I ask humbly if anyone can take me?'

Lesley immediately stood up. She was sure almost everyone knew she lived in the opposite direction but she was past caring. She needed to get Krystina on her own. Nobody said a word. Within just a few minutes she had whisked the clairvoyant out into the cool night air and into her car.

Chapter 21 - A minor hiccup

When the two women finally drew up outside the little house, Krystina felt uneasy. It was pitch dark in the living room downstairs and Zolli should really be home by now. She had been feeling unhappy all day about something she felt was connected with him but had not been able to contact him mentally, as was her usual way; her discomfiture was connected with him, it was obvious. During the evening she had carefully scrutinised his beautiful girlfriend's face, surreptitiously. Nothing there. She had even read her thoughts, strictly unprofessional of course, and found nothing of concern except happy, uncluttered musings about Zol, some stuff about curtains and quite a lot about a meal she was planning, presumably in his honour. Krystina sighed and gently eased herself out of the conversation with Lesley. It had all gone according to her plan to get Lesley on her own and encourage her to book in for a long hypnosis session. This was required so Lesley could move on with her life after her son's tragic death; they had fixed a date later in the week.

She patted Lesley's hand. A tear fell on it; it was from relief, not sadness or desolation. Oh Lord, how busy I am, the thoughts were flying around Krystina's mind. But I must not neglect my loved one. She exited as speedily as she could, and Lesley pulled away from the kerb. Deep breath.

The hall was cold, ice cold. Had he not come home yet? Why was the heat not working? She switched on the light and as she did so she heard him, a small yelp of shock, of desperation, intense but *human* emotions? Oh please, let it not be too serious.

'You are in the dark, my friend,' she murmured.

'I don't need the light for this.'

'We all need the light, my sweet one.'

He snorted and made an ugly guttural sound.

She bent down in the shaft of light that was flowing in from the hall. He had his back to it and was curled up like a frightened animal.

'Zolli, darling, what is it? Why are you doing this? You are so strong, so brave, I look up to you. Has there been a mistake? What has happened to you so you feel like this?'

He snorted again and seemed unable to answer. She twisted her head around towards him so she could see his face, faintly illuminated by the hall light.

It was shocking. He was grey with emotion. She couldn't take it in. She touched his cheek. It was wet and cold. He flinched and moved away. The next moment his whole body was bent over and huge rasping sobs sounded eerily in the silence. With his arms guarding himself against her touch, he covered his face with his hands.

She sat down on the floor next to him and closed her eyes, breathing deeply, trying to calm herself but, inside, she was panicking. She was panicking? What part of her was doing that? It felt terrifying. Some of the feeling seemed to be coming from him. It was so overwhelming. She just sat there, in the half light. He sobbed and sobbed as if he did not seem to have any control. It was unbearable. How could he feel like this? She could not understand.

Outside some young people were coming back from the pub, they were talking loudly in that particular way people have when they've had a few drinks of alcohol. It made her smile briefly. Zolli was distracted for a moment and stopped making the awful noise. He gasped.

'I am lost.'

'What?' Krystina whispered, anxious not to disturb his train of thought.

'Ah, the feeling, you know, my connection, it is lost. I need to tell you Krys, I am at the edge of the abyss.'

'Don't say that, we are in this together. What has happened? You were fine this morning.'

'It has been happening slowly for a week or so. I have been trying to ignore it, Krys ... tonight it feels like I will never, never get home. I think I will never be home again.' He looked her right in the eyes and she could plainly see the despair. Krystina was becoming more worried. This was not like something her darling Zolli would normally say, he was always so strong!

'What do you mean, we will be home soon, me sooner than you, you know this. It is fact, it was promised.'

'Ah, my head tells me that is so but something is happening here,' he pointed at his heart, 'I am feeling here that I am being disconnected from home. I cannot,' he sobbed again and his face creased up, 'I cannot remember what it feels like. I cannot conjure up the beautiful memory of home and bring it here to be with me.' He changed tack.

'You know when you go to the place of restoration, did you ever spend much time there in the past? You have had an awful life and you think you will never be whole again. Then they take you to that place and you are so tired you do not believe you will ever feel better. I remember one time I was so stubborn, I had accepted a very long assignment, I was very arrogant in those days and I arrived so faint you could hardly see me.' He seemed to Krystina to be cheering up slightly.

'Let me the light the fire so we can be comfortable. I'll get you a hot drink. You are making it worse for yourself.' She quickly went to the fireplace and lit the fire she had laid earlier in the day. She popped out into the kitchen and filled the kettle. When she returned, Zolli had wiped his eyes and was looking deep into the yellow flames that were now licking up around the logs in the grate. She sat close up to him and put her thin little arm around his broad shoulders.

'I'm glad you're here,' he said quietly.

'Keep talking to me, about when you were stubborn arrogant soul, I cannot imagine what you must have been like.' She stroked his hand while he continued.

'Yes, that is the feeling I remembered today, like I was so locked into myself that I could not recognise the healing light around me. It is strange how you can keep it at a distance, you know. It is entirely up to you. I was so certain at the time, it must have been many hundreds of years ago, that my Earth life had been the hardest, the longest, the most challenging, with the most troubles. Ha! They humoured me, the wise ones. 'Oh yes, you are so right,' they said. 'No soul has suffered like you have.' All the time they were smiling to themselves while I stayed grumpily in my place, my place of despair. At last, it must have been about 50 years of stubbornness, I remember because Ginema, another in my group who had come to retrieve me, had lost interest and gone off ahead of me, she didn't even wait, so it must have been ages.' He was breathing more easily now and smiling as he recalled. Krystina needed to know, however, the exact cause of his troubles. She had a duty to support him but also to report if anything was going terribly wrong. She kept those thoughts to herself, however.

'I realised then I was *keeping* the light out, I was actually perpetuating my misery, and when I stopped dwelling on my hard life and relaxed a bit, it was like a tidal wave. They all came to soothe me and bathe me, it was amazing. Soon I am fully restored, I drink it in so speedily, I gulp it, I am a greedy customer.' He paused, 'You see even as I am telling you this I have a sense deep inside me that something has been cut, like a chord. It is not of my doing. And I feel so homesick, I just feel so, so homesick.' He was starting to weep again now. 'I think I am never going home. But I long to go now, right this minute. I need to go Krys, I cannot survive if I feel like this.'

'It is not true Zolli, we are all going home, even when the years are long, in truth it is just like this,' she clicked her fingers, 'just a blink in eternity. What do you think has happened inside you. Have you had any message, have you changed your plan?'

'I have not changed plan but I suspect, maybe, the plan is changed for me. If that is so, then I have not been told.'

By this time the kettle had boiled and hot chocolate was being made. She brought the mugs into the warm, glowing room.

'See, we need earthly pleasures for these hard times.' They sipped and kept silent for a few moments.

At last Zolli spoke. 'I need to use my head. Oh, it is so difficult. I know what is supposed to happen, it will come soon now, the fulfilment of my plan. But why am I, of all people, feeling like this? How can *they* bear it, all those souls being here on Earth? How can they carry on if they feel as bad as me, so disconnected, so homesick?'

'It is simple, they cannot remember, you know that is true, how can you forget what we have been taught? Because *we* can have foot in both worlds, we have chance to understand both and experience both at same time. They have amnesia, otherwise they would not stay long at all. First chance, they would bail out. I do not blame them. Sometimes I wonder about all those young people, you know, the ones who end their lives. I think sometimes they get a glimpse, just a small feeling of the homesickness you describe, and before they know what is happening, they are longing to be back and are not prepared to wait a moment longer. I know someone from my group who worked with these souls, before she went on to guide, they are just overcome with longing. Is that what you feel?'

'Yes, longing, but horrible misery too, if you had not returned so soon tonight I don't know how I would have carried on.' He grinned weakly.

'Seriously Zol, I think these feelings are from your mortal heart not your immortal identity, that must mean you are meant to experience them, it is part of what you need to know, perhaps it is relevant to your path. But hold tight onto the faith, my darling, when the memory fades or the feelings are too intense, you must keep a tight hold onto what you know to be true.' He nodded and blew his nose.

'Come,' he begged, 'I'm so, so tired. Let's lie together tonight. I would not ask it of you except this is emergency. I know you need all your power for yourself, for your work, just tonight ... can I sleep with you in your bed?'

'Of course, my sweet one, that is what we are here for, to support each other, just do not be greedy tonight, as you build up your energy, I don't want to wake up and look at myself tomorrow in mirror and find I have bits missing, or I've got ragged edges, I have the appearances to keep up, you know!'

Her jokes covered her feelings of deep concern and anxiety. It felt horrible. She would watch over him tonight while he slept. There would be a lot to think about and Krystina suspected he was only telling her the very bare facts he was allowed to divulge. She wasn't permitted to know what his mission was, only the overall rules of the game were common knowledge to them both. But having feelings of despair and misery were not part of any plan she had ever worked on. That must mean something was going awry.

He was soon asleep but, every now and then, he sobbed like a baby. It would take all her energy to penetrate his sad, dark heart. Given that he was somewhat more senior to her in the matrix it would be a case of doing her best and hoping to do enough to make a difference.

Soon her arms were holding him closely and her breath was caressing his swollen eyelids and sunken cheeks. He had lost weight too. It must be bad for him to lose his appetite. She commenced with concentrating on directing light into his heart area. If it took all night, despite what she had said to him, it would be worth it.

Chapter 22 - Life between lives

Krystina woke the next morning to see Zolli sleeping peacefully with his head on the pillow next to hers. His hand had gripped a clump of her golden hair in the night and was holding on to it tightly. She rubbed his fingers briskly and he let go, opening his beautiful dark eyes as he did so. Expertly moving into his mind, Krystina probed his thoughts. This was the best time to communicate, when his human mind was still sleepy. He wouldn't be able to hide anything from her and she wanted to know as much as possible. The clairvoyant held his gaze and asked the questions, there were wordless answers in response, but satisfactory ones.

He was better, he told her. He had dreamed lucidly and something had been made clear to him. His own guide had patiently explained that there had always been this option and reminded him of the two forks of the path when he had selected this life. Zolli had, apparently, forgotten. They had enjoyed a long discussion, details of which he didn't share with her. She could tell, though, from his thought energy that he was stronger and she felt there had been a massive shift in his emotional state.

He reassured her he now understood what needed to be done. He asked her to trust his judgement. She was a little surprised when he asked this. There was a faint flicker in his eyes. They soon moved on to communicate about more mundane matters, the purchasing of food, whether they should buy more logs for the fire, what shifts Zolli was working next week. Smiling as she told him her plans for Lesley, it felt good to be back on the same wavelength and, in her mind, she let go of a tiny fear she had been keeping to herself - how and why exactly he had come to be able to feel those appalling emotions last night. She just let it drift out of her mind and allowed her attention to focus on the delightful prospect of her day ahead.

They lay together holding hands for a little while longer and then she kicked him gently out of bed, knowing that his working day was going to start at least an hour earlier than hers. He stuck his tongue out at her and lazily made his way back to his own room. A little later the sounds from downstairs indicated he was dressed and getting ready to leave.

'So long, Krys,' he called.

'So long.' She called back.

The house was beautifully quiet and Krystina decided to shower at length and take her time, she loved the hot shower, the amazing sounds of the water pounding down onto her skin. The shower cream was deliciously scented and she enjoyed rubbing it all over her. She revelled in the luxurious feelings, inhaling the scents and feeling the sensations from all over her body. It was no wonder so many souls sought Earth out as a testing ground for their skills. The intensity of experience was hard to handle at first, there was so much pain and fear but, if you persisted and made yourself take notice of the positive things, there was so much beauty, so much pure animal pleasure and so much love. She had first noticed it with the channelling group. There was love, real waves of it, yes, it was exceedingly enjoyable here. Humming to herself, tentatively at first and then, as no one was actually listening to her, she began to belt out a song she had heard many times on the radio, a pop song. It was about sex, mostly, and as the words filled the shower cubicle she started to convulse with girlish laughter, until she nearly drowned inhaling the stream of water from the shower head. Time to stop. Wrapping herself in a fluffy towel she started to think about what to have to eat. This was now another of her newly discovered pleasures, perhaps a croissant, or a warm roll and apricot jam. Her mouth was watering. For sure, these bodies were amazingly well designed, you just thought about the food and your body prepared to eat it. She pulled on her dressing gown and headed enthusiastically down the stairs to concoct her breakfast.

Lesley awoke with a raging sore throat and a huge knot in her stomach. Today was her session with Krystina, at the crystal shop in town, and it was going to involve a long 'regression'. She wasn't entirely clear about how going back in time was going to tell her the things she wanted to know. In her mind she had assumed a simple reading would do the trick but the option hadn't been offered. It had been explained to her that this was a 'once in a lifetime' chance to discover the meaning of past events, your life, your family, everything about you, including your future. The awful feeling in her throat - she now recognised it as sadness, grief.

It was a horribly familiar feeling, experienced for months after Jack died. Every morning she had awoken with it, from hours and hours of crying into her pillow, very quietly, so that Colin wasn't disturbed. It had become her little luxury. Lesley would wait until he was breathing rhythmically and it was obvious he was asleep. Then she would permit herself to start to think about Jack, his little body, lying on the hospital bed, his little face smiling to her when she would sit with him, the two of them just sitting and smiling together, even though he was wired up here, there and everywhere. Then she would remember other times, other places, her mind flitting restlessly through the scenes of their shared lives together. She was seeking what - meaning? Punishment? Someone to blame? Resolution?

The hardest images for her to cope with were the ones before he was ill, she saved those thoughts for last, they had an exquisite poignancy. She remembered being with Jack in the garden, when he was toddling. Actually, they had all this on video and she could always play it to remind herself if the memory faded. The memory, like the video, had a soundtrack, it was her voice and his, she was encouraging him, and laughing when he fell over, he was giggling and calling out in that funny high pitched squeal that toddlers have when they are excited.

The most difficult part was listening to her own voice, confident, assured, without a care in the world – because she didn't know then that he would become ill and die. Her voice had all the confidence of certainty in the future, the easy, lazy expectation that everything would be alright. And it wasn't, it could never be alright, ever again. But, she caught herself, thinking, it *could* be bearable, perhaps sometime in my future, just about. And if she could just get a hot cup of tea inside her the sore throat would subside and as for the knot in her stomach, well, only sheer force of will would make that felinease.

Lesley resolved to busy herself in the few hours before her session, she didn't want to give herself the excuse to chicken out.

The room upstairs in the crystal shop had a different light in the morning compared with the afternoon and it was always necessary to get some air into the stuffy corridor. The only access to the outside was a door to the bald tarmac car park at the rear and you opened that to get a through breeze, if you were lucky. The windows in Krystina's room opened onto the dreary 1960's shopping mall, letting in the odd combination of scents from the bakery, the camping shop and the incense from the crystal shop below. Hopefully, there would be a some fresh air, although it would be a little chilly.

Her thoughts settled on Lesley and what was in store for the day ahead. It would be useful to obtain some water and even some food that could be nibbled discreetly during their long session together. Krystina noticed she was thinking about her stomach again, she must be acclimatising. There were barely fifteen minutes to spare before Lesley was due to arrive. Water and a packet of plain biscuits were duly purchased and placed beside the comfortable couch in the corner of the room. Krys then lit the candles and closed the windows and doors. Enough fresh air until the finish, whenever that might be. Even though this session with Lesley comprised a significant part of her own personal action plan (and she had already seen a satisfactory outcome etched in the records), there remained a shred of clairvoyant's performance anxiety because, when free will was permitted, you could never totally predict the result.

Quietly, stepping lightly up the stairs, Lesley arrived at the appointed time. Krystina noticed she looked terrible and so a few minutes were spent calming her down and encouraging her. It would be fine but, for now, it was most important to get her thoughts centred and her anxiety levels reduced. When Lesley lay down on the comfortable couch, the lines of worry faded away and her face assumed a serene and peaceful expression. Breathing rhythmically and slowly she began her introduction and soon Lesley too was breathing with her. Their energy was joining and soon they would go deeper together into trance.

'I am going to move you now towards a beautiful forest, the most perfect and peaceful place in your imagination. This is a special place for you as you can feel at home here , safe and comfortable. I want you to really use your imagination to make this real for you as you walk along. Gently at first, noticing everything about this place. Look from side to side and notice the different leaves on the trees, the different colours of green. See the bark, the browns and greys and the various patterns on the trunks. Continue walking and see the branches moving from side to side in the breeze. It's easy when you know how. Maybe you can see the sunlight breaking through the canopy of leaves. Walk and feel the path under your feet, the muscles contracting and relaxing as you take the steps. Sense the aromas of the forest, the resinous smell of the conifers and evergreens and the fresh light scent of the deciduous trees. Notice the sounds, the insects and the crunch of your footfall, the swishing of the branches as they move in time with the wind. Let this scene wash over you and continue to move forward.'

Krystina continued, 'Very soon we will come to a special place, a place where you can relax totally, because in the forest is a place where you can bathe in a lake of energy, to cleanse and strengthen you ... ' she paused.

'Now, as you have relaxed so completely and so beautifully I want you to go, in your mind, to a place in your imagination, the symbolic place that your mind recognises as the place where 'this life' memories end and 'past life' memories begin. It is a hallway with doors in it, maybe two or more but there will be at least one door that your unconscious has chosen today as the past life that most requires healing in connection with your beloved child. So relax and allow your mind, which knows what is best for you, to choose. Tell me, can you sense a hallway?'

A pause. Krystina clicked the button on her digital recorder. The red light came on.

'Yes.'

'Describe it to me.'

'It's quite dark, with a doorway at the end, just one doorway and the door is dark. There are wall lights but not bright.'

'What is the door like?'

'It's dark wood and rounded at the top, with a lot of rivets on it, it looks very old.'

'Handle?'

'Yes.'

'Put your hand on it now and when you are ready I am going to instruct you to open the door and walk through. Lesley, are you ready to go into the past life that will show you things that you need to understand about yourself now? I assure you that whatever happens you will be perfectly safe, lying here, on the couch with me at all times. Are you ready to go through?'

'Yes.'

'OK, then push the handle and go through NOW.'

'Tell me, is it dark or light?'

'Dark'

'Are you inside or out?'

'I don't know, I feel a bit cold, I think it's outside, I can't see anything.'

'Look down at your feet, tell me what you are standing on.'

'Oh! It's a stone floor, I can feel it, I still can't see but I can sense it is a flag stone floor, I'm inside, yes I know where I am now. This is the temple.' The knowledge seemed to come to Lesley all at once.

'The temple?'

'Yes, I am alone now but until a few hours ago I was with my family. Oh, I am afraid.'

'What is going on?'

'Ah ... I have been prepared for this but I didn't know how it would be. I feel so foolish. And terrified.'

'Can we go back a little in time to see the days before this time in the temple, then you can tell me how it happened?'

Krystina snapped her fingers, 'Three days ago at your home, be there NOW.'

'We are sitting around the table, there is rich food prepared on it, but I am not hungry. Mother is begging me to eat; I have no appetite. A servant has just arrived from the priests. Pharaoh is sick and dying. This can only mean my time is also near.'

'Why do you say that?' Krystina wanted Lesley to give her more explanation so she could record it.

'When I was born, the priests asked my family for a gift, a gift for Pharaoh. My parents did as many did also, they promised me to be his companion, to go with him to the afterlife, whenever that would be. I was always told that would be my fate but it has come so soon. He has taken sick these last weeks and now I must face my destiny.'

'Which is?'

'To be buried in the tomb with him, to attend to his needs on the journey, to act for him if there is difficulty. I have been much with the priests to be trained. Other maidens are to be placed in outer chambers but I alone will be with him in the inner sanctum.'

'How do you feel about this?'

'I feel strange, I did not expect it so young, my mother is so sad, she told me she wanted me to grow up and have children of my own. I know that would have meant I would have been asked to give a child, my own child, in my stead. Only virgin maidens are useful for this task.'

'You are not telling me your inner feelings on this matter of life and death.'

'I am detached. I could wail but it would be no use. My mother is already weeping constantly. Father is grim faced but there is honour, too, in this and I feel a sense of destiny. Mostly I feel powerless. I am trapped by my fate, there is no choice.'

'Go forward again to the tomb, if you can.'

'I am in the dark, it is stuffy and cold. I am so alone.' Lesley started to weep at this point and Krystina placed her hand on the forehead.

'Detach yourself from these feelings so you can describe the scene to me, see yourself from outside your body.'

'Alright, I am detached now, I sense that I am close to death as I have been here for many days and nights, even though I could not count them. I am looking at myself from about four feet away. It is pathetic, I have given my life away.'

'Regrets?'

'Many, I could have done many things but I held off because of my predicted fate. I never learned the arts of reading and writing, I kept my distance from others.'

'Should you have lived your life differently?'

'Yes, and I can see now, I did have a choice, I could have been sent away to another place, where we had relatives who would have sheltered me. I'm sad to say, my pride and my fear prevented me.'

'Who is speaking to me now? The child or the soul?'

'I have moved away from my dying body and I can sense the light above me, pulling me, I wish to leave.'

'Go ahead and tell me all about it'

'I am feeling a tugging sensation. I recognise it, it feels to me that I cannot wait to go. I can move freely. Oh!'

'What is it?'

'My parents, I do feel ... I wish to go to them. I am there now, at home in the main room. They did love me, I can see them weeping and comforting each other. My father ... ah ... he is desolate.' She stifled a sob. 'I wish to see if I can comfort them.'

'Tell me what you do.'

'I have to gather myself first, I may be out of practice but I want them to know that I have passed over, that way they can know I am safe and out of pain and fear. I try to blow my energy towards my father's neck, he is bent over with grief.' She paused. There was silence for a minute.

'I am not getting through. I think it is because I am not concentrating enough. I am not fully practised at this yet.'

'Is there anything you can do to gain their attention?'

'They are so full of grief it is hard, there is like a shell of energy that I cannot penetrate. I will wait a little.'

'Can you throw some more light on this life that you have experienced?'

'I am not fully aware of all the information, the possibilities that were open to me. I sense that I had chances to take a different path but I allowed circumstances to dictate to me and I am pretty sure I didn't fulfil my life plan. Ah, I recall now. This is the second time I have experienced a life where I had to make a hard choice – yes that is what this life was about. Thinking for myself, taking risks. Oh, what a fool I have been. It is so obvious when you are back connected with your soul intelligence. How could I have missed it?'

'How does that make you feel? Disappointed, angry with yourself maybe?'

She laughed, it seemed that Krystina had made a good joke. 'Angry? That's one way of putting it. I will probably be taken to task over it. I will be annoyed with myself and she will be understanding and loving as usual. Then I will be stubborn and she will remonstrate with me.'

'Who is she?'

'My teacher, of course'

'Is she there now?'

'No, I cannot see her yet. She will be waiting for me a way off up there. But I need to do something for Mother and Father before I leave.' She sighed, deeply. Krystina was tempted to let the scenes unfold but, without her prompting, they might miss something of significance. It was important to ensure she covered all the vital questions so the responses could be recorded on the machine, in the unlikely event that Lesley didn't have full recall of her journey, when it was completed.

'Tell me what you do to get through to them?'

'I am going to wait until they sleep. I can move there now and tell you. It is very late. They are restless. I have only done this once before in practice but I remember the technique. I am going to weave my thoughts and energy into Father's dream, so I wait until that time of dreaming. If I am accurate and careful I can take control of the action and show him myself in a way that will comfort him.'

Krystina kept silent, sensing that she didn't want to disturb her subject's concentration. She knew the technique herself, she was an accomplished dreamweaver and, in fact, had mastered the skills so well her teacher had encouraged her to stay on and be apprenticed to him, perhaps even teach others. She had other plans though, and that was a long time ago. She breathed rhythmically and quietly, waiting for Lesley to tell her the result.

'He was dreaming of my empty room. I could feel his sadness. I want to show him I am still there. I show him myself lying on my bed. I am smiling. He is smiling. Then I show him myself lifting off the bed. I show him my happy face. I want to take him flying. I take his hand and , if I am strong enough, I can pull his energy out of his body and allow him to experience flying across worlds with me. Yes, I have done it, we are connected now. This is what I did to make him understand. He is feeling how it feels to be free from the body. Now I have him to myself I can communicate freely with him and tell him everything. I can reassure him. Actually, he is far more wise than I and more experienced. He shows me his energy. It is wonderful and I recognise him to be a close soul from my group.' Lesley paused.

'Finally I know I can leave. He tells me this. I understand some of our agreement with each other. I am ready to leave.'

'Have you finished comforting your Father?'

'Yes, I am ready to go. This part is finished.'

'OK, go ahead, take your time and tell me what is happening when you are ready.'

Inside Lesley's mind were the most amazing images and sensations. She felt absolutely disconnected from her body, as though all of her energy were crammed into her head. She was amazed to find that movement though time and space was instantaneous. It only required her to think and the image of the scene appeared. In front of her were misty lights, she felt as though she was travelling very fast towards them. On closer inspection, what had seemed like many lights focussed into three, one in front and two to the right hand side. She was overwhelmed with love and acceptance. The main light was brighter now, white with a yellow halo. It was her guide. She felt ecstatic.

'What is happening now?'

'I can sense my guide, she is waiting for me with two others.'

'Describe her.'

'She is tall, with flowing yellow hair, she has a long white robe on with her hands opening out to enfold me. I can't distinguish her face yet but her eyes are bright, bright blue. I know her. It is Huidor. She is my teacher.'

Tears were streaming down Lesley's face. Krystina felt enormous empathy. This moment of reconnection with a beloved teacher was overwhelming. She started to remember her own teacher and felt a lump in her throat. No use both of us crying, she thought. She allowed Lesley a few minutes to enjoy the recollection.

'What's happening now?'

'We are hugging.'

'Let me know when you're done.'

They had been working together for over three hours. Lesley had explored her return to soul home after death and spent a long time in discussion with her guide. Krystina knew she had to move the action on so Lesley could get to the place where she wanted to be – reconnected with Jack. It was a risk, but a necessary one. Only the truth would suffice, which was why no reading had been appropriate, only this, the most profound and revealing of hypnotic journeys, to the 'between lives' state. She gave the command.

'Go now to your soul group, your true family.'

'I am approaching. Huidor comes with me. I am nervous.'

'Why?'

'I sense they will chide me for those mistakes in that last life.'

'Does that matter?'

'No, huh, just wait, my group is fond of joking and they may have something planned.'

Lesley burst into laughter.

'They are sitting in a circle, grinning at me. They are tied up like prisoners.'

'That's cruel.'

'Yes, but it's true, I did allow myself to be imprisoned. It was my own lack of courage that was at fault. They are coming forward now to greet me, they stand in a semi-circle.'

'I want you to look at each soul in turn and describe them to me, you will know their soul personality, and also if any are playing a role in your life today as Lesley.'

'OK, the main figure is in the centre, I can't see the face but I sense it is a male energy, valency we call it, for there is not really male and female as there is on Earth. He is blue and tall, I know him as a strong and wise soul. He is Derthan, I admire him for his gentle and considered approach.'

'Is he in your life now?'

'No, I don't think so; now he is showing me himself as my Father in my life in Egypt. He is smiling at me. 'Good flying lesson,' he says!'

It was around 20 minutes before Lesley had explored all the relationships in her group. Around eight souls had shown themselves and it was like a merry meeting across many lives, many incarnations. But the soul Krystina had most wished would appear was not in that group. It would soon be time to move her on. It was not as she had hoped; in fact it was a disaster. There was a sense of creeping despondency, a note of disappointment in Lesley's voice, as she discussed the group's business.

Suddenly Lesley became animated. 'Wait,' she cried out, 'there is a soul running towards me from behind the group. It's Jack, I know it is.' She broke down. It was all Krystina could do to stay in control herself. It was a deeply emotional moment. At last, she knew now they could accomplish what she had intended.

'He was waiting for me to call him, he thought I had forgotten him. Oh, it has been so long. He is showing himself in Jack's little body but now I know him I can see who this soul really is. It is Simeon. I am so glad to see him.' They spent a few quiet minutes reconnecting. Soon Lesley indicated she was ready to answer more questions.

'Is he the one you most prefer to work with, your closest soul companion?'

'Oh yes, there is no doubt of that, he and I have been together many, many times. He knows exactly which buttons to press. He is the calm loving energy I need when I get headstrong and impatient. He is so good for me.'

'Do you usually take the female role to his male?'

'Yes, it was not always so but, lately, we have settled into this pattern. We are mostly partners in our lives. I know that my choice to be a mother to his son was new. I'm so glad to see him, I can't describe it.'

'What are you doing now?'

'We have moved away to a quiet place. He is his normal soul self now, I can see him as my husband from a life we had together in the American West, we enjoyed ourselves there, it was isolated, we were depending on each other for survival and we grew in strength and trust. Also,' Lesley hesitated, 'he was very, very handsome, his name was Jeff and I was Annie. I have such fond memories of those times. I'll show myself in my dress and apron, he is laughing, it is a good joke.' Lesley was quiet for a few minutes.

'Can you tell me what is going on now?'

'It's OK, we were just reminiscing. He has been reminding me of the many good times we've shared and also lives where we have gone solo. Not many lives, I can tell you. I feel so relieved that I know now. How could I have doubted it was him? He's reminding me of how much better he is at doing without me. He's looking smug, but I know better, I make him recall a life in Japan he decided to take and I didn't go with him, he made a hopeless mess of it. Ha! We're even now. It gets a little competitive from time to time, you know.'

'Would it be appropriate to ask about your life together as Lesley and Jack?'

'Oh yes, he's nodding, I feel good about it now too. OK, he's taking me by the hand; we're going towards a sort of place outside. There is a golden river, or stream I should say, it is winding and very peaceful. We stand on a bridge over the river. We hold hands; he looks out over the golden stream. Ah! I understand. This represents our future lives, not just one but many going into the future. We will always be together, we are growing together and that is how it should be, the stream meanders around rocks and its path changes from time to time, but it is our path. I can see short stretches where the stream forks into two, that is self evident, and it soon joins back. He is holding a scroll now with writing on it, but I can't decipher the words. I know it is the plan we made for our life as Jack and Lesley. I am allowed to know some things. My plan is to really get to know about overcoming sadness. I wanted to do this and he offered to give me the pain, so I could practise.'

'Why do you have to learn about overcoming sadness?' Krystina asked.

'What, generally, or me in particular?'

'Both.'

'Well, hmm ... I think I have tried before to do it, it is such a powerful emotion, it is a really hard test. I think I screwed up before and I'm having a rerun; I think I threw in the towel before.'

'What do you mean by this?'

'Oh, I took an early plane home, as it were, I just gave up, it was too hard. I didn't actually kill myself, I just sort of gave up living and in a short time I succumbed to death, disease or something. It's not that difficult, you know. It takes an immense strength of will to keep living. I was a bit weedy back then, I'm tougher now.'

'What about generally, explain to me what is the purpose of all these tests.'

'They are not tests. We love it! It is seen as an adventure but one with a purpose. What is the point of it? I suppose I know this deep inside, right at the heart of the flame in my soul. Why do we come to Earth, or any other planet or world?' Lesley became meditative. She appeared to be dreaming, her eyelids started to flutter. A tear rolled slowly from the side of her left eye.

'It makes me feel emotional to talk about it, I'm not sure I can make it clear to you but it feels absolutely clear to me. When the oneness existed and we were complete,' she paused, 'I am only telling you what I understand, because I didn't know myself then. You see - none of us were separate. The oneness was, is, so full of love, that it wanted to allow for the chance, opportunity, for that love, that perfection, to know and to have experience. Sorry, I'm not being very clear.'

'Keep going.'

'I only know this myself because I kept asking Huidor, nagging her to tell me. My curiosity gets me into trouble sometimes. One way to know love more fully is to experience the absence of it. One way to know completeness – oneness – is to know separation. So the oneness formed individual sparks of itself. In the beginning, the sparks were great, the Masters, the Great Ones, but soon the sparks were formed into souls like you and me. That wasn't enough, by itself, of course. To know love and peace and beauty you could imagine that you might need a *setting*, a sort of space to explore what it might be like to be separate. That is where different worlds come into it. Energy made into matter, like we experience on earth, for example, or as on thought worlds, just energy as purer forms. Earth has many advantages for souls, as a school. Earth is sublimely beautiful, for one thing, and the range of emotions you can experience are so wide, from the deepest misery right through to the highest and most profound love. It's the perfect playground. I love it here, but many souls find it too dense. They prefer more rarefied worlds which mimic home better, so they don't have to endure pain, for one thing. Aagh, pain. That is one thing you forget when you are home. I don't know what is worse, physical pain or emotional pain. But the pain is more than made up for by the beauty. And pleasure as well. But then you get addicted to it too, so each positive thing has a chance to trip you up. Really, when you think about it, this human experience is very well balanced.'

'So what is the real point of it all? Why do we all do this 'being alive' stuff?'

'The point? It's simple really. The point is that, by overcoming these negative challenges and by mastering these physical bodies, our soul energy grows and becomes more perfect. That perfection is added to the oneness. We are perfecting ourselves and by doing so, the oneness grows and becomes more beautiful and more magnificent, we are being given the chance to make the oneness greater, what more can a soul want or need?' Lesley stretched out her fingers and wriggled her toes.

'Are you still feeling relaxed?'

'I'm getting a bit stiff.'

'Just one more thing. Can you go back to the scroll and tell me what you can see about your life and your future.'

'OK ... I can see I am going to have a long life. I have planned to show others what I have learned too, yes, that is obvious. It's exactly what I have had in mind about the website for other parents. That is so clear. If I use the skills and the things I have learned to assist other souls in pain, the energy is multiplied many times over. It is like a great golden energy that grows and grows, energy that is replacing grey misery. Oh my, there is so much to do!'

Finally Krystina directed Lesley to bid goodbye to her soul companion, it was an emotional parting. Her guide was there to reassure her that all this was indeed as she had remembered it. Huidor spent a few moments just reinforcing the vital learnings of the 'between lives' session before charging Lesley with vigour in a wonderful energy hug. Just as she was ready to emerge, Lesley turned her head away and murmured to herself. Inside her mind, Krystina could visualise the scene as Lesley's soul mate, Simeon, was calling her and waiting for her to turn and bid him farewell, for the moment. She kept silent and waited. Then she emerged Lesley from the trance very slowly and gave instructions for grounding her in her body and in time, so that all Lesley's energy was reunited in one place. She was tired from her spiritual journey but smiling. Krystina then felt a light hand on her shoulder and knew it was her own spiritual teacher, there with them for the session, reinforcing the work. She stretched up, both pleased and relieved.

'How do you feel now?' As Lesley sat slowly up Krystina could see the earthly person emerging again and the ethereal soul personality fading.

'God! I don't know. A lot to think about, certainly.' Lesley closed her eyes for a moment. When she opened them, Krys noticed a tear welling up in the corner of her eye. 'It *was* him. I know it. When I close my eyes I can still picture him, as he was, you know, as my soul friend, my soul mate.' She started to cry more profusely so Krystina moved across and put her arms around her shoulders.

'It's alright really,' Lesley sniffed and smiled, 'it's just so overwhelming and now I'm back I realise how much I missed him, still do miss him but, really, I am OK.' She smiled a watery smile. The medium smiled back.

Chapter 23 - Nothing

It was a bright sunny day and the air had a soft feel to it, despite the time of year. Looking out of the window, Jill looked in vain for signs of the spring that was, in reality, probably two months away. Birds were still huddled together on telegraph wires, chattering madly. Her back garden contained a small bird table which she refilled from time to time. Today she had placed the rinds from bacon she used making a spaghetti Bolognese currently simmering away on the hob. Slow gentle cooking was the key to a successful Bolognese. The sauce thickened and became sweeter with a long cooking time. They would enjoy eating it together. He would complement her cooking and she would smile back at him.

There were several small birds fluttering around the table; she could identify two different sorts. Blue tits she was sure of but the others looked greener. She consulted her Handbook of British Birds. Green finches, she read, and felt pleased. The tits were shameless, hanging upside down on the perch to reach the last remains of the fatty rinds. The finches were more reserved, hanging back, and then pecking, tentatively, at the leftovers. We two are like those birds, she thought. He's the blue tit, bold and fearless and I'm the shy finch.

Later, sitting in the back room in the murky half light, it felt as if she had lost track of time. The sounds of the central heating starting up reminded her it was four o'clock. An hour late. It wasn't like him not to phone. Perhaps there was a message on her mobile, she felt around in the pocket of her jeans. Nothing. Oh well, she was convinced there was a rational explanation. She moved slowly around the room turning on the low table lamps. There were candles in the hearth and so she lit them, the effect made her feel less alone.

She must have drifted off to sleep, that was the trouble with working night shifts mixed in with days, your body clock was all screwed up. She stretched up and noticed, as she did so, a twinge of fear inside her belly. It was much, much later. The room was very warm and the candles had burned down to about half way, the wax cascading in rivulets over the smooth dark hearth. From the kitchen, the aroma of cooking was overpowering. She plunged towards the hob and, on lifting the saucepan lid, found the sauce had nearly boiled dry. Angry with herself, and then him, she tested the bottom of the saucepan with a wooden spoon. There was a thick layer of sticky minced beef but it was not burned so she put on the kettle and added some boiling water to the pot, stirring the contents until she was satisfied it was still good to eat. She tasted a spoonful, blowing furiously on the mixture so as not to burn her mouth; it was delicious.

On the wall behind her was the kitchen clock. If she kept her back to it she wouldn't have to know the time. If she didn't know the time she could hang on to the hope that it wasn't late, it was just dark early. If she didn't know the time she wouldn't have to start worrying in earnest. But, once she had thought about it, she couldn't escape the certainty that, at any moment, she would spin around to see exactly what the time was. Then she would have to do something.

Sitting on the small sofa, nursing the information that it was now eight o'clock, five hours past the time he said he would be arriving, she was faced with a variety of choices. She could phone him or text him, or phone the ward or the doctor's rest room. She could speak to one of his colleagues and check whether he was still on duty. She could just see if his phone was ringing or switched to answering service. That would tell her something. She picked it up and then put it down again. Check first to see if he was just walking down the street. She stumbled to the front door, heart pounding, and stood just inside the porch, poking her head out sufficiently far to be able to see the end of the road. Her breath was condensing in the freezing night air. There was nobody in the street at all, but she waited for five minutes anyway, to avoid having to make the phone call.

It was so unlike him. There must be a rational explanation. Perhaps he had been offered the chance to assist in theatre and had left his phone in the locker room. She prevaricated. First she would pour herself a glass of wine and then she would do it.

The irony was that four months ago she would have plagued him with texts virtually every hour they had been separated.

'Wot r u up to?'

'Luv u lotz.'

'Txt me?'

It was a wonder he hadn't throttled her. Now her hand hovered over the keypad, hesitating. She would just turn the spaghetti off in case it was going to be a long conversation. She didn't think a second burning would improve the taste. That completed, she settled herself down again on the sofa. Before picking up the phone again she turned the TV on and lowered the sound level. That way, she reasoned, when he answered, it would appear she was actively doing something rather than sitting, waiting, like some lonely fool in the dark.

It was ringing. Once, twice, it kept ringing. Nothing. Not even the answering machine message. What did that mean? Was it good or bad? She really had no idea. Perplexed, she put the phone down and pottered off to the loo. She sat in the bathroom with her knees wedged up tight against the radiator, thinking, thinking. After a minute or two she remembered why she was there and pee'd, rather absently, blotted herself with loo roll, then flushed and pulled up her pants, then her jeans. The possibilities were whizzing around in her head. It was now nearly nine o'clock.

She felt stupid and ... what was the feeling? Old. Yes, old and stupid. An old woman anxiously trying to contact her young lover, not realising he had better things to do, younger people to be with, people who were more fun. An old nurse, pining after a younger doctor, not understanding he had other, more interesting, plans for his evening. Why would he want to spend an evening eating spag bol with an old nurse when he could be hanging out with younger, cooler mates? And girls, yes, young and good looking girls, what did they call them? Ah yes, *hot* girls. Fit guys and hot girls.

She was annoyed with herself for following this train of thought, it was actually beneath her but, what else could she think? She banged her fists down on her thighs, she would not think badly of him. There was no point at all in speculating. She grabbed the phone again and redialled. Straight to answering service, she was shocked and flustered, then gathered her wits enough to leave a message.

'Darling, Zolli, have I made a mistake? I thought we were going to have dinner tonight. Ring or, if you can't, just text me, just to let me know if I should still expect you. Love you sweetheart.' She placed the phone down on the coffee table like it was an unexploded bomb. If the text alert went off in the next hour she would fall down on her knees and thank God!

It was starting to get colder; the heating had gone off at nine. Should she put it back on again, or just wait for a few minutes? It was a very tiring business, this worrying. The candles were now completely folded over with wax drooping over the stubby, burnt out ends. She extinguished them. On the television, the news was just starting, she switched it over; there was a political quiz show on the other channel. With the sound turned down she could see them all smirking and fawning over each other while, no doubt, ripping someone famous to shreds.

She couldn't go to bed, she was far too tense and on edge. It was too late now for him to come. Had she missed something? In her own mind she was sure they had made this date. It was a regular Friday evening night in for both of them after a hard working week. It only varied if it was an on-call weekend for him. When she had phoned his mobile it had gone straight to voicemail, that could mean it was switched off or he was on the phone. Perhaps she should try again. She picked up the handset of the landline, just in case he was texting her at that very minute. One ring, two rings, three and four. 'The mobile phone you are ringing is unavailable. Please try again later.' Nothing, nothing, nothing. She was angry and upset and, deep inside, she was very worried indeed.

The night sky was sublimely beautiful as he glided, weightless, over the landscape moving below him. There was no hurry now; Zolli had all the time in the world. The dark fields had a sort of patchwork quilt quality, even though, as he said this to himself, it sounded like a cliché. But the moonshine on the varied shades of green and brown threw shadows that made the small squares appear raised, like they were soft and stuffed with down. The worries of the last few weeks had evaporated and, thankfully, he could now see the bigger picture. His mind was perfectly clear, crystal clear.

He had two choices before him, now he was free of his body. To either head towards home, that way would mean hastening the inevitable meetings that needed to take place. There was a part of him that was rather reluctant to rush into that process. The second option would be to just linger a while and possibly make a visit or two. The drawback here would be ... he might actually make things worse. He didn't want to see Krystina, she might try to dissuade him and, anyway, he had made his decision on that score, there was no going back now. His physical existence was on hold for the moment. As for Jill, how hard would it be for her to feel him, to sense him one last time, before she heard the news herself?

He lifted his right arm up and directed his energy away from the fields and back towards the lights of the town. He was not a coward. He had to give her a chance. In his mind he imagined her pretty back lounge where they had spent so many wonderful evenings in love together. He had known it would be wonderful but he couldn't have predicted the sublime rapture her love would bring him.

Just by remembering, he was there. She was sitting in the room with the television on, just staring at her hands. Around her head he could see a dark miasma of thought and anxiety. Ah, it has already begun for her. He moved to position himself next to her. She remained still. He called her name. Nothing. She was looking at two telephones placed on the coffee table in front of her. He called again and blew gently against her neck. Her hands twitched and she shrugged her shoulders. She seemed to come out of her trance and got up and went to fetch a pretty, patterned wrap hanging over the back of one of the chairs. She shook and folded it so it formed a shawl and threw it over her shoulders as she sat again, staring into space.

He seized his chance and moulded his form around the shawl and hugged her. He drew all his power into the centre of his being and radiated energy into the wrap so it would be like his arms around her. Underneath the soft fabric he felt her body relax and her shoulders drop. He squeezed himself more tightly around her and Jill let her head drop back and she let out a soft sigh, the sound he had heard many times before. He caressed her.

'I love you, I love you my darling. I'm with you, everywhere you go, don't forget that will you? I love you from the depth of my soul.'

Later Jill woke up. Something had startled her. She was lying back on the sofa wrapped in the soft blanket and she was sure she had been enjoying the most blissful dream during her nap. The sky was beginning to lighten, so it must be nearly morning. In front of her were the two phones on the table. She sat up and remembered why she was there. He wasn't coming; now there was a certainty about the thought. Something would happen today so she had to be ready. She was seized with the impulse to shower and dress and prepare, so the wrap was discarded, kettle put on and clothes peeled off. In her bedroom the bed was just as she had left it, smooth and inviting, waiting for two occupants but looking at it didn't concern her now. However, something was sticking out of the top drawer of her dressing table, the drawer where she kept her most precious things, mementoes of her life. She never left it open.

Tucked just inside, next to his letters, was a soft plastic CD case. His writing on the cover; curly foreign script with a pronounced right hand slant 'For you' it said. She opened the flap and stared, it was just a plain CD, with nothing to betray its contents. There was no music player up here in the bedroom and the shower she had turned on, some minutes before, was already steaming There was no time to waste. So the CD was tucked back into the drawer. Had it been there before? There was no real way of knowing but, later, much later, Jill would take it out and play it, in the pretty lounge. Alone, as she now knew she would be. On her own in the back lounge, waiting and wanting to know the answers.

Jill was drying her hair when the doorbell sounded. It was only half past eight. Outside, in the road, was a white car, one she didn't recognise as belonging to anyone she knew. It could be a simple delivery, perhaps a parcel; couriers were often used by big delivery companies these days. Her internal mind babble was curiously at odds with the feeling of foreboding in her heart. Leaden, her feet dragged across the carpet and she felt all the strength seep from her legs. Shaking, holding on tightly to the handrail, she made her way down the narrow stairs, past the place where he had first surprised her with that kiss. It was hard to open the door. She felt as if she had been alone with her anxieties for a time that stretched into light years, yet it was only a mere 18 hours since she had first expected his arrival, whistling and cheerful, full of life.

It was Holly standing on her doorstep. Just behind was another woman who she hadn't met before, someone who looked very senior, responsible.

'Jill? Can we come in?'

'Of course, come right on through into the back.'

'Have you met Janine Thorogood? She's a colleague of ... of ... Dr Farkas.'

'Really? How kind of you to come and see me.'

'Can we sit down, sit down Jill, please, please, we have something to tell you.'

'I know.'

'Have you heard?'

'No, I just *know*, that's all. Now I need to *really know*, but I don't, if you know what I mean. Just give me a minute.' She dashed out into the kitchen and pressed her fists into her eyes. Strength. Be strong. You have to face it. She rummaged in her handbag for a packet of tissues, and then slowly walked back into the room. They were looking away from her; Holly was fiddling with a bundle of her own tissues. She was crying.

'Just tell me.'

'There was an accident. He walked out into the road - he wasn't using the crossing. It was a lorry.'

'When?' Jill needed to confirm the suspicions she had felt during the previous day.

'Yesterday at about two o'clock, he was walking towards the town centre, over the railway bridge. He must have thought he had time to cross, we all do it there. I have, I know, but he was hit.'

'What happened?'

'They sent a paramedic crew straight out and several doctors as well. Someone ran up to the ward, in case you were on duty. I ... I'm sorry you had to wait so long but, once he was in theatre it seemed no use to call you ... no news, you know. Anyway, it was out of my hands and I didn't feel able to call you, I wanted to have something hopeful to tell you.'

'Holly, just tell me straight now, I have known in my heart since late last night when he didn't arrive here, I knew he ... he wouldn't just not turn up.'

They were talking about him in the past tense.

'It's very serious, I'm so sorry.'

'He's not dead?'

'No, didn't I say?' Holly glanced at Janine.

'He's not dead? Not dead?' Jill jumped up in the air and began to dance wildly around. 'How bad is it? Is he going to die?'

'Intensive care, coma, but they have induced that while they wait to see what's going on, severe head injuries, broken pelvis, crushed ankle, but he's not dead yet.'

'Oh God! Why are we sitting here? Let's go.'

'Of course, we can go straight there, grab your bag and let's get going.'

Chapter 24 - Waiting

'How are you doing?' Beatrice enquired.

'Oh, not so bad. I'm trying to get it all in perspective. My head knows that many of the things which absolutely freak me out when I look at him are quite normal for head injuries and, in a week or so, most of the swelling and bruising will have subsided. It's the things we can't see I need to worry about. Anyway, it's really nice of you to come, how long can you stay?'

'Til tea time, I took the afternoon off.'

'It's nice to have someone to talk to,' Jill replied, 'I don't like to bother the nurses; they have enough to do already. Did you see that child in the bed next to the door, he came in yesterday, road accident too, I can't imagine what it's like for his parents. All I can really do is concentrate on being here with Zolli.'

'Is it OK for us to talk? I mean, are we supposed to keep quiet or something?'

'It's OK, honestly, this place is like Piccadilly Circus most of the time. Let's pull the screen over a bit and then we won't disturb anyone.'

They sat in silence for a while and Beatrice steeled herself to look carefully at the patient in the bed. It was hard to get her head around the mass of equipment and tubing and wires attached to him. There were things going into his head; drains she thought they were called but maybe they had a more technical name. She didn't want to ask Jill lots of questions about which tube did what. His face was very puffy and one side of his head was completely out of shape, like a rugby ball. He had a cage surrounding his whole head and some other contraption on his neck. It looked horrific and very uncomfortable.

'It's a good job he's unconscious or he'd be very pissed off about all this scaffolding.'

Jill laughed. 'You do have a way with words you know. I hope he can hear you!'

'Can he hear us? I'm always reading about people in comas who have come round when they hear their favourite poem or pop tune or even their hero comes to visit. Like David Beckham.'

'I don't think he even knows who David Beckham is.'

'Don't be too sure, the Beckhams are very big in Eastern Europe.'

'It's funny you should say that, you know. I was thinking earlier today that really I don't know what he is interested in. Apart from work and me, oh and he's very into his nosh. I've learned a lot from his cooking, we often take turns doing it, just for the fun of it. I get the impression he is really a very simple chap, easy to please, easy to get on with.'

'That's given me an idea. Perhaps you should read him a recipe for goulash, it might bring him round.'

'Or even get some from the canteen and wave it under his nose. You are very naughty, making fun of him like that. Just don't stop! I need all the cheering up I can get. However, he is actually in a medical coma right now. They know the best way to keep the patient calm and concentrate all the internal resources on the job in hand, that's healing his poor head, is to keep him in a drug induced coma. When they're happy it's safe to bring him round, they will, but not until all the internal injuries are totally settled and there is no danger of deterioration. When they bring him round, it won't be for at least week yet, if not longer, then they can tell what permanent damage has been done. I'll be a nervous wreck by then.' Jill looked away. B hadn't given much thought to permanent damage, it's strange how you just assume that if patients live, it's all going to be alright. Maybe it won't be alright. She reached over and squeezed Jill's hand.

'Want to talk more?'

'Yep.'

'Have you got time off?' Beatrice wondered what the NHS allowed in such circumstances.

'Mmm. I've got some compassionate leave, a week it says in the rules, then I can juggle my shifts. The trouble is, I can't really rest. When I go home I make something to eat and then can't eat it and I feel dog tired but I can't sleep. I'm not going to be much use to anyone if I can't recharge my batteries. Perhaps I ought to take something, at least I'd get one good night's sleep. I finally had to tell

Theo, as well. You know he didn't come home at Christmas, he got that fantastic temporary job? He needed the money. So, I didn't tell him about Zolli. I put it off. But ... I screwed up my courage. I wrote him a letter. I couldn't say anything on the phone. Beatrice ... he was so sweet. I thought he didn't care about me anymore. But I was so wrong.' Jill sniffed. Theo had never been an easy teenager. Beatrice hoped he would now step up to the mark.

'Everyone is rooting for you, Jill. This is a time of healing for all your relationships, I hope.'

'We'll see. I won't see him until Easter now. But it's a huge weight off my shoulders.'

'Yes, let's hope for the best. '

'Oh, something else. Krystina comes in at night; we sort of pass each other at about seven o'clock. She looks terrible. I don't know her well enough to know if I should try and talk, really talk to her. What do you think?'

'I think she probably feels the same way you do.'

'Did you know they lived together?' Jill stared at B. There was an uncomfortable silence. Beatrice did remember dropping her off at a little house with the thingy, charm thing, hanging in the window. Was that his house too? Why not?

'I've been to her house; I think it was where she lived. I dropped her off when I gave her a lift home, you know, when I drowned her that time, in the rainstorm. So, they share a house?'

'Yeah, and I never knew, until now. The police told me. I suppose I don't really know much about him at all.'

'But you do! You know the important bits, just because he didn't tell you about having a house share with a woman, do you think you would have been happy with that – if he'd told you?'

'Probably not. It's true. In the beginning I was very clingy, very insecure, I don't think an admission like that would have gone down very well. But, when you think about it logically, they were both here in England, on their own. It's natural to share with your fellow countryman, or woman. I'm being unreasonable, I know.'

'Why don't you talk to her? She must be feeling very alone. Perhaps he is her only friend in this country. Perhaps she feels she can't talk to you without giving something away. Look, either way, it doesn't matter now, you are the two most important people in his life and you should be helping each other.'

'OK, you win.' Jill sighed.

A brisk nurse was coming towards them with a tray of equipment. No doubt it was tube maintenance time or something like that.

'Time to head to the canteen. I might be persuaded to try and squeeze down an apple crumble and custard.'

'That's more like it.'

She was distraught. She was cut off, her source of information was just not communicating, how could he, how *could* he? Why was he not keeping his channel open. What was he up to? She could kill him, except he was already close enough to death, certainly in this body.

Krystina had come to the conclusion he was deliberately keeping her out. It was like picking up the phone and dialling an unobtainable number, you got a long flat tone that tells you there's nothing doing. She had sat there every night so far, staring at his inert form, trying every method she knew of talking to him. It had, so far, yielded precisely nothing. The police had come to her house early, around dawn, and knocked so loudly she had jumped up and banged her head on the wall behind her pillow. Krys thought he was with his girlfriend. She hadn't given his absence a shred of thought the previous evening. What hurt her most, made her furious with rage, was the way he had purposefully blocked out any communication so she didn't have the least idea of what was going on - his thoughts, his feelings, his plans. She had not felt a thing and, for that to be the case, he must have done something, put a shield in or maybe switched himself off. What was going on? Her own reaction was shocking to her, her natural coolness and reserve had been replaced with a hot fury and anyone who came near her was likely to be subjected to a torrent of anger and frustration. These emotions were deeply uncomfortable for her. They hurt her heart and made it impossible to eat. At night, her dreams oppressed her and her waking was disorienting and frightening. The days passed in a haze. Work had dried up as well which was fortunate as she was in no state to see anyone.

'So this is what it feels like,' she murmured to herself. 'My fellow human beings are seething with these unbearable emotions, buried deep beneath their sanguine exteriors. How bizarre!' As she wandered around the hospital corridors it was impossible not to observe the faces of her fellow sufferers. She stared at them, looking for clues, how to act, what to say, how to cope. It was after dark when the serious visitors arrived, the regulars. You could observe them lingering in the restaurant or haunting the kiosk, searching for a magazine to help pass the time, time spent watching, waiting and praying by another bedside, another body, some other life in tatters.

It was the hardest thing Zolli had ever had to do. It had taken so much of his energy to even *get* to the point of decision, let alone take action. When he thought about these last weeks, he could only shake his head in disbelief that he had actually carried out his plan and was now waiting, waiting for the next stage. The timelessness, however, was a relief. It took away the dreadful sense of urgency which had been dogging his every move. With each action depending on another action, and timing being so vital, he had become addicted to the clock, something he never considered would be important to him. At least he could forget about anything for a while now. His lifeless body was safely tucked up in a hospital bed. He could get on with convincing his mentors of the wisdom of his choice.

His thoughts turned to Jill. He smiled to himself and imagined her caresses, her smile, her warm and welcoming body. *She* was the reason he was here, waiting, waiting. Later, he would have to face Krys, in truth he was not looking forward to that confrontation but ... well ... he hoped she would approve.

The chosen setting for his meeting was outside, in a garden, and he wondered whether it was suggested to put him at ease. It was difficult to gauge the motivation of the Council. He knew they had infinite access to every particle of thought and feeling about this problem, they could make up their minds now if they wished but it was protocol for him to appear and present himself for their views, their good opinion and their permission.

He could see a square courtyard. In the centre was an arbour with climbing roses twined around the wooden beams; the colours were yellow and white, quite significant, he thought. Stone benches were arrayed on either side of the arbour so the canopy of flowers comprised the roof of the meeting space. There was a deep and beautiful scent in the air. One end of the courtyard was becoming brighter and, as he waited, he was aware of beings gathering there, nodding and murmuring to each other. They were tall and white, with long robes, circlets of gold adorned their brows. As he focussed he could discern differences, differing hues of colour, in their bright radiance. It seemed they had all arrived to take some part in this meeting. Something must be happening soon.

One being approached him and held out her hands in greeting.

'Welcome. I am Persidior. I have come to tell you I will be supporting you at this important time. The Council is making preparations and will be joining us shortly. Your unexpected arrival has sent many into a state of great anticipation; the deliberations of your case will send ripples of energy out to those who also work at this level of development.'

He was glad to talk about it. 'I know I must make a good job of presenting the unique circumstances. It is of great importance to me and to many whose future is bound up with mine.'

She beamed a beautiful and warming smile into his eyes. 'You are correct in your assumptions. The library and the archives have been bustling with activity. Many beings have been tasked with seeking records on which to base the Council's viewpoint. They have been preparing carefully for this moment. What is missing is your perspective. I must admit to my own curiosity. While I have incarnated on Earth myself, it was so long ago I cannot quite recall the exact amalgam of thought and emotion that would persuade me to do what you intend to do. And to wish to resign from the allotted programme! But I, too, am making assumptions; I haven't heard your case yet, only acquainted myself with the circumstances.' She looked intently at him. He was hesitant but decided to respond to her.

'I must admit to a little uncertainty myself. I wrestled long with my conscience, across many dimensions.' He paused and looked around. 'That reminds me, I was expecting Xenophia, my main guide and teacher, to be here with me at this time. We have engaged in long discussions up to this point that have greatly assisted with my reasoning on these matters. I am surprised she is not present.'

'Ah! The second matter I have come to discuss with you. She cannot assist you in this any longer; her involvement in your journey will cease as soon as a decision is made.'

'Why?' He was very alarmed and upset.

'Be calm, there is nothing to trouble yourself about. Her responsibilities are solely concerned with the progress of the project. Even though you have been with her for many times, she still retains a great number of other souls who require her diligent assistance and constant care. Your journey on Earth has been more independent. Do you not recall your vulnerability and dependence when the project first commenced? So it is with others, now you have reached the point where you have developed a self-sufficiency that is much envied among your fellows; you have progressed so fast and have a sure touch in your work. So, my sweet soul, do not feel regret, Xenophia's time with you is now at an end. I am to be your guide during this decision making process and, once matters have been resolved, you will meet with the one you are to work with, in your future, whatever that might be.'

'It sounds so final. So I will never connect with her again?' He was stunned. This was an unexpected turn of events. He was aware of feeling very alone, despite all the loving energy around him. Persidior laughed, a rich, deep sound that seemed to come from her very essence.

'Never forget *free will*, my friend, there are infinite possibilities when you include free will in the equation.'

'Does that mean I can still remain with Xenophia as my guide and teacher, if I choose?'

The being paused and sighed, seeming to be considering her answer.

'In truth, you may choose whatever path you wish, that you know already. You may remain on your existing journey and complete your part of the project. But I have to observe ... your intention in this matter seems quite clear and I do not think you would have gone to this much trouble had you intended to fall at the last fence, am I right?'

'Yes, you have observed correctly. Still, it saddens me when these partings must occur. She never gave me a clue when we were last together.'

'You must remember your form is neither spirit nor flesh at present, so your perception of reality is not entirely accurate. Any signals she transmitted to that effect would not, necessarily, have been observed by you in your current condition. However, I am informed there will be ample time for sweeter partings, later, when the business is concluded. You will be able to speak at length with her and come to your resolution together.'

Zolli was acutely aware of the momentous Council meeting ahead of him but he hadn't given much consideration to the effects of his proposal on others. It really was too late now. He just had to remain pure in his heart and accept whatever the consensus was to be.

At that very moment a clear beautiful sound filled the air, a choir of angel voices singing a song. He listened hard, they were singing a song that sounded to him like a lullaby. The kind of song a mother might sing to her child. The words were faint but unmistakable - hush a bye - he could hear it clearly now and the music was lilting and gentle. He smiled, despite his trepidation, and thought to himself , 'So they already suspect what my real intention is!' He should have known; nothing could be kept secret in this sacred place for very long. He chuckled to himself.

Chapter 25 - A new term begins

Lesley was the first one to be seated in the classroom so she had the first pick of the chairs. There was a motley assortment of what were called operator's chairs, some with arms and some without. What you couldn't tell until you sat in one was whether, during the day, some bored or frustrated student had released a catch somewhere or fiddled with a spring so that, as you sat down, the back of the chair collapsed and shot you unceremoniously towards the desks in the row behind. She had nearly come to grief several times last term because of this. Tonight she had tested many chairs before deciding on one that was intact.

The lecturer was going over the student lists. This was to be the advanced class and she hoped some of the others whom she had befriended last term had decided to stay on. They were studying more complex web design, including data base interrogation (whatever that might be) but she just wanted to *be* there, learning more and more. There was a clear plan now of her own purpose, her own direction. As she thought about the recent 'life between lives' experience with Jack and her firm conviction about what the future held, she was overcome by a wave of gratitude. It all fitted together when you considered it. First Beatrice asking her if she wanted to come to the book reading group. Then Rose choosing the book about guides and how to get in touch with your own personal one.

Lesley hadn't wanted to go at all. Secretly she thought they were all barmy, off their heads. It was Gwen who patiently and lovingly (where would she be without her?) coaxed her into joining in. Then, as if it was planned, they met Krystina. Well, first Beatrice met her by accident, then Jill found out she was the clairvoyant at the crystal shop. Now here Lesley was, she was convinced, with incontrovertible proof that her beloved son was alive and laughing in heaven or the afterlife or whatever you called it and she was his soul mate and soon they would be together forever.

Before long the room filled up and they got down to work. The first session was to be a review of the learning from last term, basic web building and using the design options to create professional quality web sites.

She didn't have the software on her home computer so hadn't had a chance to really try out her plans for this venture but she had some typed text she wanted to use which had been emailed to her college account. She opened the web design software and clicked *create web site*. Skilfully going through the procedure to manage the content and organise the folders, so her site would use server space efficiently and her images folder would be linked to the root folder, she clicked and saved through the steps like a pro. Create new HTML. The blank screen page came up. She chose page properties and set about looking at the colour options and font styles. She knew the look she was going to try to achieve – clear but welcoming, so gentle pastel colours and plain fonts were required. In her mind she had been mulling over the kinds of images she wanted to put on the site. You could trawl through masses of sterile and mildly insulting images of smiling nurses or happy doctors, looking 'caring'. They were all to be found on the websites of various hospitals. The sites for the private hospitals were even worse. She giggled to herself as she imagined placing some of the images she had seen on the cosmetic surgery sites. Perhaps a big pair of boobs would cheer up some of the parents she was aiming at, the women could plan to have breast enlargements and the men could just stare at them. Well, it was a thought certainly. Lesley shook her head, she must be going loopy.

The images she had eventually decided to use came from sites you discovered when you searched for images – angels; images – spirit. She had emailed those to herself as well. Briskly she set up a table, this was to be her template, with a main frame across the top and a frame to the left hand side for the hyperlinks. She opened 'Outlook' quickly, opened her email to herself, and copied the images into the H:drive. An angel image in brilliant white with a dark blue background, a figure pointing up to a star with beams of multicoloured light flowing back and forth, a seated figure in meditation with the heart chakra sparkling. Then she looked at images of flowers and skies and sunsets. So wrapped up in her activities was she that the tap on her shoulder nearly gave her a heart attack.

'Hi, I'm glad you're back.'

'Oh, yes, me too. Had a good Christmas break?'

'Not quite what I'd imagined actually, that's what I wanted to talk to you about. Can we chat later, do you have time?'

'Time is one thing I'm not short of at the moment.' Their eyes met. The woman she had got to know last term stood beside her appearing to have aged 50 years in the few short weeks since they had last met.

'I'm hoping you can help me. I know you have got experience of what I'm going through.'

'I'll do my best.'

The haunted look in her companion's eyes told Lesley more than any words could have conveyed. She reached across and touched her arm.

'Let's go for a drink afterwards and then we can talk in private.'

'Yes, please.'

Something was beginning already, she knew it.

Hilary sat down in the battered old chair in her beloved garden shed, her place of comfort and safety, and reflected on the last couple of weeks. Gemma was back at school. They had put last term behind them; in fact, they had stopped talking about it which was a relief. Hilary and her daughter were both intensely private people and the rather public outcry over Gemma's ordeal had alarmed them both. Fortunately, like all these things, public interest soon died down. Her friends stopped asking after Gemma in that concerned way, the Education Department finally stopped writing to her every week, the Family Mental Health Unit stopped offering counselling and lastly, but most importantly, the Head of Gemma's old school called and told Hils her daughter was to be welcomed back unreservedly, if she wanted to come. He had phoned on the 23rd December just as Hilary was wrapping up the most luxurious presents for her daughter that her budget would stretch to. Money well spent. What's an iPad when your life has been saved and your family put together again?

According to the Head (whom Hilary still regarded as a smug git) the teacher concerned had gone away; gone for good it seemed. There were no details at present but the call gave Hilary the impression there had been decisive action taken behind the scenes. The thorny question of the police and prosecution had been avoided. Hils had mixed feelings. What was right and what was right for her family were two different and conflicting things. Guilt. What if it happened to another girl some way down the line? Hils had been told by B, however, who knew about these things, that the Ruth woman would never work again in England in a teaching capacity. Hils just hoped they kept the 'register' up to date. Or that she wouldn't change her name.

She hoped the wretched woman had been given hell, even without the police being involved. But then she wondered, was she in hell anyway? Her thoughts veered off at a tangent. The clairvoyant, Krystina, seemed to think she was a sort of 'wayward soul'; someone who could only function by feeding off other's emotions. She considered for a moment whether there was a 'hell' and what it might be like. Could there be a worse feeling than the emotional torture Hilary had endured? Then, what agony Gemma must have gone through before it all came out? She must ask someone who would know about punishment in the afterlife? Rose probably, she seemed to know all about these things. She read too many books, of course, and didn't look after her garden properly (she had a man round to do the lawn and spray chemicals on the beds and borders). This was a cardinal sin in Hils' eyes. If Rose hired her as a gardener she would make the place into a beautiful, organic space with native English plants and flowers, somewhere to be inspired, to dream in and get lost in the scent and sights of nature. She was rambling, mentally speaking. Yes, Rose, she must give her a ring because she did want to find out what the accepted spiritual view of 'punishment' was. As she thought again of the Ruth woman she hoped that, whatever the punishment turned out to be, it would be nice and painful. Oh, and last for a bloody long time.

On the first day of the new term Gemma was in a quandary as usual. She had committed to the college in town and it did have many advantages in that people didn't know her and wouldn't ask too many questions. There had been a special induction day put on for her and for some other students who had fallen by the wayside in their old schools. It had felt friendly at the new college, despite the alarming size and the confusing layout. But a big part of her didn't want to go there; it made her feel like she was crawling away to hide and as though she should apologise for what had happened to her. The only part she was truly ashamed of was that she had deceived her mum. Hindsight is a marvellous thing (or so Mum was fond of saying), 'put it behind you darling, I know you won't freeze me out again.' Mum had been hurt, Gemma knew it but, at the time, she had been so involved in keeping the secret, the hiding and the covering of her tracks, trying to avoid being cornered by Ruth, she hadn't had the brain space to see anybody else's perspective.

Gemma stretched and snuggled down further under the duvet. Mum was up already, there was an unmistakable aroma of toast, that sublimely welcoming breakfast scent that made you want to leap out of bed and eat some. Gemma loved her mum, more now than she could ever remember, and what was more, she trusted her too. What judgement, what courage! I wouldn't be doing half bad if I ended up being like her when I'm older, she mused. And if I stay here, under the covers for long enough, she'll bring my toast and tea up here for me to have in bed.

She thought back to her dilemma. The Headmaster's telephone call to her mum, asking if she wanted to return to her old class, had unleashed a stream of uncontrollable thoughts and feelings. As she had lain in bed at night she found herself fantasising about being back with her group of friends, holding her head up, knowing that everyone knew what had happened, and just *seeing* if she could take it. Another dream she had was about a girl coming to find her to ask for help, someone who couldn't stand up for herself against bullies or mean teachers. She would offer advice, she could get permission to stay in the library at break times and worried students could just turn up and talk to her. Why not? The school counsellor never seemed to be around when needed and she was so strange looking you'd have to be desperate to want to unburden yourself to her or be shut in her stuffy office for more than a minute. She was so *intense* and serious. Yuck! Perhaps there were other girls like me who had secrets they couldn't tell anyone about. Or girls who needed support to cope with those feelings, the ones she had experienced, the shame and exhilaration in equal measure, the exquisite suffering you endured when you were in love.

'Bag, teeth, lunch, sports kit, have you brushed your hair? Look at that glass. What's the point of me buying that bloody orange juice if you don't drink it?' Emily looked mutinous and did an about turn and thundered back up the stairs to sort herself out. Alexa wafted into the hall on a breeze of expensive perfume.

'Can I have a pound or five to get something at break?'

'What's wrong with the snacks in the cupboard? I pay enough for your school lunch as it is, without paying more for you to get something from the snack bar. God! It's ten past already, just get in the car will you?'

The cat was lying, looking very snug, curled up in the main section of Beatrice's squashy new handbag. It was a shame to have to move her. 'I wonder if I can stay at home and sleep in someone's handbag?' Beatrice mused. She eased her hands under the light little body and replaced her in the cat basket which had now become a feature of the kitchen table décor. When the kids had their dinners, up at the table, Fluffy would stare at the plates intently for a minute or two until her desire overcame her natural laziness and she would stretch out a skinny leg and wobble over to the plates and just stick her head down and start eating, that is, if you weren't quick enough to snatch your plate away. It had become a nightly ritual. Emily thought it was tremendous fun. Beatrice made a mental note to check her for worms, and the cat too for that matter.

'Keys. Where are my keys?'

'I've got them, Mum, keep your hair on. The car's frozen anyway. I'm just going to scrape the ice off.'

'Have we got everything? Emily? Lunch box? Where is your coat? Where is your coat, child? You can't go to school without it, it's freezing.'

'I don't know, Mummy. Please don't shout.'

'Where have you left it? Is it on the peg behind your bedroom door?' She must stop yelling now.

'Mummy. I think I might have left it at school.'

'What!' At which point Emily started to cry.

'Leave off Mum, come on Ems I've got an old one you can use for today, it's a bit big but it'll do.' Alex gave her mother the most withering stare. It was true, she was a complete bitch. She had made Emily cry and she was turning into a screaming harridan in the mornings.

They went outside and B switched the engine on to warm the car up, at least it would be more comfortable for them, they might as well wait a few minutes now, they were going to be late anyway.

There had to be another approach. She couldn't stand many more of these early morning shouting matches. Was it her fault? Probably. She wondered if every house was like this in the mornings.

The living room fire was lit and Gwen had put the coffee on already. Breakfast television was a good way to wake yourself up in the morning. An intriguing mix of total rubbish and serious stories. The fire was smoking a bit, but soon the logs would catch properly and the lovely blast of heat and tang of wood smoke would combine to make this room the cosiest of places to be. She preferred to settle down in her dressing gown or an old track suit first and do some work, then, when she'd got a good hour of slog under her belt, she would go and run a bath. By then the water was piping hot too.

Outside, the traffic was building up. The start of a new school term meant the enjoyable peace and quiet on the roads of the last few weeks were at an end. The Christmas rush to shopping malls across Buckinghamshire had left the village quiet and peaceful, too. The pretty decorated cottages, the hoar frost on bare branches. Twinkling lights welcomed you as you walked back and forth to the post office or village bakery. She recalled the last of the special Christmas cake made for her by Beatrice who seemed to like making these things for her friends. It was something nice to have later, when it was getting dark again and Gwen would close the curtains and shut the night out.

Anyway, Christmas was finished and the new year begun. New year, new projects. Gwen turned to look outside her lounge window. Bumper to bumper traffic queued up to get through the T junction which joined with the main road taking everyone towards town and the older children to their upper schools. Buses growled along the narrow country roads, stopping abruptly at invisible bus stops to pick up sporadic children, shivering and hopelessly underdressed for this time of year.

She thought of Lesley. It had been over a year since her dear friend had done any school runs. No, she was wrong, of course, Jack hadn't been at school for many months before then and even when he was, they often went in later to avoid the crush, the jostling children who might push him or knock him over.

In Gwen's house there was no rush at all to get out of the house in the mornings, just the cracking of the logs on the fire and the gentle drone of the television and her thoughts. That's how it had always been. No sounds of other humans, no children, husband. Just the dogs. Thank the lord for them. She looked in her briefcase for the flash drive with the articles on it; she would be editing and proof reading them today for posting a hard copy by tea time (and the delicious cake). The laptop was glowing blue, all fired up and ready to go. The drive slotted into the side, she fumbled to get the USB part into the socket. Why do I always put it in the wrong way up first time? Her clumsy fingers did not suit this new technology, everything was too small and fiddly. She was not built for delicacy. A couple of clicks and her first piece of work was loaded, 'Mozart's undiscovered piano sonatas.' That sounded fascinating, she was a big fan of Mozart and his piano works were her favourites. What else was on the agenda? 'The Battle of the Divas – Cornelia Thorncroft and Isabella Vitalle fight for opera's top slot.' Oh, it did annoy her when journalists tried to drum up animosity where none existed. Or record companies making things up to sell more CDs. She had met both ladies, Cornelia many times at various functions and Isabella more recently, you couldn't wish for more pleasant people. They were a real advertisement for home grown soprano talent, Isabella even came from an Italian family who settled here after the grandfather had been let out of a POW camp in Wales! She hoped the piece was accurate. She sighed, no doubt the prose was going to be sloppy too. In her experience these articles were ill conceived and badly executed by idiots who had no idea how to write. Perhaps she'd hack it about so much they'd drop it from the magazine. Good, she'd see what she could do. What then? Editing of the reviews of the new releases and a couple of concert write ups. Lovely, this was the way she found out the best things to go and see and, with a judicious phone call here or there, she was usually able to procure tickets. She was a well known figure in the industry but her name never appeared on any copy. That was just how she liked it, well respected but protected from the bitchiness that existed between the 'so called' music experts who liked to see their own names in print, their views on music taking centre stage. Well, no time to waste, if she was going to do a hatchet job on the 'divas' article, she'd better get cracking!

Lesley had been up for three hours already. Colin had left for the station a long time ago and she had been shut in the office with her head bent over the keyboard without a break. She straightened up and noticed her shoulders and neck were almost completely locked in tension. Ow! That hurt. Time to get up and get some breakfast. She clicked back over her completed work. It felt very pleasing. There were six pages built already and they were looking good. The most difficult part had been the content. The design had been exciting and satisfying. It was when she had got to put words onto the pages that she realised she hadn't thought it through very well. Her first attempt had sounded like a brisk sort of 'pull yourself together' piece of text. It just didn't have the right tone. If she had been reading it she'd have logged off immediately. It wasn't good enough to publish on the web. Then she tried a more empathetic approach and it was worse - patronising and pathetic.

What had her teacher said? Check out the other websites, the self help sites on other topics, like arthritis or MS, they were well established and designed by professionals, so the look and the content were likely to be of a high standard. He had been very helpful. She'd done a screen dump of the sites she'd liked and then checked them out. Lesley had then copied some of the text which had sounded appealing and comforting, then rewrote it. Copyright existed on the internet just as it did in books and music. Her tutor had been very clear about the risks of legal action if you stole somebody else's work but he had been spot on about the sites. She was also looking at the site authors. One web design company was behind three of the better sites and she decided to look at their own website, too, for ideas.

Time to stop. Time to get dressed for a start. Colin might be home early tonight; he had a meeting at Cranfield and so she had better be dressed by then, or he'd think she needed the men in white coats again. When he arrived she could suggest a drink and a meal out. As this thought meandered around in her mind there was an unfamiliar sense of excitement inside her. Breakfast beckoned.

It was going to be tonight, no more waiting. Lesley was going to explain what she'd decided to do and show him some of her efforts so far. No need to explain about her between-lives session yet. Not now, maybe never, it wasn't something Colin could easily understand. However, for her, that afternoon she'd spent in her soul state was becoming more real every day. The memories were becoming clearer and more vivid. Just by closing her eyes she could bring up a vision of Jack (as his other self), her guide (who she could now have mental conversations with) and the amazing image of the bridge and the river. The picture would stay inside her mind forever. As she opened her eyes, back in her kitchen, she saw the milk saucepan boiling over on the hob and the naughty dogs had stuck their noses in her bowl of muesli porridge. There were a few soggy oatflakes left on the worktop, but it had mostly been scoffed, apart from the slightly chewed raisins on the floor which she knew to be mildly harmful to dogs. She really should get a grip on herself.

Chapter 26 - My new life

Was this a dream or was this reality? It didn't feel at all right; his body did not feel like his own. The last thing he could remember was the familiar rush and the thud, like a miniature sonic boom happening inside his head. He had a vague recollection of what that particular sensation meant to him, it was his returning soul, coming back into his body after a trip out, flying around, feeling freedom again.

Before that. Before that? What happened before? Zolli cast around in his mind for something he knew usually preceded it. He wanted to scratch his head, but couldn't, of course. There was something, he just couldn't locate it.

The sensations coming from his chest were very distressing. Like going too fast in a car and not being able to stop. The breathing was too fast for him, he wanted to slow it down but found he couldn't. Some invisible force was pushing the air in and out. He tried to hold it back but the process was relentless, he failed to take control of his breathing and it hurt, too. His legs were completely numb but he could just about feel something in the fingers. He wasn't sure what it was, though. He was struggling to get a grip on it. His eyelids were stuck down fast and, when he wondered about opening them, he became so frightened that his heart started to thud loudly in his chest. The resulting noise in his ears was absolutely deafening, unbearable, terrifying. A machine of some sort was bleeping next to his left ear, it was keeping pace with the thudding in his ears. He just wanted it all to shut up.

Black, black in front of his eyes, then pain, then bright light, too bright, red and blue and yellow, all together. He wanted to scream. Nothing came out.

Then a prick on the arm. He *got* it, they were doing something to him. Pressure, then a cold sensation travelling up the vein. The feeling of helplessness was shocking. He longed for oblivion again.

But they were manhandling him, talking to him, stopping him from slipping back.

'He's back now.'

'What do we expect?' Disembodied voices.

'I'm going to give him three minutes for the drug to circulate, then we'll do some tests, it's self explanatory really. Look, I know this is very hard for you, you are being very brave, Jill, but it is so vitally important for his recovery that you're here to greet him when he becomes conscious. So stay calm if you can and keep looking into his eyes when I take off the dressings. Imagine how you would feel if you came round and found me staring at you instead of the one you love?'

Jill grinned. 'You're not that horrible to look at, really.'

'No, my dear, but I am no beauty and Zolli deserves better than my ugly old mug. The wife is always complaining about my awful hair, I don't seem to be able to tame it.'

'I like you anyway. I don't care about your hair, you've been so kind. Besides, I'm not truly nervous, I feel quite confident and I know not to expect much at the start.'

'That's good. I'll tell you what to do, shall I? You've got his hand, there, he may be able to feel it now, squeeze?'

It *is* her. She's here. Holding my hand. That's what the feeling is, yes, I can feel it better now. The hand is tingling a bit but I can't move it, God! Why can't I move it?

'Are you ready?'

'Zolli? Zolli, darling, can you hear me? It's Jill.'

Squeeze harder. I'm going to do it now.

'Zolli, are you there?'

A gentle pressure on his eyelids. But they were stuck fast, it seemed to him. No, they could move, one eye open, the light was painful, he couldn't see anything other than a swimmy sort of sea of blobs. A pink and while blob hovering to the right. He couldn't keep it open by himself. Then a bright, bright pin point of light. It hurt badly. He wanted it to stop.

'Left pupil still quite dilated, let's look at the other one. Hmm, not so much, differential dilation, but that's to be expected. I'm just going to test reflex points, see if we get a response. Keep calling him. I'm told by patients who've recovered that it sounds as if you're calling from a very long distance and they have to struggle to come towards you, be patient.'

'Come on, my darling, do something, show me you're hearing me, I so want to see you smile, I have so much to tell you, can you hear me? Try to show me. Zolli, Zolli, everyone is waiting to hear how you are doing.'

A final push, all his energy was concentrated in his fingers, it took a supreme effort.

'Oh, Oh, he's moved his fingers, look, there, it twitched and I felt it.'

'Let's see, might be involuntary, of course. Zolli, it's Ben, if you are here with us move your fingers now.'

'Yes, there it is, he is back, my darling.' She sniffed and had to fumble around for a handkerchief.

Inside he was grateful, he'd made contact. At least he had shown her he was still there, inside, after this living hell of total sedation. What troubled him, though, was the way his body did not seem to be working like he expected it to. He knew he had been very badly injured, after all, he had planned it that way, but this body felt completely different to the way it had before.

Now he was back from his trip home, he had stupidly expected to be able to do more, not resume normal service, of course, that would be out of the question. Foolish of him. Now he was back he should work at his patience. Yes, patience, little steps, definitely little steps, a little patter of feet and there would, of course, be many more of them in the future.

Later Jill found her way back to the staff restaurant. It had been her comfort zone during the last weeks. Every part of the décor, all the different kinds of food, the hum of the equipment, was familiar now. There was her favourite chair, quite near the servery so she could get a refill of tea or coffee without going too far. If you sat there you could see people as they came through the door, before they saw you. It was a handy position to be in. Many friends and colleagues had come specially and sought her out, hesitant at first, wondering if she might like company, was she up to answering questions? They'd leave if she didn't feel like it. She could be ready to answer them if she saw them in advance; it had been good to talk with people she had only known by sight before. It had been a revelation to her, these weeks at the hospital. The love and concern she'd received from her own friends on the ward and the other colleagues of Zolli's, it made her feel quite overcome. It had seemed like time had been suspended, she'd been hibernating in this hospital, time had no meaning any more, days merged into weeks, punctuated by the kind words and caring responses of those souls that sat with her, sometimes just sat, stroking her hand, just in the same way that she sat, in the ICU, stroking his.

Today it was Lancashire hotpot and carrots, toffee apple pudding, mincemeat tart and then the usual regulars, baked spud, salad bar, omelette if you ordered it, kiddies menu, baby sausages, turkey dinosaurs or fish fingers. Jill reckoned she could match each customer to their choice from the menu. It was her little game to play when she wanted something to distract her mind. She had observed so many people during the last few weeks and her mind had been so empty of information, she had probably just remembered what everyone ate each day to avoid thinking other thoughts. People were so conservative in their choices. Each time they arrived at the counter they chose the same things over and over, they even said the same things, 'Not too much potato dear, it gives me indigestion.' 'Can I have my custard separately, in a jug, please?' 'Just one dumpling, I'm on a diet, but give me extra carrots.' 'Have you got any couscous today? No? Will you ever have couscous? No? Oh, alright then.'

Holly had started to join in the game. 'Here comes Mr 'Can I have an extra roast potato', he's with Miss 'I don't eat dairy'.'

'Really, are you sure? He usually lunches with the blonde one, you know, who has the mandarin yoghurt saved behind the counter, in case someone else eats it. Perhaps she's developed a dairy allergy and had to stay home, with cramps and the runs. We should slip her some Imodium.'

'You are horrible. I wonder that anyone would love you, let alone a dish like Dr Zolli.'

'Huh, it's only being bitchy and my warped sense of humour that have kept me sane lately. Anyway, it takes one to know one.'

'What's your pud like? Can I have a spoonful?'

'Mmm, it's not bad. Here.' She offered a spoonful to her friend.

'Yes, it's yummy, I think I may join you, what is it again?'

'Are you joking? Can't you tell what it is by tasting it?'

'Not really, my buds are shot to pieces after years of crisp abuse, all the chemicals, you know. C'mon, tell me what it is, I really like it.'

'Toffee apple sponge and custard.'

'Yum, I like it better already.'

After gobbling down the pudding at some considerable speed, Holly wanted to know the latest information about Zolli.

'Well, he's been brought round from his induced coma. He's very groggy but he's responded and squeezed my hand. Dr Ben's with him now, doing some tests, I thought I'd come down here so he can have a free hand. It's going to be a few days before he has a real idea. Funny, really, but I've got this unshakable faith everything's going to be OK.'

'That's just the effect of all the carbohydrate.'

'No, I mean it. Did I ever tell you about my friend Beatrice? She's been in a few times, she set up a sort of friends circle for spiritual growth. We used to meet regularly and see if we could make contact with spirits, guides who could tell us things about our lives - you know - and predict the future.'

'Really, that sounds fascinating.'

'It is, I assure you, I've never felt so intrigued. There were quite a few of us, too, all with different levels of experience. And then Krystina came. You know, Zolli's house mate.'

'No, what do you mean?'

'He lives with this friend, from Hungary, they came over together. She's a crystal healer. I met her when she came to do readings for us at the group and show us what to do. Obviously I didn't know she and Zoll were connected then. I really only found out since his accident, she was contacted as his next of kin. Oh, and, as she lives in the same house, she was down on the hospital records.

'He lives with another woman?'

'Yeah, really.'

'I don't believe it. You mean, like, you don't mind?'

'Actually, at the moment I'm too exhausted to care, but it's not important, is it? I mean, the fact that I never knew is a bit odd but, now I do know and we have talked together, I tell you, she's completely broken by this, she looks awful. She comes in at night or early evening and so our paths often cross. She's taken it really hard.'

'Are you mad? I don't mean to burst your bubble but doesn't it strike you as a bit suspicious? He doesn't tell you he's living with another woman and then she turns up and acts like it's the end of her world; she looks terrible. These are not your average flatmate's feelings?'

Jill looked across at Holly. As she scanned the young face of her friend she realised, perhaps for the first time, the feeling of complete security in his love. She searched around inside for some of the old familiar feelings, fear, jealousy, insecurity ... but, no, no sign of them. It felt rather strange. But not unpleasant.

'No, don't get the wrong idea, it's fine. They are very, very close, but not for the reasons you might imagine. And I'm totally happy about it.'

She had expected it to feel like a bolt of lightning when it happened. But the reality was very different. Krystina was tidying her room at the crystal shop. Last night had been another long vigil at the hospital. Jill had phoned earlier and explained they were waking him up, so she was on alert, waiting for some news. Anxious to fill the time, her attention soon focussed on the revolting state of her room. For the first time in many weeks she'd felt like picking up a duster. Usually there was only low lighting in the room, everyone liked it that way. But there was a fluorescent strip in the ceiling for total bright illumination. It was necessary to put it on for cleaning as the dust and fluff hid right under the chairs and behind drapes and screens. She was disgusted with herself for letting it go. The room actually smelt. Stale bodies and stale air - stale energy too.

She was going through the motions with some glass cleaner and kitchen roll. The lampshades on the side tables were giving her trouble. They were coated with a fine layer of dust which seemed to be resistant to wiping, she looked at her handiwork. Her only success was to smear a wet mark around the shade and the more she rubbed the worse it looked. She knelt on the floor, rocking backwards and forwards on her haunches. How did people put up with it, she wondered? There was just so much maintenance to be done. If it wasn't washing yourself, it was your clothes, then your house and now your workplace.

The street outside the shop was also sticky with gum and spilt fizzy drinks. She wanted to wash that, too, but she simply didn't have the energy. Actually, she had met quite a lot of humans she wanted to scrub thoroughly but *that* was way out of order. The thought of a nice cup of tea flitted across her mind. Then she was aware of another thought, one which didn't belong to her. It said 'coffee would be nicer.' She hated coffee herself but knew a person who loved it. She replied,

'I've been waiting a long time to hear from you.'

'I know,' it said.

'Where've you been then?' She felt extraordinarily happy.

'Oh, here and there, nowhere in particular.'

'You lie to me Zolli Farkas and I can see through you.' She teased him.

'Ah, I am just a shadow of my former self, you can read me like a book.' He joked back.

'So you are really back, then?'

'Yes, I really, really am back, but I need you to come and see me as soon as you can.'

'OK, what about tonight?'

Then it was gone. No reply at all.

She was left wondering all by herself, holding a roll of kitchen paper and a multipurpose cleaning spray.

Dr Ben, as she now called him, was suggesting it was time to move him out of ICU and into a quiet side room, in the high dependency unit, but out of the hustle and bustle of a main ward. She was frightened. The main ward was where she felt at home, there was plenty to look at and lots of people to talk to, more importantly, this suggestion marked a change in his treatment. While he was in ICU there was the promise of high medical support, rapid change, movement, progress. In her mind she was harbouring an inkling that things were slowing down now. Dr Ben had his hand on her arm.

'Let's pop into my office for a talk about this, shall we Jill?'

They walked in silence towards the end of the ward and out into the corridor outside. She couldn't resist a backwards glance at his bed space. He was propped up in bed looking over at her, his head on one side. The feeding tube was back now and there were supports on his right side, placed there after it had become clear he couldn't hold his head up for more than a few minutes. He didn't move, just looked. Her heart ached.

The office was some way away and within the Neurology department. Their pace was leisurely and she was in no hurry to get to their destination. Dr Ben kept up a gentle patter about general hospital gossip, who was seeing who and how the new stress counsellor had gone on long term sick leave within two months of her appointment. She mumbled in reply as they progressed. Colours changed as they walked through the various parts of the building. Yellow for Paediatrics, blue for Medical, pink for Obstetrics, then at last to green for Neurology. She passed the various specialist units, the children's section where they held the clinics for the kids with brain damage, the new Parkinson's research facility, the outpatients waiting room. They were all empty at this time of day. The doctors were either operating or making their way to their private consulting rooms. Dr Ben's Senior Registrar was standing, waiting, by the water cooler, looking at his fingernails intently as they approached. He had a patient file in his hand. She suspected it was Zolli's.

She had hurried back to the hospital right away. She couldn't wait until that evening. The Ward Manager explained to Krystina that Jill was engaged elsewhere, with Dr Ben. She wasn't worried about Jill, not at all, but, for what she intended, an audience wasn't required. When she eventually arrived at his bedside he was alone. Nursing staff were involved in a ward meeting in the large glass walled office, the door was open and the muffled business could just be heard above the gentle hum and drone and beeping of the huge array of equipment. He was propped up in his bed. It looked very comfortable, the pillows had been wedged so his weak side was supported but this left the other side of the bed empty and his arm was sort of hanging in space, the fingers limp and pale.

She could hear him as she approached. The telepathic signal was as clear as a bell, the words were rapid and animated but this contrasted with what she was seeing in front of her with her own eyes. His beautiful face was blank, the lips parted, but unevenly so, and his eyes were staring into the middle distance. Jill had obviously shaved him that morning, he looked spick and span but she had missed a bit under his nose and it looked strange.

'Hey, great, come closer, I can't wait to see you properly.'

She decided to speak her words out loud, there was nobody close by to notice her. 'Hello Zolli, you're back then?'

'Yes I'm back with a bang. It's so good to be communicating with you, my sweet one.'

'You've had us all very worried, you know.' She sat in the chair and decided to keep her voice down.

'You didn't doubt me surely? You must have known I would have a plan.'

A flickering memory of the anger and frustration she had felt at the time of his accident came into her body, her throat tightened. She looked at him levelly.

'You terminated our connection, that afternoon, it was just before you ... became injured. I felt it, it had me so mad at you, what were you playing at?'

His face was immobile, the lips silent, only his eyes showed any sign of feeling, he looked as though he was considering his answer. She waited.

'I cannot hide from you, can I?'

'Do you want to hide anything?'

'No, no I don't, but I cannot think of a way to explain it to you, I want to hug you, to kiss your pretty cheeks, but as you can see, my arms aren't working right now. If I could move I would spin you around with happiness and let the words tumble out. I would gesticulate and pace up and down while I told you my story. It would make sense to you. It would be like it was when we first came here, full of energy and hope, bright with excitement and anticipation. No, I cannot hide from you.'

'Just tell me.'

'But I am frightened of what you will say to me when you know what I have done.'

The walls in Dr Ben's office were pale green as well. The seats were much too low and wide and horribly bad for the posture. There was nowhere to put your legs without looking like you were suffering from piles. If you sat up, you looked ridiculous, if you leaned back you looked as if you didn't care and were preparing for a snooze. She felt both ridiculous and terrified, an appalling combination. The two Neurologists were sitting in normal height office chairs, spinning gently and rhythmically from side to side as they waited for her to settle. They were a good two feet higher than her and her eyes were level with their crotches. She wanted to laugh, she wanted to scream. Why do we observe these ridiculous customs? These meaningless rituals? Just tell me, won't you? She cleared her throat.

'I know why we're here.'

'Right,' the colleague opened the file, a classic delaying tactic. He shuffled the contents. Dr Ben was of a different calibre.

'You deserve the truth Jill. I just didn't want you to hear it in a public setting. I don't intend to keep anything from you or insult you by speaking in platitudes.'

She took a deep breath. 'Go ahead then.' Her heart was hammering in her chest.

'We've carried out all the tests and I double checked them myself. There is irreversible brain damage. Specifically, Zolli suffered a post traumatic inter-cranial haemorrhage, resulting in pressure which we were only able to remediate in part. There was subsequent tissue death and it is this which we are now properly assessing from a neurological point of view. Unfortunately, there are also signs of long term ventricular enlargement which, as you know, we can only manage. There may be more deterioration due to that complication.' Dr Ben leaned forwards so he was level with Jill's face.

'Now, I appreciate that we're only weeks into his rehabilitation, however, this is the first major milestone and you need to know the prognosis for full recovery is, as we sit here now, very slim indeed.

By this time most patients who will recover in the future have already made tremendous progress.'

'I see.'

Silence.

'We haven't told anyone else yet. We wanted to speak to you first.'

Numbness

'What I really want to do is to bring you up to speed with where we're at in terms of his current state and then you can perhaps help us with monitoring his progress from now on? Would you be prepared to do that? I had hoped it would be better news, but there's no point in keeping anything from you, is there?'

'No.'

'It's at this stage we usually hand over some of the responsibility for patient progress monitoring. You know this is the bit where it can seem very slow and so by having the charts and the prospective range of outcomes, you can at least be involved in the whole process. Is that what you'd like?'

'Yes. Yes. You've been very kind. Thank you.'

He reached over and squeezed her hand.

'Hey, it's not over yet. Don't speak as if you've given up, we haven't, have we Geoff?'

'Certainly not. What I was going to show you were the test results and some of the latest data we've got on outcomes. They're doing magnificent work in the States on brain damaged patients. The Christopher Reeve legacy has been a tremendous boost and of course our own Government has already sanctioned the necessary research using stem cells. We're making dramatic strides every week.'

'That's right Jill,' Ben was squeezing her hand harder now, 'I can't open the pages of my Neurology Journal without reading about miracle results or, certainly, what we used to think of as miracles.'

She looked up, seeing their earnest faces for the first time. They smiled, in unison.

'Really?'

'Yes, really.'

'Can I take the information home so I can look at it later? I feel a bit overcome at the moment?' Jill wasn't sure how to get away without her emotions overwhelming her.

'Please, do, be our guest. I've put copies of everything significant into this folder for you. It will help you to put things in a proper perspective.' Geoff handed the folder over to her.

'So, when you've had a chance to look at it, I'll get the Senior Rehabilitation Therapist to make contact with you and decide on a way forward. Of course, Zolli will be moved tonight into a high dependency bed in the Neurology Ward. It's a small unit, I don't know if you've ever seen it. Very comfortable though and much less stressful than ICU.'

'Yes, much less stressful than ICU.' Geoff nodded in agreement.

'Alright, I'll do as you suggest. Can I come back to you if there's anything I don't understand?'

'Yes, of course you can, my dear.' They rose out of their chairs and made preparations to leave. She too got up, she felt lighter and less oppressed. It was really quite bad news but, now it had been delivered, she felt better. She turned to go and smiled at them both. It felt strange being on the receiving end of one of these talks. She wondered, as she walked back down the corridor on her own, what it was like for other people who had received bad news, perhaps terrible news, in that office. As she imagined this she had an insight, a vision, of rooms all over the hospital, all over the country where news was being delivered in such a way.

'There's no easy way to tell you.'

'I'm afraid I have some bad news.'

'We've tried everything to no avail.'

'There's been a serious deterioration.'

'There's nothing left for us to do.'

'We'll give you the option of taking him home, but it's just palliative care now.'

'There's always a chance of some new drug or treatment.'

It made her feel small and humble just to think about it. She wouldn't cry. There'd been enough crying done in the beginning. Now was a time for patience and fortitude. How the hell could she explain it to Krystina?

'Did that go alright do you think?' Dr Ben, as he was fondly called, even by his colleagues, looked tired.

'Yes, it's always the same for me though, Ben. I'll never get used to it, as long as I'm in practice. If I had my way we'd only deliver good news.'

'I know what you mean. Just when you think you've got it cracked, you have to see the parents of a brain damaged child and explain the worst to them. Do you remember that case I had a couple of months ago, that gymnast who'd fallen in training and cracked her head. I almost sent her home, you know, it all looked quite normal. Then she fitted and had a bleed. I didn't get to it in time, it was only a matter of 30 minutes delay, but enough to change the prognosis completely. How could I explain to those parents I was actually at home ordering a takeaway at the time. The surgical duty team were trying to phone me and I was bloody well choosing chow mien and spring rolls. I was bleeped of course but they'd waited that crucial few minutes for me to get off the phone. Life can be a bastard.' They sat in silence for a minute or two, thinking about Jill.

'We did give her something though, the one thing we cannot predict. It's changed more things in more surprising ways than I can recall.'

'What's that Ben?'

'Hope, dear boy, hope. It's a human thing, you know, we can't survive without it. But with it, God willing, so called 'miracles' can become reality.'

Jill walked straight out of the hospital and carried on walking the half mile or so to her house. The file was under her coat. It hurt her fingers to clutch it to her chest, to stop it falling out and disgorging its contents onto the wet pavement.

Two floors up at the back of the building Krystina was helping to push his bed through the ward to its new resting place. There were four berths and only one was currently occupied. Overall, it was a pleasant setting and, unlike ICU, it had a window overlooking the quadrangle in the middle of the building. There was a garden and seating. In the summer patients would sit outside and talk, smoke, and listen to the birds. She wondered if they'd still be here in the summer to see that, maybe she would be pushing him around in a wheelchair if things went well.

Zolli was keeping up a slightly manic commentary on the action, occasionally making her giggle out loud with some rude or bad taste remark. She was getting used to not replying out loud.

'Don't forget to reconnect my saliva drain or I'll dribble all down this new outfit I'm wearing. Nurse took ages to get me into it, she does like her patients to look neat.'

'I wonder what's for dinner tonight, Mash or mash? Or maybe mash? Or would soup be too daring?'

'I hope to be looking forward to another bed bath, before I go to sleep tonight. I can't wait for the personal parts. It drives me to ecstasy.'

'Shut up will you, you're maddening with this talk. Just because you can't speak out loud doesn't mean you have to keep up this inane nonsense.'

'Don't be hard on me Krys, I'm just getting my skills back. I feel like I've been cut off for weeks, well, indeed I have, haven't I?'

'Just slow down a bit. And don't say anything unless it's important. I've got a headache now because of all this noise.'

'Ooohh! No sympathy from you then.'

'No, the more I think about what you've done the more headstrong and foolish it seems. You say they, your Council, were expecting you. Doesn't that seem odd to you?'

'No, I got the impression they had been watching for some while. So when I made my crazy decision to jump, it was accepted.'

'Crazy, yes, you can say that again. Hmmm.' Perhaps there was more information to be prised out of him. 'You never really told me exactly what your original plan was, perhaps it doesn't matter now, but at what point did it diverge from the proper sequence of events?'

'I don't think it was at a particular point, you know. It was more like I noticed that the rules, the set of certainties we were drilled in, seemed to be shifting.'

'Sorry, I don't get you.'

'Well, one of the rules I'd always had complete confidence in was that I would always been able to distance myself from it all - the human emotion stuff. I have never felt any of the things people say they feel, not in any previous body. All that ridiculous stuff you read about in the newspapers.'

'You used to read newspapers?'

'Oh yes, only in the staff room. Things like 'Agony of Coronation Street Star' or 'Courage of transplant girl' or stories about broken hearts or true love or passion. To me it had always been unreal. Look Krys, we know human emotion is just a pale imitation of the real thing, and corrupted by the worst excesses of human negativity. People can't have love without jealousy or possessiveness or pain of some kind. Well, I can admit to you now, I have always been pretty dismissive of all that trashy emotional stuff. And I never once got caught up in it. Then I noticed a small change in myself. It's hard to explain but, I started to feel *involved*.'

'Was that just with Jill?'

'Funny you should say that but, actually, it wasn't. I was treating an old chap in the fracture clinic one weekend. He was in his seventies. I sorted him out and just for luck I checked into his future, I was only being curious, but I saw his end, alone in his flat, with nobody to look after him or miss him or notice he'd gone. I felt regret. I actually felt a connection to his humanity. I could hardly believe it at the time but I've now progressed, or deteriorated if you like, to a completely different level of perception about human emotions. In a strange way, I have more respect for them. The people that is. This is *hard* Krys, really hard. Being in a human body with no memory of ... you know ... the bliss and beauty above ... and being so cut off from it.'

'I hope you weren't tempted to change that old man's future?'

'No. I know they watch out for that!'

'My teacher used to repeat it, day in, day out, 'never try to change events, it's not your responsibility.'

'Makes it boring though, doesn't it?'

She glanced up at him, the expression of vacancy was still there, he was focussed on some object towards the window, not on her, but something in his mental voice reminded her that he was powerful still, and could achieve much. Perhaps this wasn't the end he had wished for, or changed his plan for, or was it? She felt tired and thirsty, maybe she would go now and get a nice cup of tea and then go home. It had been a very long day.

'Don't go just yet. I need to talk to you about something.'

'Talk! You haven't stopped from the moment I came in today. You are exhausting me.' She smiled. She didn't mean to be harsh with him. She was just trying not to be sentimental or sympathetic. He would hate her to show those feelings. They had only ever had that one incident. The time she'd found him sitting in the dark, keening like a wounded animal.

'I mean it. I don't know if I will be able to do this tomorrow. I can't assume the knowledge will stay with me. Perhaps they'll give me some medicine to stop it, so I need to clear a few things up – big things.'

'Like?'

'Like ... I don't know how to start.' He appeared to hesitate. 'Do you understand I did it deliberately? I knew what I was doing.'

'Yes, the police have been talking. I assumed you had calculated you could discarnate for a while if you were comatose. Am I right?'

'Yes, was it that obvious?'

'Oh, yes. But poor Jill, what have you put her through? I can't understand how this, what you have done here, could possibly be better than the original plan?'

'Jill. I have done it all for her.' He stopped for a moment and Krystina noticed a softness creep into his telepathic voice.

'I had very high ideals, I had it all worked out in my mind. You have no idea how much thinking has gone into this. I explored every possible way I could imagine to stay here but retain my status. I sent a proposal to them before my visit. It had all the benefits and costs weighed up. It was with this in mind that I decided to step off the pavement.' Krys could see how difficult this was for him. She leant over and stroked his hand.

'Of course, when I arrived and we had the meeting, there had already been decisions made in principal higher up in a different Council. I didn't expect it. I went to explain my proposal to them. Then they informed me – you know how they do this, they are so loving and wise - they told me there was a trade off. It isn't possible to make the change I wanted without there being an opposing transaction. It's part of balancing the energy. I had to offer something. I knew what they wanted, it was as clear to me as the sun in the sky. So I offered this.' He cast his eyes down towards his chest, his arms with the tubes attached, his paralysed legs. ‘It is the perfect balance is it not?’

‘You offered this? This useless, broken body? Are you crazy? You say you did it for Jill. If I were she, I’d prefer to be going to your funeral.’ She was so angry with him. ‘I am astonished, no ashamed, of your *arrogance*!’

‘Don’t shout at me, please Krys, I need you to help me. There’s something you don’t know yet. Even Jill doesn’t know, but I do. It’s why I need to stay to see it through. Soon everyone will know. It cannot remain a secret for much longer.’

Chapter 27 - Another new life

He was sitting at a café bar by the main road. The air was soft and there was the promise of a warm spring day in the light breeze. It would still be freezing cold in England. How stupid they all were, plodding on, day in, day out. They could be here, sitting enjoying a morning coffee and a read of the newspaper. Printed in France and costing 2.50€, of course.

The man at the tobacconist always kept David's copy back for him as English papers were in limited supply. It had become a habit. They exchanged a few words, adding to their vocabulary each day. They'd almost reached the stage of commenting on the weather. 'Il pleut' wasn't going to be much use to him down here. 'Il neige' was pretty useless as well. Unless he hired a car and went into the snow capped mountains in the distance. Somehow it didn't quite appeal just now. The feeling of sunshine on his dingy skin and the way he had established this routine around the bar and the market and his small hotel room, all of it was building him back up to some sort of state of good health. Madame Genroche who owned the hotel and had seemed so frightening in the beginning, even she was part of his routine. She had taught him how important it was to speak the correct greetings to every French person he came upon. Bonjour before he asked for his coffee. Au revoir ... bonne journée when he left the supermarket checkout. Bonsoir at the internet cafe/bar. Merci ... bonne soirée when he paid for his beer and left. He was getting into the flow of it and the familiar patterns of the compulsory greetings were making him feel he belonged to something. All of it was doing him good, he just knew it. He didn't want to change anything at the moment.

He'd been reading a book about Van Gogh, he'd found it in Heidi's English Bookshop in Old Antibes. He was drawn in by the images of sunflowers on the cover but he found it was not a sunny book at all. He tended to keep it on him when he went out for his morning coffee or a lunchtime beer. It wasn't a book you wanted to read on your own at bedtime. From what he had gathered, Van Gogh had seemed to lurch from one disastrous thing to another. He wondered if many young men of those times had lived similar lives. It made him think about his own rather uneventful existence. Van Gogh had been an art dealer, a Methodist preacher, then failed his theology studies. All this by the time he was 24. Then he went to be a missionary, living in a poor area of Belgium, choosing to live in poverty in a squalid hut. He was then sacked from that career for some inappropriate behaviour. Then came the mental illness that drove his father to try to get him committed to a lunatic asylum.

Van Gogh began painting in earnest later on in his life after studying Impressionism in Paris. He was manic and extremely prolific, by then producing works in oils in his familiar style. But he was afflicted by mental illness, bordering on madness, with manic episodes and confinement to mental hospitals. Even in hospital his painting continued. His final months were spent alone in the village of Auvers-sur-Oise near Paris. David had checked out the famous location on his journey south. Van Gogh spent 70 days there and painted 70 oils. Each morning he would set out and walk up the hill to paint. But his depression had deepened. He felt himself to be a failure. David knew what that felt like. One day the troubled painter walked into the fields and shot himself but he even failed at that. He walked back to the little room he rented and lay on the bed. The Doctor could do nothing for him. He took two days to die. The barman took pity on him and, during his last days, fixed his beloved paintings around the room so he would die looking at the views that inspired him. He died having never sold one painting.

What could that feel like? He couldn't make himself understand. It was so far removed from his own experience of life. His misery had only made him more and more inactive, he had shrunk his world down to his bedroom and the chair in the lounge, gazing aimlessly at the television, sometimes he didn't even turn it on.

When he tried to remember it properly, he found he could only pick out brief scenes, odd things that varied from his usual routine. There was no doubt the drugs had made the last six months of his life at home utterly unbearable. He was off them all now and, although he had felt pretty bloody awful during his journey down south, he'd been compelled to keep going and reach his destination. He was glad he was clean. No more Prozac type drugs messing with your brain chemistry. No weird sounding metals that might or might not work, but could also kill you. There was something inside him that wanted to live, to find out what another day might feel like. Whereas Van Gogh had run out of whatever it took to keep going. His end had been a complete tragedy. If he'd been alive today he would have been treated and could have had a normal life. Hard to say, though, whether he'd have painted anything.

David could empathise in a small way. Those last weeks at the house had been the worse he'd ever endured. He tried not to dwell too much on what he'd intended to do but, sometimes, his mind got hold of some thoughts and wouldn't let go of them, like a dog with a bone. Pippa, he kept thinking about her. Her face in the light from the streetlamp, on the night he left. What does she think now? Every night when he lay in his single bed he made a promise to himself that he'd write to her the next day, just to tell her he was alive. But every morning he woke up to the sound of Madame bashing the crockery about in the dining room downstairs, the scent of coffee and croissants and the promise of a spring day ahead. Each day he put it off.

Later on he left the café and made his way back to his little room. It was charmingly drab in a way that only the cheap hotel rooms of France could be. He had negotiated a weekly rate of 90€ which allowed him to eke out the cash he'd taken from their bank account so it would last a bit longer. It was low season and he knew that once May arrived, his special rate would suddenly be raised to an astronomical and unaffordable level. Even in this dull little grey hotel. The address was after all 'Avenue de Cannes'. There was a bank in the main street and a cash machine at the post office but he rather suspected his card would be rejected if he tried to use it. The thought made his heart start to jump about. Here on the border between Golfe Juan and Juan les Pins he was close enough to the enchantment of the best the Cote D'Azur could offer but far enough removed to feel like he was entitled to be there. A dull man in a rather uninspiring part of the South of France.

In his room he could look out at the tiny park used by early morning joggers and people walking their dogs. How the French loved their pets. It gave him much pleasure watching them walking their little dogs. The hotel was opposite the Parc Exflora, another place he loved to spend time. The park was locked at night, though, and didn't open until 9.30 in the mornings, so the tiny offshoot across the road had to satisfy anyone wanting green space outside these times. The main road was busy all the time but this had advantages. David wasn't sure he wanted peace and quiet.

Downstairs Madame would be stirring the soup, tasting the cassoulet or making a similar rustic dish and turning out the crème caramels. It was a comfortingly familiar menu every night. The thought reassured him and so he allowed himself to lie down for a few minutes. Turning his attention back to the room, his eye travelled up to the ceiling. The plasterwork was grey, probably from age rather than design. He guessed the dust and fumes from traffic had hastened the deterioration. A continuous crack spanned the junction of the ceiling with the walls. He now understood something about French building techniques from watching one of the new developments across the road towards the sea. Prime building land; the apartments were going to be very posh and have sea views. He often stood and stared at the sales boards advertising the new building - Domaine Juan Flore. It looked spectacular.

The buildings in that part of France were formed from solid concrete, poured in during a seemingly haphazard process involving shuttering, chutes and lots of shouting. Concrete, hence the greyness in his room and the slightly uneven walls. And the crack, he didn't think they had taken much care when building it. He was more used to British houses made by jaunty bricklayers building upwards, measuring their work carefully as they went. But, of course, all building techniques were changing these days, steel frames, multi-storeys, massive basements. Perhaps this method of construction would soon be used widely in the UK.

The hotel building he was staying in was only about thirty years old, three storeys and square, and joined in a row of buildings with some apartments and finishing with a scooter workshop at the other end of the small parade. Like the majority of French building, all the residential parts had shops underneath, except the hotel which had its bar and small dining room/cafe at ground floor level facing the road for passing trade.

In the corner of his room an ancient spider's web had long since been abandoned. Three walls were the uniform grey and there was wallpaper on the wall behind the bed, the like of which he had never seen on an English wall. It was stripy and predominantly orange and brown. Fortunately, time had dimmed the effect so you could look at it without getting a migraine. Over in the corner was a basin, large enough to wash almost all of your body in. A mirror above was new and plain and square. That's how he knew his face was looking better each day. His hair was clean and, since he hadn't been to the barbers for many months, had reached his collar and now sprung curls which gave him a slightly bohemian look. He liked it. The eyes were clearer too and he could look at himself without feeling afraid. Despite the cool season he had the glow of a slight tan. The sun was surprisingly warm during the day and it was hard to stay indoors, especially with the continuous warm baking smell from the Boulangerie Eucalyptus just to the side of the hotel. With the best croissants in the area, of course. He knew this from Madame.

The narrow bed he lay on was an iron bedstead with a rock hard base and a sagging feather mattress on top of that. He'd taken a week to get used to it and had woken every morning with a dreadful aching back but now, the snug nest he could create when he sank down into the mattress, made him feel secure. From his position in bed he could observe the lights and activity from the traffic outside. It was a busy road with lorries, frequent buses and commercial traffic rattling along until early in the morning on their way between Nice and Cannes and all the romantic sounding towns in between. The bright orange street lights cast a comforting glow on the ceiling. The thin curtains and ill fitting patio windows were no defence against the noise, the sound of car horns and the clamour from below. People laughing and talking loudly, not caring who heard them. He was drawn into the feeling he was part of it all. Was he? He had been two months in this place. It was just a normal part of the south of France, not fashionable, not touristy. But the people who he observed everyday were residents. He assumed this area was composed of the workers who went each day to make the beds in the Carlton or staff the bar in the Belle Rive. Many apartments in the huge blocks behind the hotel had families in them with children. As well, of course, as their little dogs. He wasn't sure about children being raised in apartment blocks but, as his thoughts meandered around this topic, he pictured his own garden at home and wondered if Pippa knew how to look after the lawn. It was time to get the scarifyer out and get rid of the moss. Why, when you were just quietly thinking, did your mind do that to you? Why did he suddenly care about the moss? How many years was it since he had done any scarifying? The whole thought process was ridiculous and beginning to draw him into another long debate with himself about what he had done and where his future lay. The only way to stop it happening was to get up and do something. Something that didn't cost anything. He would walk through the park and go under the railway line to the sea, via one of the many underpasses on this stretch of coastline between Antibes and Cannes. It was ironic, he thought, that the developers in the early twentieth century had built the line so close to the sea, not realising how all the surrounding landscape would be developed in just a few decades. The main railway track cut through the potentially beautiful 'littoral' creating a barrier between the sea and the towns. He got up and brushed himself down a bit, before collecting his sunglasses, his book and his beach mat, in case he felt like sitting down somewhere. Perhaps there would be a few people on the sand today, just for the joy of being there.

Later on, before dinner, he usually did a bit of washing, just pants and socks and suchlike. Things to be washed in the little basin then hung out on his meagre balcony or 'terrasse'. Madame disapproved of sand in the rooms, she seemed to have a sixth sense about it so he had taken off his shoes and socks, both quite sandy, and walked up the stairs bare footed. Sand removal subterfuge was needed before he could even think about dinner. He stupidly hadn't invested in pegs so his washing was precariously hung on a tiny line between hooks in the wall inserted there by previous occupants. This had led to an unfortunate incident with some pants which had blown off his line and slumped onto the top of the awning below. Fortunately you couldn't see them from the road. Madame would be angry if she knew they were there. He hoped to enlist the young chambermaid to help him retrieve them, as it was only a matter of time before Madame was on the upper floors and happened to look out of a window. Until he could remember to buy pegs he had developed an ingenious way of stopping his laundry escaping. He tied it all to the line. It meant things were more creased but at least they were still in his possession.

Very soon, in that area, the magic hour of eight o'clock would arrive when everything came back to life. People would walk slowly and decorously down the road, greeting their friends as they did so. He was greeted now by almost everyone. He nodded and smiled. A few words of French to make conversation. This ceremony over, the restaurants filled up, not too busy in the mid week but comfortably alive with local families and couples, even a few single men like himself. Widowers he assumed, or bachelors perhaps, not everyone was suited to marriage. Then the noise from multiple conversations would take over and the wonderful smells would waft into the dining room.

He took his place in the window looking out onto the few tables on the pavement occupied by the hardened smokers who would rather be cold than do without a cigarette.

'Monsieur?' He looked up and saw Madame smiling at him, holding the half finished bottle of wine from last night.

'I 'ave surprise for you.'

'Really? I mean c'est vrais?'

'Regard là.' She nodded towards the back of the room and her hair did an alarming wobble on her head.

'C'ete mademoiselle là!'

'The one on her own?'

'Oui, oui. Anglaise, monsieur.'

She winked and grinned at him, he supposed she meant him to do something now. He looked again. Fortunately, the girl or woman was reading the menu intently and peering at the blackboard with 'plat du jour' written on it. The dish of the day was the same, varying with the day of the week, rotating dependably so he now knew it off by heart. She looked like a modern girl, probably about 25 years old, quite self assured he thought. She had the most vibrant red hair he had ever seen. It shone like an elfin cap in the dim light at the back of the room. With an effort he got up and walked slowly towards her table.

'Hello!' She pre-empted him. 'I'm Ruth, how do you do?' She stood up. 'Do please join me, I understand you're a permanent fixture here, Madame has been filling me in on the mystery of the Englishman.'

'What?'

'Oh, didn't you know? Your turning up here unannounced in the middle of winter without any family or explanation and staying for over two months has caused a great deal of speculation, well, certainly for Madame, anyway. She's just nosy and I think she wants some kind of notice about how long you're going to be here. She mentioned the desire to redecorate your room before the season.'

'Really?' He shuffled around to the chair opposite and hurriedly sat down, sensing Madame's eyes on him again.

'I take it you only have rudimentary French? Mine's quite good, I studied for six months in Paris as part of my degree so I'm reasonably fluent. She gave me the lowdown on you within five minutes of me booking in this afternoon, can't wait to know where you're from and what you're up to. Her money is on broken romance.'

'I can't believe it. God, that's made me feel, well, trapped somehow. I thought I'd, sort of, become anonymous.' He sighed. She poured him a glass of red wine.

'So,' he continued, 'Madame and her cronies who prop up the bar most days have been watching me and speculating about me?'

'Don't take it so seriously, it's harmless. Remember this is the low season and there's not much to do, I guess they don't have much else to think about, well, not the old ones anyway. Don't let it bother you. I'll tell her to mind her own business if you like.'

'No, wait, I'll have to think about it. Do you mind if we talk about it? I haven't really had much chance to talk things over with anyone since I've been here.'

'I'm OK with that. I take it there's a story, then? You don't need to spill the beans unless you want to.'

He leaned back and picked up the wine glass. Looking at her intent little face, wildly attractive too, he felt flattered and excited. But it was all going too fast. One minute he was a sad, depressed, old git running away from his family and the next he was sitting chatting with a stunning young woman who seemed to want to get to know him.

'I'd think I'd like to stay and talk if you don't mind. I, well, I don't want to disturb your meal if you'd intended to be alone, but it'd be great to have a proper English person to chat with.'

'That's a deal then, is it? Do you want to bring your wine over then we can get our meal ordered.'

Madame was looking very pleased with herself as he collected the wine from his table and returned to sit with his new companion. Smug even.

There were just two of them sitting at the kitchen table. Washing up was stacked in the sink. Several school bags were heaped on the floor.

'Life goes on you know.'

'Yes, I do know. Don't make me feel even more guilty.' Pippa looked at the floor.

'It's just that you seem to be going round and round in circles, Mum, and I've got my GCSE's to worry about next term. Over Easter I've got to spend the whole holiday revising for them. We got our revision timetables today and by next week we'll know the exact dates of the exams.'

'I'm sorry darling, I know I'm not being much help. I just hate the not knowing. It's taking up so much time to think about possible avenues of enquiry to follow up, I should stop for a while and we'll all sit down together and think about what you children need from me for the next few months.'

'I just want you to be here, Mum, body and soul. Even when you're with us, you're a million miles away. Can't you just forget it for a bit. It'd do you good to get out maybe, have some fun. With your friends?' Leanne was staring with a look of genuine concern on her face. Tears pricked in the corner of Pippa's eyes.

'Bless you darling. You're right of course.'

My friends, my poor friends, Pippa thought. I'd been absolutely awful to them. I'd had Beatrice running around doing research into missing persons. We wondered if David would even use a false name! B then went down to London and did the homeless shelters for me when I asked her to. At least she knows about those places, I couldn't face it, myself.

Rose had come to the studio for the last three weeks to help clear the backlog of jobs. She phoned all the customers and explained there'd been a personal matter that I'd had to take time off to deal with and she reassured them all their photographs would be ready on time. I couldn't have spoken to them, myself. Then she sorted through all the proofs, sent out the invites to view and handled all of that while I just sat and stared into space. Poor Julie hadn't known what to do with me. Rose had explained it all and got Julie set up with doing all the routine admin and finance so I still had money to spend. Just as well.

Even Jill, who I hardly knew until this year had called around with some information from the hospital about the kind of counselling I could have if I wanted. In the end I just wanted *her*. She looked so understanding and nice. I cried and raged my way through all the details of our married life and all the things that'd happened. She was fantastic to me and even now she emails at least once a week to make sure I'm not cracking up. All that while she was nursing her poor doctor friend.

And Polly, who I actually loathed up to now and thought was shallow and self-obsessed, she researched the internet for methods of tracing people who've gone missing and even came with me to the police station, that awful step I'd been putting off and putting off.

Polly has turned out to be strong and determined, not at all like I imagined her to be. Perhaps we all hide our true selves from the world. What am I really like underneath? I don't know anymore. I thought I was a feisty, reasonably talented, photographer with a fantastic business and a goodish marriage. Until last summer anyway. Everyone has relationship problems at some time or other, some men run off with girls half their age, some get fat and go bald, others are bullies or are selfish and mean to the children. David was just prone to gloomy spells, sometimes they got a bit out of hand.

Nothing that I, strong, spirited Pippa, couldn't handle. Nothing I couldn't solve if I put my mind to it.

The memory of the things he'd said to me still stung me when I thought about them, but not because they hurt my pride or made me feel stupid (although stupid was exactly how I felt most of the time), but because I had seen for the first time the hurt and pain he was suffering and that I'd been part of the problem, not the solution. In a few words he'd shattered my idiotic idea of myself as some sort of saviour. I was the problem. I had been made to understand I was deluding myself, thinking of him as my project, something for me to fix.

Leanne looked across at her mum who was staring at the papers strewn around the kitchen table. Her fists were balled up and digging into her thighs. Pippa was lost in her own world again, excluding everyone. Poor Josh was upstairs, quietly panicking about University while trying to be tough and manly and keep going for all of them, waiting for his offers but with no idea whether he should go to college or stay or get a job locally for a year.

'Whatever, Mum. Do your best. If you don't feel up to it, I understand. But, just don't keep *sitting there*, just thinking. It doesn't solve anything.' She scraped the chair back and stooped over the table, pushing the papers together and gathered them up.

'I'm taking this lot away from you anyway, they need to be sorted out so I can see where we've got up to and what we can do next. I'll put everything in a box file, is that OK?'

Pippa nodded. It was all she could do to keep from breaking down.

Candles were flickering on all the tables, red candles in small green glass jars.

'So, what do you recommend from the extensive menu tonight David?' She smiled an ironic smile over the single sheet of grubby typed paper she held in her hand.

'Aha, Mademoiselle, I believe I can recommend the cassoulet this evening, over everything else on the menu, then followed by the crème brulee, crispy on the top and creamy underneath. Actually,

I'm lying, it's a packet mix. The cheese is very good though but it rather gives me a nasty headache - and funny dreams - so I laid off the cheese quite early on. Oh, another warning, the cassoulet is very garlicky, so if you are planning any close liaisons tomorrow I'd cancel them.'

'Really? So from your familiar tone I can infer that you've been eating this dish for some time now?'

'Ah, yes, but only every Thursday. Sunday we sort of do for ourselves and we get a cold spread with a lot of nasty pickled things out on the table. I make sure I have lots of bread or I get heartburn later. Monday is usually veal in breadcrumbs with creamed potatoes or frites if we're lucky. Tuesday is chicken with green beans, Wednesday is lamb, last week it was lamb shanks in red wine but more often than not it's a sort of stew, very tasty with herbs, Thursday you are about to experience for yourself, Friday is fish, odd fish, I've never seen fish like it in England, very firm and meaty and sort of barrel shaped.'

'That could be eel,' she interjected.

'Eel, hmm, not sure I like the sound of that. Perhaps I'll ask about it before I tuck in again. Saturday is 'specials night' so we have an extra course and everyone who seems to be related to Madame comes here to dine. Madame pushes the boat out rather and we all get as merry as hell. I often accidentally have cheese on Saturday, then regret it.'

'It sounds as though you eat here every night. Haven't you been trying out other places? I mean, there are restaurants all along the front, on every corner. There is even a McDonalds up the road at the roundabout.'

'I do eat lunch out, so don't think I'm not adventurous. But I'm on a very special rate and it includes an evening meal, I just pay for my wine.' He realised too late how odd and lame that sounded.

'OK, well you are obviously well in here. I think you've probably made the right choice. The menus at the restaurants on the front, just two courses and they're charging 30€ some of them. I don't understand the French, their economy is in the doldrums but they'll eat out most nights at 30€ a head. Anyway, that's a whole different topic. Let's stick to tonight. From your description, it all sounds very jolly to me and I'm sure I'm going to enjoy myself immensely.'

They sat in silence for a few moments. Madame was hovering. She fluttered over and, in due course, they ordered the dishes from the menu du jour, as was expected. Any attempt to order anything else would have been met with shrugs and dissent or the plain lie that it had already all been eaten by other guests so was unavailable.

'So, do you mind telling me what you are doing in this part of the world?' He decided to wade in to satisfy his curiosity.

'I'm on holiday actually. I know France well enough to travel about comfortably and I just have, sort of, gravitated south. Paris was horribly damp and depressing so I left two weeks ago and have finally fetched up here. This little hotel was recommended by the Tourism place in Juan. I was looking at the lower end of the rate spectrum. I'm on a budget too. The longer I can eke it out the better. So this will suit me fine for a while. I'm enjoying the air and the sun and the outdoors. Also, it's not like the resorts is it? It's almost like a little separate community here, not Juan and not Golfe Juan. And sooo convenient for the buses!'

'Ah yes, very frequent, very noisy but only 1€.'

She stared right at him and picked up her glass, pressing it to her lips and drawing the deep red liquid into her mouth.

'Hrhmm,' he cleared his throat. 'Actually, I'm sort of taking a break, from my ... life, I suppose. I sort of ran away.' There, he'd admitted it.

'Ran away, that sounds exciting. If you'll admit to that ... so will I, I'm running away too.'

'Really, where from? What from?' He felt energised by this confidence.

'Well, I had a teaching job until recently and I made a mess of it. I decided to leave before I was pushed out. And I also had to spend a little time in emergency psychiatric care which wasn't exactly a picnic, but hey, here I am, almost back to normal and looking forward to spring in the lovely South of France.'

He admired her honesty. She deprecated. He felt more relaxed than he had for many months. He decided that, as she seemed to think that talking about one's mental problems in this matter of fact way was OK, he would plunge in before he could stop himself.

'I had a breakdown too.'

'Did you? Well we are like two lost souls then, aren't we?'

'Yes, I suppose we are.' He couldn't decide what to say next. 'Look, I haven't had anyone to talk to about it and if you wouldn't mind ...'

'No, I'm a nouvelle expert on matters of the mind, let's pool our resources and see what we can come up with.' She grinned again and his felt his doubts evaporate.

'I'm a depressive. Have been all my life and my mother was too. Of course, I didn't realise it at the time but I can look back at it with a degree of understanding.'

'Go on.'

'I'm married to a wonderful and successful woman who, how can I put it without seeming churlish and ungrateful, she loves me - I don't doubt that - but she sees me as a sort of project to be worked on. I definitely felt, certainly as I slipped down more into those feelings, you know the ones, I felt trapped by her goodness and she just wouldn't let me be. I couldn't just be depressed in my own way.'

'And what would that mean exactly?'

'I just wanted to be myself, I know I was pretty low but I just wanted to deal with it in my own way. But she made me feel this awful expectation all the time, she used to watch me and her eyes would be calculating what needed to be done next. Like should she get my tablets changed, or should we have more therapy. I hated the therapy. You do know that you can't have it on your own now, it's all 'family centred'. The idea being that everyone is to blame.' He was becoming heated. 'That's it really, it was my problem not hers or the kids, I couldn't even have my own bloody depression without someone interfering. Pippa and the damn smug family therapist.'

'Sorry to disagree but, don't you think if you're depressed, the whole point is that you're not capable of making balanced decisions about what should be done. It's up to people who are more mentally healthy to decide. The whole of the psychiatric system in the UK is based on that premise. So, are you the best judge of whether she was right to treat you like that?'

'But, it's my bloody life you know, it's up to me to decide. I hate that patronising attitude. Surely you know what it feels like to be patronised, yes and pitied, that's the worst thing.'

'You're getting angry.'

'No, I'm not, I'm just not agreeing with you.'

'It's OK, calm down. I was just testing you. Anger, you see is the opposite of depression, so if you can get angry about something it's a sign you're not really depressed, or that you're on the mend.'

'Really?'

'Yes, I am sorry, I shouldn't have riled you up, I just wanted to see. You are on the mend, I can tell, just by looking at you. Come on, tell me more about why you're here.'

'How can you tell?'

'Your eyes and your body position, depressed people tend to look down all the time, it's a way of connecting with their depressed feelings. You look down and you can wallow in your misery. And the shoulder position, slumped and curling inwards, to protect the centre, that's a typical body position for depression. It's obvious really. Look, you're on the way up, you must know that for yourself. Otherwise you wouldn't be here, you'd be back in your old life sitting slumped in a chair with your eyes locked onto a square of carpet, wallowing in your feelings or whatever you used to do.'

He laughed, despite himself. She was direct to the point of offensiveness but her sweet appearance was so at odds with the things she was saying. He couldn't be angry with her. She was insulting and he was feeling challenged but, in a way, she was right. He felt an energy inside, rising up into his chest, anger maybe, or excitement, a rush of adrenaline. It felt good, he wanted to continue.

'OK, I'll tell you more about me and then you must tell me about you, deal?'

'Of course.'

It had been one bloody visitor after another, each like an inquisitor, wanting her to do something, think something, feel something.

'I think you're depressed, Pippa.'

'Of course, I'm depressed, my husband has left me and I'm a failure. I failed him. So he walked away.'

'No, you misunderstand. You are clinically depressed, like he was or still is. It's when your emotional systems kind of shut down and you draw your world into yourself, so it gets smaller and smaller. And you stop being able to do anything about it.'

'I don't know. I don't care either. I just feel so tired all the time and I can't face going to work. It doesn't seem important anymore.'

'Darling, the bills will need to be paid, you can't stay away forever.'

She sighed and pulled her dressing gown closer around her. Why wouldn't Polly just go away.

'I'm not here to pressure you, honestly, just to make a few helpful suggestions.' Polly dug her nails into her palms to stop herself leaping up and shaking her friend. It would be necessary, in the near future, to think things through a bit more carefully. What should be done? She didn't really know enough about the subject but she could easily find out.

'Please Polly, I need to have a sleep now. I can manage, honestly. I'll be better in a week or two, just when I stop feeling so tired and run down.'

Polly got up and patted her friend on the shoulder. She'd leave it for now.

'I'll see myself out, darling, you just snuggle into bed and I'll be around tomorrow.'

'Oh, not tomorrow, please, let me be for a while, come at the weekend and Leanne will be here. She can make you some lunch, perhaps.'

'Alright, the weekend it is, Saturday lunchtime, I'll come and see you.'

As she walked out into the hallway, she made a snap decision and quietly opened the draw of the hall table and picked out what looked like a spare front door key, silently slipping it into the lock to check as she left. She slammed the door and she pocketed the key. She might need it later. If things got worse.

The next day was even more promising than the last. Spring was truly arriving and David woke with a fantastic feeling of anticipation. Ruth would be sleeping, perhaps, on the floor above, where the rooms were larger and slightly more expensive. They had plans. He'd see her at breakfast and they'd decided to find out if they could hire bicycles at the scooter place on the corner. If not, there was a place on Raymond Poincaré towards Juan les Pins. The early morning noises were drifting up and in through his window. Delivery vans of all kinds were pulling up outside, honking their horns, the men were chattering away. The bread, the meat, the laundry, the milk. It made him feel secure, he belonged, this was his life now.

As it turned out, the scooter garage up the road had a selection of quite good bikes and they chose two, with gears, as they intended to go on the new cycleway along the coast, aiming for Cagnes where there were fantastic new cycleways going along the coast for miles. Ruth seemed to know a lot about it.

'If you only read Nice Matin instead of the Daily Express you'd know these things.'

'How do you know I read the Express?' David asked. Ruth wiggled her eyebrows mysteriously.

They would cycle on the coast road as far as Juan then cut across to Antibes before picking the coast road up again towards Villeneuve-Loubet Plage. Some parts of the ride would necessitate being exposed to the French driving behaviour that had, according to Nice Matin, (Ruth had summarised last week's news for him) killed 22 young scooter drivers in the last 12 months over the Alpes Maritimes region. (Quelle tristesse!). Ruth did not seem at all concerned about this so he would have to trust her. He found his naturally anxious nature poking him in the chest where he now had a dull pain. He was not sure the helmets and fluorescent jerkins would make the slightest difference, only perhaps make them, as targets, more noticeable to M Dubois or Mme Dupont as they cycled along the roads through Antibes.

Madame had packed up a picnic, without even being asked. He had a tricky moment, though, when he realised there was no way to take it on his bike. There were no panniers. Soon, however, an old rucksack was produced by Madame and inside was a bottle of wine and two glasses, wrapped in plenty of paper napkins, to go with whatever Madame had already prepared. Ruth added a large bar of chocolate to their picnic lunch and they were off.

The early morning weather was hazy but with a promise of sunshine later. They soon had to discard their winter jackets and put the hi-viz jerkins back on. Ruth had packed a nylon backpack so she elected to carry the coats. Down the Boulevard Bijou Plage, along the coast road, with the red cycleway taking them to Juan les Pins. Past the many beach restaurants, shut up for winter and protected from high tides by huge banks of sand, forming an informal sea defence. Intriguingly, the sea was very close to the land here with stretches of sand sometimes only ten metres away from the water, it was not like the beaches in Norfolk where he had spent his childhood summers. He wondered if those sand banks could possibly offer any protection if there was a storm.

They were in the centre of Juan les Pins in just twenty minutes but Ruth signalled she wanted to stop for a while.

'Can we stop here for a bit? There is something I want to do.'

'OK, I'm always up for stopping!' He grinned, hoping he had said the right thing.

'I want to get a coffee? A proper one at the best place to get it?'

'Where's that, then? It must be good coffee.'

'Oh, it is, but it's the place more than anything. Le Crystal. It's been here for years, never changing and I couldn't pass through without stopping. I have fond memories from my youth of evenings spent here. Juan was considered quite a go-to place in the past. It's like Antibes's naughty little sister. If we walk up this little street,' she elegantly pulled the bike up onto the pavement, 'we can have our coffee outside and keep our bikes with us, that way they won't get nicked.'

Le Crystal was far less romantic or racy than David had anticipated. Set at a junction of three small roads, lined with other shops, cafés and restaurants, it formed one triangle of the junction. It looked like a slightly scruffy 1930's building that had not been maintained, except at customer level with window dressing. He liked it. Tables were set inside, in the dark wood interior, or outside under a thick vinyl awning so you could keep warm while looking out for the sun. Several people were lingering with coffee or what looked like delicious breakfasts. Cigarette smoke was thick under the awning. He felt mischievous, like he had bunked off school but was now really enjoying it. When had he last smoked? As if Ruth had read his mind, she pulled a pack of slim looking cigarettes out of her pocket.

'Omé,' she said, ' I hope you don't object. My vice, or one of them anyway.'

'They're so thin!'

'Yes, you can only get them over here. I love them. Don't you think I look fabulous, darling?' She twirled the long thin cigarette around her fingers, pouting suggestively.

'One long drag and it's gone, I assume?'

'No, not at all, they last as long as a Superking. I would say they are very, very satisfying indeed, on so many levels.'

I am flirting but feel so out of my depth, he thought. The dull chest pain returned. He cast around for a change of subject just as the waiter took their order for tiny espressos.

'It will come with a glass of water to sip so you don't get a heart attack or die of dehydration,' Ruth offered.

'What's that place across the road?' David noticed a colourful frontage. There were Caribbean birds and coconuts painted on the bright sign which said Pam Pam.

'What, that place there that says Pam Pam? That's Pam Pam,' Ruth smirked.

'Very humorous,' David was getting the hang of it now.

'Oooh! You want to know what *Pam Pam* is? And you have never heard of it?'

'Obviously.'

'How long have you been here?'

'Just over two months, I think.'

'You really don't get out much, do you?'

He looked away.

'Sorry, I must stop trying to be clever or get one over on you. It's a bad habit. I know it already.' She poked his knee.

'Forgive me? Or I'll stub my fag out on your hand?' She laughed very loudly.

David breathed deeply. Why do I take things the wrong way? Why can't I be like her? He felt hurt.

'Pam Pam. It's a bar, it will be open tonight but, during the season, it is open pretty much all day. Cocktails. Served in coconuts made to look like monkey heads. That sort out thing. All the cocktails come with different but bizarre serving ... you know ... methods. You can't call them glasses! I love it there. And,' she was running out of breath, 'you get simply loads of snacks so you don't have to eat dinner. Like curry popcorn. Odd fishy fried balls. Quite big,' she made a circle with her fingers. 'We must come! Weekend is probably best. More customers. More fun!'

The idea of cocktails out with Ruth was appealing. But he felt he was a bit old to be joining in with the kind of enthusiasm she was showing.

'Oh, and if we come at the weekend they have dancers.'

'Dancers?'

'Mmmm. But don't worry. They won't be naked.'

Ruth took her small camera out of her breast pocket. 'Smile,' she said as she snapped. 'Your face! It's priceless!'

I am so truly old and dull and irrevocably out of my depth, he thought.

They set off again and, powered by their tiny coffees, they made for the main road to Antibes. There was a lovely scenic route round the Cap but, if they wanted to sample the delights of the municipal cycleways of Cagnes, they needed to step on it. Ruth stayed ahead as she seemed to know where they were going. They cycled and puffed around the coast road until Ruth signalled to him she was pulling in. There was a little inlet and beach from where you could see the lovely bay and all the boats currently anchored there.

'I'm not sure if this is Billionaire's Bay but look over there. That yacht. Well ... if it was 99% smaller you could call it a yacht. It's the largest private vessel in the world, I think. That Russian, you know, who owns Chelsea football club. He has an estate just up there.' She pointed inland. 'Next to the Eden Roc. And that smaller boat next to it, that's his old one!'

They stared. Thinking. It was overwhelming. Even the smaller one had massive missile defence systems on top, radar, a helicopter. Both were a grim shade of grey and very imposing. Like warships. David wished he had binoculars, then wondered if watching the boats through binoculars was wise, given the menacing, military style, hardware on the deck. He couldn't comprehend what it might mean to be that wealthy or that security conscious.

'I wonder what he does all day?' Ruth was thinking out loud.

'I don't know anything about him. I'm not a football fan.'

'Well you've seen his 'fuck off' boat now, so you know one thing. We can Google him later and nose into all aspects of his rich life.'

'Yes, maybe he spends all day updating his Facebook page. What else is there to do if you have people to do everything for you?'

'I have a friend who works for a company that manages people's web sites and Facebook accounts. You know, famous people. They delegate it all out.'

'So he can't even enjoy the pleasure of posting pictures of his massive boat to the world?'

'No, sad isn't it? Rich people have different rules to us. He probably spends most of his time at his desk making loads more money. Or playing real life fantasy football with his real life players.'

'It is beautiful here, though. The bay, not the boat. You can see why he likes it.' David looked away and noticed the sparkling water, the bright buildings along the coast, jaunty parasols set out on the sand for prospective customers despite the season, the sea mist hanging on the horizon.

'Yeah, this is just the nicest time to be here, I think. Not too many tourists, lovely fresh air and not too hot. Ready to go again?' They set off.

David was enjoying the exercise, the amazing views of both the sea and the wonderful houses, set into the wooded landscape. You got a glimpse of a beautiful garden, the elegant corner of a huge house, a workman trimming greenery at the front of an unknown estate, an old lady walking nimbly towards the little Intermarché for her groceries. Every minute held a surprise. He was also gratified Ruth wasn't any fitter than him. She was puffing and struggling up the hillier sections, just as much as he was. He tried to relax into it. They were just enjoying this day, having fun, and he felt more alive than he could recall in a long time.

They finally got off their bikes at Antibes railway station and Ruth slumped down on a bench. David soon joined her and they sat quietly for a few moments.

'Will you think I'm a sloth if we get the train? We can take our bikes.' She lit another of her Omé cigarettes. 'And I really need a bottle of water. Have you got some change, there's a drinks machine in the station?'

David smiled to himself. He half ran into the station ticket office, glad to be of use and glad they were both tired of cycling. He hadn't wanted to give in first. They sat sharing a bottle of water and sweating silently.

'What about going down into Antibes, to the harbour? I'll buy you a beer then we can eat.' Ruth suggested. He nodded. 'We'd better leave the bikes here though. We can lock them up over there.' Walking felt strange after cycling so far. Soon they found the central square Charles de Gaulle and headed for Old Antibes. They strolled wordlessly down the dark little streets which smelled of baking, fish, drains and disinfectant. Steps were being washed and stalls set out. Waiters polished glasses at sunlit tables, ready for lunch service. If you looked down the passages between the tall houses, women in floral aprons were hanging baskets of washing out in tiny sunlit back yards. A number of dogs were being walked briskly through the bustling old town. Dogs met other dogs, there was yapping and the odd growl.

Ruth was entranced and kept stopping to point out a pretty view, an attractive window or the odd cat, sitting in a patch of sun, washing itself. He was very contented, just letting her do the talking. As they progressed up towards the market area there were more sunny squares and shops and cafés. He looked upwards at the buildings, above the line of the shops below. Ramshackle apartments with multilayered peeling paintwork and washing strung about their rusted metal balconies stood alongside bright new renovated blocks in greys and creams with modern windows and smart new railings. The effect was fascinating. He wanted to look inside each one and find out what they were like. He tried to imagine living in one of them. Would he choose a quaint run down old studio or a safe modern flat? Probably the latter. He'd set up a chair or two by the French window at the back and just allow himself to be mesmerised by the comings and goings of all the inhabitants. And from the upper floors he would spy into the gloomy depths of the old blocks opposite and see for himself what went on.

Ruth was sitting patiently at a pavement bar while he stared at the buildings.

'Is here OK? If you spend too long looking at the views above you'll end up stepping in something unpleasant ...'

'Fine, shall we enjoy a beer and then I'm all for finding somewhere to eat our lunch. Let's see what's in the rucksack, it smells like spicy sausage or salami type stuff.' He rustled and checked the contents.

'Yes please, is there water as well?'

'Sorry, no, Madame seems to think we only need alcohol. We can get a bottle here before we go.'

'And I need a wee.'

Later they wandered down towards the harbour. They had already cycled close by on their way through to the station. There were plenty of benches looking out to sea and many luxury boats docked in the harbour. Deckhands, cleaners, mechanics and staff were all busy on board. It was interesting to watch and have another glimpse inside the superrich lifestyle all around them.

Ruth lit her cigarette while David set out the food. They had little plastic glasses for the wine.

'Is there anything more satisfying than a drink and a smoke after some physical toil? And such a view. I'm in heaven.'

'Mmmm. People watching. My favourite.' He paused. He wanted to tell her something but didn't want to spoil the light mood.

'You know when we were talking about my depression, our depressions, last night? Well, I think this area around here, and the, well, what I mean is, the kind of mood of the place, can be credited with a fair amount of my improvement.'

'It's amazing isn't it,' she said, 'I actually don't think it would be possible to sit here in this sunshine and feel anything other than *glad to be alive*. Mountains behind you, sea in front of you. They weren't wrong, you know, the ones who came and starting building it. And then they had to defend it.' She pointed over to the huge fortifications beyond the harbour. 'I think they spent a lot of time fighting off invaders by the look of things. The walls of the fort and around the old town are pretty massive. We can look later if we walk up towards the Picasso Museum. I'd like to go in and look around, if that's OK with you?'

She smoked and drank and he watched her.

She hadn't referred to their conversation last night but he knew she had taken in what he'd said.

'You've reminded me of something I was thinking about before. I was reading a book about Van Gogh. He was very mixed up wasn't he? You probably know more about it than me. Art and all that.'

'Yes, it's something you study with your classes around year nine. I took my lot to Paris last year for a trip to Monet's garden and Van Gogh's room, in that place above the café. It's very moving. You can still see the marks on the wall where the paintings were put up so he could die looking at them. Put's our little problems into perspective rather, doesn't it?' She lit another cigarette.

'Yes, and I've been thinking about what you said.'

'What?' She squinted at him through the smoke. He had to say it.

'About being almost cured. And I think you're right. I have experienced a gradual change inside me while I've been here. Part of it, I am sure, has to do with being completely on my own and not having anyone to compare myself with. It's made me start from the beginning again, with the simple things like making myself go out every day, finding somewhere to have coffee and forcing myself to speak to the waiters or Madame. It's like I've relearned how to be alive in the simplest terms, with nobody telling what to do, except Madame of course, and because I've done it for myself, I feel I can call myself cured, or better at least.'

'I'm glad if I've helped. Talking about it. Yes, I am glad for you.'

She looked away and stared out to sea, then abruptly got up and starting brushing the crumbs off her lap.

'Shall we continue now?'

Much later, around the time all French towns go for a lunchtime nap and the shops shut down, they found themselves in the now deserted square outside the English bookshop. Customers had finished their lunches and the restaurant tables had been cleared. The shutters of most of the shops were closed. A few tourists were hanging around, looking for something to do. There was nothing for it except make themselves comfortable and wait for an hour or two or trudge back to their bikes, hopefully still locked up at the railway station. The wine had made him sleepy, however, and so they sat. Ruth had already bought her newspaper and so they found the most comfortable bench and she read, relating snippets of news as she translated them for him.

Pippa was lying in bed listening to birds clattering along the gutters and chirping to each other. The first sounds of spring. In the garden there was a large and expensive bird table, neglected and bare. She should put some bread and nuts out, she supposed. Just the thought made her recoil. The kids were at school, it would be lunch break by now. She turned over in the bed, her back was aching from staying too long in one position. Her head seemed glued to the pillow. It was so heavy. Her eyelids were stuck together, it was such an effort to open them. Her arms were leaden, they couldn't push the duvet up so she could get out. Her lips were dry and cracked, she hardly had the energy to lick them. She wondered how long it would take her to die if she did nothing at all from now on.

'You must go back.' Ruth broke the silence without moving.

'Go back where?' David asked.

'You know where I mean.'

She had been lying on the green bench with her feet on his lap and her eyes shielded from the late afternoon sunshine by the shade from the buildings. He thought she'd been asleep but, obviously, she was thinking. He watched as her mouth moved in her face while the rest of her was immobile.

'Trust me, I just know these things.'

'But, you've no idea what it was like.'

'Really?'

'Just thinking about it now makes me feel, oh, I don't know, as if my energy is all draining away.'

'Don't think about it, then, just do it.'

'I can't.'

'Can't or won't?' Ruth was warming to her subject now. 'Look, just stop being pathetic will you? This isn't real, you know, being here with me, sitting in the sunshine, it's just *playing*. Time to go back to real life now and explain yourself.'

Annoyance and the familiar feeling of guilt mixed together in his mind. It reminded him of listening to Pippa.

'I don't think it's up to you to make me decide.' It came out like a challenge. He was even more annoyed with himself now.

She fell silent. As he looked at her lying there, her brown legs exposed to catch the sun, her bright clothes scrunched up around her hips and her elegant little hands lying clasped in her lap, he felt overcome.

He couldn't say any more. He couldn't trust himself not to say something to make her get up and walk away from him, he didn't want that, at all.

Pippa must have dozed off again. The phone was ringing downstairs. Before she could wake up properly she'd stumbled out of bed and banged her knees against the bedside cabinet. It hurt. One of her arms had gone numb from lying in a strange position. She was all at sea.

It stopped. Then started again. Three rings. Then it stopped. It was like a stupid horror movie. She stood in the hall with blood trickling down her leg onto the hall rug, watching it. 1471.

'You were called today at 15.36. The caller withheld their number.'

Her hand hovered over the handset. It started ringing again and she pounced on it.

'What do you want, for God's sake?'

'Pippa, is that Pippa?'

'Who is this?'

'My name, oh, my name doesn't matter. I just need to know if, if your husband, well, if you would take him back?'

'What, what do you mean, take him back. I have no bloody idea where he is, he could be dead for all I know. Do you know him?'

She was shaking.

'Who the fuck are you anyway? Are you with him? Where is he? What's going on?' The line went dead.

They ate that evening in a little café with a section outside under a pergola of climbing plants that would flower later in the year. Green shoots were spreading out over the canopy of tangled mature branches. The atmosphere was strained. He gained the impression she was bored with him now, just when his interest was growing into something more serious.

Ruth smoked incessantly and criticised the food. It was lovely food, however, he'd never tasted better, certainly not from Madame's kitchen. She commented on the other diners and was loud and rude in front of the shy girl who had served them. What was going wrong?

'Are you angry with me about something?'

'Why would I be angry with you? You've been the perfect gentleman.'

'You just seem as though you don't want to be here.'

'Don't take it all so seriously, David.' She stubbed the cigarette butt out, grinding it into the ashtray.

'What am I taking seriously?'

'Look, it's not about you, you know. This is what I'm like. Think of it like the Van Gogh problem. Feel sorry for me if you like but don't think it has anything to do with you.'

He was stung. He called for the bill and paid. They left in silence.

Pippa was so shocked she stayed stuck to the floor in the hall for about fifteen minutes before she could decide what to do. It was nearly time for the children to come home from school and she was still standing in her nightclothes like a mental patient. The horrible feelings inside her oscillated between naked fury and blind panic. She couldn't decode them. She couldn't understand what the phone call meant. She looked down and saw the bloodspots on the rug and the wooden floor, time to clean up, at least, before being discovered. She hobbled into the kitchen and reached for a dish cloth. As she bent down to wipe off the evidence of her incompetence, there was a sound from the other side of the door and the key turned in the lock. A flash of sunshine and Polly stepped through the door. Her indecision was over in a moment.

'That's enough, sweetheart. It's time to stop this silliness and get you sorted out.'

'Pol,' she needed to explain, 'wait, I've had a phone call, from someone who knows David, maybe even knows where he is.'

'Christ, look, let me get that.' Polly took the bloody cloth and lead Pippa into the kitchen. 'Come on then. Sit down and you can tell me what happened.'

It was a few hours yet before dawn and David just couldn't sleep a wink. He lay in his bed feeling as if the world had turned itself upside down. The imprint of Ruth's shape was still clear in the mattress right next to him and her clothes were strewn around the room with such abandon, he just marvelled at the events that had lead them here.

It had been alright in the end. Her mood had evaporated as quickly as it had begun. She'd been right. It wasn't about him, it was just her way. Women felt things far more keenly, it was just a female thing he supposed. He'd had plenty of time to reflect on the evening. She'd gone back to her own room some hours ago to get some sleep, she'd said. Scurrying away wearing his old dressing gown. She didn't seem to care she'd left her clothes. Later, they'd meet for breakfast. He'd never felt such anticipation, such hunger, so brilliantly alive.

Much later, he drifted in and out of sleep. Dreams floated around in his consciousness. Dreams without endings, just abruptly disconnecting. He woke to the usual clattering coming from the street downstairs feeling faintly unsatisfied. The first thought that came into his mind was Pippa. What the hell. Pippa? Talk about bad timing. She was the last thing he wanted to think about.

The moonlight was fading as the first rays of cold bleak daylight appeared over the mountains to the east . Ruth had never been up at this time of night before. Always a late riser, often because of the drugs that sapped all of her manic energy away, she marvelled at the way the dawn light made the landscape look. There was a threatening quality about the low dark buildings that had seemed so bright and cheerful just yesterday. The cold sand under her feet was greyish green. She felt her surroundings merging with the bleakness inside.

It was almost over. As she thought this, she realised how pathetic it sounded. No point in being dramatic. She was just a little cog in a much bigger plan. She'd tried to do her bit, atonement, whatever that meant but, last night, it had all come unstuck. She knew she was heading for another episode and was unlikely to be able to keep it to herself. So her cover would be blown anyway. It was very sad to have to do this and part of her even now was making up objections to her scheme, laying alternative traps in her way.

She could just leave, or do it tomorrow, there might be a doctor who would prescribe her medication without questions or referrals. That would delay matters for a few weeks. She swept away these mental delaying tactics. No, it had gone too far.

'I'm sorry David. I really am. I never meant to make love to you. It was selfish of me. I just wanted to *feel* something, maybe just the feeling of my humanity, before going. But if I've screwed it up, well, it wouldn't have been the first time.'

She whispered out loud, connecting in her thoughts to her most recent bedtime companion. 'Forgive me, be brave and go back. It will be fine now. We can't escape our connections no matter how hard we try. Your life is there now, and mine? I've compensated in a small measure, not as well as I had hoped. You can't teach an old dog new tricks, so they say, and I'm an old dog in a young body. Too long in the tooth to change my interfering ways. I can't hang around because, in a few days, maybe a week, you wouldn't recognise me and I can't have that. My pride wouldn't allow it.'

Her thoughts plunged back to a year ago, in a bedroom in the afternoon, the soft feeling of another body entwined around her own in ecstasy. A face, a soul, the one hurt she could never heal. She felt a raw tug inside as she thought about her former love. The love of her life, if that wasn't a bit overdramatic.

'Forgive me, my wonderful darling Gemma, for how I hurt you, how I tortured you. Just totally selfish of me, as usual.' She fished around in the pocket of David's old dressing gown for the photo she had retrieved from her room; the one memento she always carried with her. It was crumpled and creased. Fine lines criss-crossed the young face of a beautiful girl.

'I had to do it, you know. I had to make you hate me. Otherwise we would both have been consumed and I love you far too much to have allowed that to happen.'

It was icy in the water but she didn't notice. The feeling was exactly what she'd been waiting for. The opposite of all her waking emotions. Numbness. Cold. Just as she'd planned.

Chapter 28 - The last meeting of the channelling group

I had been trying to arrange another meeting for ages. I particularly wanted to have a get together with Jill before the baby was born. It seemed to be the right thing to do somehow, like putting a full stop at the end of a sentence. As it was my idea to learn how to channel in the first place, introducing the book at the first meeting, it fell to me to bring the subject up and make sure everyone was invited. Beatrice was, as always, full of sound common sense.

'Can you get rid of Charles, then Krystina can come and we don't have to worry about him making remarks.'

'I'll do my best. He's not totally insensitive, you know. He just seems that way.'

I had doubts about Krystina. I really wanted her to come so we could show her how much we cared about her and how grateful we all were for her help. She had become part of our lives. In the short space of time I'd known her she'd changed my life completely and her own had been turned upside down too.

I worried she might disappear, go back to her homeland or just decide to settle elsewhere. Every time I had spoken to her in the last month or so, she'd been evasive. I didn't have the nerve to ask her what she thought about the baby and Zolli. So I gave vague and soothing answers to her questions.

Why did she need to come?

We all knew what to do, did we not?

It would be hard to get a lift, perhaps.

No, I said, I'd come especially and pick her up.

Alright, she'd think about it.

Text when you have decided what date it will be.

I could hear her hurting and wanted to rush over and hug her but I knew how uncomfortable she'd be with that arrangement. Her Eastern European bluntness and the tough exterior would kick in. So

I made do with planning a gift for her, something beautiful to show her how I felt.

Beatrice coolly informed me last night that she'd been practising and had worked her way through all the channelling tapes on her own. She had an image of her guide in her mind, she didn't know if it was the right one, but it kept appearing and she had actually done several readings for people at work. She never fails to surprise me. Where she finds the time I have no idea. The woman has a full time job, for goodness sake, and she spends at least two evenings a week visiting the hospital and learning how to carry out some of the nursing procedures so she can support Jill when the baby is born.

Zolli is due to spend his first weekend out of hospital very soon, as long as he doesn't get an infection or anything, so Jill and Beatrice are going to look after him together. I feel exhausted just thinking about babies, let alone caring for someone who is severely disabled as well. But there must be many women doing just that, or caring for elderly relatives while their own children grow up, just like mine are. It makes you understand just how powerful love is, I suppose. That must be the energy behind it all. When I remember seeing Jill last, just a few weeks ago, she seemed to be floating rather than walking. Despite the obvious bump she was sporting on the front. She looked radiant. I know they say all pregnant women look like that but, with Jill, there was almost a supernatural glow. When she told me about her plans for Zolli to be with her part time her whole body was shining. Call me barmy if you like but I saw it with my own eyes. What's more, I even felt it. I felt like I was standing in sunshine, that's the only way I can describe it.

She loves him so very much. I hope he is able to understand about the baby. If he was just able to recognise it as his ... something wonderful he did before his accident. His gift to her. I've only been to see him twice and each time his face has shown no emotion or expression at all. Then, maybe, there is a very subtle shift that you can only see if you really look carefully or you really know him.

I made sure I gave everyone lots of notice so they could put the meeting date in their diaries. People are so busy, I don't know where they get their energy from. Polly was flaky and peculiar as usual but Pippa said she'd make sure she came and she'd bring Polly as well.

Which I thought was odd because Beatrice told me they hated each other. So what was Pippa doing volunteering to do that, you'd think she would be glad if Polly didn't show? Polly's terrible at coming late and upstaging everyone. I don't know how B can bear her but, then, she always was too forgiving about other people's faults. Perhaps even mine. I mustn't overlook my own failings.

Hilary wanted to bring Gemma when I said Krystina was coming. I couldn't see any reason why not. The group kicked off with Gemma and her problem so it will be good to get them together. I did get Hilary to explain to her, though, that we'd be spending quite a bit of time meditating and then doing our stuff, doing readings with each other. Gemma offered to make the tea and be a guinea pig if anyone didn't have a partner.

Lesley has been out of the loop for a while. She's not really my friend though, so I had no idea about what she'd been doing lately. B told me that she's going to tell everyone properly when we meet. She's just heard that the NHS trust have agreed funding for her to have an office in the new paediatric cancer unit, with all her IT thrown in and the support that goes with it. And they want her to write up what she's done so other similar facilities can see what she's achieved.

Who else is coming? Well, Gwen, of course, she'll come with Lesley. I think the two of them are pretty close. I don't know what Gwen gets out of it though. She's a funny old fashioned thing. She wouldn't be my choice of friend. It's hard to tell what goes on between other people, though. Like marriages. If anyone really knew what marriage was like they'd never do it. Or am I being stupid? Perhaps it's just my own situation I find so maddening. So, I wonder, do we really know what goes on in other people's relationships? In other people's hearts? Somehow I doubt it.

It annoys me that B has been practising. No, I'm only joking. Actually I'm annoyed with myself. I haven't put the kind of effort in I would have wished. I've just let these last few months drift. I guess it's complacency. I did so well in the beginning despite that mad first time when my guide nearly knocked me out. Then that amazing reading from Krystina. I thought it would all follow on easily. Lately, however, I've found myself grasping the air for answers to questions about my life. Before, I'd get a sense of him, my spirit guide, being there, ready with a simple phrase or a feeling to help me. Now he seems to have gone. It feels very alone here in my life. I sometimes think I've been parachuted down into the wrong family, the wrong life. It doesn't fit me anymore. But I don't know what the hell to do about it.

'Come on then. Get under the porch, Gemma. You're going to get soaked if you stand around for much longer outside.'

'For God's sake Mum, it's only rain you know.'

'But Rose has a very *grand* house darling. She's got cream sofas and I don't want you to drip on them. It's not like our house at all.'

'Have you rung the bell?'

'Yes, someone's coming, just slip your shoes off will you?'

'OK, keep your hair on.'

'Is it down this road or was it the turning back there?'

'I don't know, dear. Didn't we get lost last time?'

'Trouble is, I can't see very well in this weather. Why don't they have bloody street lights in the countryside. It's not even proper countryside, just a commuter village trying to be up its own arse.' Lesley was animated.

'I don't know where you get these vile turns of phraseology!'

They both laughed. Gwen was well spoken and a bit old fashioned. She didn't approve of her friend Lesley using such bad English out loud.

'I think I've had my vocabulary expanded, lately. In the support group they say things like that about the doctors. I have to get them to say it quietly, or we'll get chucked out. I love it, though. And I'm so happy. Shall I tell them about all of it? You know, the child? Or is that insensitive to Jill?'

'You've no need to worry, I think, just tell them enough. That's my advice.'

'Oh, here we are, it's just tucked away down this little close, right here.'

'Good girl. We're still in one piece, I'm glad to say.'

Beatrice gathered up the tiny frail body in her arms and breathed in the scent of her warm fur for the last time. Fluffy was virtually weightless. In death she had lost the tight knotty muscles and the wriggling determination to be elsewhere. The cat rested, peaceful, in Beatrice's arms. She'd already been up to her chest of drawers and taken out her best, softest and most colourful jersey, a turquoise coloured cashmere, and lain it on the kitchen table. She placed her darling Fluffy down on the soft resting place and, with a shaking hand and much regret, covered her over and placed her in a cardboard box which she carried, tenderly, to the garage. Bill would bury her in the garden. They had a special corner for all the graves of her lost pets. She would not cry now, there was too much to do, but later, much later, she'd bury her head in the pillow and weep for the last twenty years and what she'd lost. It was the cruellest thing that your beloved animal companions passed away too soon.

They had dimmed the lights in the ward for the evening. It made the room feel more homely.

'I'm going now my darling.' Jill leaned over his bed.

'Where did you say you were going again?'

'To Rose's house. You didn't know her until your accident but she's been in to see you a couple of times, or to see me anyway. She's very elegant and wears beautiful suits. Her husband is quite well off.'

'I remember. She was nervous. I don't blame her, I look like a road accident.'

'Idiot. You are a road accident.'

'Will you just hug me again before you go? I can't get enough of it and the nurses don't touch me as much as they used to.'

She gave him an exasperated look.

'If I didn't know you better I'd say you were developing an unhealthy interest in sex.'

'No it's perfectly healthy I assure you. It's called physical rehabilitation.'

'Alright.'

She slipped off her shoes and took off her cardigan so her arms could be bare. She cradled his head in the crook of her arm while sliding onto the bed sideways and laying his head onto her shoulder.

The tubes flopped away towards the other side. This was the most comfortable way to do it. Then she slid her hands down to his hands and stroked them rhythmically, then moved towards his chest, bare under the thin T-shirt he wore, underneath the fabric, stroking and murmuring as she did so.

'I love you so much. It will be alright, I know it. You'll see. Soon there'll be the three of us, I can't wait.'

'I love it when you do that. It makes me think of that first time we were together. I can lie here, when you're not around, and dream about that time for hours. It just takes me away from here.'

'Do you know I had the cot delivered today?' She continued caressing him. 'The delivery men assembled it for me. The alterations to the front room - your room - are looking so good. The colours you chose are just right. I can't wait for you to see it. For you to be at home again with me.'

He smiled with his energy, even though his expression was blank.

'Can you play me a little of my music? Put it on and I will dream about you as I go to sleep.'

'Which disc do you want?'

'You know which one, my darling.'

She took it out of the clear plastic case. It had sustained her through dark times, many difficult nights, and she never tired of hearing the tracks he'd assembled for her. That day nearly four months ago, when he was in turmoil, he had left her a clear message in this music. Just in case he never came back at all.

He was quiet and she knew he had blocked her for a while to be in his own thoughts. He had a lot to think about and she mustn't go too quickly. She was used to him blocking off his telepathic communication from time to time. At first she had been offended, but soon understood it was only the same as the conversations most couples would have - talking had pauses in it too. Couples didn't tell each other all their thoughts, they kept some things to themselves. She didn't want to be able to know every tiny thing he had in his head. Otherwise there'd be no mystery, no anticipation, no relationship.

On a dark road on the other side of the town a different conversation was taking place.

'I'm really looking forward to this evening. I know Rose doesn't much like me but I'm determined to behave myself.' Polly announced.

'I do hope so, otherwise people will think it's my fault for bringing you. Have you actually any idea of what we are going to do tonight?'

'Of course! I'm not completely without sensitivities you know. Although I don't have the book that you've all been working to, I have done the odd course in the past, during my new age phase I suppose. I did a ten week psychic powers course in Somerset somewhere, that was when I was living with Zak, my handsome Australian, and he was amazing in the sack.'

'Don't tell me the details, I'm not interested.' Pippa stopped her.

'Really? Come on, at our age we need to take all we can get, even if it is only a memory in the distant past.'

'Please Polly, spare me the explicit stuff, I haven't been near a man except my lovely son, for some months.'

'OK, I accept I'm being insensitive *now*.'

'Sensitive to your psychic powers but insensitive about my feelings?'

'Yes, right on both counts.'

'Let's stick to the psychic powers discussion. How did you get on with it – your course in Somerset?'

'Oh, fabulous darling. I was made for it. But I think it helps when you have the right setting. This place we were at, it had presence, if you know what I mean. I was glad I wasn't staying there at night! The woman who ran it was called Letitia, or Letzina or something. She was very deep, dear. But I loved every minute of it. We had to bring an object that belonged to someone else and the group would all meditate and see what everyone could pick up. The person who brought it had to write the details of the thing and its owner in a sealed envelope and we'd open it at the end, with some ceremony I can tell you. I just opened my mind and let the ideas flood in, nine times out of ten I was right, or close anyway. Have you done any of that in your group yet?'

'No, nothing like that, it's all talking and listening. What you've done sounds more intense. For myself, I don't think I have enough confidence yet to just let go and say what comes into my mind. Do you know what I mean?'

'Mmm. But that's the exciting part. You don't know if you are right. You have a picture in your mind of something, or some words - it's pictures for me - and you just blurt it out, then you find out if you've hit the nail on the head. I liked it when we had the sealed envelopes. It meant we were all in the same boat. I'll tell you something funny. Often, when we talked about it afterwards, we found we had all got the same picture in our minds. How spooky is that, I ask you?'

'How do you mean, tell me more about it.'

'Well, say we had an object that someone had brought. We'd pass it around and have some time feeling it quietly. Then it would be placed on a cushion in the centre of the circle, that's how we would sit, in a ring. Then Letitia would lead a meditation. I loved that bit. It always felt like I was sitting in the cinema when I was a child, waiting for the film show to begin. I would just let myself go and see what vision came into my mind. Sometimes it was just light but, if you allowed yourself to drift, you often got a picture of something. Then you would have to interpret it. So, say I had a picture of field, for example, I could just say field but, more often than not, some words or meaning would come along with it. The field would just be a symbol and I had to talk about the meaning of the field.'

'Doesn't that make it hard? I mean, you could say anything.'

'Exactly, anything, but what I said all made complete sense at the time, so I'd say something like, ... it's connected with things growing. Everything is here, from the smallest seed and bug right up to the wind and the clouds and the sunshine. It's a metaphor for life and growth ... that's not a very good example. Let's see if I can think of something else. Perhaps a bee, yes I had that once, I saw a bee. I said something about the thing being connected with a busy person who is very industrious and always on the go. I said they could be irritating when you were with them but had a good intention. Something along those lines. I was given the image but I had to interpret it. In this case it was spot on. I think the object we had was a bracelet, yes, that's right.'

'But wouldn't it be easier to get words, so you just listen and then repeat the words out loud?'

'Oh yes, and indeed some people do get that, so they can just open their mouths and give the message or reading. But I've always had pictures. I suppose it's a bit like dream interpretation. You get used to certain symbols having certain meanings. I've got a book about dreams and it has some useful stuff in it. Anyway, what about you, have you been successful with your channelling?'

Pippa was silent for a few moments. Her thoughts were elsewhere. She'd been to hell and back in the last few months but Polly had dragged her up from the depths of despair. Then the stupid phone call. They'd decided in the end it was from a kid, perhaps a friend of one of her kids, someone who clearly didn't realise the seriousness of what they were doing. She could imagine the scene, two or three of them bored and looking around for some mischief to make, perhaps they'd been at the vodka shots, not an uncommon scenario. Perhaps they had truanted off school and got into some poor parent's cocktail cabinet. Anyway, the person was definitely not in their right mind. So Pippa and Polly had dismissed it.

Channelling, she needed to concentrate on the channelling. She didn't want to be ridiculed by Polly but, at the same time, she had come to trust her and knew the shallow exterior hid a solid dependable heart. So she knew she could be honest.

'At the start, I didn't come to meetings. I was wrapped up with David, he was very depressed at that time. When he left, B sent me an invitation to go to Gwen's house, miles out in the country and I made up my mind to give it a wide berth. I didn't know her anyway, so I didn't feel obliged. But something funny happened. Two nights running, I was woken up at about 3 o'clock in the morning. I don't mind that, I'm used to odd hours, David was often up in the night, and that's when he chose to leave me. This time I was woken up by an unmistakable feeling of being shaken. It felt like I woke up with the bed moving about and the covers being tossed around.'

'God, that's horrible.'

'Yep, I thought I was being burgled or raped or something. It was awful and my heart was beating and I had to get up and walk around for a while just to stop myself shaking. Then, when I went back to bed and closed my eyes I had a loud voice in my ear saying 'Get to the meeting, phone Beatrice and go there.' Or something like that. When it happened the second night I decided to phone B and say I would come. I was just hoping it would stop. I couldn't cope with that happening every night.'

'No, how awful it must have been for you. It makes me shiver. I wouldn't want to be one of those ghost hunters, you'd never sleep, dear, it's too terrifying to contemplate. Did you get any more funny turns, then?'

'No, of course it stopped when I did as I was told.'

'Oh, yes, I see. Isn't your house old though? You don't think you had a little night time visitor? Somebody who doesn't know they're dead yet.'

'No, don't scare me, Polly. Actually, I think it was my guardian angel telling me to get off my butt and do something. So I did. That's not all, though.'

'Ooh, tell me all about it.'

She needed to get this off her chest. Polly was asking for the whole story; she might was well go for it. Polly wouldn't be happy though – this was even more odd. And she'd kept it a secret, so far.

'I don't want anyone to know this, alright?'

'Yep, my lips are sealed, honestly.' Polly winked, rather disarmingly.

'I dream that I can see David and I know where he is.'

'Yes, that's understandable; it's just a dream though?'

'No it's not a dream, Poll. It's like I'm really there. And when I wake up I know I've visited him in the night.'

'Hang on, when did this start, because either we were wasting our time at the Police Station and trawling the internet and you were leading me up the garden path or it's a recent innovation?'

'Don't get huffy with me, I wanted to tell you but I thought you'd laugh. And you have laughed at me, haven't you. And now you're annoyed.'

'Oh, sorry. I really am, just take no notice. Now tell me, how can you tell it's not a dream?'

'Well, I didn't realise at first but, after the third night of it happening, not in sequence, say over a fortnight, I sort of put two and two together. First, it's the same sort of beginning each time, then the next thing is, it's very logical and believable, not random and odd like a dream. Thirdly I can control it. I did that last night.' Polly pulled the car over to the side of the road and put the handbrake on.

'Well, come on, tell me exactly what happens.'

'Right,' Pippa was breathing rapidly now and her eyes were glittering in the darkness of the car interior. 'I feel myself sort of flying very quickly about, quite low, just above the level of the houses, like when you're on a plane coming in to land and you can see all the gardens. I know where to go. It's a warm place by the coast. I fly in across the sea. It's very built up, this place, so it must be a popular resort somewhere with a mix of modern buildings and old. I've never been to a place like that before but I'm sure I can work it out from what I have noticed as I get there. Then ... I can hover outside his window and just slip in, through the glass if necessary. He's always asleep.'

'So he is asleep as well?'

'Yes, he looks sound asleep but I suspect it's to do with his mind being free when he's asleep, so he doesn't, sort of, stop me. Or maybe he's calling me and I'm responding, I really can't say. Then I sit on the bed and talk to him.'

'Is that all?'

'No, he answers.'

'In his sleep?'

'Yes, honestly, his body just keeps sleeping and looking very relaxed and we just talk. Last night we talked about when we first met and all the things we did together.'

Polly sighed. She was perplexed. It had got to be wishful thinking. After all the practical things she'd done to help, Pippa had gone barmy and started to make things up. Maybe to keep herself hoping, or maybe to assuage some of that great load of guilt she was carrying.

'Look. I think if I'd been through the things you've been through I'd be having those kinds of dreams too. It's natural, but you mustn't think they mean anything, it's just your emotions doing a final sort of wishful thinking, hoping he'll come back.'

'No, no, listen to me.' She grabbed Polly's arm. 'I think I know where he is. Last night, when it was happening, I made myself go outside again and look around the place I go to, I have some road names and a sign, the town name and even the name of the place he's staying. It's in France, Poll, the south, near the Cote D'Azur, all the signs are in French. I flew out towards the ocean to judge what part it is.'

'Now you're scaring me. OK, what's this place called then?' She had to humour her.

'It's Antibes les Pins, next to Juan les Pins. I've checked on the map. It exists.'

She turned off the engine and stared at her friend in disbelief.

'Juan les Pins. You're just thinking of that old song. Come on Pip. It's too ... *convenient.*'

'I want to go there. It can't hurt. I'll soon know if it's real. I don't have to tell anyone that's what I'm doing. Not the children anyway. You can fly out easily from Luton to Nice and be back in a day. I've checked. I didn't say anything before but, now you know about it, I've finally made up my mind. I need to see him and thrash this out face to face.'

'Oh, bloody hell.'

'There's more.'

'You're joking.'

'Just before it ended, his thoughts and words changed. He went from being comfortably relaxed and chatty to, sort of, distressed.'

'Distressed, how?'

'He showed me a picture.'

'Of?'

'A beach. With an area cordoned off, yellow and black tape. A pile of round stones, in a heap, with some flowers placed around it.'

'Oh God, Pippa!'

'So, you see, I need to go as quickly as possible.'

'I'm coming with you.'

Krystina was dressing herself very carefully tonight. The bedroom was strewn with floaty tunics and little shimmering scarves. She was listening out for Rose's car, it was expected any minute now. In the next door room all his possessions were packed up in boxes, ready for her and Jill to move them over to Jill's house in the morning. It would be the end of things, then, for her. But the start of something else for Zolli. Her beloved Zolli. She'd known him for over a thousand years but only worked with him for one year, one Earth year. But it seemed as if this one year had more meaning and more realism than any other time they'd spent together in any dimension.

Had she accomplished all she'd set out to do? It was hard to say with any confidence because the action had revolved so much around Zol. He'd hijacked the project, turned it around, stood it on its head and shaken it until he'd got what he wanted.

She had to sit down abruptly as a wave of emotion washed over her. She observed it carefully. It was joy mixed together with a sort of poignant regret. Regret that they couldn't go all the way back to the beginning and start it all over again. Because she wouldn't have missed any of it. But these overwhelming feelings now reminded her it was time to move on before she got entangled and couldn't detach herself. It would be best for everyone if she moved on, even for Zolli. She knew about the baby a long time ago, of course. And, unlike Jill, Krystina knew the reason for it. Her agile spiritual mind had journeyed far into the baby's future to satisfy herself that the sacrifice was worth it. So it was with a sense of completeness that she could turn her attention to her own future on this planet.

She was nursing a small secret from her spirit companion. Jill was now talking to her baby telepathically as if it was second nature to her. In fact, the baby had completely opened up Jill's natural clairaudient capabilities. Krystina and Jill had discussed it many times and she had given advice on how to tune in to greater effect; how to distinguish one's own thoughts from the ones you were tuning into and how to block your mind to keep parts of it to yourself. So Zolli didn't know about Jill communicating with the baby. Jill had a mischievous glint in her eye as she enjoyed this new power. She had deliberately kept it a secret. They were all going to have such fun together after the birth pretending they couldn't understand one other. It was hysterically funny, really. It was a shame she'd not be around to see it.

The baby was a little girl. It was to be called Agathà. A child of light with a destiny to match. No wonder Zol had decided he had to hang around to see it through. Who would want to miss out on that?

There had been a last gift from her to Jill – the soul to whom she was handing over all her responsibilities in relation to Zolli. The gift of an insight into the future. One night last week they had come together in this house and sat in the little room downstairs. For this reading, Krystina had decided to channel without consciousness. This meant she would move out of her body and away from all recollection of the content. It would be completely private for Jill. She could then ask anything she wished.

When Krystina came to after her trance, Jill was jotting notes down in a small notebook. Their eyes met.

'Did you find out what you wished to know?'

'Very much so. There is a lot I have to prepare for so I can be a good mother for Agathà and a strong partner for Zolli. I mustn't forget what I have been told.' They hugged. Their energies were intense and vibrant. It was as if Jill had graduated into a higher dimension. She heard the car drawing up outside and stopped her musing. Time to go.

At last they were all assembled. Rose had poured each one a small glass of champagne, even Jill. They toasted the baby and wished mother and baby luck for their momentous journey with Zolli and their new life together. Then Beatrice produced a present wrapped in gold paper. They all turned their eyes to her, and Krystina knew it was a going away present from them all. She unwrapped a large wand of beautiful crystal - yellow Citrine - vibrating and sparkling in her hands. The lines of light were concentrating waves of energy towards the pointed end. Krystina had the feeling this gift would be well used in her future projects. It was one of the most beautiful things she'd ever seen on Earth. A tear tricked down her pink cheek. Words eluded her.

Within moments hands were patting her, stroking her and drawing her into a warm embrace. They were soothing her and she could feel their warm, loving energy around her. It was wonderful to be here and among these friends. She sighed and released the feelings of sadness she'd been holding on to.

Krystina knew she would be leaving them stronger and braver; their new-found knowledge driving them on to greater things. Who knew where it would end? She suspected Rose would carry on and find herself growing at an accelerated pace. There was a restless impatience about her now. Beatrice would, no doubt, use her energy to love and support Jill and Zolli. B had grown in energetic stature too displaying both resolve and strength so that Krystina surmised she was also to play a significant part in future events, in little Agathà's destiny.

Lesley's energy was bubbling like the champagne. She had earlier told the group how she and Colin, her husband, had decided to put themselves forward to foster or adopt a child who had been orphaned by cancer. The joy and anticipation on her face was wonderful to behold. Lesley's mission would be to support parents of children with this illness and to love and cherish a new child of her own. She would use her energy to lighten the journey of the souls who were treading the difficult path of physical illness. The embrace ended and they all looked serenely at her. It was wonderful to have known these souls. It had been her privilege. Now it was time to get on with the business in hand - their final channelling session with each other.

They were seated in their meditation positions. Rose noted they were almost exactly in the same places as they had been for the first meeting. Polly was wedged up against the right arm of the big sofa but, aside from that, the placements were all as before. Krystina then started the process by clearing their energies, grounding their souls and connecting each with their higher purpose. She led them deep into themselves using their breath and images of waves of coloured light and thus encouraged awareness of their guides, drawing the higher energy down towards an earthly plane. Each guide was imbued with different qualities, characteristics and energy. Each one was uniquely suited to be the spiritual teacher of their human charge. Soon, she thought, they would have enough confidence and enough awareness to speak about their guides and teachers, compare notes and, by doing so, increase their understanding of how the spirit guide system operated. Krystina settled back to the task of leading them.

Beatrice, having made the difficult decision to, temporarily, wipe the recent sad memory of poor Fluffy from her mind, was getting lost in a violet wave of light inside her. It looked like a donut with a black empty hole in the centre. She kept looking, it was drawing her in, and each second she focussed she was aware of feeling more and more elevated. She'd lost her breath. In fact, it almost felt as if she didn't have to breathe any more in order to continue.

'Draw your energy up into your third eye and concentrate on imagining a golden thread of thought reaching upwards into the higher realms. In your mind, recall a picture of your guide's face and call him or her towards you. Feel the energy coming now into your own aura.'

Beatrice suddenly found she couldn't concentrate any longer, the donut was still there but she had a tickle on her leg that needed scratching. She reached down and felt where the itch was, ready to scratch, and then get back to the matter in hand. She opened her eyes in shock. Around her legs, weaving a figure of eight about her ankles, was the image of a young Fluffy. She could sense the soft fur caressing her skin. She gasped and a lump formed in her throat. Biting her lip to stop herself from crying out, she just watched in awe. The cat stared back, right deep into her soul, those yellow eyes looking unblinking into her own. The furry dance continued around her feet and she could feel the cat purring with pleasure. She tentatively placed her hand on Fluffy's back and cat energy arched up to meet her. B wanted to scoop Fluffy up and squeeze her tight but she knew this was a magical moment, not a real one. The tears trickled down her cheeks as she just kept concentrating with love at the vision in front of her.

The room was quiet. She was aware that the sound of Krystina's voice had faded, yet, as she looked up, she could see the mouth moving as the words formed. The clairvoyant was quietly guiding the group towards the part of the meditation when they would open themselves to channel.

As Beatrice looked at the scene before her, the figure of Krystina turned to look at her and, all at once, intense light flooded the room. It was a struggle not to turn away. Now they were just two souls watching each other, everyone else had faded to invisible. Krystina grew bigger and brighter. Her image lifted off the chair and seemed to hover in space. For a second she was aware that the cat at her feet was moving towards the light, drawn by the celestial brightness. Krystina held out her hands to meet it and Fluffy, young in both energy and spirit, jumped onto the clairvoyant's shoulder. They stared right at her and it seemed to Beatrice as if a slow smile was spreading on both their faces. Her mind opened. A light, sweet voice called to her in the silence.

'From now, never doubt what you see with your eyes and feel in your heart.'

Time stood still. The words rang in her ears. This moment of revelation was the culmination of all the hard work done over many weeks and months but all she could do was hold her breath and gaze at the vision in front of her. Eventually, against her will, her lids closed, eyes stung by the brightness. But, when she opened them again, the room was back exactly how it was before. The light was dim and only the table lamps were glowing in the corners of the room. The soundtrack was back to normal and everyone, including Krystina, their teacher and guide, was seated on chairs and sofas meditating deeply. Fluffy was nowhere to be seen.

Acknowledgements

I would like to thanks all my friends who read this book while it was germinating. Thanks to their input, the story has improved and become more rounded. Thank you to Juliet for taking up competitive trampolining so I could while away your training sessions tapping away on my laptop, writing this story. You were just a youngster when this tale began to unfold and now you have just passed your driving test and got your first car. How time flies.

Becky, you are an inspiration to me and I love your determination and ambition. The insights you shared into the daily life of a teenager and lately, an amazing young woman, have given this story extra zing.

Thanks to Dad, retired proof reader and patient teacher, for his invaluable input which has allowed my uncertain grammar to be corrected, in some measure, I hope! I have learned more about acceptable fonts, margins and ellipses (to name a tiny fraction of the things Dad has gone over with me) than any person should, ordinarily, know.

Mark, without your support I would not have been able to get this book into print - thank you.

The Channelling Group will be reconvening soon, to support the friends and their families through other challenges. Look out for the next instalment, *The Walk In*, coming to Kindle and paperback late 2015.

38605976R00161

Made in the USA
Charleston, SC
14 February 2015